Darren Coleman

author of the smash hits, *Before I Let Go* & *Do or Die*,

introduces a future legend of the Hip-Hop lit genre...

Proudly presents:

Fast Lane

A novel by **Eyone Williams**

An nVision book

nVision Publishing an imprint of **Power Play Media®**

A division of nvision incorporated
P. O. box 274, Lanham Severn road, Lanham, Md 20703

Nvision Publishing and the above portrayal of a boy looking to the moon and the stars are trademarks of nvision incorporated.

This novel is a work of fiction. Any references to real people, events, establishments, or locales are intended only to give the fiction a sense of reality and authenticity. Other names, characters, and incidents occurring in the work are either the product of the author's imagination or are used fictitiously, as are those fictionalized events and incidents that involve real persons. Any character that happens to share the name of a person who is an acquaintance of the author, past or present, is purely coincidental and is in no way intended to be an actual account involving that person.

Book and Cover design by Darren Coleman & Keith Marion

Library of Congress Cataloging-in-Publication Data;

Williams, Eyone, A novel by
Fast Lane:
   For complete Library of Congress Copyright info visit the nvision publishing web site.

www.nvisionpublishing.com

isbn digit 978-1-934230-00-8
Copyright © 2007

Fast Lane

A novel by **Eyone Williams**

This book is dedicated to;

**My Mother and my Brother,
who lost their lives in the unforgiving
streets that I write of.**

In Memory of;

**Tawana D. Lattisaw
and
Markelle D. Wilson**

My love remains true.

"I'd love to go back to when we played as kids but things change...
That's the way it is."

-2Pac

Part I

One

    The summer sun was blazing down on the DC streets as his rims set off a glare that got the attention of everyone he passed. Mann was leaned back in the driver's seat of his jet black 1988 Nissan 300ZX Turbo, speeding up 5th Street NW, better known as *Uptown* in the Nation's Capital. N.W.A.'s *Fuck Tha Police* was blasting out of the speakers as he turned the air conditioning up in the car. Mann was in deep thought about what he had to do before the day was out. He wanted to sell his last 4 ounces of coke in order to buy another half of brick from his man Silk.

    Money and honies seemed to be raining from the skies like the sunshine this summer and Mann was going to make sure he did everything necessary to ensure that his pockets stayed fat. With money came respect and Mann loved it. Making a quick left turn on 5th and Rittenhouse Streets, Mann pulled into the alley behind Kisha's house. Everybody and they momma was outside. Mann parked his car and as he was walking down the alley toward the crap game, he saw his cousin Black and his partner Dre. Passing by Kisha's backyard, he saw her first, then Kelley and Metra sitting on the back porch.

    Kisha was a light skinned girl with a well-shaped body and a behind like a donkey. Her house was what you could call the hang-out spot around the way. Her buddy Kelley was the best looking one out of the bunch by far. She was the one that everybody thought was going somewhere in life. She had a thing for Mann, always clear by the way she smiled at him whenever he was in her presence. Metra was the youngest out of the crew at only 15. Being the youngest didn't mean a thing because she had been around and knew how to survive in the streets.

    "Mann!" Standing up Kisha called out.

    "What's up?" Mann said as Kisha and Kelley walked up to him. Kisha hugged Mann tightly and kissed him on the cheek. Kelley did the same but she was bold and kissed Mann in the mouth. "I know y'all want something," Mann said knowing something was up.

"We tryin' to use your wagon to hit da Metro Club tonight," Kisha said with a smile. Thinking about it for a minute, Black and Dre came to mind. They went on a caper in the wagon last night and it was no telling who was looking for it. Mann knew it wasn't safe to let the girls ride around like that.

"I can't let y'all see da wagon, but I'ma see if Dre'll let y'all push his joint," Mann said.

"Let us know before it gets too late," Kisha said, as she and Kelley walked away, swinging hips and thighs like only a broad out the hood could.

Mann went on down the alley to see what the dice were hitting for. Dre was down on one knee shooting the dice surrounded by Black, Silk, Smoke, Serge, Onion, and Quick the young gun of the hood. Dre was picking up his money as Mann walked up on the crap game. He had just struck Onion for $500.

"What's up?" Dre said.

"Ain't shit what da dice hittin' for?" Mann said.

"We shootin' some small shit," Dre said.

Mann threw $20 on the ground, stepped on the money and said, "Who fadin' me?" as he grabbed the dice.

His man, Silk, threw $20 on the ground and said, "Shoot young nigga!" Smoke and Serge were side betting with Silk against Black, who was betting with his cousin. Money went from hand to hand until Silk got a beep and had to leave.

It seemed like everyone in the whole neighborhood was gathered around Mann's ride as Black lit the weed and began passing it around. Mann took notice when Black passed Quick the blunt. As the younger dude took a deep pull of the smoke, Mann said, "What your lil' ass doing smokin?"

Blowing a huge cloud of weed smoke into the hot summer air, Quick said, "I'm grown nigga! I do what I want! Suckas do what they can!" Everybody burst out laughing.

Short, brown skinned with a wild afro and not a trace of hair on his face, Quick was before his time at 12 years old. He had been in the streets for a long time now. Living with his grandmother, Quick ran the streets going and coming as he pleased. His grandmother tried to lay law but Quick was out of control and never listened, he chose the way he was streets. Quick's grandmother didn't have the money to get him the finer things in life, so Quick hit the streets and started hustlin' for his. In the process of running the streets with the big boys, Quick grew a love for the gunplay, and that made him dangerous.

Stepping away from the crowd, Mann and Dre walked down the alley to talk about their next move. It was time for them to step it up in the streets and the first move was to get a whole brick of coke from Silk now that they had the money to do it. Black walked up behind them and tapped Mann on the shoulder saying, "Slim! I gotta move out Maryland. Let me use da wagon joe!"

"Who you takin' wit you?" Mann asked, always concerned. He knew Black didn't have it all. Everything was done with the trigger of a pistol in his world.

"Smoke and Serge rollin' wit me on da move. They know where da joint at," Black said.

"Watch yourself joe," Mann said as he gave Black the keys to the wagon.

Dre headed for his baby's mother's house when he was done talking to Mann. Now walking back down the alley to his car Mann asked Quick if he wanted to go find Lando with him. Like always, Quick was down for whatever. Hopping in the Z, they flew out onto Rittenhouse Street. At the end of the block they saw a lot of pipeheads in the alley. Mann slowed down and pulled into the alley to get rid of the last of his coke.

"Let me get some of dem sells young!" Quick said.

"Come on shorty," Mann said as they hopped out and started serving pipeheads left and right. In minutes, Quick was sold out and back in the Z counting his money. Sliding his money into the pocket of his Guess Jean shorts, Quick looked over at Mann through the car window. That nigga getting paid, Quick thought to himself. It wouldn't be long before he would be making money like that Quick told himself.

Tall, slim, and dark skinned, Mann was what the young women wanted in a man. At 16, Mann had the street sense of a nigga that had been in the game for years. At 12 years old, Mann hit the streets looking for the dollars. Mann met Silk through his older cousin Dez, who got shot in the head during a drug deal that went bad. After killing the nigga that killed Dez, Mann was known for being a smooth killer when it was time to put that work in, but over all Mann was about the "Dollars". From 10 packs of heroin to $50 bags of shake coke and now crack rock. Mann always had whatever made dollars.

Eyone Williams

packs of heroin to $50 bags of shake coke and now crack rock. Mann always had whatever made dollars.

Snapping Quick out of his deep thought, Mann hopped back in the car with a hand full of cash. "You finished your shit?" Mann asked.

"Yeah, I'm done joe. I'ma call Wee and re-up."

"You fuckin wit Wee huh? Dat's alright," Mann said.

Lando rode up on Quick's red and white CR-80 dirt bike and said "What's up wit y'all niggaz?"

Mann turned to his little brother and said, "Ain't shit shorty. Where you been?"

"I was up da Ave. looking for Baby-D. We suppose to go over some broad house he know."

"I'm bout to go get something to eat, you trying to go?"

"Yeah, meet me down Kisha's house," Lando said as he let the clutch go and took off flying down the alley.

Jumping in the hatch back of the Z Lando told Quick to pop something in the tape deck. Quick slapped N.W.A. in the tape deck making "Fuck tha Police" hit the speakers as Mann whipped the speeding car out onto Georgia Avenue. Looking back at Lando through the rear view mirror, Mann said, "What you want for your birthday?"

"I'm trying to get me a dirt bike," Lando said.

"I got that shorty!" Mann said, as he pulled into the McDonald's parking lot. Cutting the car off, Mann pulled his Browning 9mm from under the dashboard and slid it in his waistband as they got out the car.

As they walked in the door, Mann scoped the whole spot out with one quick glance. Two cops were all the way in the back, drinking coffee. Across from the pigs were Marvin, Ant, and Ric. They were from 13th Street. Mann went to junior high school with them a few years back. Mann stepped in line to order his food followed by Lando and Quick. Looking back at the 13th Street niggaz, Quick tapped Mann on the shoulder and said, "Check dem niggaz out joe." Mann turned to look back at Marvin and his partners. They were acting funny. Most of the time they would speak when they saw Mann, but this time they just left like something was up. Mann thought about it for a minute and brushed it off after a while.

After getting their food and sitting down, Mann's beeper went off. It was Dre's code followed by #911. It had to be important, Mann thought. He had just seen Dre no more then an hour ago. Mann got up telling Lando and Quick that he had to use the phone. Outside on the pay phone

"What's up Tina? Dis Mann, where Dre at?"

"Yeah!" Dre said into the phone sounding angry.

"What's up joe?" Mann said.

"Slim! Some niggaz ran up in here while Tina and my son was in here sleep."

"Is they okay?"

"Yeah, they just a lil' shook up joe."

"So what da fuck went down?" Mann asked.

Dre put Mann down with what had happened. Tina told him she was in the bed sleep with Lil' Dre when she heard some kicking on the back door. She got up to see what was wrong and before she could get out of the room she saw two niggaz in ski masks standing in her bedroom with pistols pointed at her. She screamed waking Lil' Dre. One of the dudes grabbed her, smacked her in the face with a pistol and slammed her to the floor. While Lil' Dre was screaming, the other dude snatched the phone cord out of the wall and tied Tina up with it. Leaving Lil' Dre on the bed screaming, they tore the apartment up looking for coke and money. They found $15,000, a .357 magnum, and 62 grams of coke. When they were done, they ran out the back door. Tina got herself free and ran to the window crying and saw a dark brown Nova roaring down the alley with two dudes in it. She couldn't tell who they were, but one was light skinned and the other was dark skinned. Tina had seen the exact same car a day before with 14th Street Tate in it, sitting in front of the apartment. He had to have something to do with the caper. Mann let Dre know that he would be over Tina's house right away with Black after he dropped Lando and Quick off down 5th Street, and hung up the phone.

Mann had that look of concern on his face as he drove back down 5th Street. He knew that beefin' always led to other things. Most of the time somebody had to die and maybe even catch a body. However it went, it got in the way of making money, and Mann didn't like that at all.

Lando and Quick could tell that something was wrong with Mann, but they said nothing on the ride back. They knew he would tell them when the time was right. As the jet black 300ZX pulled up in front of Kisha's house, Mann then let Quick and his little brother know that he had to take care of some business and he would catch up with them later on. As they got out of the car, Black walked up right in time, followed by Kisha.

Black hopped in the passenger seat, while Kisha walked around to Mann's window. "What's wrong wit you boy?" Kisha said, seeing the look on Mann's face.

Eyone Williams

Black hopped in the passenger seat, while Kisha walked around to Mann's window. "What's wrong wit you boy?" Kisha said, seeing the look on Mann's face.

"Ain't shit. What's up?"

"Did you say somethin' to Dre about da car?" Kisha asked. Mann had forgotten. He had something else on his mind. Shaking his head no, Mann said "Somethin' jive came up, I ain't get a chance to holla at Dre." Turning to Black, Mann said, "Let Kisha use your car 'til later on tonight."

Looking at Mann like he was crazy, Black said, "What?"

Kisha cut in and said, "Come on nigga, I'ma take care of your shit!"

Handing Kisha the keys to his black '88 Acura Legend, Black said, "Don't let nothin' happen to my shit girl!" Kisha took the keys and walked off smiling. Mann began to tell Black about Tina's door getting kicked in as he slammed the Z in first gear and shot up Rittenhouse Street.

Kelly and Metra were laying on Kisha's Bed talking about Mann and listening to Rare Essence blasting out of the speakers on the wall. Kisha walked in the room and said, "I got us a ride for the night!"

"Dat's right girl! I'm bout to go get dressed!" Metra said, as she got up and headed for her house across the street.

"Who car you got?" Kelley asked Kisha, once Metra was gone.

Walking over to the closet, Kisha said, "Mann got Black to let me push his Acura for da night." Kisha began to pick her clothes out for the night when the doorbell rang.

Downstairs, Kelley let Quick and Lando in and said, "Where y'all comin' from?" Sitting down on the sofa with Lando, Quick said, "Mann dropped us off a lil' while ago."

"Where he at?"

"You askin' too many questions; who you work for?" Quick said.

Frowning up her face as she stormed up the steps, Kelley said, "You lil' muthafuckas think y'all so grown!" Lando and Quick had to laugh.

Picking up the phone to call his cousin Wee-Wee, Quick pulled out a thick knot of cash and started counting it. Wee-Wee answered the phone and Quick began talking in codes about buying some more coke. After taking care of his business Quick hung up the phone and asked Lando what he had to do. Lando let him know that he was chilling for the day.

"You trying to go downtown wit' me to pick dis coke up from Wee?" Quick asked.

Pamila gave him everything he ever wanted, and Mann gave him everything else. "What you need some coke for joe?" Quick asked.

"I want my own shit. I ain't gon' keep depending on Pamila and Mann to look out for me. Fuck dat!" Lando said. Quick thought about what Lando had said for a minute and decided to go along with his man, even though he didn't believe Lando needed to hustle.

As the night rolled in, sending most of the average, law abiding citizens inside, Mann, Black, and Dre were riding through the streets in Mann's huge green station wagon with dark black tinted windows, making them unseen to the outside world. Dressed in black, wearing bulletproof vests, and strapped for war, the plan was laid down. They were to get into 14th Street Tate's grandmother's house and find out what he knew about the brown Nova that Tina had seen him in. After that he was a dead man one way or another. Dre checked the clip of the old AK-47 that he had laying across his lap and asked if everyone was cool with the plan. No one objected so it was game time and somebody would pay for Tina's door getting kicked in.

Lando walked into the house a few minutes before eleven p.m. with over four hundred dollars in his pocket. His first day of selling drugs was one that got him paid. It was easy, he thought. All he had to do was hang out on the block, like he did everyday, and the money would come from nowhere. It was so simple, and in just one day, Lando felt as though he had the game mastered.

Lando's Aunt Pamila was in the kitchen drinking a glass of orange juice when he came in the front door of the 3 bedroom house that sat in the middle of 5th Street, no more than 3 blocks away from the drug strip where Lando had just took his first lesson on "how to get paid".

Pamila was the sister of Mann and Lando's real mother who passed away in '83. Since that day, Pamila was the only mother or father the two brothers ever knew. The love between Pamila and her kids was a strong one and when it came to raising two young black males in the city, it was a love that would have to stand the test of time. Nowadays, Mann was a man in Pamila's eyes, even though he was only 16. He did for himself and never needed anything. He had always been that way. Pamila only had to focus on her daughter Tyesha and Lando. Tyesha was only 2 years old and she was no problem. The only one Pamila had to worry about was and she was no problem. The only one Pamila had to worry about was Lando, now that he was showing all the same signs Mann showed her when he first hit the streets.

Coming out of the kitchen, Pamila looked down at her watch and said, "It's 11:00, I ain't seen you all day boy, where you been?" Lando knew that Pamila did not like for him to run the streets all day without at least checking in with her to let her know what was up with him, but once he was out the door it was a whole different world on the streets.

Looking at Pamila, Lando said, "I been riding around with Quick on his dirt bike all day."

Walking pass Lando, Pamila went up the steps asking, "Where is your brother?"

"I think he went to take Dre somewhere, he should be home soon," Lando said.

"Well if I don't see you before you leave the house tomorrow, happy birthday!" Pamila said as she headed for her bedroom.

The humid, but cool, night air was hitting Quick in the face as he stood up on his red and white dirt bike flying up 14th Street on his way home with a .38 revolver in his waist band, and a pocket full of drugs and money. Bending the corner on Summerset Place, Quick switched gears and took the bike flying onto the sidewalk. The only sound in the air was the roar of the little bike while it picked up more speed as Quick went from gear to gear fearlessly. Coming to a stop at the corner of 13th Street, Quick looked up and down the street, and then let go of the clutch, again sending the bike high into the air as he shot down 13th Street at top speed under the street lights. Pulling up at the corner of 13th and Piney Branch Road, Quick leaned over on one leg as he came to a stop with a serious look of concern on his face.

Looking Quick dead in the face from across the street was two "jump outs" in a brown unmarked Ford Crown Victoria. The cops could tell that Quick was no more than 12 or 13 years old, and by the look in the eyes of the two young white boys, Quick knew he was going to have to show his skills on the bike if he planned on making it home tonight.

The "jump-outs" rushed Quick, almost hitting him with the car. With ease, Quick shot around the car and went flying down Rittenhouse Street and out onto Georgia Avenue. Pissed off and embarrassed, the "jump-outs" made a quick U-turn and the chase was on. Flying down Georgia less then two cars lengths away and gaining every second, Quick could feel the rush of adrenalin rapidly pumping through his body, and he loved the feeling. Wasting no time, Quick made his move. Swerving hard to his left, at top speed, he shot up on the sidewalk. Looking down Georgia Avenue, he saw a Yellow Cab coming up the street in the far left lane. Swerving back out into the street in front of the speeding Crown Victoria, with the Yellow cab coming head on, everything came down to a split second decision between life and death. In a flash, Quick made the amazing life threatening turn and cut right in front of the cab, escaping certain death by only 10 feet or so. The "jump-outs" didn't make it. Smashing head on into the cab, making a huge explosion of crashing metal and flying glass, the Crown Victoria sat in a heap of twisted metal in the middle of Georgia Avenue, right in front of the 4th District Police Station. Quick looked over his shoulder while he kept flying down the street, and laughed at the deadly mess that he left behind.

Black popped the clip into his .45 automatic as Mann pulled up in back of Tate's grandmother's house on 14th Street. Looking around to make sure no one was outside, they all slid on ski masks and walked up to the back of the house.

After Black slipped into an open window and let everyone in the house through the back door, they crept downstairs to Tate's room in the basement. With their burners out they walked right up on Tate who was asleep on a sofa in the basement. Black walked over and put Tate into a deadly headlock while placing the .45 to the side of his head. Waking up to an unrelentless chokehold, the first words Tate heard was Black hissing through clenched teeth in a menacing voice saying, "Wake your bitch ass up! You know what time it is nigga!" Tate couldn't believe what he saw. At 6'4" behind a ski mask, holding an AK-47 was Dre. Right beside him was Mann, 5 inches shorter, in a ski mask but just as deadly holding a smoke gray MAC-10.

Tate tried to talk, but he couldn't get a word out due to the chokehold Black had around his neck. Mann walked up and knelt down in front of Dre, calmly tapping his finger on the trigger of the MAC-10. Pure fear went through Tate's body at the sight of Mann's action. Mann could tell that he had Tate's attention.

Smoothly rolling his ski mask up on his head like a skull cap, Mann said, "I ain't gon' play no games with you. I'ma ask you one time, and one time only. Whose brown NOVA was you in the other day in front of Tina's house?" Black lightened up on the chokehold in order to let Tate talk.

Taking a deep breath, Tate said, "It was Marvin and Ant, they said they was suppose to be getting some coke from Dre. I wasn't wit dat shit joe! For real!"

As soon as Tate was done telling on Marvin and Ant, Mann stood up and said, "Let's go." Black let go of Tate and walked around in front of him, pointing the .45 in his face. Tate looked up at the three young killers that stood in front of him with fear in his eyes. Balling up in a knot, he looked between his arms at Black who was still pointing his pistol at him. He could almost feel the bullets slamming into his body before the gun even went off. Without a blink of the eye, Black pulled the trigger sending two hollow point slugs into Tate's head. BOOM! BOOM! The sound of the powerful pistol shook the whole house before the killers ran for the car.

Two

Through all of the madness the night before, Lando was at home in the bed sleep. It was 11:00am by the time Lando got out of the bed. The bright sunshine hit him right in the face as he wiped the sleep out of his eyes. He was 12 years old today, yet he felt no different then he did the day before. Lando wasted no time getting in the shower and getting dressed in a fresh red, white, and blue polo short set, white polo socks, and a pair of New Balance 995's. Going down stairs to get himself something to eat, he stopped dead in his tracks. In the middle of the living room floor was a shiny white Yamaha YZ-80 dirt bike with little red stickers on it that read "YZ".

"Damn!" Lando said out loud as he ran over and jumped on the bike. That nigga Mann always came through, Lando thought. Lando had to go downstairs to holla at Mann about getting him the bike.

Downstairs, Mann was already up and dressed. Sitting on his bed reading the Metro section of the Washington Post, Mann wore a look of experience. In the Crime and Justice column there were three killings in the city streets last night. Only one concerned Mann. That was the one that read Donell Johnson, 18 years of age from the 6700 block of 14^t Street was found shot in the head twice in the basement of his home at approximately 12:00am. There were no suspects or motives in the slaying. That was all Mann really wanted to see at the time, yet he knew that things never stayed the same when murder was a part of the game. Even so, Mann was a thinker and he was sure that he would be able to think his way through whatever came his way.

Closing the newspaper, Mann saw Lando standing at the bottom of the basement steps and said, "What's up shorty? You like da bike?"

"Yeah! I love it young! I'm 'bout to go find Quick right now. Thanks joe!" Lando said. Mann had made his day once again.

With his dirt bike, Lando was like a puppy let off the chain, always on the go, exploring the city looking for adventure beyond his block. Pamila would even have to send Mann to find him some nights. With school out, Mann knew what all that free time could lead to growing up in the city. Lando was a thinker just like he was. If Lando saw a way to "make it happen" he would. Lando had met a young girl by the name of Nakia that lived just across the city line in Silver Spring, MD. Nakia was a cute young girl with a lot going for her. Her family had money and she lived in a big old house with just her mother, as an only child. Whatever she wanted she got. Over the past few weeks her mother, Karen, had taken a quick liking to Lando. She had only 2 small problems with him. She didn't like him flying down the street with her daughter on the back of "that damn bike of his" as she put it, and she didn't like the little thug that he kept with him all the time. Quick always got a bum beef when it came to grown-ups. He was always in black, his pants were always hanging off his ass, and he kept a lot of cash. Other than that Karen thought that Lando was a sweet boy.

Lando sat on his dirt bike in front of Nakia's house for about an hour kickin' it with her. He was really diggin' her. He always got a good laugh when they were together. She thought she knew so much about the streets. Lando, on the other hand, thought she was still wet behind the ears. He was still young himself but had seen a lot, and he was doing a lot more as the summer grew old. Him and Quick had started buying coke together from Quick's cousin, Wee-Wee. Mann knew nothing about it at the time, so for what it was worth Lando was making a way for himself lately. While Lando and Nakia stood outside, Quick pulled up on his dirt bike.

"What's up young? I knew I would catch you out here. Let's go around the way. Bring Nakia with you!" Quick said. He didn't like being away from the hood for long, it made him feel out of place. Lando thought about what he said and decided against it.

"Na, I'm 'bout to roll out anyway young," Lando said, as he leaned over and kissed Nakia on the lips, sending a chill down her spine. "I'll holla at you a little later okay?" Lando said.

She hugged him tightly and said "Call me when you get around the way." Lando kicked his bike to life and took off behind Quick flying down the street while Nakia looked on.

With the coke flowing in and out Mann and Dre had been making a killin' for the last few weeks, even with the beef still in the air. Black had seen Ant and Marvin coming out of Marvin's baby mother's house and bust shots at 'em, but they got away. Since then they hadn't seen them niggaz, Mann wasn't taking the situation light at all. He knew they would resurface. They had to. Their money wasn't long enough to stay low-key too long, and when they did it would be time to put an end to the situation once and for all.

The air condition was pumping hard in Dre's white Nissan Maxima. Blunt smoke filled the air as they cruised up 5th Street. Mann was leaned back in the passenger seat nodding his head to the music. Rare Essence was blasting out of the huge speakers that surrounded the car. Black laid in the back seat puffing on the blunt with a .44 revolver on his lap. Dre was trying his best to catch up with the black Nissan Pathfinder ahead of them. It was two bad ass females in the truck, and Dre had his mind set on meeting them. As Black raised up to pass Mann the blunt, Quick and Lando went flying by on their bikes. Everybody's head turned for a second as they went by. Mann laughed as he took a deep pull on the slow burning blunt. Letting out a cloud of gray smoke he said, "Lando think he slick. Him and Quick bad ass been buying coke from Wee."

"How you know that?" Dre said.

"I went down 7th Street yesterday to pick that shit up from Silk and Wee put me on point. I know shorty gon' do his thing, and I ain't gon' get in his way but I ain't gon' let 'em make the mistakes we made coming up. I been meaning to pull up on 'em about that shit but he stay gone on that bike all day, plus he in love with some little girl out Maryland so it's been hard to catch 'em."

Black burst out laughing and said, "Shorty tryin' to get his dick wet!" Everybody else burst out laughing. Mann's beeper went off. It was Corey's code "500". Mann knew what he wanted. Corey was buying OZ's from Mann damn near twice a day now so that was at least a quick $800. Mann said, "It gotta be pumpin' around the way joe. That nigga Corey just hit me on the box for the second time today for an "O"." Black couldn't stand Corey for some reason. He didn't know why. "That nigga getting' money now huh?" Black asked. Mann and Dre looked at each other with smiles, knowing what was on Black's mind. Only a year younger than them, Black was far more aggressive when it came to the gunplay. He had always been that way. When he was 12 years old he had shot a nigga dead in broad daylight for running off with Mann's coke and he got away clean. Since then it was like he couldn't put his pistol down.

Mann looked back at Black and said, "Leave that man alone, joe. You gettin' more cash than he is and you ain't even out there everyday. You need to slow down and flip some of that shit you keep stickin' niggaz for. You making too many niggaz scared of you. That ain't good slim. No bullshit!"

Black wasn't trying to hear none of that, he responded with a, "Yeah whatever. You always protecting them punks!"

Finally Dre caught up with the Pathfinder. Pulling up beside it he rolled down his window, letting out a huge cloud of smoke and said "Hi, how you doing miss?"

Niggaz were everywhere when Dre pulled up in the alley. They all got out the car and quickly mixed in. Onion and Corey were sitting on a small brick wall that surrounded the fence at the beginning of the alley.

"What's up joe?" They said at the same time when they saw Mann coming out of the alley.

"Ain't shit!" he responded as he gave them "5". Onion and Corey were jive like partners. They were always together, but inside they didn't trust each other at all. The thing that kept them close was that they trusted everybody else around the way even less. Mann and Corey stepped off together to take care of their business and Onion spotted a pipehead coming down the alley and rushed the sale. Dre and Black had headed straight for Kisha's porch. All the young niggaz was in front of Kisha's house. Black stepped straight to Lil' Garvin and threw his hands up. "What's up sucka ass nigga!" he joked as they started slap boxing. Lil' Garvin and Quick were running neck to neck when it came down to who stayed in the most shit. Lil' Garvin had just come home from Oak Hill's Juvenile Detention Center days ago for Assault with Intent to Kill. Him and Quick had robbed some college niggaz at a Howard University football game last fall. The niggaz bucked and they let 'em have it. Quick living up to his name got away when the feds came. Lil' Garvin got away as well, but a hot ass bitch saw his car leaving after the shooting and ran her mouth. The feds caught him days later in the alley hustlin' behind Kisha's house. When questioned about the shooting and who was with him, Lil' Garvin ain't say shit, he played by the rules of the game.

"Damn joe! You got big as shit shortie!" Dre said as he stepped between Black and Lil' Garvin and hugged him. Everybody was happy to see shorty home. "Quick and Lando seen you yet?" Dre asked.

"Na, I ain't seen them niggaz yet. I only been out for a week now. They got me in a group home around the corner from my house. I'm on a weekend pass, I gotta be back tomorrow night by 9," Lil' Garvin said.

"You got some money?" Black asked.

"Na, get me joe! They say you and Mann doing y'all thing!"

Black cut Lil' Garvin off saying "Shit, it's more like Dre and Mann doing they thing. I'm livin' by the trigga!" Everybody burst out laughing, as Black and Dre pulled knots of cash out of their pockets and hit Lil' Garvin off. Mann was coming through the cut when he heard the laughter.

"What's up young nigga?" Mann said when he saw Lil' Garvin.

"Ain't shit young! What's up?" Lil' Garvin said as he hugged Mann. Mann had always dug shorty's style. Now that he had gone down on a beef and kept his mouth shut, Mann dug his style even more.

"Where your brother at?" Mann said.

"He down 9th Street. He took me shopping this morning."

"Tell that nigga Dex I said come holla at me."

"Cool, I got that," Lil' Garvin said. They all sat on Kisha's porch and kicked it until everybody went their own way. As they left, Mann got Lil' Garvin to hang out with them.

The evening sun was setting. Pamila and Tyesha were just coming home from the mall. She carried Tyesha up stairs and laid her in the bed. A long day of shopping always put her to sleep. Coming out of Tyesha's room she wondered where Lando could be. It seemed like he was only in the house when he was sleep nowadays. Pamila opened the door to his room, walked in, and sat on his bed. She began to think deeply about Mann and Lando. Lando was growing up over night and he was 12 years old now. Mann was the same age when she started finding drugs tucked in clean socks. Pamila got up and started to look through his drawers, but there was nothing. Something inside of her soul was inspiring her to keep looking. She looked under the bed, went through all his pockets, and all of his shoes. Nothing was to be found. Pamila started to walk for the door still feeling like she was overlooking something in Lando's room that would explain why he was never around anymore. Right before she was out of the door she looked over at Lando's stereo. She walked over and picked it up. She looked straight in the battery compartment. Inside was a small plastic bag with a rubber band around it. Pamila pulled the rubber band off and opened the bag. There was a rack of small white rocks in tiny bags. Her fears were true. Lando was going down the same road as his father, and his brother. Pamila was going to do something fast. She took the coke and flushed it down the toilet. Pamila picked up the phone and beeped Mann. She knew she would need his help with this. Pamila went and laid down. She was a very strong woman, but she didn't know where to start with this one. She had run Mann away when she went off and started throwing shit at him in this same situation just four years ago. She didn't want things to go that way with Lando, but even so, she was going to lay law one way or another.

Mann got the beep and told Dre to pull over at the gas station.

"Hello?" Pamila said in a voice of concern. Mann knew something was up. He hated being in suspense about anything.

"What's wrong?" he said. Pamila went on to tell him how she found the coke in Lando's room, and that she wanted Mann to find Lando and bring him home. Mann hung up the phone and went to find his little brother.

Dre dropped Mann off at his car. Mann was floating through the hood in his black 300ZX. He bent the corner on 5th & Rittenhouse Streets, noticing it was dark on the long street. Mann knew that everyone was in the cuts now that it was dark outside. Pulling up in front of Kisha's house, he saw Kelley sitting on the porch with Metra. Mann rolled down his window and called Kelley. Walking up to the car in a white Polo t-shirt and a pair of tight blue Guess jeans Kelley said, "What's up boo?"

"Ain't shit," Mann said and continued, "you seen Lando or Quick?"

Kelley looked up and down the street and said "I heard them damn bikes out back a few minutes ago."

"I'm jive on a move right now, but I'ma call you later on. Okay?" Mann said before pulling off. Around back, Mann got out in the dark alley.

Baby D was the first to see him, "What's up young?"

"Ain't shit D. Where Lando?" Mann asked. Lando was leaning on the fence that separated the two yards that the cut was between when he heard Mann. Coming out of the cut he saw Mann and asked, "What's up Mann?"

"Pamila want you. She found that shit."

"What shit?" Lando shot back. Mann wasn't about to play police, he already knew what was up.

Fast Lane

"You know what shit I'm talkin' bout joe. Let's go see what she got to say." Mann and Lando hopped in the Z and rolled out.

Marvin was sitting in Ant's green Dodge station wagon blowing the horn in back of his apartment building. Ant came to the window and said, "I'm coming young, stop making all that noise!" Marvin was coming to pick Ant up from his house on 13th Street, they had a lot to talk about. Ant had been locked up ever since the day Black had shot at him and Marvin in front of Marvin's baby mother's house. Ant and Marvin went back down 5th Street, but the "jump-outs" had got on their backs. They both got out and started running. Ant got caught in the alley leading to Georgia Avenue with a Tec-9. He had just made bond last Friday thanks to Marvin. Marvin had been laying low waiting for Ant to get out so they could take care of their business. Now that Ant was home it was time to see if Mann and them could stand the pain.

"What's up?" Ant said as he jumped in the wagon with a lit blunt in his mouth. Marvin pulled out of the alley and began to put Ant down with what was up as they passed the blunt back and forth on their way down 14th Street. Marvin let Ant know that he had got word that Dre and Mann knew they ran up in Tina's house. He let him know that they killed Tate for showing them where the spot was. After putting 2 and 2 together, he let Ant know that Black had bust at them for that very reason. Ant leaned back in the darkness of the tinted windows and took in all that his partner had said. When Marvin was done talking, Ant looked over at him with his blood shot eyes and said in a *Tony Montana* voice, "They wanna play ruff? Okay! We play ruff!"

Though Pamela was laying down the law about her rules for the upmpteenth time Lando's mind was somewhere else. Mann had heard what Pamila was saying far too many times. "Do you hear me talkin' boy?" Pamila yelled, and went on to say, "I'm not going to let you throw your life away with that bullshit out there! You don't have to be out there selling that shit. Do you hear me?"

"Yeah I hear you!" Lando yelled out of frustration.

Pamila walked up and got right in his face yelling "Well if you hear me, then don't bring that shit in my house no more! Do you understand?"

Eyone Williams

Lando got up from the dining room table saying, "Yeah I understand!" and went up to his room leaving Mann downstairs to deal with Pamila's wrath alone. Mann stood leaning on the dining room wall looking at the floor with his arms folded. With tears in her eyes sitting at the dining room table, Pamila looked over at Mann and said in a shaky voice "You gotta talk to him for me Mann. He'll listen to you Mann. Don't let him get caught up in that bullshit. Do that for me." Knowing that Pamila was right, he agreed. Deep inside, Mann knew he was going to have to step in. He also knew that if Lando was going to hustle, the only person that could tell him anything would be his big brother. Mann thought back to when he was going through the same shit with Pamila. In the end, he still did what he wanted to do. Shit....it even got him paid, he thought to himself.

Quick and Lando were flying up Georgia Avenue angerously swerving in and out of the evening rush hour traffic. Lil' Garvin was on the back of Quick's bike. They were now on their way back uptown from taking Lil' Garvin to take his weekly piss test at the court building. Their plan was to get him down the court building and back around the way as fast as possible so that he could get some pussy before they took him back to the group home. Mann had convinced Lil' Garvin not to run from the group home since all he had left to do was a month. He would be out by the end of the summer. Lil' Garvin was cool with it. Between Mann, Dre, and Black, he always went back to the group home with at least $1500 tucked in his draws.

Lando wasted no time shooting over to Nakia's house after dropping his man off over Metra's house for some quick pussy. Quick decided to hang around the way until it was time to take Lil' Garvin back to the group home. Now laid out on Nakia's bed watching TV, Lando finally slowed down for a second. He had been moving 100 miles per hour all summer, and to him, the quick $4500 he had hustled up was worth it. The long lecture that Pamila had given him days ago was old news now, and the more Mann tried to keep the big brother watchful eye on him, the more he was determined to prove his manhood by being able to hold his own. There was no love lost between the two brothers. In fact, the whole thing seemed to bring a new understanding between them. Mann began to see, with a new light, how much Lando was like him when it came to growing up in the fast lane. Already, Lando was about the dollars, and not the name. On the other hand, Lando understood why Mann got money and kept it. Mann never played big like Dre, buying car after car, and spending G's on women and clothes. Early on in the game, Lando was saving his cash, just like Mann. Everything he did in the game was modeled after Mann; sub-consciously.

Nakia walked into the room wearing a pair of cut off Polo shorts displaying her thick young thighs, and an oversized black Madness T-shirt tucked in. She was a cute brown skinned girl with her features of womanhood already developed in the right places. Lando couldn't take his eyes off of her body when she came into the room. She walked over and kissed Lando on the lips as she lay down on the bed beside him.

"What's up boo?" she said as Lando took her into his arms and rolled over on top of her. They began to kiss passionately, rolling over and over in the bed. Lando's hands were everywhere. He began to try to unbutton her shorts, but each time she would quickly grab his hand and softly say, "No don't." After a few more tries, Lando had Nakia down to just her bra and panties. He started to take his pants down when she stood up and said, "I can't." Lando rolled over and sat on the edge of the bed in front of her.

"You can't what boo?" he gently said as he softly grabbed both of her hands and pulled her closer to him.

"I'm not ready for this Lando." Nakia stopped and looked away from him and went on to say, "I want to wait awhile. I don't want to be some freak you hit and forget." Her eyes were beginning to fill with tears but she quickly wiped them dry, not wanting Lando to look at her as a little girl.

Lando flashed her a quick "take it easy" smile and said as he stood up and hugged her tightly, "Don't cry. We can wait as long as you want to boo. I ain't in no rush. I plan on being yours for a long time. You hear me?"

Nakia felt the realness in his words as she hugged him back and said, "Thank you for understanding. I love you." Nakia kissed Lando and put her clothes back on.

Everyone was chillin' in front of Kisha's house. She was sitting on Onion's lap talking to Kelly and Metra, who were also sitting out on the porch with them. Mann, Dre, and Black were all sitting right in front of them on the steps leading to the sidewalk. Chained to the fence that separated Kisha's yard from old lady   Mrs. Barns' yard, was Quick's vicious black pit bull "Killa". The dog had earned the name by killing a much bigger "pit" when she was 4 months old. Along the side of the porch, in the darkness of the cut that ran to the alley behind Kisha's house were Quick, Baby D, Smoke, Serge, and Corey. They stood lined up along the brick wall of the porch, passing two weed-packed Backwoods back and forth.

A dark blue Buick of some kind bent the corner and was slowly rolling up Rittenhouse Street. There were dark black-tinted windows all the way around the car. No one could see who was in the car, or knew right off hand whose car it was that was pulling up on them in the darkness. Black being the first to peep the bucket bend the corner reached under his T-shirt and tightly gripped the .44 magnum he had tucked in his waistband. "Who the fuck is this?" he said excitedly, standing up and walking out toward the sidewalk with the huge magnum in open display. Mann and Dre did the same. Kisha hopped off of Onion and started walking quickly to the front door followed by Kelly and Metra. Onion stood up and snatched a Glock from under his T-shirt, and walked down to the sidewalk with Black and them. The pit bull sensed something was wrong and began to growl. Quick and everyone else poured out of the cut and into Kisha's front yard with pistols in hand. Truthfully speaking Kisha had a small army of thug niggaz in black in her front yard.

About two houses away from Kisha's house the car suddenly slammed on brakes making the tires scream. The passenger side window slowly came down. Somebody yelled out of the window "Hold! Hold! This Dex joe!" Black recognized the voice and put his pistol up. It was Lil' Garvin's big brother. Everybody put they shit up as the car pulled up. Mann and Black walked up to the car laughing.

"You almost got this joint lit up young!" Black said to Dex, reaching out to give him "5".

"Yeah, I see y'all on point. I like that," Dex said, and looked over at Mann continuing, "What's up joe?" Looking up and down the street, Mann leaned against the double-parked car.

"Ain't too much going on slim. A nigga trying to get this money 'cause I ain't gon' be out here slangin' this shit for the rest of my life joe. I'ma get me a store or a car lot or something," Mann said.

"I feel you slim. If I can get my hands on enough loot, I'ma do the same thing joe, but for right now I gotta do my thing," Dex said. They went on catching up on old times until Silk pulled up next to the car on the other side of the street. Mann told Dex that he would catch up with him, and got in the black Benz .190 with Silk. They pulled off and parked a few spaces down the street.

Silk had been around for a while, and he didn't trust a lot of people. Mann knew how to keep his mouth shut, and Silk learned that long ago. That's one of the reasons why he loved dealing with him. Knowing that Mann knew where his ass was in the streets, Silk knew to come to him when he needed a hand. Silk had a move to cop 20 bricks of raw coke from a New Yorker that he had met in Atlantic City at the Mike Tyson fight, but he was going to cop 2 first to see what he was dealing with. The only thing was that he didn't trust the bamma. Therefore, he wanted Mann to go along for his brains, but he also wanted Black to come as well for the muscle. Silk was hip to Black. He had been hearing his name in the streets for a while now. Black was just a little too wild for him to deal with on a "one on one" kind of time. Deep in his heart, Silk thought Black would try him and if he did, Silk would have to get his head hit. So to avoid something like that from ever going down, he always dealt with Black through the security of Mann.

While Silk was laying the spill on Mann about the move, the street started to get a little too busy for that time of night. Cars seemed to just keep going back and forth. Mann glanced back over his shoulder to see what was going on in front of Kisha's house. Everything was the same. Dex and his 9th Street partners were still double parked in front of the house. Dre and Black were leaning against the car kickin' it, and Quick along with everybody else was still in the cut along the side of the house. Only now, Quick had unchained Killa and was holding her by it. Mann and Silk went on talking and suddenly they both jumped. POW! POW! Gunshots rang out, again another POW! POW! Followed by a BOOM! BOOM! Shots filled the air non-stop for a second. Silk and Mann looked back after pulling their pistols and saw a white Ford LTD right beside the Buick Dex was in, with a flame of automatic gunfire jumping out of both cars. Somehow the Buick went flying up the street with the tires smoking. Quick, Baby D, Smoke, Serge, and Corey ran out into the street bustin'. Off of Kisha's porch, Onion did the same until his Glock stopped. The LTD was desperately trying to escape the hail of gunfire that was coming its way non-stop, from what seemed to be everywhere. Miraculously the LTD made it to 5th Street and bent the corner in a flash of light. When the shooting was over, Silk and Mann slowly raised their heads. They were in a bad position. It was too many bullets flying in their direction for them to do anything but get low. Looking once more they saw the street was empty. Quick and everybody else had bloomed through the cut to avoid the feds when they came. Out of all the shooting no one was hit that ran with Quick and the rest of the niggaz around the way, but they would have to check on Dex and the niggaz in the car with him. Silk was pissed off to say the least. He looked at Mann with murder in his eyes and a .50 cal Desert Eagle in his hand and said in a most concerned voice, "What the fuck goin' on around here?"

"I don't know who the fuck that was slim! But you can bet I'ma find out real quick!" Mann said as he slid his Browning 9mm between his waistband. Silk started up the Benz, and him and Mann got ghost before the strip was crawling with police.

Dre, Black, and Quick were all sitting on the sofa in Mann's room in the basement telling Lando what had just went down around the way. Everybody had some idea of who could have been in the white LTD, but no one knew for sure. Black swore it had to be Marvin and Ant. They were the only people, he could see, that would have a reason to come through bustin' like that. Dre thought the same, but he had doubts. Quick really could care less, he just wanted somebody to put the blame on so that he could vent his anger "quickly". Mann came down the steps with Silk. Looking at Dre, he said "What the fuck is up young?"

Before Dre could answer, Black stood up and said "I'ma tell you what's up! Them 13th Street niggaz tried to catch a nigga slippin'!" The open conversation continued as Black went to call a number back that kept coming on his beeper back to back 911.

"Hello!" an angry voice spit into the phone from the other end.

"Yeah this Black, who dis?"

"This Dex joe! Where you at?"

"I'm over Mann's house. You ah-ight?"

"Yeah, I'm cool, my man Doo-Doo got grazed on the arm. We tryin' to put that work straight in. What's up? Who the fuck was that?"

"I think it was them 13th Street niggaz. We jive got something going on wit dem niggaz right now, but I ain't sure slim." Black finished rappin' to Dex and walked back over to see what everybody was trying to do. It was going down.

Fast Lane

They were going to take a trip   up to 13th Street even though Mann insisted that if it was Marvin and Ant that they wouldn't be outside. Even so, everybody was headed for the door, even Quick. Lando stood up feeling left out and said, "I'm tryin' to go too!" Everyone stopped for a second, and left that up to Mann. In his eyes, hustlin' was one thing, but killing was something all together different. Mann was going to let shorty grow up, but he wasn't about to take his little brother on a move like this with them. Besides that, Lando didn't even have a pistol yet, which meant that one of them would have to give him one, and Mann wasn't having that at all.

Mann turned to Lando with a look of seriousness never seen before, and said "Hell no! You ain't going! You can get mad as you want, but you ain't going!"

As Mann jogged up the steps behind the crowd, Lando kicked an old pair of shoes against the basement wall. "Shit!" he exhaled. Out of all of the hustling he had been doing this summer, he never thought to buy a pistol of his own, being as though his partner Quick kept a huge .38 revolver with him all the time. That wasn't good enough anymore, due to this very situation. It wouldn't have been so bad if he didn't see Quick roll. That alone, made Lando feel left out. Tomorrow, he was sure that he would never be left out again.

Silk's car appeared as he bent the corner at the end of the dark alley behind Mann's house, as he was leaving. Black had beeped his man Smoke, and told him to pick everybody up behind Mann's house. Smoke and Serge had pulled up in a huge family size Ram van, with a sliding door. They were ready to roll. Being only a year younger than Black, they had met him way back in the 3rd grade when they all went to school together down the street from Black's mother's house on Maryland Avenue NE. Black had stayed back that year and they clicked off the top. Smoke and Serge always had a caper, even back then. They started breaking into houses down Georgetown and in Rock Creek Park in the early 80's. As crack and gun play grew prevalent later on, they stepped it up with the times in the fast lane. Everybody hopped into the van with a small arsenal of murder metal, from AK-47's, AR-15's, Mann's Mac-10, all the way down to Quick's .38. Smoke gave Mann the wheel since he was the best driver. He had never been caught by the law behind the wheel of anything and he never crashed either. Swiftly, yet always on point, they made their way

Eyone Williams

up 13th Street. Mann had put the plan together. He would drive through one time to see what they were working with, then pull around 14th Street, park and creep on 'em from behind. Mann knew everyone would be beside the middle apartment building in the shadows of the cut that led to the alleys. They would come through that very cut blazing. Carefully, Mann pulled onto Georgia Avenue, watching everything closely. They were riding too dirty for any slippin' to be taking place along with the fact that they had too much heat on board for the police to pull them over. It would be none of that. Mann let everybody know that they were going to bust first if the feds got on their back. Turning on to Ft. Stevens Drive they could see flashing sirens and police cars everywhere on 13th Street. Yellow "Do Not Cross" tape was surrounding an area right in front of the cut where the niggaz hustle. Two white homicide detectives were inside of the taped-off area. One was taking pictures of the body. The other one was writing down information about the shooting that had just taken place on a small note pad. An old black woman in a nightgown and bedroom slippers was pointing in the direction that the car had gone after the shooting. Mann would later find out, through Black, that Dex and Doo-Doo had put the work in and killed a nigga that be with Marvin and Ant, named Dirty. He was serving a pipehead out on the sidewalk when the shooting started. He caught slugs all in the back running for the safety of the cut, trying to get the pistol tucked in his waistband. He never made it. Mann kept going on by after seeing that the block was hot. They would make their move at another time.

Three

Lando was up before anyone in the house. After taking a shower and getting dressed, he was off to scoop Lil'Garvin up from the group home. The sun wasn't even all the way up yet. It was still chilly outside when he stepped out of the door into his backyard. Walking through the grass to his dirt bike, he could feel the wetness of last night's late rain coming through his K-Swiss tennis shoes. He kicked his bike to life, filling the early morning air with the loud buzzing roar of the engine. He had learned to ride the bike well this summer. Quickly, he floated through the back streets until he pulled up in front of the group home. Every few minutes, a couple of young dudes would come out of the door on their way to summer school or summer jobs. They all gave Lando a quick look of suspicion as they walked by. Sitting on his bike with his arm-folded, in a black Madness baseball cap, a black Hugo Boss T-shirt, and a pair of blue Guess Jean shorts, he looked like he was up to no good. Lil' Garvin and an older young dude came out finally.

"What's up young?" Lil' Garvin said, as he walked over to Lando and gave him "5". Lando didn't like new faces and Lil' Garvin saw it in his face. "This my man Poochie, he cool peoples joe," Lil' Garvin said. Poochie was a short brown skinned nigga that had a look of a young dude that had been around for a while. Poochie met Lil' Garvin down Oak Hill Juvenile Detention Center. He had taken a liking to the younger dude when he found out how Lil' Garvin had robbed some niggaz with Quick and ain't tell on his partner when he got locked up. Poochie was telling Lil' Garvin how he had some pistols for sell, some were dirty, but some were in the box. Lil' Garvin put Lando down with the move, and now all they had to do was go around Martin Luther King Avenue with Poochie and buy whatever they wanted.

Eyone Williams

At first glance, Poochie thought Lando was a Mexican or something because of his light skinned and curly hair. He stepped to Lando, gave him "5" and said "What's up shorty? What, you a amigo or something?"

"Hell no, I'm black young!"

"So you trying to buy a pistol huh?"

"I'm tryin' to get two for real," Lando said. Poochie looked him up and down. He saw that shorty was no more than 12 or 13. Even so, he was going to make sure shorty got something that would hold him. A shiny black Pathfinder pulled up with Rare Essence blasting out of the speakers. Poochie told Lando and Lil' Garvin that was the ride. Poochie and Lil' Garvin got in. Lando shot through the alley and parked his bike in Lil' Garvin's back yard, which was a block away from the group home. They pulled in the alley behind him and scooped him up.

Poochie had taken them to an apartment off of M.L.K. Avenue. The apartment looked like no one lived in it. Lando came to the conclusion that the joint had to be some kind of stash house. In the one bedroom apartment, there was only a bed, a TV, and a refrigerator. Walking into the bedroom, there were 3 black bulletproof vests lying on the old bed. Poochie moved them and flipped the mattress over exposing 2 old beat up .44 bulldogs, a Glock that he said was dirty, and 2 smoke grey Tec's, one was a 9mm and the other was a 22 cal. Lil' Garvin asked "How much for tha .44?"

Poochie picked them both up and said "I'll give you both of them for $400".

"Bet!" Lil' Garvin said as he took both hammas and gave him 4 $100 dollar bills. Lando had his mind set on the Tec-9. The long clip that was hanging out of it drew him to it. It was still in good shape.

"How much for this joint?" Lando said aiming it at the wall with both hands and one eye closed.

"Gimme 3 for it," Poochie said.

Lando paid him $300 and said "I thought you got some fresh shit too?"

Poochie went into the bathroom and came back with a brand new Glock 17 in the box. "What you think about this shorty?" Poochie said while he was pulling it out of the box.

Lando set the Tec down and got the Glock from him, and said "This is what I'm looking for!" While Lando was checking out the pistol, Poochie pulled a 35 shot extended clip out of his grey Polo shorts.

"This will give you 35 shots, shorty. I'll give you everything for $750. That's cool?" Without anymore talking, Lando paid him again and they were on their way back uptown.

Days later, Marvin was on his way to the Days Inn on the DC/Maryland line. Ant had beeped him and told him that he had a vicious freak bitch with him. Fifteen minutes later, Marvin was letting himself in the door. All he could see was Ant stretched out on the bed ass naked, blowing weed smoke into the air. A short light brown skinned broad with short curly hair, and a fat round ass, was on her knees between his legs. Her head was going up and down with a blur of speed. Ant saw Marvin and winked his eye, saying, "She vicious young." Not knowing who was in the room, the broad slowly pulled up off of Ant popping her thick lips. Turning around, Marvin saw it was Metra. He knew Ant had been fucking her, he had hit her and got the head a few times himself, but since running up in Tina's house he hadn't thought about fucking a broad from down there where Mann and them be at.

Knowing full well about the beef between them and the niggaz around her way, Metra slapped her ass cheeks with her hand while looking Marvin in the eye, enticing him to get with the action. She was vicious by nature, but she was a bitch in heat when high off the smoke. She motioned with her hand for Ant to slide back on the bed so she could climb up onto the bed herself, giving Marvin a better shot at her ass hole. Seeing her climb up onto the bed while never coming up off of Ant turned him on. Only dropping his Nike shorts down over his Timberland boots, Marvin crawled onto the bed behind her. Firmly grabbing her waist, he plunged deep into her tight ass hole with vehement passion. Metra's head shot up off of Ant as the seductive pain generated an instant climax for her. "AHHH!" she moaned. She dug her nails into the mattress as Marvin pounded her asshole, in and out. Getting impatient and close to cumming, Ant reached behind her head and slammed it back down. Metra let out a quick gagging sound as her mouth was stuffed with manhood all the way to the back of her throat. She was becoming faint as she took the punishment from both ends. Her mouth was filling with pre-cum and her asshole felt like it was on fire. She began to wildly slam her ass against Marvin's every thrust, taking him all the way inside of her until she felt it in her gut. Out of nowhere, Ant exploded in her mouth sending cum bursting out of her nose. She struggled to pull up off of him, but he kept her head pinned down, making her swallow every drop of his climax. Seconds later, Ant let her head go and it flew up in the air as she let out a scream, "Please! Please!" She tried to catch her breath. "I can't take it! You are tearin' my ass open!" Her pleas only gave Marvin more drive. "My ass is burning!" She screamed. When she thought she was about to pass out, Marvin came inside her. He kept plunging in and out until he could no longer stay hard. After Marvin pulled out, Metra rolled over on the bed beside Ant and said "Roll some of that shit up!"

Later on, Silk, Mann, and Black, were on Rockville Pike headed for the White Flint Shopping Mall to meet the New Yorker named "Supreme" that Silk had been talking about. Black was in the back seat of the old tan Buick 225 that Silk only drove when picking up weight or dropping it off somewhere. Gazing up at the bright, full moon, Black was already thinking of ways to rob Supreme without Silk or Mann finding out, despite the fact that Mann clearly told him not to try anything stupid. Silk was telling Mann how Supreme was going to give him the first two bricks for $32,000. He felt as though that was sweet for a test run.

Pulling into the parking lot behind Bloomingdale's, Silk pulled up behind a dark blue Ford Bronco. A slim dark skinned dude smoothly jumped out of the big truck in a bright red Fila sweat suit. He walked up to the car, cautiously scoping out the whole situation. Once he felt that things were cool, he gave Silk "5", flashed a gold tooth smile and said "Follow me god." They took a 10-minute back road trip to a remote old house, on a dark road not far away. Supreme and a chubby brown skinned dude, carrying a tan M.C.M. tote bag, got out. Silk got out and waved his hand for everyone to follow. For some reason he felt a little uneasy, but he always felt like that at times like this, even more so when dealing with out-of-towners. He pushed his thoughts aside and focused on what was going down. The chubby dude and Black had locked into an ugly staring match.

Silk leaned back on the hood of the car beside Mann, looking at Supreme saying, "Let's do this slim." Supreme called his man, who came over looking back at Black like 'Fuck you nigga!' He opened up the M.C.M. bag and handed Silk a fat zip-lock bag of white powder. Silk nodded his head for him to hand it to Mann. Supreme folded his arms and said, "This is the best shit up top right now son, the Fishscale gon keep'em comin' back. Watch what I tell you!"

Silk took the bag from Mann and tasted the coke, saying "I'm cool with this, gimmie the other one." The chubby dude handed him the other zip-lock bag of coke, as he signaled for Black to get the cash. It was good that Silk called him when he did because Black was fucked up about the way the chubby dude had looked at him and was thinking about killing the nigga. Black got the brown paper bag with the money in it out of the back of the car and gave it to Supreme. Silk told Supreme that he would be getting back at him if he liked the outcome of the coke. They shook hands and went their separate ways.

Two homicide detectives knocked on Tina's door. Boom! Boom! Boom! The loud knocks scared her; she jumped out of the bed and ran to see who was at the door.

"Who is it?" she said as she looked through the peephole seeing a short black man and a white man that was a little taller.

"It's the police, open up the door please!" said the black detective, in a voice of authority.

Tina opened the door only revealing her cute face. "What y'all want?" She said in a shaky voice. The detective went on to tell her he had a warrant for Dre's arrest, for first-degree murder. After finding out that he wasn't home, they told Tina to tell him that it would be best for him to turn himself in. Once they left, she ran straight to the phone to beep Dre.

Mann and Dre were sitting in Dre's new 1989 turquoise Corvette ZR1 with white leather seats, talking about how good the Fishscale coke was that Silk had given Mann a brick of after they got it from Supreme. It had pipeheads coming from way across town to get a hit. The word was out, Mann and Dre had Fishscale. While talking, Dre's beeper went off. It was Tina's "911". He got out of the car and jogged across the street to use the phone in Kisha's house.

"Hello!" Tina said, clearly excited.

"What's wrong boo?" Dre said.

"The police just left. They say you wanted for murder!"

"What?" Dre snapped, not believing what he was hearing.

"You heard me, they looking for you. They want you to turn yourself in."

"Fuck that!! Look here, don't worry yourself. I got this. Okay?" Dre said before going back to the car. Things were not looking good. Mann and him were getting money like never before and through Silk they had a

Eyone Williams

Fishscale connect but now he was wanted for a body and they were beefin' hard. Not a day went by that they didn't go hunting for their prey. Walking back to the car, he thought about whose murder they could want him for. He knew it was no one to tell on Tate's murder because the only eyes to see it were Mann and Black. Besides that, Black did the shooting so they would want him first, Dre thought. That left room for only one other body that he could think of and that was the Jamaican that he smashed outside of the Black Hole in the beginning of the year. After Black hit the nigga in the middle of Georgia Avenue with the car he was driving, they got out and finished him off with 12 hollow points. Dre was sure that's what they wanted him for. He got in the car and told Mann the fucked up news while pulling off.

Lil' Garvin had been out of the group home for a few days, all he had to do now was get in school when it started in about a week. He didn't like the dirt bikes that his little partners got around on, so he took $2500 and bought a black Chevy Impala and got the windows tinted dark black. Lil' Garvin was taking Lando over Nakia's house so that he could stash the Tec-9. He didn't want to take a chance with leaving it in the house anymore. He knew in his heart that Pamila would find it sooner or later. He decided to keep the Glock on him. He now packed it all day, extended 35 shot clip and all. Quick laid in the back seat playing with the Tec while he was "jonin" on how Lil' Garvin could hardly see over the wheel, holding it with both hands. Pulling up in front of Nakia's, Lando got the Tec from Quick and told them he would beep them when he wanted them to pick him up.

Lando crept into the house through the back door that Nakia always left open when she knew he was coming. Nakia was sitting on her bed in nothing but a T-shirt and panties, eating ice cream when Lando walked into the room with the Tec-9 in his hands.

"Boy! What you think you doin' wit dat?" Nakia said, as she stood up displaying her thick brown skinned legs.

"I told you I needed you to put something up for me boo," Lando said reassuringly.

Nakia took the Tec-9 and walked into a huge walk-in closet, swinging her hips enticingly saying "You gon' get me in trouble. If my mother find this gun and all these drugs, she gon' put my ass out!"

"She ain't gonna find it," Lando said as he laid across the bed, and went on to say "If she do, I'll buy us a house." Lando had an "8th a Ki" bagged up in a Nike shoebox along with $6800 now. Wee-Wee was selling him 8th's for $2800 now and he was seeing his little money stack by the hour hand-to-hand on the block.

Nakia came back, laid down beside Lando on the bed, and said "How you think you gon' buy us a house boo?"

Staring at the spinning ceiling fan, he responded in a "matter of fact" tone. "Pretty soon, I'ma be able to buy us whatever we want!"

Kelley walked through Takoma Park, in a tan loose fitting linen Armani short set. She was just getting off from work, so she decided to go hang out at Kisha's house for a little while and then go in the house before it got too late. Kelley grew up with Kisha and Metra; they had been girlfriends their whole lives. Now that Kelley was growing up, she felt herself being pulled away from them by her plans of going away to college next year. She wanted something out of life and nothing was going to get in her way if she had anything to do with it. As her mind reflected on her future, she couldn't see herself being like Kisha, running the streets and living off of Onion. She damn sure couldn't see herself being like Metra, selling ass and living day for day. She promised herself that she would always love them, but she would never be like them. Her thoughts were abruptly interrupted by a loud car horn.

"Kelley! Kelley!" Metra yelled out the window of a little Toyota. With her cute fat face behind a pair of fresh Gucci sunglasses, she said, "Come on girl, get in!" Kelley got in the backseat and shut the door. The strong smell of Weed smoke hit her nose as they pulled off.

"Where you going?" Kisha said from the passenger seat.

"I was on my way down your house. What's up with y'all?" Kelley said, as she stretched her sexy legs across the back seat. Kisha went on to tell her how they had been shopping all day. Metra had been dying to ask her about Mann, she swore they were fucking.

"What's up with you and that fine black muthafucka?" Metra slipped in.

"Who you talking 'bout?" Kelley said with a smile.

Cutting in, Kisha said, "You know she talkin' 'bout Mann fine ass."

Kelley was 'diggin'' Mann, but she wasn't going to chase him like everyone else. They had been talking a lot this past summer, but she wasn't even thinking about giving him the pussy yet.

"Is y'all fuckin'?" Metra said.

"Bitch please!!" Kelley said. They went on talking, Metra somehow started talking about how she thought Mann and them was suckas and that Black was the only one with heart. Kisha knew better, she had seen all of them work before. She told Metra that she was "lunchin." Metra went on to say that she seen them work before too, but they were fakin" and if they weren't they would have done something about Marvin and Ant coming through shooting out of the LTD. She told Kisha that she heard them talking about it one night at the hotel. Kisha and Kelley were fucked up that Metra knew they had done the shooting and didn't say shit. Kisha was even more fucked up than Kelley being as though bullets flew through her living room that night. Both Kisha and Kelley were determined to hip Mann and the rest of the niggaz around the way that they knew who did the bustin' that night.

Black was laying in the bed sleep with a freak bitch he had pulled the night before. Something kept telling him to wake up. He opened his eyes and saw that it was still dark outside. Rolling over, he sat on the side of his bed and grabbed his beeper off of the nightstand next to the bed. Wiping the sleep out of his eyes he saw that it was only 5:45am. He ran his hand through his long hair thinking that he would get the broad to cornrow his shit for him later on. He got up and grabbed his blue Perry Ellis jeans off of the hotel floor, pulling a half smoked 50 bag of skunk weed out of the pocket. Black had been laying low in the Walter Reed Inn on Georgia Avenue since Dre told him that he had a warrant on him. Unlike Dre, Black was sure they were going to be looking for him next and knew why.

Dre and Black had robbed a Maryland bamma in the beginning of the summer. Dre was under the impression that they weren't going to have to kill the dude being as though he would never know who they were behind their mask. A broad had told Black that she knew that it was $50,000 in cash in the dude's grandmother's house. Wasting no time, Black scooped Dre in Mann's old station wagon, put him down with the move telling him how it was sweet and that they wouldn't have to kill the bamma. They had slid in and out with ease, but they didn't put their mask on until they were at the door. While they were coming out, the dude had got strong and popped the phone cord they had tied him up with. Black grabbed him and slammed 6 inches of Buck knife steel into his gut. Black was sure that he died, but the only person that could be telling was the broad that gave him the lick. He was going to have to kill her.

After smoking a blunt to the head, he got back into the bed with the cute brown skinned broad. Suddenly, the hotel door burst open, A.T.F. agents in all black, with Mini-14's swarmed the room. The broad jumped out of the bed naked, titties bouncing everywhere, screaming hysterically. An agent rushed her and slammed her to the floor face first. He then pressed her face hard into the dirty carpet, smashing his knee into her back. He couldn't help but to look at the woman's fat brown ass. Five agents rushed Black choking him out as they wrestled him down on the bed, and handcuffed him placing him under arrest.

Mann was fucked up about Black. He knew the Feds would be charging him as an adult for the body. Black had been in and out since he was 11 years old, but this was the first murder that he had ever been boxed up for. As Mann cruised down Georgia Avenue, coming back from dropping Dre off at the hotel way out Virginia, he felt his anger and frustration boiling. His cousin just went in on a murder, and his partner was on the run for it. To add to the night's problems, he saw Ant on the pay phone across the street. He was slippin'. Mann glanced around to see who Ant could be with. He saw that his Dodge wagon was the only car in the mini mall parking lot. Now was the time.

Mann calmly passed by the mini mall and doubled back into the alley behind it. He quickly tied a black bandanna around his face and pulled his black Madness baseball cap down over his eyes. With the slickness and precision of a crocodile on the hunt in murky waters, Mann crept back around the corner with his 9mm in hand. Step after quiet step, he tip toed up behind Ant until he could almost reach out and touch him. Ant sensed someone was behind him, but it was too late. His senses had failed him and his slippin' would cost him his life. He dropped the phone and swung around to see nothing but the eyes of a dark skinned killer with some kind of pistol in his face. He broke and ran for his car. Mann started "dumpin" as he ran behind him. POP! POP! POP! One by one, Mann tagged him over and over, slug after slug. Ant felt his legs getting weak, yet he put his all into making it to the car. Behind him, the sound of gunshots just wouldn't stop. He could no longer feel the pain of the hot hollow points that were murderously slamming into his body. He fell hard on his face, sliding on the black top. The gunfire stopped and he rolled over to look up

Eyone Williams

into the star lit sky. A million thoughts running through his mind. Most were dreams of living to see another day. He looked up as a shadow covered him. Then next thing he saw was Mann, who stood right over top of him and put an end to any hopes of survival. Two shots point blank to the head left Ant blood soaked and dead, lying beside his car waiting to be found.

Four

The phone began to ring as Pamila sat in the living room playing with Tyesha. She picked the tall lean child up and answered the phone. "Hello," she said as she sat down and placed Tyesha on her lap. "You have a collect call from Black at the Central Detention Facility." Pamila accepted the call and called Black by his real name as she always did. "Richard!" she said, not surprised at all, "what are you locked up for now boy?"

"I ain't do nothing Aunt Pamila, they talking about I killed somebody I never heard of."

"Killed somebody?"

"Yeah, I don't go back to court for another 9 days. They got me on an 8-day hold right now, but weekends don't count. I'm cool though, it ain't nothing to worry about. I'll be out soon. I need to holla at Mann right now, is he home?"

"No, you know him and Lando are never in here. Call back later on, Mann should be in here about 10 or 11. Do you need anything?" Pamila said.

"Na, I'm cool, just tell Mann to be in there when I call. Okay? I love you," Black said and hung up the phone. Pamila shook her head as she hung up the phone. That boy ain't never going to learn, she thought.

Marvin was sitting on the steps in front of Ant's apartment building surrounded by his partners Ric, Will, and Jammie, who was Ant's younger brother. They were fucked up about Ant getting smashed and they knew that them 5th Street niggaz had something to do with it. Ric, the youngest one, was in a murderous rage about his man's killing. He was trying to kill everybody down 5th Street. Jammie and Will wanted to do something about the murder, but they needed Marvin or Ric to push them. Marvin began talking in a no non-sense voice telling everybody how shit was going to get straightened, and that they were going to do it. Marvin got up and walked to Ant's car followed by his niggaz and left.

Eyone Williams

It was 2:30pm Monday afternoon and Lil' Garvin was outside of Quick's grandmother house blowing the horn. His timing couldn't be better. Quick's grandmother had found a box of bullets under his bed and went off.

"You no good boy! You sell them drugs, you don't go to school, you just a bum!" She screamed as Quick slammed the door.

"I ain't tryin' to hear that shit!" Quick said as he ran down the apartment steps and jumped in the car with Lil' Garvin and Baby D.

"What's up young?" Baby D said, sitting in the passenger seat.

"Ain't shit joe. My grandmother beefin' and shit, but I'm chillin'," Quick said. Lil' Garvin pulled off headed for Paul Junior High School to pick Lando up. School started a week ago and Lando had gone everyday. He would get a ride from Lil' Garvin, drop his books off, and hit the strip to hustle until nightfall. For now it was working.

Lil' Garvin pulled up in front of the school as it was letting out. Lando was coming out of the big green beat up doors with a gorgeous young girl, with long silky brown hair, a light honey golden complexion, and beautiful brown eyes that made her look like she was from the Philippines. Lando got her number and got into the car with his niggaz. "Who was that bad ass bitch young?" said Baby D.

"Her name is Jazmin, she cool as shit joe. I been jive rappin' to her in class but she on some real laid back shit," Lando said.

As they rolled around the way, everybody was asking Lando about Black. What was he in for? When was he coming home? How could they go see him? Lando let them know that he was charged with murder, but he hadn't talked to him or went to see him yet. Lil' Garvin brought up the beef between them and 13th Street, telling everybody how the dude Ant had got his head hit a few days ago. "Fuck dem niggaz young!" said Baby D, with a mug on his face.

"No bullshit, fuck them niggaz! We should ride on them niggaz wit out Mann and them!" Quick snapped. Everybody agreed. Lando began to think. He had never shot a nigga before and he was itching to bust his Glock dead in a nigga's ass. His wait wouldn't be long now, he was sure of it.

Dre was playing everything by ear until he heard from Black. That way he could take care of any loose ends on the streets and then turn himself in and beat the case along with Black. Being as though he was now on the run, he only came in the city to make a drop off or to collect some of his cash. On this windy fall morning, he was coming through Rittenhouse Street to serve Smoke a "half a brick" of Fishscale. Pulling up in his white Nissan Maxima, he parked on 3rd Street, two blocks away from the heat of the strip on 5th Street. A short, stocky, black dude, in a dark blue Nautica jacket, with the hood pulled over his head, came walking swiftly up behind Dre's car from out of the alley. Being on the run had Dre's senses on blast. He tightened up the grip on his Colt.45, and swung his head around to see who was walking up on him like that. It was clear that it was Smoke. He had been smoking an early morning blunt in the alley while he waited for Dre to come through with the coke. "What's up slim?" Smoke said, as he flopped his heavy body down in the passenger seat of the car, sending a strong smell of weed smoke into the air.

"Ain't shit slim. Here you go," Dre said, as he passed him a folded zip-lock bag with coke in it. Knowing that Dre was on the run and that he couldn't stay in one place very long, Smoke stuffed the coke into his big jacket pocket. Smoke looked around and combed his surroundings as he pulled an "overweight" stack of cash out of his inside pocket.

"Here you go slim, that's right there," Smoke said as he passed Dre the money and went on to say "You know I talked to Black last night."

"Oh yeah? What's up wit' em?" Dre asked, very interestingly.

"I ain't talk to 'em that long, he said they was about to count. He told me to tell you to send Tina to see 'em, or tell Mann to come see 'em so he can holla at you. He say that they ain't give 'em no bond, and he don't go back to court until January 18."

"Next year?" Dre said, with disappointment in his voice.

"Yeah slim, next year! I was fucked up too, but we can't do shit but wait until something gives. I'm down for whatever, I'ma make sure he come home. Other than that, I just sent him a $100 and told him to send me a package slip so I could get 'em some gear and shit." When they were finished, Smoke got out of the car and Dre went straight over Pamila's house to drop off $200 for her to send to Black since he knew that's who would be on top of his business for him.

DC Jail's visiting hall was packed with FAMILY members of all kind coming to see their confined loved ones. The young females that were coming to see their men had the spot looking like a small fashion show in all of the top-flight gear that was on the streets. On the other side of the scratched up old Plexiglass that separated the two very different worlds, were men from all walks of life. Every face that had a phone to its ear, on the other side of the glass, told a very different story of survival through their expressions. Some told stories of long nights of pipe smoking, some told stories of a hard life struggling on the streets, and some told stories of men already convicted of crimes that would have them legally fighting for their freedom for the rest of their lives.

As Black came through the powerful sliding iron door that lead back to the cell blocks, his face told a story like no other in the room. There wasn't a trace of a worry in his face as he sat down and picked up the phone and said "What's up joe?"

Picking up the phone on the other side of the glass, Mann said "What's up with you?"

"Ain't shit, I'm just waiting to go back to court. I think they gon' throw this shit out. My lawyer say they got me on some hearsay shit, we should know more at the next status hearin' though." Black looked over Mann and saw Kelley walking toward him waving, with a huge smile on her beautiful face. Black couldn't take his eyes off of Kelley's well-shaped body. Her thick thighs looked so good in her tight Gap jeans. Mann looked over his shoulder and saw that Kelley was just coming back from the bathroom. He turned back to Black with a big smile on his face, as Kelley sat down beside him.

"What's up with you and Kelley joe?" Black said.

"We cool...." Mann said and before he could finish, Kelley snatched the phone and said "What's up Black? Don't listen to him. We more then cool nowadays." Kelley rapped to Black for a few more minutes before giving the phone back to Mann. She made sure she told him all about Metra and her knowledge of Ant and Marvin shooting at them out of the White LTD. Black never trusted Metra, but he now felt he had a reason to kill her. Mann got back on the phone and let Black know that everything was going to be cool and that as soon as they found out who was talking to let him know so he could take care of business. Just as Mann was about to hang up the phone, Black looked at him with a smile, while Kelley was on her way to the door and said "You ran into Ant didn't you?" Mann didn't even open his mouth; he smoothly hung up the phone and winked his eye as he put his hand up to the glass to give Black "5" as he left.

Mann was watching Kelley's hips shake all the way up the steps to her front door. Once she was in the house, he popped his 300ZX into his first gear, lighting up the dashboard as he went flying up the street. Turning on to Georgia Avenue, he saw that the Avenue was full of life tonight. Niggaz were everywhere, cars with music blasting were double-parked, and pipeheads were sadly rushing back and forth up and down the Ave. in search of a way to get a blast. Overall, this was a perfect picture of the Government's "War on Drugs". Parking his car in the mini mall parking lot, he got out to holla at a few niggas he fucked with from the Ave. He saw that the Ave. was pumpin', money and crack were exchanging hands with velocity. It had been a long time since he had been out on the block grindin' hand to hand. His man Pat-Pat stepped to him, giving him "5" saying "Let me holla at you". Mann and Pat-Pat stepped away from the crowd in front of Sam's Liquor Store. Pat-Pat was all about cash and could always relate to Mann. They had been cool since they were kids. Pat-Pat was a tall dark dude and when he spoke it was always with "sense".

"I been hearin' about this shit between you and Marvin and them since this summer. You done let that shit ride to long. I was over there in the cut the night Ant got his head hit. I saw the whole thing go down and I peeped you double back, so I can put 2 and 2 together. I know how you work. My thing is this, you got to get the shit over slim. Now that Black is in, they gon' be tryin' to catch you slippin'!" Pat-Pat said, with the sound of real concern in his voice. Mann's beeper went off as he started to respond.

"You right slim. I'm on top of that shit joe. Believe dat! I gotta call this number back, so I'ma catch up with you." Mann gave Pat-Pat "5" and ran across the street to use the pay phone in the mini mall parking lot with Pat-Pat's words still fresh on his mind.

Mann got on the phone and called Silk back. He turned and leaned his back against the white brick wall of the drug store so that he could see everything moving, he was in no mood to get caught slippin' tonight or any other night.

"What's up Silk?" Mann said, as he watched a beautiful young woman walk into the drug store.

"I just came from seeing Supreme. Come get your break down," Silk said, and quickly got off of the subject of business on the phone. Silk began asking Mann about Black and Dre. While he was talking to him,

Mann got a strange feeling in his gut and slid his hand under his thick gray Polo hoody, wrapping his fingers around the fresh Ruger 9mm tucked in his waistband. He began to think.... He was on the same pay phone he had caught Ant on almost two weeks ago. He glanced over to the drug store door and saw Marvin coming out.

His first thought was to start shooting on the spot, fuck witnesses and all. Marvin was out of the door when their eyes locked for what seemed like forever. Standing right outside of the door that just swung shut, Marvin thought about running back inside, but in his heart he knew it was do or die. Mann dropped the receiver to the pay phone, while Silk was still talking. That set it off. At the exact same time, they both pulled their pistols in what appeared to be slow motion. Mann got the first shot off, catching Marvin in the chest. Marvin staggered backward as he let his first shots go, knocking Mann against the wall. Pat Pat was servin' a pipehead across the street when he heard the shots going off. He saw Mann and Marvin standing no further then 10 feet apart, with flames of gunfire between them. Mann fell to the ground, still shooting, but he was hit bad. Marvin was running now. He flew across Georgia Avenue, with bullets still flying by his head. Mann emptied his pistol and looked at his blood soaked shirt. He could see the huge holes Marvin's .45 had put in it. His head began to spin. He believed that what goes around comes around, but he never thought he would die on the same pay phone he killed a nigga on.

Pat Pat ran across the street to help Mann. He knelt down beside him and grabbed him in his arms saying "Hold on slim! You gon be okay!"

Mann looked him in the eyes and said in a last breath voice "Get rid of this pistol, I hear the bodeans comin!" Pat Pat took the pistol, threw it down the sewer, and came back. Mann was looking into Pat Pat's face as he screamed "Hold on!", but Mann couldn't hear a word he said. Mann tried with his all to hold on, but everything went black as he slumped in Pat Pat's arms.

Marvin sat on Ric's bed, breathing like a raging bull. As Ric helped him to take off his shirt, Marvin was already telling him how he killed Mann up on the Avenue. Ric was "cised", he couldn't wait to finish the rest of them niggaz. Pulling off his bulletproof vest, Marvin could see that his whole upper body had dark purple bruises all over it from the slugs that had slammed into his chest.

Fast Lane

"Damn joe! Your shit all fucked up!" Ric said as he saw the damage the Ruger did to Marvin's body through the vest.

"I'm cool young! I just gotta lay low now. It was a rack a muthafuckas on the Ave tonight. I know somebody know me," Marvin said. He decided to stay over Ric's house for the night, and slide out of town in the morning. He knew that way he would be far enough away to see what the Feds would do, without staying in a hotel where somebody might see him that knew him. All he could do right now was wait for the next move.

Everybody in the house was asleep when the phone rang and broke the peaceful silence of the night. Half asleep, Pamila rolled over wondering who the fuck was calling her house at this time of the night. "Hello!" she snapped, in a pissed off tone.

"Sorry to disturb you at this hour, but this is Detective Brown, from 4th D. I need to know if a Mark Mills lives at this house," a deep voice said through the phone. Pamila knew what kind of life Mann was living, so she didn't want to give the Feds any information she didn't have to.

"Why do you need to know that?" She said, very concerned.

"Well ma'am, Mr. Mills has been shot very bad and this is the phone number on his I.D.. I'm trying to contact a family member," the detective said in a "straight to the point" way. Pamila began to feel faint. She was speechless for a moment. This was the very phone call she had dreaded for years.

"This is his mother. Is he alive?" she said, praying that she would hear him say yes.

"I really can't say ma'am. They took him to Washington Hospital Center by Medivac. You will be able to find out how he is doing down there." Fighting tears back, Pamila quickly got dressed and rushed to the hospital, leaving Tyesha and Lando asleep.

After sitting in the emergency room waiting area for hours, she got up and called Lando on the pay phone. While the phone rang, she could see the early morning sun just beginning to shine into the lobby window.

"Hello?" Lando said, wide awake. The sound of his voice somehow put a sense of hope in Pamila's heart about Mann making it.

"Lando, look. I got a problem, so I need you to stay home and watch Tyesha 'til I get there." Lando had no problem staying home from school. He agreed and Pamila walked back into the waiting area. As soon as she sat down, an old white man emerged through the emergency room's double doors wearing latex gloves, and a long doctor's robe. Pamila felt her heart pounding rapidly as she awaited the verdict.

"Ms. Mills, your son has just come out of surgery," the doctor said. "We can't say how things will turn out at this time. Mark has slipped into a mild coma, so it's all in God's hands now. We have done our best. We have moved him up to the 3rd floor in room 311. You may see him."

Tears ran down Pamila's face in a steady flow as she walked down the hall to Mann's room. She stepped into Mann's room and was horrified by what she saw. Mann laid in a white robe, with all kinds of tubes coming out of his body. Even one long tube was inserted into his nose pumping a thick green fluid out of his stomach. Pamila could hardly look at Mann; he looked like he was dead already. Looking around the room, Pamila had never seen a person hooked up to so many life support machines in her life. Ever since Mann was able to walk, he always found a way to do for himself. That's how he got the nickname from Pamila years ago. Pamila slowly walked over to his bed, placing her hand softly on his forehead. Silently she prayed. "Lord, please spare his soul. I know that this life is but play and amusement, pomp and mutual boasting. Even so, I beg you. Please don't take him away like this." Pamila pulled up a chair beside the bed, and talked to Mann until she fell asleep, knowing that he could not hear her. It was just good to know he was alive, in whatever condition he was in.

Tyesha was lying on Lando's bed in a pink pajama set, watching him play Super Mario Bros., when Pamila walked in the front door. They both got up and went down stairs to see where Pamila had been all day. Tyesha ran and jumped straight into Pamila's arms, not noticing the look of desperation in her face. Lando on the other hand, quickly caught on. He knew Pamila well and it was very rare to find the strong woman perplexed about anything. The burden she carried was openly displayed in her body language, even though she tried to hide it.

"What's wrong wit you?" Lando said, becoming very concerned and uneasy. Pamila kissed Tyesha, and sat her down, telling her to go play Nintendo for a minute while she spoke to Lando. The little girl ran off, leaving them alone. As Pamila sat down on the couch, she searched for the right words to say and the right way to say them. Again Lando asked. "What's wrong?" Pamila began to speak in a slow and serious tone.

"Lando, you are growing up fast. You've seen a lot. What I have to tell you, may upset you but...."

"What's up Pamila?" Lando cut in.

"Mann's in a coma. He got shot last night." As Pamila spoke, her words echoed through Lando's ears. He couldn't believe what he was hearing. It couldn't be true. Mann was never slippin', he was always on point. Lando's thoughts of Mann's "Game tight mobbin'" were coming from every corner of his mind.

"Shot? Who the fu.... Who did dat?" Lando asked, as his anger began to boil over. Reality hit Lando when Pamila spoke again.

"I don't know who shot 'em. I don't want to know. All I want is for Mann to come out of this shit alive. I don't want you out there trying to find out who shot 'em either."

"When can I see 'em?"

"Tomorrow."

Pamila talked to Lando for awhile, trying to get him to leave the whole situation up to Mann. By no means did she want Lando out in the streets trying to straighten his big brother's beef, but some how she knew it was nothing she could do to stop him. His love for the realest nigga in his life was too deep.

Lando sat on his bed staring at the floor for a long time. The mere thought of Mann laying in a coma with bullet holes in his body was a thought that wouldn't allow him to think about anything other then pay back. "Fuck dat!!" Lando said out loud, as he got up and went down the basement to get his Glock out of the stash spot in the ceiling. He sat on Mann's bed and took the clip out, sliding the 35 shot extended clip in the pistol. Cocking the Glock, he swore to himself that one of them 13th Street niggaz was dying tonight and every other night until Mann was able to take care of his business or until all of them niggaz were 6 feet deep. Lando needed a ride. His bike would make too much noise for what he wanted to do. He used Mann's phone to call Lil' Garvin.

"Hello?" Lil' Garvin answered the phone with N.W.A.'s Gangsta Gangsta playing in the background. The house was live and Lando could hear it.

"I need you to come get me young," Lando said, sounding more serious than ever.

"What's wrong?"

"I'll tell you when you get here. I'll be on the corner at the top of my block," Lando said and hung up the phone, leaving the house.

Eyone Williams

The night was cool and windy. Lando stood on the dark corner of 5th & Tuckerman Streets, in a black Eddie Bauer windbreaker, black Gap jeans, and a pair of black Timberland boots. If a person got close enough, they could see the print of the long extended clip in the Glock poking out of his waistband. In less than 10 minutes, Lil' Garvin was pulling up in his black Impala, with Quick and Baby D. Lando hopped in the back with Baby D and they pulled off. Lando could hardly see Quick's face in the darkness of the car when he turned around in the passenger seat and said "What the fuck is up young?" Lando told everybody about Mann being shot. None of them could believe that Mann was in a coma. They all loved Mann like a brother. He had looked out for all of them as they grew up under him. Lando didn't have to ask anyone if they were "rollin". Baby D spoke for the whole car when he said, "We gotta see them bitch ass niggaz tonight young!!" Already showing traces of the quick thinking of Mann, Lando told everybody that the 13th Street niggaz would feel safe now that they thought Mann was dead, with Dre on the run, and Black locked up.

"Them niggaz gon be out in the open. They ain't expecting no get back yet!" Lando said, pulling the Glock out and laying it on his lap before going on "Everybody strapped?"

"Naa, take me around the way. I gotta pump stashed in back of the crack house," Baby D said.

Lando looked at Quick and said "What about you?"

"I got my .38," Quick said.

Lando looked at Lil' Garvin through the rear view mirror and said "I know you strapped!" Lil' Garvin responded by waving his huge .44 Bull Dog in the air.

After stopping around the way to get Baby D's pump, Lando told Lil' Garvin to slide over Nakia's house to get his Tec-9 for Quick. Lando knew how blood thirsty Quick was, he always reminded him of his cousin Black. This was one time that Lando was in support of Quick's ruthlessness and to show it, he was going to arm his partner with the 32 shot Tec-9. It's murdaaaa!!!!

13th Street was pumpin' tonight. Ric had sold out twice and went in the house to bag up another "62". Will, Jammie, and a few younger dudes sat on the steps in front of the apartment building smoking weed while they were hustlin'. Boo, a 6-foot tall, dark skinned, heavyset nigga from 13th Street walked up. "What's up?" He said to his niggaz. Everybody said what's up at the same time. An old Cadillac Seville pulled up right in front of the crowd and stopped. Quickly, everybody turned to see who was in the car. Will squinted his eyes to make out the driver. It was a pipehead that he always served. Picking up a half way empty bottle of Cognac beside him, Will got in the passenger seat to serve the fiend, leaving the door open with one leg hanging out of the car. Two more pipeheads walked up. Jammie jumped on the sells. The rush was on. Sells were coming from every direction. Ric came jogging out of the building, coke in hand, and quickly started servin' left and right. In the heat of the "rush", Quick, Lando, Baby D, and Lil' Garvin exploded out of the dark cut behind them, wearing black ski masks.

Boo, being the closest to the cut never had a chance. Standing with the blunt in his mouth, in a state of shock, Baby D blew him off of his feet and kept bustin' at the crowd. Lil' Garvin came right behind him finishing Boo with two devastating blasts from the Bull Dog. Ric dropped his coke and money, as he jumped over a car followed by Baby D's shot gun blasting. Panic set in, everybody scattered. Quick was in the middle of 13th Street waving the Tec-9 from side to side with both hands, spraying everything moving with vengeance and intensity. One of the young dudes that were running caught a slug in the back and tumbled to the ground helplessly. Never subsiding on the trigger, Quick showed no mercy to his prey. Running up on the young dude, Quick pumped 5 quick rounds into him, snatching his last breath, and then turned and went after Jammie who was fleeing down the street. Lando aggressively attacked the Cadillac Will was sitting in. 9mm slugs flew through the car striking the pipehead in the face, instantly killing him. The car started to drift down 13th Street, with Will balled up in the passenger seat, while the driver laid slumped and lifeless behind the wheel. Lando jogged along side the car, firing the Glock through the window, now that Will had slammed the door seeking refuge. Lando filled Will with 20 or more hollow points before the car smashed into a tree at the end of the block. In seconds, the four teenage killers were gone as quickly as they came, leaving 4 dead and many wounded.

Five

A week later, Black was walking down the top right tier in the North 1 cell block of the DC Jail, with the top of his pressed blue jumper tied around his waist, like 'Fuck the world two times!' He got on the phone to call Kisha's house collect, turning his back to the wall so that he could face the day room that was full of young killers charged as adults, just like himself. As the phone rang, Black lit a Newport and adjusted the buck knife on his waistband that he had bought from a pipehead C.O. he knew from around the way.

"What's up nigga?" Kisha said in an excited, high-pitched hood rat voice.

"Ain't shit. I'm chillin', this shit ain't nothing. You seen Mann?"

"Mann?" Kisha asked, sounding confused, and added, "You ain't heard about Mann?"

"Heard what?" Black snapped, already becoming angry by not being informed.

Kisha watched her step, picking her words very carefully, "Mann uh..."

"Mann what?" Black snapped.

"He in the hospital. He got shot last week."

Black couldn't believe his ears. He swore she had the facts mixed up. Kisha went on to tell Black all that she knew about Mann being shot. She told him that Marvin did it, how he did it, and where.

"Where the fuck Dre at?" Black yelled through the phone.

"I ain't seen him in over a week. He only come through in spots. You know? But Lando and them got the hood hot as shit! They been lighten shit up every night since Mann got shot," Kisha said. Black finished talking to Kisha and hung up the phone burning with anger. He had to get out and quick.

Silk was pissed off that Dre wasn't returning his beeps. He had been trying to catch up with Dre since he heard the shooting over the phone. Silk had got word from the streets that Mann was in a coma, but he wanted to know who put him in a coma. It had been years since Silk had put some work in. Since he had started getting bricks by the 10's and now the 20's, he tried not to get his hands dirty. He had too many young niggaz that loved the gunplay. Yet and still, he had grown a love for Mann. He was going to find out who shot him and have something done about it. His first step was 5th & Rittenhouse Streets.

As soon as Silk's Benz turned on to Rittenhouse Street, he saw that the "jump-outs" had a group of dudes against the wall in the alley searching them. Looking closer, he saw that Lando was one of the dudes that they had hemmed up. He pulled over and parked, waiting for the Feds to let everybody go, so he could pull up on Lando.

Everyone went their own way as the "jump-outs" left. Lando and Quick came walking out of the alley together. Silk blew the horn to get their attention. Seeing Silk, they walked over and got in the car.

"What's up?" Lando asked from the backseat.

"I'm tryin' to find out who shot your brother," Silk said as he pulled off.

"We found out this nigga named Marvin did it. We been going through that joint every night, tearin' shit up, but the nigga don't never be around. Just some niggaz he fuck wit. We walked through there today, about 40 minutes ago, on the way home from school, that joint a ghost town," Lando said.

"Oh, yeah?" Silk responded with a smile. He had been hearing about Lando getting a little bit of money all summer, but it was like he started firing pistols overnight. Quick, on the other hand, he had been hearing about for the longest. These two young niggaz would be able to hold it down until Mann was back on his feet, Silk thought. He would make sure that they needed nothing in the streets.

"Look here," Silk said, handing Quick his beeper number, and continued, "I want y'all to hit me if y'all need anything."

"Cool," Quick said. After Silk had made his loyalty to Mann clear and his support of Lando and Quick known, he dropped them off on 5th Street and rolled out.

Kelley had gotten tired of hearing all the rumors about how Mann was dead or how he would never walk again, so she called Pamila's house early one morning telling her who she was and how she thought she was in love with Mann. Pamila, being a sagacious judge of character, quickly dissected the girl's morals & principles and decided to take her to the hospital with her.

Pamila stood over Mann, talking to him, as she had done everyday for the last week. Kelley stood behind her, fighting back tears. The one nigga that she could see herself with was hooked up to beeping life support machines with tubes coming out of his body. The sight made her somewhat understand why Lando and the rest of the young niggaz around the way seemed to be shooting every night after dark. Looking at Mann, she thought about what Lando told her after he and Quick had come from seeing Mann the day after they sprayed 13th Street. Lando told her that he wasn't going back to that hospital until Mann came out of that coma. And if he died, he only wanted memories of Mann at his best. He would pay his respect by "bustin' ass" every night. The knock on the thick wooden door behind her snapped her out of her daze, as a doctor came in and asked to speak to Pamila in the hallway.

Pamila stepped out into the busy hallway with the tall African doctor. As speeding nurses and doctors hurried by, the doctor gave Pamila the bad news that she had been asking him for. "Ms. Mills, we've been doing a lot of tests on your son. He's suffered 5 critical gunshot wounds, one of which lodged itself less then an inch from his spine damaging the lower part of his cerebral cortex..."

"What are you telling me?" Pamila angrily snapped cutting the doctor off.

"I'm saying that if your son comes out of his coma, he'll never walk again." Pamila didn't want to hear that and she didn't believe it either.

Walking back into the room with Mann and Kelley, Pamila saw Kelley rubbing Mann's forehead, talking to him. Pamila stood silently looking on. "You gon' make it boo," Kelley said, with tears running down her cute face, "You got too many people pullin' for you boy." Pamila walked up beside Kelley and held Mann's hand. That doctor don't know shit, Pamila thought. Her faith in the Creator was too firm. She knew Mann would be fine. As soon as those thoughts went through her mind, Mann showed the first signs of life. He turned his head, letting out a moan. Kelley screamed out of excitement, while Pamila only smiled as her faith was strengthened.

Mann struggled to open his eyes. Immediately, the pain of the bullet wounds shot through his body, causing him to frown up his face in anguish. Kelley rushed to his aid, caressing his weak body softly. Mann rested his head and looked up at Pamila and said in an exhausted voice,

"Why y'all look like somebody died. I know y'all ain't count me out." Pamila and Kelley laughed. Mann's strength took a huge burden off of their shoulders.

"I'm in bad shape huh?" Mann said, as he looked at all the tubes that were running through his body.

"You're alive, that's all that matters," Pamila said. Mann thought about what she had said. He remembered the whole shooting and he began to wonder if Marvin got away or not. He remembered tagging him, but he saw him break across the street that night and that's all he remembered. Pamila was right, he thought, he was alive.

"Where Lando at?" Mann asked. Kelley looked away from Mann to Pamila, wanting her to answer the question. She knew that the 411 she had on Lando couldn't be talked about in front of Pamila. Mann read this in her actions and looked at Pamila. She on the other hand, was already hip.

"Lando's bad ass runnin' around wit Quick and them wanna be gangstas, playin' payback. I pray that you get outta here soon. You gotta do something to let 'em know that you got things under control. Every night I stare out of my bedroom window wishing Lando was coming down the street, but with you lying here shot I know what he's doing," Pamila said, giving up a look that showed she wasn't as green as they thought. Mann laid in pain talking to Pamila and Kelley, thinking about Lando, knowing he had to hurry up and get back on his feet.

Handcuffed and shackled in the back of a U.S. Marshal's van being extradited to the DC Jail to face murder charges, Dre sat in a daze. Over and over again, he heard Mann's voice telling him how his dick was going to get him caught up one day.

Funky ass bitch!! Dre thought. He had wanted some pussy so bad that he danced with the devil. After beeping Tina all morning, not knowing that she had went to see Black like he told her to, Dre called around the way for the quickest fuck he could find. Despite all of her cruddiness and snake ways, Metra had some smoking' pussy, bomb head, and she could fuck for days in whatever position you were trying to hit it in. Dre paid her cab fare all the way out Va., smoked an ounce of skunk weed with her, fucked her in the ass, came in her mouth, and paid her cab fare back to DC. An hour after she left, Va. State Troopers and FBI Agents kicked his hotel door in. On his way to the Alexandria Jail, a cocky red neck FBI Agent told Dre that a Metra Wilson had called him in and collected the $1,000 reward money for his arrest.

Black was taking a shit smoking a Newport looking out on to the pitch black tier when he heard 48 cell slam open, hungrily waiting for it's next meal of 'Young Black Male'. Wiping his ass, Black quickly got up and looked through the side of the bars, with his hands hanging out of the tray slot. Just like everybody else standing at their bars, Black was trying to see who it was that would be in the cell across from him. Black had done too much dirt to be slippin'when a new nigga came on the tier. He kept his cell jammed and if the new comer was "opposition", he was good as "hit" before the tier door slid shut.

Coming in the dark No.1 Sally port, Dre could feel butterflies in his stomach. Never showing the least sign of fear, Dre walked up to the bubble. When the lights came on, Dre saw pipehead Ronnie in his C.O. uniform. The short, big belly, dark skinned man emerged from the bubble with a smile and told the C.O. that walked Dre up from R-n-D that he had everything from there. Knowing Dre and Black from around the way, pipehead Ronnie knew that he would be smoking good as long as they were locked up, because he would be their only connect to the streets.

Dre's 6 foot 4 frame stepped through the tier door into the darkness. Step-by- step, Dre walked past the tiny dark cells looking into the eyes of the unfriendly faces behind the bars. "Where you from cuz?" A husky voice called out. Looking around the tier to see where the voice had come from, Dre responded, "You got me fucked up slim!" Black recognized his voice off the top.

"Dre!" Black called out.

"What's up young?" Dre said as he jogged up to Black's bars, dropping his goodie bag and bed roll on the floor.

"What's up nigga?" Dre said, as he gave his man "5".

"Ain't shit joe. How da fuck you let them peoples catch up wit you?" Black said.

"That snake ass bitch Metra! I had her out the hotel wit me, fuckin' her and shit. The bitch left and called the Feds on me for da cash."

"That bitch knew who was bustin' at us that night in the white LTD and she ain't say shit! I'ma hit dat bitch head as soon as we hit da brix!" Dre had no doubt that Black was serious, he ain't play that snake shit at all.

"You talked to Mann?" Dre asked, not knowing that he had been shot, being as though he got locked up a day before the shooting.

"Where da fuck you been? Mann got shot 'bout a week and a half ago?" Black said.

"Damn, I been out Alexandria for 'bout 10 days. Who da fuck shot Mann?" Dre asked with anger in his face. Black gave him the run down on everything around the way, from who shot Mann, all the way down to how Lando and his little mob put the work in about it. When Tina came to see Black, she brought Lando and Quick with her, so he now had all the facts as he put his man down with what was going down.

"So what dis case look like from your end?" Dre asked, moving on.

"Shit cool, but we might gotta get somebody to hit the bitch head that put me down wit the move. She the only person that know anything, even so, she ain't see shit so whatever she say is hearsay," Black said. The cell door behind Dre began to shake, as the morning shift was coming on. Dre stepped in and continued rappin' to Black until they got tired.

Mann was pissed off. He had just cursed the doctor out for telling him that he may never walk again, despite the fact that he could move his legs. He just wasn't strong enough to try to stand up yet. As Mann got better, Pamila went back to work and only came to see him in the evening. Mann had a lot of time to think now. He was still getting use to the idea of Lando being in the street's "putting in work". There was nothing he could say, he would be doing the same thing if Lando were in the hospital shot. Mann didn't even try to tell Lando to stop doing what he was doing with his little mob. Lando had got word that they had killed Boo, Will, some young dude name Dug, and a pipehead the night they lit 13th Street up. Ric got shot in the back twice and Jammie got shot in the arm. Mann could hear Lando's words in his head as if he was still talking. "I ain't gon stop tearin' that joint up til dem niggaz dead!" All Mann could do was put his little brother on point about the new side of the game that he was now in. Over all, what he told him summed up to: "Watch your back and leave no memories." Thinking of witnesses, Mann's mind flew to DC Jail. Tina had put Mann on point about Dre and Black's murder case. The Feds knew that a broad had told Black that $50,000 was in the house and they knew that Black did the stabbing. Dre's name was implicated only as being part of the robbery, never the less, he was charged with murder. Mann knew the case was weak from what he had heard from Pamila and Tina, yet he still wanted the broad dead. That way he felt sure that his cousin and partner would make it home.

Mann's thoughts were interrupted when Lando, Quick, and Nakia came strolling in his room. Mann smiled when he saw Lando with his arm around Nakia's shoulders. The young girl was cute, Mann thought.

"What's up nigga?" Quick said as he hopped up on the bed beside Mann.

"Ain't shit shorty. How y'all get down here? Y'all could'na rode y'all bikes." Mann asked.

"We rollin' in big boy shit!" Quick said. Mann looked at Lando with an expression of curiosity.

"Black told me where the extra keys to his Ac was," Lando said, playing it cool. Every move he made had to be smooth when Nakia was around.

"Black told you that you could push his shit? You know he don't play 'bout that car," Mann said.

"Yeah he know, but check dis out," Lando said and continued. "We just left from around the way and Tina was beatin' Metra's ass out there. I mean fuckin' her around young! She done busted da bitch mouth all open and everything!"

"Fuck is all that about?" Mann said, as he pressed a button to raise the back of his bed, making him sit up straight.

Quick stood up and said, "You know that bitch got Dre locked-up!" Tina had failed to hip Mann to that fact when she came to see him, they spent so much time talking about the case Black and Dre had that she left without telling him.

"She did what?" Mann asked. He knew Metra was cruddie; she had been like that since they were kids, but she had never been "hot."

"Yeah slim, she turn big boy in for a G," Lando said. Mann turned his head to the right looking out into the clear fall afternoon, thinking how a lot of shit was going to change as soon as he was out of the hospital.

Skipping the subject, Mann looked over at the shy young girl sitting on Lando's lap and said, "So this is the girl you crazy about huh?"

Lil' Garvin had just parked his car in front of Kisha's house when Wee-Wee zoomed around the corner on a shiny black Ninja 900, dressed in all black, with his unbuttoned leather Hugo Boss jacket blowing in the wind. He had heard that his little cousin Quick was beefin' with some niggaz up 13th Street.   Wee-Wee pulled up right beside Lil' Garvin's Impala, as he and Baby D got out. Leaning on one leg, still revving the loud engine of the powerful sports bike, Wee-Wee gave Lil'Garvin "5" saying, "What's up shorty? I hear y'all beefin' wit some bammas up here." Lil' Garvin shut the door behind him and put Wee-Wee down with how Mann got shot, who did it, and who they were beefin' with. Wee-Wee knew Mann and everybody down 5th Street, but his main concern was Quick, who was his Aunt's son. Wee-Wee told Lil' Garvin to let Quick know that he was trying to holla at him as soon as possible. When they were done talking, Wee-Wee revved the bike aggressively, sending the RPM gauge into the red as he popped the clutch making the Ninja fishtail straight up Rittenhouse Street. The 130 horsepower bike flew from 0 to 60 in 3.7 seconds, propelling Wee-Wee's tall and lean body out of sight in a raging roar.

After watching Wee-Wee fly up the street, Baby D and Lil' Garvin walked up the street to pipehead Old Tima's house. This was the "crack house" on the block. Many nights niggaz would sit in Old Tima's house hustlin' till the sun was up or until they finished pushing all of their coke. Now that it was getting cold at night, everybody that had coke to sell could be found "slangin that shit" when the sun went down.

Stepping in the door, they saw Old Tima sitting in the living room hitting the pipe. The tall, gray-haired, old man saw the young dudes come through the door and said, "Where y'all been at? It's pumpin' like shit. Karen been spending money all day. Big Busta down the basement trying to smoke all her shit up now. Y'all better get some of that cash, just hit me off real quick and get me out the way." Baby D and Lil' Garvin both hit Old Tima off with a fat 50 rock each and began hustling.

One after another, pipeheads rushed Old Tima's house for their 15 seconds of fame at the end of the "glassdick." Two hours after Baby D and Lil' Garvin had come in the crack house; they had both made over $1200 each. Pipehead Karen had spent $1000 of her income tax return between the both of them. They had caught a good rush while nobody was around. They were on their way to get some "smoke" when pipehead Ronnie came through the door in his C.O. uniform.

"What's up scrap?" Ronnie said, "jeffin" hard.

"Ain't shit. What's up?" Baby D said in a rush to go get some "smoke." Ronnie told them that he worked in the cellblock that Dre and Black were in up the Jail. He said that they had sent him to get some weed and money. Lil' Garvin was always on point for game.

He folded his arms and said "Don't be playing no games!" Ronnie assured him that he was serious. Lil' Garvin gave him $100 and told him to wait in the crack house until they got back so that they could send Black and Dre some "smoke."

"So what do they got on me?" Dre angrily said to the tall white lady that sat across the table from him on his legal visit.

"They have a young woman that says she knows that you and Mr. Mills robbed Mr. Sutton and afterwards Mr. Mills fatally stabbed him. They know that you didn't kill Mr. Sutton, but if you don't tell 'em what really went down that day, you're going down for murder with your buddy. As your lawyer it's my job to give you the best..."

Dre quickly cut her off. "Fuck dat! You got me fucked up. I think you on the wrong side of the fence already. I'm outta here." Dre got up and left the woman in the room alone. He couldn't even think of flippin' the script on his man. He had made up his mind. He was going to fire the bitch and get him a paid lawyer and if Black didn't have enough money saved, he would get him one too.

After being up the jail for the last two weeks, Dre had already gotten use to the madness. It was just like the streets, the only difference was having nowhere to take cover when the drama hit. Dre was far from a punk, but he was not as aggressive as Black on the inside. Knife, knuckle, or burner, Black was down for whatever, whenever. Dre was more like Mann when it came down to the drama, he liked to strike when least expected. Black had already had them beefin'. Black stabbed a dude in the face in front of the bubble that the C.O.'s sat in. Even so, Black was his man and against all odds, Dre was going to ride to the bloody end.

Walking through the sally port door, Dre saw Black on the phone with a smile on his face. Black waved his hand for Dre to come up the steps and see who was on the phone. "Hold on shorty!" Black said into the phone, as he gave it to Dre.

"Hello?" Dre said, hearing Rare Essence blasting in the background.

"What's up young?" an excited voice said into the phone.

"Who dis? Lando?"

"Yeah joe. You know Mann walking and everything slim. He should be home in a few days," Lando said. Dre cut his eye at Black and flashed a smile. They both knew that things would move the way that they were suppose to with Mann back in the game. Lando gave Dre the run down on what was going on around the way. Ric and Jammie were back on the move again. They had shot at Lil' Garvin's car at a red light on Georgia Ave. about 2 nights ago. Nobody had seen Marvin since he shot Mann.

"I heard Tina beat Metra's ass," Dre said.

"No bullshit! She fucked dat bitch up. She don't even be hangin' down Kisha's house no more. She got a mob of new bitches she be wit. They all be sittin' on her porch. Dem bitches jive like dat too!" Lando said.

Dre finished talking to Lando and walked down the tier with Black. "We gon beat this shit joe," Black said and added, "Mann gon make sure shit right. But uh... anyway, what your lawyer talkin' bout?"

"That bitch full of shit. I'm bout to get rid of that bitch. How much cash you got saved up?" Dre asked.

"I got like 15 stashed over my mutha's house. What's up?"

"We gotta get a real lawyer..." Dre started to say, as Black cut him off.

"We ain't gotta spend no money on a lawyer. Mann bout to be home, we gon get that bitch head hit, and we outta here!" Black pulled a bag of weed out of his drawers and said, "Let's go smoke joe. Shit gon work itself out."

While Lando and his mob were bringing major drama to 13th Street, Marvin had been laying low for the last 3 weeks in North Carolina. He had a cousin down there that was getting some money from selling weed. Through his cousin, Marvin met a New Yorker named Solo that had all the coke in the small town of Greensville. It didn't take long for him to cut into the hood rats and find out where Solo kept all his coke and money. Once Marvin was on point about the whereabouts of the stash house, he wasted no time. With an old book bag, a roll of duck tape, and a .45 automatic, Marvin made his move late at night. Leaving Solo duck taped and shot in the top of the head twice, Marvin left town headed for the Inner State in a used red '87 Porsche 911 Cabriolet with paper tags along with 3 bricks of coke and $10,000 in murder money.

Marvin's first stop was over his baby's mother's house. Nicole was a short, slim, dark skinned girl with a head on her shoulders. She went to school with Kelley and knew all about the beef between her baby's father and Mann. She had always found Mann to be a good nigga and had even gone out to eat down Georgetown with him a few times. Mann had earned a spot in her heart one day after her and Marvin had a big fight.

Marvin had smacked her in the face,   blacking her eye, and put her out of his car downtown in the rain. Coming from paying Pamila's phone bill, Mann pulled up at the light on 16th & M Streets and saw Nicole soaking wet, crying, and trying to flag a cab down. Mann took her home and told her to call him when she wanted a man that was going to treat her right. Nicole loved Marvin, but she was crushed when she found out that he shot Mann.

Nicole was sitting on the sofa in a tight pair of blue Perris Ellis jeans and a white Banana Republic T- shirt, with her pretty feet propped up on the coffee table, watching cartoons with her son. Marvin came through the front door carrying the old book bag full of coke and money. His son jumped off of the sofa and ran into his arms. Nicole got up and hugged him tightly, kissing him in the mouth.

"I missed you boy!" Nicole said with her arms wrapped around his neck.

"I missed you and my lil' man too, but I'm back now. Let me put this up and I'll be right back," Marvin said and then went up to Nicole's bedroom to call Ric. Once Marvin heard that Mann was alive, he told Ric that he would be on his way home, but when Ric called down N.C. telling him that he had got shot along with Jammie and the rest, Marvin hit Solo and came straight home.

"Hello?" Ric said picking up the phone.

"I'm back joe. I'ma be over Nicole's house all night. Come holla at me," Marvin said, sitting on Nicole's bed.

"I'm on my way young!" Ric responded. He hung up the phone and was gone.

Mann was home now, still weak, but he was home and he was ready to put things back in their proper place. Mann knew that all eyes were on him, and he had no plans on doing anything while the world was waiting. Mann had to sit Lando down and tell him that since he was out of the hospital that didn't mean he was going to go on a rampage. He told Lando that if he were to act out of his anger, instead of using his mind, he would slip along the way, costing him his life or his freedom. Lando listened, never cutting him off. Lando looked up to Mann all his life. He knew Mann knew where his ass was. Yet and still, Lando was firing pistols now and he had fell in love with the superficial power of the gunplay. At first he couldn't understand why Mann wanted him to chill out on stalking anybody that was from 13th Street, but then he thought that Mann would put him down with everything when the time was right, he always did. Now the plan was for Lando to stay strapped and on point, but not to go looking for Ric or Jammie, but if he was to catch em slippin' it was a green light to "split they wigs." Lando was with it, Mann could do no wrong in his eyes.

Mann had been out of the hospital for 3 days. Pamila had allowed Kelley to stay in her house, after getting to know her while Mann was in the hospital. Kelley was going to Coolidge High school, which was right across the street, so she was never far away. Every time she showed her face, Mann felt himself growing closer and closer to Kelley. She was a female that a man could fall in love with. While Mann was thinking about Kelley, she came walking down the steps with her schoolbooks in hand.

"What's up beautiful?" Mann said, as he laid across his bed, wearing nothing more than a pair of grey Polo boxer shorts.

"I'm okay, just tired as shit," Kelley said as she sat her books down and threw her Nautica jacket across the sofa. Walking over and laying down beside Mann on the bed, she rubbed her soft hands across Mann's chest saying, "Sometimes I wonder if I'm wasting my time with the school thing. So many people go off to school with all these big hopes and dreams, only to come back to the city and work at Safeway or 7-Eleven somewhere. I ain't trying to be like that Mann."

Looking into Kelley's beautiful eyes, Mann raised up off of the bed, leaning back on his elbows. He could see that the "future" truly meant a lot to Kelley.

Rolling over on his side, Mann rubbed the back of his hand against Kelley's smooth cheek saying, "Shorty, the question ain't whether or not school is worth it. The question is, are you worth it? I feel as though you are, but you gotta feel as though you worth it."

"Mann, I know I'm worth it. Shit is just so hard! I ain't got nobody helping me, then on top of that, I only got $4,000 saved up for college. That's only enough for like one year...." Mann sensed Kelley's frustration building.

Softly, he placed one finger over her lips and said, "Shhhh, slow down boo. You looking too far down the road. Deal with today for right now and plan for tomorrow. Don't worry about it. Just do what you gotta do to get into the college you trying to go to. As long as I'm around, money ain't a thing." Kelley felt every word that Mann said. She was touched by his display of care for her. She pushed on Mann's chest, slowly making him lay on his back again. Lying right beside him, she passionately kissed him in the mouth. Her hand exploringly caressed its way down into Mann's Polo boxers. As things got heated, Pamila called Kelley from the top of the basement steps.

"Kelley. Are you still going to help me make dinner?"

Mann and Kelley both smiled, as Kelley responded. "Yeah Pamila, I'm on my way." Kelley sat up on the bed fixing her clothes, thinking of what it was going to be like to make love to Mann. As she got up to go help Pamila, she looked back at Mann saying, "We gon finish this later."

The phone rang as Kelley ran up the steps. Mann painfully rolled over and answered it. "Hello." It was a collect call from Dre. Mann accepted the call before the recording finished.

"What's up nigga!" Mann said.

"What's up wit you joe?" Dre said, with all the noise of the DC Jail day room in the background.

"I'ma little weak, but I'm getting stronger everyday. I been home for 3 days now, why you just calling?"

"Tina just came to see me and told me you was home. We got a lot to talk about, but that can wait. I told Tina to come holla at you, so she gon put you on point, but hold on, Black wanna holla at you." Dre put his hand over the phone and yelled out on the tier for Black. Black came pimpin' in the day room wearing a fresh pair of tan double sole Timberland boots, with his jail jumper on up to his waist with the sleeves hanging at his side. In his tight tank top, with his blue-black arms "on swoll" from doing push-ups and his hair picked out into a Comrade George afro, Black looked like "Black Power" in the flesh.

"What's up joe?" Black said.

"Ain't shit slim, I'm in rehab," Mann said with a laugh.

"Yeah, I'm fucked up bout that, but we gon be outta here in bout 3 months. First day I'm out..." Mann cut Black off.

"Ho! Ho! Hold! I feel ya, but we can keep dat on da hush. Don't even worry about me, I got dis. Trust me. We gotta worry about getting y'all out." Mann finished talking to Black and Dre, letting them know that everything was going to be fine, because Mann was home.

Six

Lando was deep in the game now. To Lando, he was a big nigga "gangsta muthafucka" and nobody could tell him anything different. At 12, he had two bodies under his belt and everybody around 5th Street knew it. At school, he was the only young nigga driving an Acura legend in the 7th grade. His money just wouldn't stop stacking, 2 grand away from $10,000, Lando was making a killin' in the crack house at night, along with his mob. Not realizing it, Lando was really letting his hair down and even more so now that Mann was out of the hospital. He was staying out hustlin' all night, he was going to school only to show off his fresh gear and Black's Acura, and he was even neglecting Nakia now. She would have to beep him over and over again before he would find his way to the phone, only to tell her that he was busy and he loved her, but had to call her back later. Mann had made sure that Lando got rid of the Glock he killed Will and the pipehead with up 13th Street. Wasting no time, he shot over Martin Luther King Jr. Ave to see Poochie and copped a brand new Taurus .45 automatic and two 18 shot extended clips. Lando was quickly becoming a ghetto superstar. As Lando, Quick, Lil' Garvin, and Baby D all became more notorious in the neighborhood, the police became more familiar with the up and coming gun slinging, dope dealing, and murderously violent tempered younger generation that would run the 90's and leave the late 80's with a murder rate never before seen in the District of Columbia. Mann had warned Lando of this, but now, he would see for himself and never forget it.

As the cold chill of another fall night fell upon the DC streets, the "dope game" was in overtime and everybody from 5th & Rittenhouse all the way up to Georgia & Rittenhouse was grindin' hard for "most valuable player". On the 5th Street end, things had changed a little bit over the past weeks with Mann in the hospital and Dre in jail. Onion had got his hands on 2 bricks of coke from somewhere. The pipeheads were talking bad about the coke Onion had on the streets while Mann and Dre were gone, but it was the only thing they could buy when Lando and his little mob were not around. Corey, Smoke, and Serge were all buying coke from

Onion at the time and they knew it   was bullshit. This had Smoke and Serge fucked up. They had even talked about robbing Onion, but passed the idea up. Corey really didn't care about the coke being bullshit. His only beef was with Lando and the young niggaz around the way. By Lando and Quick buying coke from Wee-Wee, they had much more clientele when they hit the strip. Lil' Garvin and Baby D were buying coke from Lil' Garvin's big brother Dex and they had good clientele also, but it was nothing like Lando's or Quick's.

All the young niggaz started hanging a block over from Rittenhouse Street on Roxboro Place, which was a small one-way street with a cut between every set of row houses. After hanging out on Roxboro Place during the daytime for a few days, before hitting the crack house at night, the young niggaz had turned it into a strip almost over night.

Pulling up in the alley in Black's Acura Legend, Lando and Quick along with his pit bull got out and hit the block. Stepping out into the streetlight, they saw Lil' Garvin and Baby D sitting on the hood of Lil' Garvin's car. Further down the block they saw Smoke and Serge servin' pipeheads. Walking up to Lil' Garvin, Lando gave him "5" and said, "What shit look like out here young?"

Lil' Garvin let Lando and Quick know that the money was coming through. Hearing somebody behind them, they quickly turned and saw Corey and Onion coming up the alley. As they came out of the alley, pipehead Karen bent the corner. The first person she saw was Corey. At 5'10" & 240 lbs., Corey was a heavy weight and a knock out artist as well. He rushed Karen, knowing that she had been having money lately.

"What's up?" Corey said.

"I'm tryin' to get 6 for 100," Karen said. Corey pulled a bag of rocks out of his drawers, and began to open it. Looking across the street, Karen saw Quick and told Corey that she was going to holla at him.

"What da fuck you mean you gon holla at him, after I got my shit out?" Corey yelled as he followed behind Karen.

Becoming scared, Karen jumped behind Lando who tried to calm the situation down by saying, "Come on man, she tryin' to holla at Quick. What? You gon make her spend her money wit you?" The younger dudes' words just added to Corey's anger.

At 20 years old, Corey had been to prison and back before any of the younger niggaz started hustlin' around the way. They were in his way. They had the block hot and police stayed on the strip. They were shooting every time he turned around and now they were taking money out of his pocket. He couldn't take it anymore. His anger and frustration made him feel as if the young niggaz were taking him for a sucka. Knowing that he could beat all of the young dudes into a coma, Corey went off.

Putting his finger in Lando's face, with his right hand balled up into a fist, Corey said with anger, "I'll knock your lil' ass da fuck out. You a lil' boy Lando!"

Baby D and Lil' Garvin jumped off the hood of the car, as Quick struggled to hold Killa back, who was trying to lock her jaws on any part of Corey that she could get her teeth into. Onion grabbed Corey to try to pull him back, but he snatched away, getting back in Lando's face. Knowing that Corey was too big for him to fight, Lando's first thought was the .45 automatic in his waistband.

"You betta pipe down big boy!" Lando said, trying to warn Corey of the danger that waited for him if he put his hands on him. While Killa became more aggressive and angry, Corey continued to press his luck.

"I better pipe down or what?" Corey said as he got closer up on Lando setting him up for a short 6-inch hook; that would no doubt put the younger dude straight to sleep. Realizing Corey was sizing him up for a knock out, Lando swiftly stepped back, whipping out the huge chrome .45 automatic with the extended clip.

Pointing the gun in Corey's face, he said, "Nigga! I'll smoke your big ass out here!" Smoke and Serge walked up on the situation, as Lil' Garvin pulled Lando back, warning him it was too many people outside for him to smash Corey right in the middle of Roxboro Place.

Killa yanked away from Quick and lunged straight for Corey's thick neck. Throwing his arms in front of his face to protect himself from Killa's potentially lethal bite, Corey felt the first lock jaw bite of Killa's teeth sinking deep into his forearm as he screamed out in pain and fear. Recklessly swinging his arm to get the angry dog off of him, Corey saw blood hitting the ground. Killa let go of his arm and lunged at his chest wasting no time. Corey kicked the dog in the mouth as he tried to run. Raging with anger Killa caught Corey's leg and locked her teeth deep into his thigh ripping a huge chunk of bloody flesh. Quick finally got a hold of Killa's chain and pulled her off of Corey, allowing him and Onion to run down the alley.

While Smoke and Serge were dying laughing, Lando slipped his pistol back into his waistband saying, "Fuck dat nigga!" Quick gave Baby D Killa's chain so that he could go ahead and serve Karen. Smoke and Serge talked to the young niggaz for a minute about what had just went down. Then they went on their way back down the street. Lando walked down the alley fired up. His pride was hurt. With one hand on the steering wheel of the Acura Legend, sitting in the car with the door open, Lando tried to calm himself down. Lil' Garvin walked up and said, "Chill out young. Fuck dat nigga!"

"I can't stand dat nigga. I'ma end up poppin his ass!" Lando said.

"Damn young! You came off down da country!" RIC said as he sat in the passenger seat of Marvin's Porsche admiring the way he had went down North Carolina and came back with a Porsche 911 Cabriolet, 3 bricks, and $10,000. Sitting behind the wheel, Marvin let Ric know what the next move was as they flew along the beltway headed for Marvin's apartment in Bowie Maryland.

Taking a deep pull of the blunt Ric had just passed him, Marvin said, "The nigga Mann out da hospital now, so shit gotta come to a head. I known slim since we was kids. He done always been a thinker. He gon lay until he get better and then he gon strike in a way that we ain't gon expect, but he gon be comin' for me first...."

"But what about dem young niggaz? Quick and dem?" Ric asked, cutting in.

"Don't worry bout dem!" Marvin snapped as he went on, "Mann out da hospital now. He callin' all shots. He ain't gon have them young niggaz shootin' shit up for nothing, makin' da hood hot, when he know I ain't around. Them young niggaz came through there and caught y'all slippin' cause they felt like dat's what they 'pose to do at the time. I got a spot out here by my apartment where we gon push dis coke and get paid. You gon pass out weight to da young niggaz around da way, they can keep shit pumpin' til I kill dis nigga Mann." Ric was down with the plan. He had trust in his man and he was down to die with him if it came down to that.

"What about Jammie?" Ric asked, as he grabbed the blunt and popped N.W.A. into the tape deck.

"I got Jammie. He gon come out here wit us," Marvin said. The plan sounded good, Marvin thought to himself, but he knew Mann was like Air Jordan down 3 late in the 4th. It was no telling what he would do next...

Silk was just getting out of his Benz in front of Mann's house, as Kelley and Tina were coming out of the door carrying two boxes.

"What's up ladies?" Silk said, stepping to the side as he let them pass by. Always fly, Silk saw how the girls were checking out his black leather Armani jacket.

"What's up Silk?" they said.

"Where y'all goin' wit da boxes?" Silk asked.

Tina, looking so good in her tight blue Guess jeans said, "We on our way to the post office to mail these boxes to Dre and Black."

Pulling a knot of $100 dollar bills out the pocket of his black Perry Ellis jeans, Silk handed Tina $300 and said, "Send 'em a lil' cash for me." Tina let Silk know that she would make sure that they got the money, as her and Kelley got in Dre's new Corvette ZR1 headed for the Post Office.

Walking down the basement steps, after Pamila let him in the house, Silk overheard Mann talking to Lando and Quick, who were sitting on the sofa.

"I'ma see y'all later. Take y'all ass to school and don't forget what I said," Mann said as he ran in place on the treadmill Pamila bought for him so that he could get back in shape. Headed for school, Lando and Quick got up and left.

"What's that all about?" Silk said as he sat on the sofa.

"I jive had to pull Lando up on pullin' pistols on niggaz and not using 'em. Shorty had some words wit Big Corey the other night, and pulled a joint out on him," Mann said.

"What happened?" Silk asked.

"Corey was fucked up that some pipehead ain't want to buy his shit, so he went off and act like he was going to do something to Lando. They say shorty was 'bout to bust his big ass. Somehow Quick let his pit bull go on da nigga. I gotta go around there and make sure Corey leave that shit alone before dem young niggaz kill 'em." Mann got off the treadmill and grabbed a towel. Wiping sweat off of his face, Mann asked Silk, "What's up wit you?"

"The question is what's up wit you!" Silk said.

After being out of the hospital just over a week, Mann was already on top of what he had to do to get things straight. Tina gave him the rundown on the girl that was talking to the police on Black and Dre's case.

Eyone Williams

He had to make sure that he took care of her even though he knew he had to get himself in some better shape before he could deal with her or Marvin. He told himself that he would take everything one day at a time. The Feds had been to his house twice, since he left the hospital before it was time for him to check out. Before the Feds knew he was out of his coma, he was gone. The first time they came looking for him, Pamila told them that Mann was out. The second time, Mann let them in and got straight to the point, telling them he had no idea who shot him. They, on the other hand, told Mann they knew DeMarvin Scott shot him and that if anything was to happen to him that they were coming for Mann since he called himself "being true to the game." Mann paid them no attention, knowing that when he caught Marvin, nobody would know shit.

Mann looked at Silk and said, "You know what's up wit me slim. I'm back on my feet now. It's time to get that money. They say that nigga Onion got a rack of bullshit out there. I'm trying to get back out there and lock shit down."

"What's up wit dis nigga that shot you?" Silk said.

"I got dis nigga. He walkin' dead, I'ma push 'em in his grave when the time is right."

"I think you taking this nigga lightly," Silk said.

Mann smiled at Silk and said, "You done known me too long joe. I got dis." Mann asked Silk about his connect with Supreme. Silk let him know that he was getting 30 bricks a week now. Supreme was charging him $480,000 for every drop. Paying $480,000 for 30 bricks rounded off to $16,000 a brick at a time when coke was short and a brick could go for $25,000 to $30,000 depending on your connect. Silk was dropping 20 bricks in the city at $25,000 a piece and 10 more out Va. for $30,000 a piece. He was killin' 'em.

Mann was drunk off of all the dollar signs that were flying through his mind. Hearing Silk talk about the way he was "flippin bricks" had Mann ready to get down to business. "I'm ready to get that cash. What's up?" Mann said.

Giving deep thought to what Mann said, Silk responded, "How much cash you got right now?"

"I got about 90 in cash right now," Mann said as he walked over to the weight bench.

"This is what I'ma do. Gimme 50 now and I'ma give you 5 joints. When you finish, just hit me wit 30 more. Dependin' on how you push da shit, you gone see well over 125. After that, you can do your own thing wit Supreme every time I see 'em." Silk laid the cards on the table. Mann was ready and he already knew what he was going to do.

The 4th District Police Chief stormed into the office of Detective James and his partner Detective Hall. The short, overweight, white Police Chief dropped a thick folder of paperwork on Detective James' desk and hissed at him angrily, "Downtown is all over my ass about these latest shootings! These little wannabe gangstas are making my job hard! I want you and Hall on top of finding anything to lock their black asses up for!" The Chief stormed out of the office slamming the door behind him.

Detective James, an older black man, opened up the folder that contained information about the string of shootings that had taken place on 13th Street NW Over the past month, there were 4 unsolved murders and 7 assaults with intent to kill. Flipping through the papers, Detective James ran across the names DeMarvin Scott and Mark Mills.

Turning around to his partner, he said, "Hey Hall, didn't you have that Mills shooting?"

"Yeah, he's some big dope boy down on uh... 5th Street, uh....5th & Rittenhouse. Another young guy named uh.... Scott, DeMarvin Scott got into a shootout with Mark Mills. Why you ask, that's what that's about?" Detective Hall asked.

"Yeah, these shootings seem to occur as soon as Mr. Mills gets shot and then they stop as soon as he gets out of the hospital. He's gotta have something to do with it," James said. Hall had been trying to get a murder case on Black for the last 3 years, but no one would live to talk. He knew all about him.

Thinking about Black, Hall said, "The Mills boy gotta cousin they call "Killa Black", but he's locked up for murder right now. He's the only one I think could be responsible for some shit like that."

"It's gotta be someone else that's close to the Mills boy. These murders are related to him being shot," James said.

"Looks like we gotta hit the streets then," Hall said.

Seven

It was back to business for Mann. Days after talking to Silk about the coke he was pushing, Mann was in the basement bagging up. Mann had cooked 5 bricks of powder into solid pies of crack rock. He decided to keep a brick for himself and break it down to ounces. This way he would get all the cash possible when he stepped back on the strip.

Dusting his hands off, Mann stashed the bricks in the ceiling along with his money. Walking over to the bed, Mann pulled his T-shirt up to look at his healing bullet wounds. He felt blessed to be alive, but payback was in the making, he thought, as he pulled a heavy black bullet proof vest over his head. He grabbed a thick grey Polo sweat hoody off the bed and pulled it over the vest. Sitting down on the bed, he picked up the huge black Desert Eagle that Silk gave him and slid a clip of .44 magnum bullets in it. Sliding the pistol into his shoulder holster, Mann grabbed his big blue Eddie Bauer down coat and hit the streets

Winter was now in town and only true hustlas were on the block. Bending the corner in his black Nissan 300 ZX, Mann got everyone's attention. Standing at the end of the alley in the middle of the block wearing thick black skull caps, big Eddie Bauer coats of all colors and tan double sole Timberland boots were Smoke, Serge, Onion, Corey, and Kevin who must have just made parole, Mann thought.

Slowly pulling up on the crowd with one hand on the wheel and the other on the Desert Eagle lying across his lap, Mann could tell that his presence was making Corey nervous. Sliding the pistol under his seat, Mann rolled the passenger window down at the push of a button and spoke to everyone. From the sidewalk everybody spoke back to Mann. Smoke and Serge pulled up on Mann and asked if he was back "on". Mann let them know he had coke and told them to beep him later. After talking to Onion and Kevin, Mann called Corey over to the car. Cautiously, Corey limped to the car using a cane, still feeling the effects of Killa's vicious lock jaw attack.

Watching Corey walk over to the car, Mann reflected on his years of knowing the older dude. When Mann came off the porch, he was Lando's age and Corey was his age. Back then, Corey and Kevin had the block locked down. Mann was only getting ounces from Silk at the time. Corey had always looked out for Mann when he was just coming off the porch and still green to the streets. Mann never forgot those days. Mann could still remember when Corey caught his big drug case and went to prison. Fighting the case, Corey spent over $20,000 and still ended up taking a cop to 0-to-30 years, spending two years in Atlanta's Federal Penitentiary. While he was locked up, Corey's girl had a baby by a Prince George's County police officer. She married the cop, taking the $80,000 that Corey left with her, and moved to L.A. with the money. Corey came home in 1988 broke as a bag of glass.

"Mann, I ain't got no beef wit..."

Mann shook his head and waved his hand cutting Corey off saying, "I ain't beefin' slim. I'm tryin' to make sure it ain't no beef. I already talked to Lando and Quick. I told them to leave da shit alone. You know they think they big boys now. I'm asking you to leave the shit alone for me joe." Corey was more than happy to let the beef slide, not because he was scared, but because it was too much trouble to beef with Lando. He would have to kill Mann, Quick, Lil' Garvin, Baby-D, then he would have to turn around and kill Black and Dre when they came home. After a little thought, Corey saw it as a no win situation. The whole thing could only get worst for him. If one of them didn't kill him first, he knew he would be back in prison before he was done beefin'.

"So how you livin' out here?" Mann asked Corey.

"Shit ain't like it use to be, but I'm making it."

"Check dis out, beep me later on. I'ma do something wit you," Mann said. Mann talked to Corey and the rest of the dudes on the strip, never once talking about the beef with him and Marvin. While they were talking, a white van rode by with Virginia tags. The flash of a camera went off and everyone turned their heads quickly. "Damn! It's hot like dat out here!" Mann said as the van kept rolling down the street. Onion let Mann know that the same white van had been riding through taking pictures for the last week or so. That was all Mann needed to hear to let everybody know that it was time for him to leave.

"So what Mann gon do 'bout dem bammas?" Quick asked Lando, laid back in the passenger seat of the Acura Legend, on their way over Nakia's house.

"Mann say leave da shit alone," Lando said as they pulled up in front of Nakia's house.

"Leave da shit alone? Fuck dat! I ain't gon let a nigga shoot me and get away wit it!"

"Mann ain't gon let a nigga get away wit shit! Mann gon see all dem niggaz!" Lando said, as he became upset about Quick doubting Mann.

Sensing the frustration in Lando's voice, Quick said, "I know Mann gon see dem niggaz, but he suppose to smash dem niggaz off da top." Lando could see what Quick was saying. He really didn't understand why Mann was waiting to get on top of the beef, but he knew Mann knew what he was doing.

Nakia took their attention off the conversation as she came out of the house along with another cute brown skinned girl. Dressed to impress, the two young girls got in bringing the cold night air with them, as Quick got in the back seat with the brown skinned girl, allowing Nakia to sit up front with Lando. Nakia unzipped her big grey Polo coat as the car pulled off headed for the movies. Turning back to Quick with a smile on her face, Nakia said, "Quick, dis my girl Trina. She da one I was telling you about."

"Oh yeah?" Quick said as he slid an arm around the cute girl. "So dis Trina huh?" Quick moved closer to Trina and began to get very familiar with her. Before they got to the movies, Quick had his hand in Trina's pants, kissing her in the mouth while he played with her clit.

Cutting the Acura off in the White Flint Mall parking lot, Lando pulled his .45 automatic from under the seat and got out of the car along with everyone else. Looking all around the three level parking lot, Lando saw a red Porsche 911 Cabriolet with dark tinted windows and said, "Dat joint right there like dat!"

Turning to look at the car right beside theirs, Quick said, "Yeah dat joint knocking' young" as he shut the car door behind him, tucking his 10mm Ruger in his waistband.

Mann pulled up in the alley between Roxboro Place & Rittenhouse Street and cut the head lights out, leaving him and Corey plunged into the darkness of the tinted windows on the Z. Handing Corey a fat zip-lock bag with a half a brick in it, Mann said, "Dat's 500 grams. You gon get your money's worth wit dat there." Corey pulled two stacks of cash out of his blue Eddie Bauer and handed Mann the money. Sliding the rubber band off the money, Mann flipped through it and saw that it was $10,000 on the nose in big bills. Mann and Corey talked for a minute then Corey got out the car and went to bag his coke up.

In the car alone, Mann pulled the Desert Eagle .44 from under the dash board of the Z along with a zip-lock bag full of 50 rocks and got out the car cutting through Kisha's backyard headed for the strip.

Pipeheads were commuting in and out of Pipehead Old Tima's house, in a numbed daze. As the cold winter air blew, Mann pulled his thick black skull cap down tight on his head and quickly observed the surroundings. He didn't feel good on the strip knowing that the Feds had been coming through taking pictures. Sitting at the end of the alley in the middle of the block, Mann saw Smoke and Serge waiting for their next dollar. Seeing Mann, they waved their hands in the air. Mann responded in the same way as he looked across the street at the crack house. Seeing Lil' Garvin's car parked right in front of the crack house made Mann shake his head in disagreement. He didn't play the crack house at all. He always needed to see and know what was going on around him and he felt that sitting in the crack house took his eyes and ears away from him, leaving him vulnerable to an unexpected attack from the Feds or some niggaz trying to rob or kill him. Looking down the street, Mann saw Metra and four other bad broads in big coats standing on Metra's porch. They must be waiting for someone, Mann thought. Dre came to mind when he saw Metra. She had to get dealt with but now wasn't the time or place. Turning to the side, Mann saw Big Busta and C.O. Ronnie.

"What's up Mann? Boy I done missed you. Dees niggaz got a bunch a bullshit out here." Big Busta said, as he gave Mann "5". Ronnie walked up and gave Mann "5" too, as Mann led both pipeheads into the dark cut beside Kisha's house to serve them. Once in the cut, Mann asked them what they were trying to get. Big Busta wanted four 50 rocks. Mann pulled the zip-lock bag of 50 rocks out of his pocket and gave Big Busta four huge 50 rocks for $170. As Big Busta headed for Old Tima's house, Mann served Ronnie two fat 50's for $90 and asked him how Black and Dre were doing up the jail.

Ronnie began to tell Mann how he was taking Black and Dre weed and money up the jail every time he went to work. Mann let him know to beep him every night before he went to work so that he could send his niggaz whatever they needed. Ronnie went on to tell Mann how Dre had pulled a young C.O. broad and was fucking her every night. She would come get him before the last count of the night and take him on a medical run to the infirmary. After making sure that everyone that had to be seen was gone back to their block, the cute young woman would make sure Dre got caught up in the count. They would go in the back of the infirmary in the empty holding cell and fuck until the count was clear, while a buddy of the C.O. broad would watch their back.

Black was the same ole nigga inside and out. He was on administrative segregation again. Black had a fallout with an old timer that had come back to the jail on a writ from the Lompoc Federal Penitentiary. The old timer had been locked up for the last 20 years. He had it in his mind that the younger generation was soft because all they did was use guns. Black was the only nigga in the block with weed and the old timer had asked him for a few jays. Black sent him a few times but the old timer wore out his welcome and ended up taking Black's kindness for weakness. Black wasted no time letting the old timer know that he wasn't about any games. Late one night, Black got Ronnie to let him down on the adult tier. Ronnie popped the old timer's cell while Black ran down the dark tier and caught the old timer taking a shit. In seconds, Black slammed the buck knife deep into the old timer's body over and over, hitting him in the neck twice, and all over his back and arms. Black would have gotten away with the whole thing, but a young dude that was scared of Black told on him and checked out of the block.

When Ronnie was done talking to Mann, he headed for Old Tima's house. Mann's beeper went off and he went in Kisha's house to use the phone. Lando was beeping him 911. Something had to be up.....

People flooded out of the movie theater into the crowded mall when the movie was over. Nakia was tired; she fell asleep twice during Friday the 13th and was now half asleep on Lando's shoulder as they walked out into the mall.

"I got to use the bathroom boo," Nakia said to Lando.

"Me too," Trina said, as her and Nakia bent the corner on their way to the bathroom.

Fast Lane

Waiting for the girls, Lando asked Quick what was up with Trina. Leaning on the pay phone as people walked up and down the huge hallway with shopping bags, Quick let Lando know that Trina was cool as shit.

"I dig shorty," Quick said. While Quick was talking, Lando began squinting his eyes, looking down by the Eddie Bauer shop.

"Ain't dat Marvin and his baby mutha?" Lando asked.

Turning to look at what Lando was talking about; Quick reached for his 10mm and said, "Yeah dat's dat bitch ass nigga. We can smash dat nigga right in da parking lot young!"

"Naa, I got dis nigga. Wait here for Nakia and dem joe," Lando said as he jogged down the hallway, following Marvin and Nicole out into the parking lot.

Hand on his .45 automatic, with it hid inside his big Eddie Bauer coat, Lando cocked the hammer as he trailed behind Marvin and Nicole unnoticed. Cautiously, Lando looked all around the parking lot. No one seemed to be around. This was the perfect time to blast Marvin and his baby's mother, Lando thought. Stalking his prey, Lando followed the couple up a pair of dark steps that led up to the 2nd and 3rd levels of the parking lot. Pulling his pistol out in open display Lando watched as the couple walked through the door on the 2nd level. "Damn!" Lando said as he smacked the .45 against his leg while running up the steps. Peeping through the door, Lando saw that Marvin and Nicole were walking toward the Acura Legend that he was driving. Walking up to the red Porsche beside the car he was driving, Lando saw Marvin stop and point at the Acura. "Ain't dat Black's car?" Marvin asked Nicole, as he carefully looked around the parking lot.

"Yeah but his lil' cousin Lando been drivin dat car since he been locked up."

"You talking 'bout Mann lil' brother?"

"Yeah."

"I thought he was a lil' boy."

"He ain't a lil' boy no more. He runnin' around wit guns and shit now. Anyway, let's go. I got school tomorrow," Nicole said as they got in their car and left. After overhearing Marvin and Nicole, Lando ran back into the mall and beeped Mann.

As Lando was telling Quick why he couldn't smash Marvin in the parking lot, the pay phone rang. "Yeah!" Lando said into the phone.

"What's up shorty? What's wrong wit you?" Mann asked.

Eyone Williams

"I just saw da nigga Marvin out here at da mall wit his baby mutha. I coulda smoked da nigga, but he was parked right beside Black's car."

"I told you to leave da nigga alone. Let me deal wit dat," Mann said as he went on to let Lando know that he had been in the streets long enough to take care of a situation like this one. Lando was pissed off about the way Mann was dealing with the whole beef and in his mind, he told himself that if he caught the nigga Marvin slippin' one more time he was going to blow his brains out no matter what Mann had to say.

Mann spent the next two days making money and checking his traps on the streets. Mann had got word that Marvin had ran across some bricks out of town and now had a little spot out Bowie, MD locked down. After running into Nicole one day after school, he had also found out that Ric had been making a lot of money out Bowie along with Marvin and Jammie. Ric had bought a silver '88 Acura Legend coupe with tinted windows, while Jammie had bought a light blue '89 Nissan Pathfinder with chrome B.B.S. rims. After a little thought, Mann could remember seeing the car and the truck a few times within the last two weeks. It was time to make his move.

Now that Mann was back on his feet, his money was starting to stack again. He ran into two old friends name Da-Da and LeRon that he used to sell coke to a while back. They had found a New York connection and started buying bricks from him sometime last year. Come to find out, the New Yorker had got robbed and killed about two months ago, leaving Da-Da and LeRon with no sweet connect. Mann moved right in and started selling them both a brick each for $25,000 a whop. Onion was also buying coke from Mann now that he saw how Mann had the best deal on the streets at the time. Onion couldn't beat a brick for $20,000. Silk couldn't believe how fast Mann had locked his block back down. Mann was coming at Silk with $80,000 strong every Friday. Silk was pleased to have a for sure buy once a week for 5 bricks and Mann was showing no signs of slowing down. It was back to business.

Mann felt that he was well enough to take care of the broad that was telling on Black and Dre now. Picking Tina up from her house, they both slid up the jail to see Black and Dre. While Tina sat and talked to Dre, Mann got the run down on the government witness. Mann let Black know that he needed more information on the broad because she was never at the address that he had been going to. Black let Mann know that the broad could be found at the club called the Black Hole every weekend. Mann told Black that he would be on top of the situation by the end of the week for sure.

Just before the visit was over, Black began to ask Mann about the beef with Marvin. "So what's up wit da nigga Marvin? I hear he back in da streets," Black said, wondering why Mann hadn't taken care of his business.

"I got dat nigga joe. That's small shit to me," Mann said.

"How da fuck is dat small shit? If I was home, all dem bitch ass niggaz would be dead now. You taken dem suckas lightly, dat's what da fuck is up!"

"Look! I know what I'm doing. I been bustin' ass just as long as you, but I never been locked up for murder. Not once! I know what I'm doing, so let me do dis," Mann said, checking his younger cousin, who seemed to be acting more like his younger brother at the time, Mann thought.

Things weren't getting better at home for Lando. Pamila was at the end of her rope with him. Two days ago, she had to go pick him up from the police station. He had been arrested for driving without a license and truancy. When Pamila arrived at the police station to pick him up, the police let her know that Lando had $8000 on him when he was arrested. The police let Pamila know that Lando's name was popping up a lot lately and if he didn't watch himself, he would be in a lot of trouble. Lando paid the Feds no attention at all. The only thing that got to him was that Pamila took his money, put it in the bank in his name, and it was no way for him to get it.

Standing in the kitchen cooking dinner, Pamila voiced all her frustration to Kelley. "I don't know what's wrong with that boy. I know boys will be boys, but Lando lil' ass is out of control," Pamila said. "He's out of fucking control. He comes and goes as he pleases. He don't go to school but every blue moon. Mann was nothing like this at his age."

Kelley didn't know what to say, so she said the only thing she thought that made sense, "Why don't you get Mann to talk to him?"

"I tried that. Lando still do what he wants to do, I want to put his lil' ass out of my house, but I know that my sister would turn over in her grave. Something is going to have to give. I'm not going to keep living like this!" Pamila said as her anger began to boil over.

Outside of Paul Jr. High School, Lando, Quick, Baby-D, and Lil' Garvin leaned against the brick wall in huge Eddie Bauer coats that looked twice their size. Lil' Garvin was waiting for some young girl that he was trying to pull while everybody else was talking about the fight that Baby-D had tonight at the boys and girls club. Quick was telling Baby-D that he better not get knocked out in front of everybody. Baby-D looked at Quick and said, "Nigga is you lunchin? I'm the quickest young nigga up town. Bet on me!" Everybody burst out laughing. Lando walked over and told Quick that he needed to talk to him and they stepped off while Lil' Garvin and Baby-D pulled up on the young girl Lil' Garvin was waiting for, along with another young light skinned girl that was with her.

Lando put Quick down with how Pamila had put all of his money in the bank and he was now broke. "So what you gon do?" Quick asked.

"I got a move for us young!"

"A move? You ain't gotta go on no moves! Mann got bricks," Quick said.

"You right! Mann got bricks! I ain't got shit! Is you wit me or not?" Lando asked. Quick was down with his man; win, lose, or draw, he was with it. Lando went on to tell Quick how it was a Jamaican that had moved in the apartments that Jazmin lived in. He was pumpin'weed out of his apartment by the pounds. Lando wasn't sure how much money was inside, but whatever it was, it was a quick caper. When Lando and Quick were finished talking, Jazmin walked by and flashed a smile at Lando. Lando told Quick that he would see him later on at the fight as he ran to catch up with Jazmin.

Jogging up behind Jazmin, Lando called her, "Jazmin! Hold up beautiful."

Turning around smiling, Jazmin said, "Oh, you got time for me today, huh?"

"What you mean today?"

"You always on da run, you ain't never got no time for me," Jazmin said as the two began to walk toward the Acura Legend that Lando was pushing.

Putting an arm around Jazmin, Lando said, "It ain't like dat wit me. You always seem to be on your way somewhere when I see you. Where you going now?"

As they walked up on the Acura, Jazmin said, "I'm on my way home. You think you going that way?"

"Yeah, I think I am going dat way," Lando said as they hopped in the car headed for Jazmin's apartment.

Inside of Jazmin's bedroom, Lando looked around the room at all of the fashion designs on her wall and asked if she drew them all herself. "Yeah, I draw those things all the time. One day, I'ma have my own fashion line," Jazmin said. Lando started laughing.

"You think my dream is a joke?" Jazmin asked, becoming dead serious.

"Naa, I just never thought you were some kinda fashion designer."

"Is something wrong wit dat?" Jazmin asked.

Lando stood up and grabbed Jazmin's small hands saying in a no nonsense voice, "Look here, I ain't say nothing was wrong with that. Everybody needs a dream. I support yours. Shit! When I get one myself, I'll be cool." Lando sat and talked to Jazmin for a while, really getting to know her. For the first time in his young life, Lando had run into someone that made him think about the future, even if it was only for a minute.

Inside the boys and girls club, Baby-D was already gloved up, ready to go into the ring. Lando came in the front door in his over-sized blue Eddie Bauer. The spot was packed. Niggaz from all parts of town were in the stands. Lando looked all around the gym. All the way at the top of the stands, Lando saw Mann, Kelley, Quick, and Lil' Garvin. He headed in their direction.

After showing his love to everyone, Lando sat down beside his brother. "What's up shorty?" Mann asked.

"Ain't shit young," Lando said.

"I heard Pamila took all your money and put it in da bank. I don't want you out there doing no wild shit, I'ma do something wit you."

"Naa, I'm cool young. I got a move I'm bout to go on tonight," Lando said.

"A move?" Mann said, not understanding why Lando would want to go on a move when he knew that Mann would give him anything he needed.

"Yeah! A move. I got a caper up da Ave," Lando said. Mann and Lando got into a heated argument about the whole situation. Mann became frustrated with Lando's idea of being his own man. Lando was on some kind of tip where he didn't want anything from Mann. Mann understood where his little brother was coming from, but he couldn't see any sense in the mindset that Lando had grew into over the last few months. One thing that Mann did understand was that Lando was going to do what he wanted to do no matter what he had to say. The only thing Mann could do to keep his little brother close to him was to get him to come at him with the money when he made whatever move he had in the making. Lando agreed to that and the stage was set. Lando was calling his own shots before he was old enough to drive.

The bell rang. It was round one of three. Baby-D came out with his game face on. With his face greased up, no more then 125 pounds, he was still just as dangerous as his bigger opponent, who was 5 pounds bigger than him, as well as 4 inches taller. The bigger fighter was from another boys and girls club. Everyone that came to support him called him "Champ." Tall and very dark skinned, Champ looked like a young Zulu warrior.

Pow! The first punch of the fight was thrown sending a loud smacking sound echoing through the whole gym. Champ caught Baby-D with a lightening hard jab on the chin. The stands went crazy, screaming, "You da man Champ!" Mann's voice was the only other voice you could hear that was supporting Baby-D, but he sounded like a crowd of people when he was screaming, "Dat nigga fakin shorty. Knock his big ass out!" Baby-D knew that he would have to use his speed to win this fight. Champ was packing too much power for him to go toe to toe. Champ rushed Baby-D, seeing that he was much smaller. Swinging two powerful left hooks off of his jab, Champ became angry when Baby-D slipped every punch and landed two quick stinging right hands to his face before shuffling backwards like Muhammad Ali himself. The stands went crazy once more. Baby-D thought Mann was ringside by the sound of his voice screaming, "Dat's right young nigga!" Fish-bone, Baby-D's trainer, gave clear instructions for him to use his speed and stay away from the bigger fighter. Baby-D did just that. Using the divine speed of youth, Baby-D popped his quick jab and danced around the ring, every now and then he would stop with a little shake and dig straight to the body and then slam a right hand down the pipe. The fight was going exactly how Fish-Bone had planned.

At the start of the third round things took a turn for the worse. Champ threw a solid overhand right taggin' Baby-D flush on the chin, ringing his bell. Dazed and off balance, Baby-D caught a thunderous upper cut that shook his brain painfully, somewhat putting him out on his feet. By the mixed sounds of the loud emotional crowd, Baby-D knew he was in deep trouble. Out of nowhere, a devastating leaping left hook took Baby-D clean off his feet, slamming him to the canvas. Fish-Bone went crazy. As Baby-D got himself together Fish-Bone got his attention and told him that the fight was his if he could survive the rest of the round. Baby-D could care less about surviving the rest of the round. All of his niggaz were in the stands and they saw him hit the canvas hard. Going against everything, Fish-Bone had said, Baby-D went straight at Champ. This change in his fight game so late in the last round shook Champ up and he was taken off guard. Baby-D popped two jabs and slammed two over-hand rights against the side of Champ's face. Champ shot a powerful right hand back at Baby-D as they got into a nasty clutch. Pure anger kept Baby-D safe in the clutch. His mind was made up, somebody was going out. Punch after punch was thrown and no one seemed to be slacking at all. Fish-Bone became hysterical. He couldn't believe Baby-D was throwing the fight away out of pride, he had taught him much better than that. "Get outta there!" Fish-Bone screamed at the top of his lungs, while the stands went off. Something told Baby-D to slide out of the clutch. In a flash, he stepped back and slid out of the clutch as everything seemed to move into slow motion. Off balance, Champ ran straight into a murderous right cross that put him straight to sleep. As his big body lifelessly hit the canvas, all Baby-D could hear was Mann, Lando, Quick, and Lil' Garvin screaming, "Dat's right young nigga!!!" The fight was over, Baby-D had taken a chance that could have gotten him hurt, but he was a gambler and this time he hit 7 on the first roll.

Hours later, Lando and Quick sat in the Acura Legend in the darkness of the night on a side street a block away from Jazmin's apartment with their pistols in hand as they put the plan together on how they would get the Jamaican dude to open the door.

"Dis what we gon do," Lando said, "We gon act like we trying to buy some smoke. When da bamma open da door, we gon go in wit our joints out."

Quick thought about what Lando had said for a minute, and then said, "So we gotta pop da nigga."

Eyone Williams

Cocking his .45 automatic, Lando said, "Yeah, you right. Let's do dis young."

Lando knocked on the door with no fear at all. Quick stood on the other side of the door, out of sight, with both hands on his huge 10mm.

A deep Jamaican voice said, "Yeah mon! Wha yah want?"

Lando wasted no time saying, "I'm tryin to get a 50 bag."

The Jamaican said, "Hold on, mon." In seconds, the door cracked and a 6 foot big black Jamaican dude with long dread locks peeped through the door. Lando and Quick kicked the door open with their pistols pointed at the big man.

"Back da fuck up nigga!" Lando ordered, as he and Quick walked into the apartment.

The Jamaican dropped the 50 bag of weed on the floor with his hands in the air saying, "What ya want mon?"

"You know what da fuck we want nigga. Where dat shit at!" Quick said as he began to look through the apartment. Lando held the big man at gunpoint while Quick tore the place up. In less than a minute, Quick came out of the back room with a Foot Locker bag full of weed.

"I got at least two pounds in here young!" Quick said to Lando.

"Oh yeah?" Lando said as he turned to the Jamaican and said, "Where da money at nigga?"

"Me ain't got no money in here shorty!" the Jamaican said.

"Watch dis nigga," Lando said as he went to take a look in the bedroom. Seconds later he came back out with a shoe box of cash. The Jamaican dude gave in to his anger. He tried to rush Quick and take his pistol. Dropping the Foot Locker bag of weed, Quick popped three quick 10mm slugs straight into his chest, sending the big man flying back against the wall with his arms swinging in the air.

Wasting no time, Lando let the .45 auto go, sending six .45 slugs flying into the dude's chest as well. The slugs went straight through the dude, and hit the wall. The Jamaican dude fell dead to the floor. Quick picked up the Foot Locker bag of weed and ran behind Lando out the door. Running down the hallway with their pistols still in hand, they didn't even see that Jazmin was looking out of her apartment door.

Once in the car, Lando got him and Quick out of there in seconds. Pulling up in the alley behind his house, out of breath, Lando said, "Dat nigga was lunchin! What made dat   nigga think he was gon get away wit some shit like dat?"

"Man, I don't know what was up wit dat nigga, but he dead as a muthafucka now!" Quick said with a murderous laugh.

Opening the shoe box full of money,Lando said "Let's go break dis shit down young."

Eight

The Black Hole was packed. Mann walked through the door without a search because he knew the dude that was patting everyone down. So he walked in the go-go with his Desert Eagle tucked in his waistband. The small dance floor was packed with people and through the darkness, Mann couldn't tell who was who, so he kept his hand inside his Hugo Boss jacket with his finger on the trigger of the .44 he was carrying. Mann saw a few old friends in the spot. All they wanted to know was who had shot him and if he had put that work in yet. Other's asked about Dre and Black and when they would be coming home. Mann told no one more then they needed to know, then he began to pull up on the females.

Leaning against the wall sipping a cup of Hennessy was a beautiful dark skinned girl in a tight pair of blue Gap jeans and a soft leather Armani coat on. Mann pulled up on her smoothly and got her phone number. Moving to the back of the dance floor, Mann ran into a small cute light skinned girl, with long black hair. She looked as if she could be from an island somewhere in the Caribbean.

"How you doin?" Mann asked, as he flashed a smile.

Turning to look at Mann, the cute girl responded, "I'm chillin'."

"So what can I call you? You gotta have a name."

"You can call me Mika, if I can call you something."

Rubbing his hand seductively through the girl's hair, Mann said, "You can call me New Yorker."

"What?? You from New York or somethin'?"

"Yeah, why? You don't like out of towners?" Mann asked the cute girl.

Smiling up at Mann she said, "Naa, they cool. I just never messed wit one before."

Fast Lane

"Well look here. It's a first time for everything in dis world. So check dis out, can we leave here, maybe go get something to eat and then you show me a good time?" Mann asked.

"Sure, dat sounds good to me, let's go," the cute girl said, as they left the Black Hole.

Days after Lando and Quick had killed the Jamaican dude in Jazmin's apartment building, they were walking down the hallway of Paul Jr. High School about to sneak out for lunch. They had came off with a nice little bit of cash on the caper. It turned out to be $10,000 in the shoe box that Lando found and three pounds of weed in the foot locker bag that Quick had found. The two of them broke the money and weed down 50/50. They decided to keep the weed for smoking and to buy some coke from Mann with the money. They hadn't gotten around to buying the coke yet and they seemed to be in no rush either. Waiting for their chance to run across the school yard to the Acura that they were riding in, Jazmin walked by. Lando saw that she wasn't trying to speak, so he told Quick to hold up and ran up behind her.

"Jazmin, what's up wit you? You act like you beefin' wit me or something," Lando said.

Turning to face Lando with her books in hand, Jazmin snapped, "You ain't no different then Quick and dem. I was a fool to think you were different then dem wanna be gangsta ass niggaz you be wit...."

"Hold up! What you talkin' 'bout?"

"You know what I'm talking 'bout Lando. I saw you and Quick runnin' down my hallway the other day! I know what y'all did!" Jazmin said. Looking around to see who could hear, Lando saw no one. He was shocked by the information Jazmin had just given him. He didn't know what to do.

Looking Jazmin in the eyes he said, "So now what's up? You saw us and what?" Jazmin was still very upset. She had feelings for Lando but she didn't want to get involved with a dude that was living like he was living.

Looking Lando in the eyes, Jazmin said, "I can't fuck wit you Lando. When you make up your mind what it is you want to do wit yourself, then we can be more than friends. Until then, we just cool." After letting Lando know how she felt, Jazmin walked down the hall on her way to the lunchroom.

Eyone Williams

"So what was Jazmin talkin' bout?" Quick asked Lando, as they were riding down 9th Street.

"She saw us smash dat nigga the other night." Lando answered.

"So what you tryin' to do about it?"

"I ain't tryin to do nothing, she ain't gon say shit about it. Her beef wit me young," Lando said, as he turned down Rittenhouse Street.

At the top of the block, Lando stopped the car and quickly tapped Quick on the arm, saying, "Look down there young!" Rittenhouse Street was packed with FBI, DEA, and Metropolitan Police. Cars and vans were parked all on the sidewalk and in front yards, up and down the street. It was a full scale raid, DEA agents were bringing Corey, Onion, Smoke, Serge, Lil' Garvin, Baby-D, and Kevin out of Old Tima's house in handcuffs. DEA and FBI agents were bringing Kisha's mother out of her house in her bed robe and slippers, hand cuffed as well. "Let's get da fuck outta here young!" Quick said, as Lando backed out of Rittenhouse Street and shot down 9th Street.

Mann was just getting off the phone with Black when Lando and Quick came down the basement steps with the news of the raid.

"So the Feds had everybody huh?" Mann asked.

"Slim! They even locked Kisha's motha up! They ain't playin' down there young!" Lando said. Mann knew a raid was in the making and had been laying low for that reason. Catching cases wasn't his thing. He knew that out of all the people that had just got locked up, somebody would give a few names. He didn't want Lando and Quick hanging out until he could find out what was what around the way. Lil' Garvin and Baby-D would most likely be the first to get cut lose being as though they were under age and the Feds always wanted someone they could build a good case on.

Rubbing his hand on his chin like he always did when he was in deep thought, Mann said to Lando and Quick, "Look here, I want y'all to stay away from da strip until we find out what da fuck is going down around da way. Y'all got dat?" Lando and Quick were both in accord with that. They both knew the strip was too hot at the time.

"So what happened the other night on da move y'all went on?" Mann asked. Quick looked at Lando, not wanting to say too much about the killing. Lando gave up a deadly smile and told Mann all about how the caper went down. Mann shook his head. He didn't agree with how they went about the whole thing and he would have been even more upset if he knew that Jazmin had seen them kill the Jamaican dude that night.

"If y'all wanna be big boys, y'all gotta think more than y'all thinkin'!" Mann said, as he gave the two young killers the game, "In dese streets, the man dat think da best on his feet gon live da longest. Everything ain't what it seems to be. Y'all coulda ran in dat joint and lost your life. Y'all ain't case da spot or nothin'! Y'all ran in there wit y'all little pistols and just so happen a nigga like Black was in there. Some niggaz don't care about life or death. It coulda been four or five niggaz in da joint! Y'all ain't know! Y'all can't just think y'all gon shoot ya way out of everything. Da game don't go like dat!" Lando and Quick paid close attention to every word that Mann said. This was the first time he had ever spoken to them as if they were on his level and by him doing so, they took the whole lesson to heart.

Black came back from his legal visit smiling like he had just been found not guilty on the murder case that he was facing. Once locked back in his cell, the cell doors on the tier opened, allowing the general population out. Dre came over to Black's bars and said, "What da fuck you so happy about?" Black's lawyer had just told him that the government's only witness had been found dead with her neck slit from ear to ear. The government was in a no win situation now. It was no way they would be able to indict Black and Dre with no one to testify at the Grand Jury.

"Yeah?" Dre said, full of excitement, "So we out of this joint for sure when we go back to court?"

Black pulled out some paperwork that he brought back from his legal visit and showed it to Dre, saying, "See dis? This says found dead! Dat means no witness to testify!"

Dre smiled and said, "Dat nigga Mann done took care of business already!"

Taking off his fresh jail jumper and sitting down on his bunk, Black said, "Yeah, my cuz must have put dat work in. I can't wait to get back out there. I'ma murda dat nigga Marvin and all da rest of dem bitch ass niggaz!"

Ric had started putting his   guards down a lot lately. He was even hanging out on the Avenue, knowing that Mann was out and about. It had been awhile since anyone had run into each other, so Ric had began to take Mann lightly. Mann on the other hand was on top of his game. Watching every move Ric made when he was in the city, Mann knew exactly how to catch him slippin'. This made Marvin much harder to catch then Mann had planned, so he went after Ric first.

Laying in the bushes besides Ric's mother's house, late at night, dressed in all black, Mann put his first move in effect. The front door was open and Mann could see Ric coming out of the house with a brown shopping bag in his hand. As Ric walked down the walkway to his car, Mann waited for the right moment and then quietly crept up behind Ric putting his huge Desert Eagle to his back.

Ric's first words were, "Damn!" he thought he was being robbed. Putting his hands in the air, he dropped the shopping bag and said, "I ain't got no cash on me slim!"

Putting a tight grip around the collar of Ric's leather jacket, Mann leaned over, pressing the .44 deep into Ric's back and whispered into his ear, "I don't want no money nigga." Then with a little laugh of revenge, he said, "You ain't think dem yesterdays was gon come back and get you. Did you?" Ric tried to snatch away when he realized Mann caught him slippin', but it did no good. Mann had him and he wasn't letting him go.

Marvin and Nicole were in the bed cuddled up under the sheets. Nicole hadn't felt so close to him in a long time. They had just made love for hours. With Nicole in his arms, Marvin looked her in the eyes and said, "I'm tired of da streets boo."

Not believing what she was hearing, Nicole raised up and said, "Are you serious?"

"Yeah, I'm sick of dis shit boo."

"So what you gon do?"

"I'm thinking 'bout moving down Virginia Beach. I got da cash to do it now, but you and my son gotta come. What you think about dat?" Rubbing her soft hands up and down Marvin's chest, Nicole thought about what he was saying. It sounded good, very good the more she thought about it.

"I like it. I like the thought of us moving down there together. I'm wit it," Nicole said.

In the middle of their deep conversation about the future, the phone rang. Nicole reached across the bed and answered the phone. Turning to Marvin she said, "Here, it's for you."

"Hello!" Marvin said, wondering who was calling him this late at night, over Nicole's house at that.

"Marvin! Dis Ric young!" Ric said, sounding very nervous, "Mann just shot at me right in front of my mother's house!"

"You okay?"

"Yeah, I'm cool slim, but I'm tryin to go get dis nigga! I'm bout to come get you. Be ready!"

"Where da nigga at right now?"

"He over his mother house right now! I saw his car in da alley."

"You sure?"

"Yeah! Man!"

"Okay den, come get me! I'ma be out front!" Marvin said, as he hung up the phone.

Marvin stood out front waiting for Ric to come get him, so he could put an end to Mann, once and for all. Everything would work out fine. He would kill Mann and then take his money and move down Virginia with Nicole and his son, leaving the streets to Ric and Jammie. Mann was slippin' Marvin thought. It wasn't like him to just be shooting at a nigga and letting him get away. Marvin thought that Mann must be acting out of his anger and that would be exactly what would allow him to kill him with ease. Even the best had to die some day Marvin thought as Ric's silver Acura Legend bent the corner at the top of the block. It was time to put all this beefin' behind him Marvin thought as he walked up to the car looking at his reflection in the dark tinted windows of the Acura.

Looking back over his shoulder as he opened the door, Marvin hopped in the car and shut the door. Rubbing his hands together to heat them up, Marvin turned to ask Ric how he wanted to go about getting into Mann's mother's house and almost shitted on himself. Smiling at him with a huge Desert Eagle .44 pointed right in his face, Mann said, "Pay back's Eh-muthafucka!!" Pulling the trigger of the .44 one time as he pulled off in Ric's car, Mann blew Marvin's brains all over the passenger side window. The rest of Marvin's body lifelessly slumped against the dash board, bleeding all over the place. Mann carefully drove up to the Fort Totten woods and set the car on fire, leaving Marvin shot dead in the passenger seat and Ric shot dead in the trunk. Mann walked back to the main street, after wiping all finger prints off of the .44 and tossed it down the sewer hole before catching a cab home. The killing was over for Mann. If Jammie wanted to find him some heart overnight, Mann decided that he would let Lando and Quick deal with him since they were firing pistols now or Black would be more then happy to kill him now that him and Dre would be coming home thanks to Mann slicing the throat of the only government witness.

Inside the 4th District police station, Officer James came into his office very upset and slammed a bunch of paperwork on his desk. Seeing something wrong with his partner, Officer Hall walked over and asked him what the problem was.

Flipping through the paperwork, Officer James said, "What's not wrong? First of all, everyone that got busted with that big raid on Rittenhouse Street has made bail and were now right back down there pushing more drugs in the neighborhood. On top of that, the DEA has no real case on any of them. The only scumbag that was caught with any drugs on him was the one they call Onion or something like that!" The younger officer knew Onion well, he had arrested him once before.

"So what did they find on Onion?" Hall asked.

"He had at least 62 grams of crack on him when the Feds ran up in that crack house." James responded.

Thinking back to the time when he had arrested Onion, Hall said, "That guy Onion owes me a favor. We can cash in on it if you need to." James looked up at Hall with a look of relief. That was what he needed to hear. The Chief was all over him about finding out who had all the coke down 5th and Rittenhouse Street, as well as who was doing the killing. Downtown was making a big fuss about the Rittenhouse raid being a big fluke. The Feds wanted no more to do with the case unless 4th District could produce a bust of a kilo or better. That meant that the whole case load of the last raid, as well as all other investigations on Rittenhouse Street had to be done by James and his partner Hall.

Pamila's house was packed. Upstairs in the living room, Pamila, Kelley, Kisha, and young Tyesha sat around the TV, while Pamila talked to the younger girls about life and how she use to run the streets just like them when she was young, but she realized that life had more to offer as she got older.

Downstairs in the basement, Mann had music blasting, while him, Lando, Quick, and Lil' Garvin played Nintendo on Mann's 60" inch TV. Mann asked Lil' Garvin what the Feds had locked him and everybody else up for. Lil' Garvin let him know that Onion was the only one dirty that day, everybody else went downtown for petty stuff like no identification or in the case of him and Baby-D, they had well over $1,000 in loose cash on them with no way to prove how they made it at a work place.

"So what they catch dat nigga Onion wit?" Mann asked.

"They caught dat nigga dirty as shit! He just cut up a fresh 62 before da Feds hit da joint. I don't know how that nigga got out when everybody else did," Lil' Garvin said. The first thing that came to Mann's mind was that Onion was talking to the Feds. Mann didn't trust him as it was but now he told himself that he wouldn't sell Onion a dime rock.

Jammie was scared to death when Nicole called him crying and told him that Marvin and Ric had been found shot in Ric's burnt up Acura Legend. Jammie first thought was to take all the money and coke they had stashed over Marvin's house and leave town, but he knew he couldn't stay away from the city for long so he did the next thing that came to mind. He made a phone call to the 4th District police department and told Officer Hall everything he knew about the beef Mann had with Marvin and how Lando and Quick were the one's doing all of the shooting in retaliation for Mann's shooting. With no real evidence, Officer Hall got a warrant for Mann and Lando's arrest since he knew their whole names off hand. All Jammie knew Quick by was Quick, therefore, Hall would have to catch up with him after questioning the other two, if he could get any information out of them.

Waking up in the bed next to Mann was something that Kelley had grown very use to over the past weeks. It was not only something that she had grown use to, she was in love with it. She was in love with everything about Mann. She had seen none of the horrible things that people had told her about Mann being a killer and even though she knew he sold drugs, she never saw him with any or even heard him talk about selling any. The Mann she knew was the smooth dark skinned man of her dreams that made love to her every night and then held her in his arms and listened to all of her worries, giving the solution to everyone as if he was always divinely inspired with Universal Laws about living life. Mann was wide awake when Kelley opened her eyes this morning. He had things to take care of and was out.

Mann had seen Nicole walking down Georgia Avenue with her son Lil' Marvin. As Mann passed by in his Z, they caught eye contact. Mann had never seen so much hurt and pain in a person's eyes in all of his life. For a second, he felt bad that Marvin had forced him into a situation where he had to take his life. Nicole flashed Mann a look of more then a thousand words and Mann read each of them in one way or another. He knew Nicole knew that he was behind the murder of her baby's father, yet she somewhat had a look of understanding that what goes around comes around and this time around Marvin got the short end of the coming around. Mann really couldn't find the balls to overplay his hand and speak to Nicole so he waited for her reaction to seeing him. Sadly she understood that Mann wasn't trying to add any more pain to a painful event and she waved at him as if to say "Why?....." Mann could not get that haunting look that Nicole gave him out of his mind and for the first time in his life he understood why his little cousin Black went through life saying fuck the world, it made times like these much easier. Even so, Mann had a heart and this was one move that he had to make in life that he would never forget.

Rolling over on to Mann's chest looking beautiful as always, Kelley saw something was on Mann's mind.

Rubbing her soft hands on his arms, she looked up into his eyes and said, "What's wrong boo?" Mann was quickly turned on by the feeling of Kelley's soft body against his. Sliding his hand down under the covers, Mann softly caressed Kelley's soft ass.

"Ain't nothin' wrong wit me. I was just thinkin' 'bout what we was talking about last night. I'ma get into dat G.E.D. class I was telling you about." Kelley was pleased to hear that, it made her feel like she really had a say so in Mann's life since she had been pressing him about getting back into school.

Smiling at him, Kelley said, "You ain't nothing like everybody be sayin' you is." As she threw her thick thighs over Mann's body and climbed on top of him.

Pushing her hands down on Mann's chest, Kelley raised her sexy body up into a sitting position on top of Mann, with her well shaped breast sitting enticingly in his face. Mann grew full of sexual excitement instantly.

Rubbing his hands slowly up and down Kelley's smooth back, Mann said, "What do everybody be sayin' I'm like?"

Raising up off of Mann sliding him slowly inside of her with her hand, Kelley let out a tiny sigh of pleasure as she said, "It don't even matter right now."

Placing both of her hands back down on Mann's chest, she began to wiggle her body up and down. Opening her mouth as she threw her head back in the air, Kelley started to move faster and faster on top of Mann.

As her ass started to slap against Mann's thighs, she began to moan and scratch his chest, saying, "Ohh..... I love you so much. I love what you are doing to my body. Ahhh...... don't stop Mann, I love you so much." Mann slid his hands down around her hips and locked an unrelenting grip around them as he began to push himself deeper and deeper into Kelley's accepting body. Kelley couldn't take the act of Mann's aggressive desire to push her off the cliffs of ecstasy. She came in seconds. Mann continued at the same pace, making Kelley come over and over again. Grabbing Kelley tightly as he could, Mann pulled her down to him as he reached his climax. Looking into Mann's eyes as she felt him exploding inside of her, Kelley smiled and said, "I love you so much!"

Officer Hall was out riding around with the "jump-outs". Since his partner Officer James was in charge of all affairs that had anything to do with Rittenhouse Street, Hall had the authority to carry things however he chose to. Being as though he was much younger then James and closer to the streets, James put his trust in him when it came to finding out who was who. On top of that, Officer Hall was glad to work the Rittenhouse investigation because it gave him another shot at making a case stick to Black when he got out of jail this time around.

Hidden behind the tinted windows of Black's Acura Legend, Lando, Quick, Baby-D, and Lil' Garvin sat on the corner of 5th and Rittenhouse Streets smoking weed and talking about how the Feds had to have somebody telling them something. Baby-D was telling everybody that when they took him back into the interrogation room, the only people they wanted to know about was Mann and Dre.

Lando turned back to Baby-D and said, "What they was saying bout Mann and Dre?"

Baby-D blew a cloud of weed smoke out of his mouth as he said, "They was talking bout they know Mann got all da coke around the way and they trying to get somebody to tell dem dat they buyin coke from him or Dre. I told dem crackers dat I ain't know Mann or Dre, but somebody done told dem muthafuckers something."

While Baby-D was talking, Quick peeped the "jump-outs" bending the corner, and said, "Jump outs!!!" Even though the four of them were hidden behind the tinted windows, they all slid down in their seats.

Across the street, standing in front of Kisha's house, was Corey, Onion, Smoke, Serge, and Kevin. Corey was servin' pipehead Big Busta when the "jump-outs" bent the corner in the black four door Cadillac Seville. "Jump outs!!!!" Kevin yelled, as everybody broke through Kisha's yard, running through the cut and into the alley going their separate ways. The "jump-outs" made a quick turn into the alley and jumped out, each one of them picking one person to run down. In a black Polo sweat shirt, blue jeans, and high top Air Jordan's, Officer Hall ran after Onion.

Onion hopped the fence across the alley from Kisha's house and ran across Roxboro Place and into another yard that led to another alley. Hall was right on his back, no less than three or four steps behind him.

Pointing his Glock at Onion, Hall screamed, "Freeze! Mother Fucker!" Onion kept running and cut into a yard full of bushes. Throwing a zip lock bag full of 50 rocks, Onion hopped the fence that led to the street in front of the house. Hall came running through the yard seconds later, never seeing Onion throw his coke. Running out into the front yard of the house, Hall saw Onion running down the sidewalk. Hall took off after him, showing no signs of fatigue. Onion was slowly but surely running out of gas. Hall ran up on him and tackled him to the ground like an All Pro free safety.

"Where you think you going?" Hall said as he wrestled Onion down to the ground.

"Get da fuck off me!" Onion yelled as he tried to get Hall off of him. Choking Onion out until he calmed down, Hall stood him up and slammed him against a car, while pulling a ready made bag of dime rocks from under his black Polo shirt. Seeing Hall pull the coke from under his shirt, Onion said, "Dat shit ain't mine!"

Throwing the coke on the hood of the car, Hall said, "Oh, yes it is. Now I could get rid of these nice little rocks if you let me know something."

"Let you know what?"

"You know Marvin and Ric from 13th Street?"

"Yeah I know 'em. Why?"

"Who smoked 'em?"

"I don't know who smoked dem niggaz!" Onion said.

Hall became angry and smashed Onion's face into the cold hood of the car, saying, "Don't play dumb with me you piece of shit!"

"I don't know who smoked dem niggaz!"

"Look here! I know Marvin shot your homeboy Mann. I also know that Black is the only one of you little wanna be gang bangers that got the balls to murder a motherfucker in cold blood, but he's locked up now so who the fuck is the next in line to be the trigger man around here?" Hall said. Onion really didn't know who had killed Marvin and Ric, but he had a feeling that Mann did it. Hall got fed up with Onion telling him that he didn't know who shot Marvin and Ric. By the time the rest of the "jump-outs" pulled up, Hall had his mind set on taking Onion in for the bag of dime rocks that he had planted on him. Asking Onion one last time about Mann, Hall told him that if he didn't tell him something, he was going back to jail. Onion knew that he had just been caught with 62 grams of coke just over a week ago. He wasn't going back in at all. Onion gave Hall the only information that he had, telling Hall that Lando and the young niggaz around the way were the ones doing all of the shooting and killing around the way. Hall questioned Onion for a while getting everything he needed to know about Lando, Quick, Baby-D, and Lil' Garvin then he let Onion go, telling him that if he was to ever act like he didn't know what was going on around the way, that he would let everyone know that he was dropping dimes.

Later on, Mann sat at the kitchen table eating pizza, while Lando told him everything that Baby-D had told him in the car, just before the "jump-outs" came through.

"So da Feds askin' bout me, huh?" Mann asked.

"Yeah slim. Baby-D say they askin bout you and Dre."

"Do they know anything?"

"I don't think so. Baby-D say they tryin' to get a nigga to say they buyin' they shit from you," Lando said. Mann began to think about what

Eyone Williams

his little brother was telling him. Mann knew that things were going to be "hot" around the way ever since he saw the Feds come through taking pictures in the van a while back. Mann knew what he had to do and it wasn't hard at all. Mann told himself that he would get all of his coke, money, and guns out of Pamila's house just in case the Feds wanted to play dirty and kick the door in.

Officer Hall had decided to take a ride down to the Homicide Branch. He knew the detective that had the case that Black and Dre were about to come home on and wanted to find out how in the world did the system let Black slip through the cracks once again. Hall walked into the office of his old high school buddy, Detective Walt Brown. Brown had gained a lot of weight since Hall had seen him last, but he still had the look of a young man.

Sitting down in front of the desk of the short black man, Hall said, "I see you been living good."

Brown leaned back in his chair, lighting a Newport Long, laughing as he said, "Yeah, I've gained a little weight now that I'm not running down those thugs anymore. So what brings you to see me?" Hall got straight to the point and asked Brown how did he let Black get away from him?

"Well" Brown said, "It's like this. No witness, no case. In fact, I never really had a case. All I had was some young girl saying that she told Black that there was like $50,000 in the guy's house that he killed. I thought that maybe Black would get scared of being charged as an adult and take a cop or even act like a big boy and go to trial, where anything goes. But he done got somebody to kill my witness so I'm back at the drawing board." When Brown was done talking, Hall gave him the run down on all the information that he had picked up from Jammie and Onion. He let him know that there was an arrest warrant out for Mann and his little brother Lando. Brown was very interested in the information. He had the "Marvin and Ric" double murder case.

"So what's up with the guys Mann and Lando?" Brown asked. Mixing opinion with the truth, Hall told Brown that Mann was the big dope boy around his way and just so happens to be the cousin of Black, not to mention that he was shot by DeMarvin Scott about two months ago. He went on to tell Brown that Mann's little brother Lando was an up and coming killer, with a gang of side kicks. He believed that Lando and his gang of juvenile delinquents were behind the murder of the government witness as well as Marvin and Ric. He also let Brown know that he didn't believe Mann was behind the murders because he was a pretty boy that was used to telling someone else to kill for him.

"So why do you have a warrant out for his arrest? Why not just his little brother?" Brown asked.

"Because if I'm right and the youngsters are behind it, then Mann is putting them up to it. He has all the brains in the family," Hall said.

"Let me ask you this," Brown said. "If we bring these brothers in, what can we charge them with?" Hall was stuck, he had nothing on them but hearsay and Brown let him know flat out that his boss would not support another hearsay case right after the bad gamble they had taken with Black and Dre.

"Get something that will stick to these brothers and then I'll pull some strings for you since you seem to be taking this whole thing with the Mills boys so personal," Brown said. Hall rolled with the punches and let his buddy know that he would nail this one for sure. Hall got up and shook Brown's hand as he headed back up to the 4th District Police Station.

Mann had been taking G.E.D. classes for a week now. He was into the little work that he was getting. Besides that, going to school for a few hours a day, three days a week gave him a break from the madness of the streets. Silk had found it very pleasing that Mann was taking G.E.D. classes. He had been telling Mann all year how easy the G.E.D. was for him and that Mann should take the test so that he could get into the Business Management class that he was taking. Silk always told Mann that he was going to have to put the dope game to the side sooner or later and go legit. Mann and Silk came to an agreement that when they both got $1,000,000 out of the game they would go legit. Silk was to start a chain of restaurants called Silky's and Mann told him that when he hit the million mark he was going to open a night club in the city that would have local bands performing in it and he would also rent it out for parties and cabarets. Thinking of all that the future would hold when they both hit the million mark, Silk decided to pay Mann a visit at school.

Mann had to smile coming out the door of the Armstrong Vocational Center. Smooth as always, Silk was leaning against a cherry red Ferrari 355 Spyder, in a thick black Hugo Boss leather coat and a pair of black Polo jeans that were hanging down over his black Timberland double sole boots. Mann walked over to Silk, hugged him and said, "What's you doing up here?"

"I came to check on you. I went by your house and Kelley told me you were down here. I see you gon go ahead and take that test," Silk said. Mann talked to Silk for a while about how he had been talking to Kelley about school and it made him think about his night club and the agreement they had made about the million mark. Silk was pleased to hear that. Mann was like a little brother to him. Mann switched the subject to the raid on Rittenhouse Street and how the Feds were trying to get somebody to say that they were buying coke from him. Silk knew that once the Feds were on your trail they wouldn't leave you alone until that got you for something if you were the type that was never caught dirty, like him and Mann. Silk asked Mann what he planned to do about the situation, and also let him know that he couldn't pass out weight around the way being as though anybody could be working with the law. Mann let Silk know that he was going to lay low and only serve coke to his old buddies Da-Da and Leron out Maryland. Silk was in accord with that, he told Mann to do whatever it took to duck an indictment. Before leaving, Silk asked about Black and Dre.

Mann smiled at him and said, "They gon be home soon."

Silk understood exactly what Mann meant by the smile. Opening the door to his Ferrari, Silk said, "Let Dre and Black know that it's a rack of money out here to get. I'm sure you can show'em how to get it."

Mann turned the head lights to his Z on as the night grew dark. On his way home he was thinking about what Lando had told him. The Feds were on his back. He knew they had nothing on him, but he didn't like the heat on him. He was all about the money, not the fame.

Looking into the rear view mirror, Mann saw a patrol car pulling up behind him. He wasn't dirty so he played things cool even though he could tell that the pigs were running his plates. The pigs hit their lights as a white uniformed officer got out of the car and walked up to Mann's window.

"Shit!" Mann said out loud. Tapping on the window of Mann's car, the officer pulled his radio out again. Mann rolled the window down and

said, "What's up?" The officer asked for his ID and told him that there had just been a shooting a few blocks away and his car matched the description of the car that fled the scene. After Mann gave the officer his ID, the officer on the passenger side of the car got out and walked up beside his partner.

"Would you mind stepping out of the car sir?" the other white officer said. Mann got out while the officer with the radio was running his name. "Mr. Mills" the officer with the radio said, "You're under arrest."

Downtown inside of the Homicide Branch, Mann waited for Detective Brown to come into the interrogation room. Handcuffed to the floor, looking around the tiny room, Mann had never been questioned for a murder before. Even so, he knew that the best answer to a question from the Feds was no answer and that's exactly how he played it when Detective Brown walked into the room with him.

"So mister bad-ass" Detective Brown said as he sat down in front of Mann, "What do you know about ah.....a mister DeMarvin Scott and Ric Jones?"

Mann smiled, this would be easier then he thought. "I don't know nobody by those names slim!" Mann said with no sign of fear.

"Well here's the deal smart ass! You and your little brother, uh.......Lando, y'all are suspects in three murders, so if I were you I wouldn't be acting so damn tough."

"Yeah? Well I guess dat's why I'm cuffed to da floor and you ain't! Dat shit you talkin' don't scare me at all, if you ain't gon charge me with something you gotta let me go, and if you is!.... you gotta call my mother so I can get a lawyer because I ain't nothing but 17! You dig?" Mann said with a very no nonsense look on his face.

Detective Brown was stung by Mann's aggressiveness, not to mention shocked by his age. Officer Hall never once told him that Mann had just turned 17 years old. By the way, Hall talked about Mann he assumed that he was in his twenties. Mann had Brown in a do or die situation. He was a juvenile, therefore he was right, his mother had to be notified that her child was under arrest, meaning that Brown had to charge Mann or let him go. Brown wanted so bad to charge Mann and take him through the procedures because of his slick ass mouth, but he had nothing on him and he knew that Mann knew it. Uncuffing Mann, Brown let him know that he had the double murder case that he was a suspect in and that he was going to be on his back until he could place the beef on him. Mann knew he had played his cards right once again. Walking out of the interrogation room, Mann did something that he had never done before; he played big saying "You can do what you want to do. You'll never place a beef on me. Believe dat playboy."

Nine

The rest of the year seemed to fly by at the speed of light. Mann stuck to his plan and cleaned all of his coke, money, and guns out of Pamila's house. He made sure that he didn't sell a crumb of coke on Rittenhouse Street. Every brick he sold went for $30,000 now and they were all sold through Da-Da and LeRon. They had their White Oak apartment complex locked down. Mann was never dirty now. The only thing the Feds could catch him with was a G.E.D. book. All his coke, guns, and money were in a one bedroom apartment right around the corner from where Da-Da and LeRon lived and they didn't even know it. The only people that had ever been to the apartment were Silk and Lando. All was going well for Mann. Dre and Black went to court in days, the Feds hadn't bothered questioning him again about the double murder, and life was what it should be in his eyes.

Lando on the other hand was a different story. He brought the new year in with a murder. Him and Quick got into a fight with some older Maryland dudes inside of a party they went to for New Year's Eve. One of the dudes had bumped Lando coming into the party. Lando turned around and punched the bigger dude in the face. The Maryland dudes tried to jump Lando and Quick, but they ran outside. Once in the parking lot, they ran for the Acura Legend and got their pistols. By the time the older dudes got into the parking lot it was no way out. Lando and Quick unloaded they pistols at the group of five. As they tried to run, Lando ran the dude down that had bumped him in the party, shooting him in the back until he fell between two cars. Walking up and standing over top of the older dude, Lando shot him in the head twice and ran back to the car where Quick was waiting behind the wheel.

Pamila had grown very close to Kelley over the past few months. She believed that the young girl was going to do something with her life and Pamila loved to see a young person go after their dreams. Mann had inspired Kelley to go to school to be a lawyer. Pamila was in support of the idea. Pamila told Kelley that as long as there were little bad asses like

Eyone Williams

Lando running the streets that she would always find work if she knew the law.

Pamila was fed up with Lando. She hadn't spoken to him in at least two weeks. His school was calling her at work every other day. Lando would go to school when he wanted to. Pamila didn't understand how Lando could go from a regular kid to and out of control young thug over night. Pamila had to get Mann to help her understand Lando these days. She truly believed he had lost his mind and wanted to get him some psychiatric help. Mann assured Pamila that Lando would slow down once he became sure of his manhood. Pamila had decided to go with Mann's theory and she prayed that if he was right, Lando would live long enough to see true manhood.

The District of Columbia Superior Court was busy on the morning of January 18th 1990. Pamila, Mann, and Kelley walked into the court room of the Honorable Judge John H. Suda. Black and Dre were already in the court room sitting down beside their lawyer, a tall white lady named Mary Armstrong. Black turned to look back at his aunt Pamila, Mann, and Kelley, as the judge began to speak.

"Does the government have an indictment for the two defendants?" Judge Suda asked the D.A.. Fumbling through her papers, the slim white D.A. tried to beat around the bush.

"Either you do or you don't!" the judge said, becoming very angered. "I'm throwing this case out if there is no indictment!"

"Your Honor, all I need is two weeks and I will have the ..."

"No! Ms. Miller, this case is dismissed as of today. The defendants are to be released from the DC Jail. Good day Ms. Miller. Next case!" Judge Suda said as the Marshals took Black and Dre back into the bullpen.

"I told you we was outta here nigga!" Black said to Dre once they were in the holding cells downstairs in the court building, waiting for the bus ride back to the DC Jail.

Smiling, Dre hugged Black and said, "We outta dis muthafucka. I can't wait to hit dem bricks. Mann say da money comin' like shit out there." Sitting down on the hard metal bench inside the holding cell, Black and Dre talked about what they were going to do when they were back on the streets. Black had his mind set on killing Metra for turning Dre in to the Feds for the money. Dre let Black know that it was too much money out in the streets to be thinking about Metra. He told Black to leave the "hot bitch" alone. Skipping that subject, Black started talking about Lando and all of the young dudes around the way. Black couldn't wait to see what was up with his cousin. Lando's name was kicking all over the streets for the five months that Black and Dre had been up the jail. While Black was talking about Lando and his little mob, Dre stood up at the bars and looked over to the bubble where all the Marshals were.

"Ain't dat da homicide nigga dat had our case?" Dre asked Black, sounding concerned.

Standing up to take a look himself, Black said, "Yeah, dat's dat nigga."

The Marshals opened the gate and let Detective Brown into the bullpen. Behind him was Officer Hall. They both walked over to the holding cell that Black and Dre were in alone, being as though they were still juveniles. Hall leaned against the bars smiling while Brown began to speak. Black and Dre stood on the other side of the bars with their arms folded, anxiously waiting to see what the pigs had to say now that the murder case had been thrown out.

"Well Dre," Brown said, "Looks like you were the lucky one this time around kido."

Confused, Dre said, "What da fuck do dat suppose to mean?" The door to the bubble where the Marshals were opened and a big blond haired young white Marshal came walking up to the cell with a pair of hand cuffs and shackles dangling from his hand.

"Who's going?" The Marshal asked Brown as he opened the holding cell.

Unable to pass up the pleasure of breaking the news, Hall let out a little laugh and said, "Mr. Mills." The Marshall told Black to step out of the cell. Coming out of the cell, Black asked the Marshall what was going on. Pointing at Brown, the Marshal started handcuffing Black.

"Mr. Mills," Brown said, "You are under arrest for murder."

Looking back at Dre with a look of defeat, Black said, "Y'all fucked up dat da judge threw dat weak shit out so y'all come at me wit some fake shit like dis huh?" Dre watched as the Marshal walked Black out of the bullpen with Brown and Hall, who was reading him his rights.

Dre walked out of the gates of the DC Jail happy to be free, but fucked up that Brown and Hall had played dirty with Black, hitting him with another body right after the case they were on was dismissed. Mann,

Lando, and Quick were sitting outside the gates in Quick's big brown Cadillac Fleetwood. Hidden behind the dark tinted windows of the old "bucket" that Quick had paid $2500 for, Mann watched Dre walk out into the parking lot, not knowing where Mann was, being as though he had never seen the car Quick had just bought a week ago.

Rolling down the window, Quick said, "You lost or something?" Looking over to the car, Dre smiled as he ran over and got in the back seat. Weed smoke filled the car, as Rare Essence blasted through the speakers.

"What's up nigga?" Mann said full of genuine love for his partner, as he reached over and hugged him.

"Ain't shit," Dre said. Quick and Lando turned around in the big front seat showing nothing but love. Quick passed Dre a fat blunt full of weed.

"Where da fuck Black at?" Lando asked Dre as he took a deep pull of the weed smoke. Dre let out a long sigh of disappointment.

"What da fuck is up joe?" Mann asked, sensing that something was wrong. Dre broke the news, letting everybody know how Brown and Hall had came and rearrested Black downstairs in the court building right after the case was dismissed.

"What da fuck they arrest him for in da court building?" Lando asked, not understanding how a person could be arrested for a crime inside the court building.

"They playin' dirty wit slim. They done charged him wit another body." Dre let everybody know that he had just seen Black in R-N-D when he was leaving. Black let him know that he had already been arraigned and that he went back to court in a week for his preliminary hearing.

"Who da fuck they say he smashed?" Mann asked. Black had told Dre that he knew the dude they were saying he killed but couldn't remember his name. He knew he had shot a nigga down SW on Half Street at the weed spot in the middle of the summer sometime last year. Black assured Dre that there would be no witnesses at all on the case because the only person that was out there that night was one of the dude's partners and Black said that he had ran into him at the Black Hole two days later and dumped 17 hollow points in his body while he sat in his car lighting a blunt. Mann remembered the whole situation and was sure that Black would come home on his first court date.

Kelley walked into Kisha's house and hung Mann's huge Eddie Bauer coat up on the back of Kisha's chair.

"What's up girl?" Kisha asked as she turned around blowing weed smoke into the air.

"I see y'all getting y'all smoke on," Kelley said as she sat down at the dining room table with Kisha and Tina.

"I hear Dre came home yesterday," Kisha said, looking at Kelley, "You ain't even tell me dat."

"I ain't seen you since he been home, Mann and dem ain't go get him 'til last night some time."

"So why Black ain't come home? You know dat's my boo," Kisha asked with a smile. She always ran to get Black when a nigga got out of line with her, she had been like that since her and Black were kids. Kelley gave her a funny look. Kelley knew that Kisha wanted to fuck Black, but Onion always seemed to watch her when Black came around.

Smiling at Kisha, Kelley said, "They charged Black wit another murder." Tina shook her head.   Black was trouble in her eyes. She had always told Dre to stop hanging with him. The three beautiful young girls went on talking about Black until the conversation somehow moved on to who fucked the best around the way.

The "jump outs" had just hit the block causing Smoke, Serge, and Onion to take cover inside Kisha's house. Coming through the door they smelled the weed smoke in the air. Onion ran over to Kisha and grabbed her.

"Get off me boy! You cold as shit!" Kisha said. Everyone laughed. Smoke and Serge sat down on the floor in the living room watching HBO. Tina and Kelley were sitting on the sofa watching TV as well. Onion picked Kisha up out of her chair and carried her into the living room with everyone else.

"What bring y'all niggaz inside?" Tina asked.

Wrestling Kisha while kissing her all over, Onion said, "The jump-outs out there." Smoke pulled a big zip-lock bag of skunk weed out the pocket of his big blue Eddie Bauer.

"Y'all tryin to smoke?" he asked. Everybody let it be known that they were trying to put something in the air.

"Where dem Backwoods at?" Smoke asked Serge.

"Here they go," Serge said as he tossed Smoke the pack.   In seconds, four fat Backwoods were floating around the room. Smoke was feeling the effects of the strong weed in no time. Kelley began to look more attractive than usual. Smoke had always had a thing for Kelley, whose attention had always been on Mann.

Smoke looked up at Kelley from the floor and said, "What's up wit you?"

Not knowing if Smoke was coming on to her or not, Kelley said, "What you mean what's up wit me?"

"You know what I'm saying," Smoke said. While everyone seemed to be waiting for her reaction, Kelley quickly set things straight.

"Look here!" Kelley said as she began to check Smoke, "It ain't dat type of party wit me nigga. You ain't just gon come in here and blaze a lil' bag of bud and think you gon get some pussy from me. You got your people mixed up." The room went silent as reality seemed to smack Smoke in the face, this was not Metra he was talking to, it was Kelley, and male or female, she would stand firm if she felt disrespected or taken for granted.

Onion broke the tension by looking out the window and saying, "The Feds gone, let's hit da block."

Once outside in the cold night air, Onion, Smoke, and Serge got right back to business. No longer playing Old Tima's house since the Feds had raided it about three months ago, they hustled out of the cut beside the house now. Pipeheads came from every direction as soon as they stepped back on the strip. Now that Mann was no longer passing coke out on the block or hustlin' on the block, Onion was somewhat the man. He had everyone buying coke from him once again, just like he had done while Mann was in the hospital. Onion walked down the alley with pipehead Karen, leaving Smoke and Serge alone in the dark cut beside Old Tima's house.

"What's up wit dat nigga Corey?" Smoke asked.

"I don't know, but Onion was talking to 'em da other day 'bout some money he owed 'em. It was like $15,000," Serge said. Smoke had wanted to rob Corey for the last month. Money wasn't coming like him and Serge wanted it to. Mann was to blame for some of their problems being as though he kept telling them that he was laying low until the Feds let up off of the strip and Onion was the other part of their problem being as though he always found a way to lock shit down when Mann and Dre weren't around. Onion would've been their first choice for a quick robbery, but seemed to give them whatever they wanted due to the fact that he was scared of them turning on him. This meant that Corey was the one person other than Mann that they could rob and that would be worth robbing around the way. Smoke had even said something about robbing Mann and Dre, but Serge wanted nothing to do with that move. Serge couldn't see himself crossing Black like that, and not crossing Black was a safe thing to do.

Corey and Kevin had become very close again since Kevin had come home from prison. They both walked up on Smoke and Serge in the dark cut behind Old Tima's house. Showing no signs of the snake shit that they were just talking about, Smoke and Serge showed Corey and Kevin much love.

"Y'all know Dre home," Corey said. Smoke let him know that he heard, then asked if they knew about Black.

"What's up wit Black? Why da fuck he ain't come home if him and Dre was on da body together?" Kevin asked. They all began talking about how the Feds had hit Black with another body the day him and Dre got their case dismissed. Onion walked back into the cut a few minutes later with a lit blunt of weed. Passing the smoke around, the five of them started slippin'; as the smoke took effect.

At the end of the block on 5th Street, two young dudes in ski masks were getting out of an old silver Nissan 280 ZX with paper tags. They walked straight over to the cut beside Kisha's house.

"I thought you said da niggaz be out here," the short stick up boy with the Tec-9 said.

His partner, a fat dude, just a little taller than him, said, "They might be up there by Metra's house. It's a crack house 'bout two houses from her house. I saw some niggaz in da cut up there last time I dropped her off. She say they be hustling up there at night." Creeping up the street to Old Tima's house, the two stick up boys overheard the group of dudes talking, they could even smell the weed smoke strong in the cold air.

"Let's go!" the short dude said. They ran up in the cut catching everybody off guard.

"Lay da fuck on da ground!" the fat dude said. Smoke acted as if he wanted to buck, but the Colt .45 automatic that the dude behind the ski mask held, quickly talked him out of it. Laying everybody down in the ice cold dirty grass, the two stick up boys checked everyone. They took pistols from everyone but Onion. The short dude was so upset that Smoke had a

Glock .40 on him that he smacked him in the back of the head with his Tec-9.

Lando and Quick were just coming back around the way from dropping Lil' Garvin off down Crittenden Street where he had been hustlin' with his brother Dex since the Feds had brung so much heat down on Rittenhouse Street the last few months. Getting out of the Acura Legend, Lando and Quick headed for Old Tima's house. Pipehead Sheila was coming down the street. She had watched the stick up boys run up in the cut with ski masks on.

Walking up to Lando and Quick, she grabbed Quick's hand and said, "Baby, you and Lando be careful going up there. Some boys got Corey and them up there in the cut beside Old Tima's house robbin' them." Lando pulled a brand new Mac-10 from inside his Eddie Bauer. Quick pulled a 10mm from out the pocket of his Eddie Bauer. They both crossed to the other side of the street so they could walk in the shadows of the tall trees, while looking across the street where Old Tima's house was. Lando had never fired the Mac-10 or any other fully automatic weapon at the time and he was dying to spray it, all 36 shots of it. Seconds later the two stick up boys came running out of Old Tima's yard. As soon as they stepped foot on the sidewalk Quick and Lando ran side by side into the middle of the street firing their joints with both hands. The short dude with the Tec-9 started firing back. His partner never had a chance. As soon as Quick let his first couple of shots off the fat dude caught a slug in the side of the head and fell to the ground with his pistol sliding out of his hand. Gun fire filled the night. As the stick up boy ran down the sidewalk sideways shooting at Lando and Quick, they ran down the street shooting back at him while shooting car windows out and everything. Running and gunning for his life, the stick up boy cut through a yard and disappeared into the darkness of the alley. Lando and Quick began to follow him but a police car came roaring around the corner with no lights or sirens on.

Two young black officers jumped out of the car and started shooting at the two little gunmen. Running right in front of the pigs as they crossed the street shooting at them and their police car, Lando and Quick ran through the cut beside Kisha's house and were gone in the night. The officers called for back up and in no time the whole block was covered with Feds.

At 10:00am, the next morning the National Guards came rolling in dressed in army fatigue carrying M-16's. 20 deep in four Hummers they shut the block down. Two Hummers pulled up at the 5th Street corner and placed 60 cal. Machine guns on stands in back of the Hummer. The other two Hummers did the same thing. Not a rock was sold on Rittenhouse Street all day, they made sure of that.

At about 12 noon, Officer Hall and his good buddy Detective Brown were on the murder scene. Yellow tape was all in front of Metra's house where the body of the stick up boy turned murder victim was found. Hall was walking around with Brown trying to get him to see that whoever was doing the killing now was different than all the killings before. Hall told Brown that Black was the known killer around Rittenhouse Street and that he had never left so many shells at a scene.

"So what are you trying to say?" Brown asked. Hall told him that this meant that there was a new breed of killers and it had to be Lando and his buddies Quick, Baby-D, And Lil' Garvin.

Looking at the back of the shell casings that he had picked up around the murder scene, Brown said, "We are going to have to do something about these little motherfuckers. They are running around here with fully automatic weapons. That poor son of a bitch that they took to the morgue last night had two pistols on his waist line and a .45 no more then three feet away from his body and he still had 20 .45 slugs in his ass when he got to the morgue."

Lando and Quick were no longer little boys around the way. Smoke, Serge, Onion, Corey, and Kevin watched the whole shooting up until the cops came. It was the first time they had seen the young dudes in action alone and they held their own. They were all pissed off at them for shooting at the police and bringing the National Guard around but it was nothing they could say.

The whole shooting was all over the news for the next four days. This scared Lando and Quick. They were staying in a hotel just across the Maryland line until things cooled off, whenever that would be. Lando sent a cab to pick Nakia and Trina up from Nakia's house and drop them off at the hotel. The girls stayed there with them the whole time.

Mann could no longer stand by and watch Lando and Quick run wild. They were both family as far as Mann was concerned. Before going to the court building to see if Black was going to get his murder case dismissed, Mann and Dre stopped by the Days Inn Hotel to check on the two younger dudes. Mann knocked on the door as he blew hot air on to his hands to heat them up in the cold winter air. Quick answered the door in his boxers with his 10mm in hand. "What's up wit y'all niggaz?" Quick asked as he stepped back and let the two older dudes in.

Inside the hotel room, Trina was laying in one bed asleep with the covers pulled over her head. Lando was in the next bed rolling a blunt with his Mac-10 laying out in the open on the nightstand. Nakia was in the bed next to Lando knocked out sleep. Lando and Quick smoked too much for the young girls, they had passed out late last night and hadn't come back around. Dre couldn't believe how much Lando and Quick had grew up in the short five months that him and Black had been up the jail. The last thing he remembered about Lando was when he wanted to roll on the 13th Street niggaz and Mann wouldn't let him, now the same little dude that he had watched grow up was running around killing niggaz and busting at the Feds, things seemed to change over night in the fast lane.

Mann got Lando and Quick to step in the bathroom with him and Dre so that he could talk to the young dudes about what was going on.

"Look here," Mann said to his little brother and Quick, "Y'all gotta slow da fuck down. I understand dat y'all caught some niggaz robbin' niggaz around da way, y'all was right 'bout putting dat work in and no matter what y'all lil' muthafuckas get into I'm wit it but y'all gotta stop runnin' around here like dis da wild west or something. Shit all over da news. Pamila worried as shit." Mann went on to tell the two young dudes that they had to lay low. He felt that somebody that was on the strip that night was going to tell the Feds something. Mann made it clear that he didn't want Lando and Quick to do anything wild if the Feds were to start looking for them. He told them that if they were to get locked up for the murder and assault on two police officers that they would only go down Oak Hill for 2 years being as though they were only 12 years old. Everything Mann said to them eased their worries, because despite how much Lando and Quick acted like they ain't care about what was going down, they were a little shook by seeing the shooting on the news and hearing things like "manhunt" and "wanted for murder." When Mann was done talking he made the two young dudes give their word that they would lay low and only leave the hotel when the two young girls left so that no one would know where they were except him and Dre. Whenever they left, Mann told them to go to his apartment out White Oak Maryland and hang out until they heard from him. Lando and Quick agreed to the plan that Mann had laid down.

Pamila couldn't sleep for the past week; all she did was toss and turn. Even at work, all she could do was worry about Lando. The Rittenhouse shooting was all over the news. Pamila knew that Lando had to have something to do with it because he hadn't been home since the night of the shooting. Then Quick's grandmother called her looking for him and told Pamila that she hadn't seen Quick in a week as well. Pamila knew that the two sweet little boys that she had known for the last 12 years were the two gunmen that the police were looking for. The mere thought brought tears to her eyes.

Kelley had picked Tyesha up from school today and was just walking in the house when Pamila got off the phone with Quick's grandmother. Wiping the tears from her eyes, Pamila told Kelley to take Tyesha upstairs. Kelley did just that, then she came right back to see what was wrong with the loving woman that she had grown to look at as a mother over the past few months.

"What's wrong Pamila?" Kelley asked. Pamila told her everything, even though Kelley already knew without a doubt that Lando and Quick were the ones that did the shooting that drew so much heat to the neighborhood. Kelley gave Pamila a firm hug and told her that everything would be fine.

Pulling herself together, Pamila looked at Kelley in the eyes and said, "No Kelley, everything won't be fine. I done lost my baby to the streets and I don't know if I will ever get him back." Kelley had never seen the strong woman so shook up. As strong as Pamila was, Lando filled her soul with pain and didn't even know it.

Killa Black was back on the loose and dying to get into something. On the way to Mann's apartment to go see Lando and Quick, Mann let Black know that shit was too hot at the time for him to come home with that trigger happy shit. In the back seat of Dre's Nissan Maxima, Black let Mann know that he was trying to stay out in the streets this time around.

"It ain't easy to get two bodies dismissed in two weeks slim. I ain't tryin' to be in front of no judges for a while joe," Black said.

Eyone Williams

Dre looked back at Black through the rear view mirror and said, "I damn sure hope you mean dat shit cause shit hot as Eh-muthafucka out here. I ain't made a dime yet." Mann began to tell Black about everything that was going on in hopes of making him understand why he needed for him to chill out. Black told Mann and Dre that he was going to chill, but he was going to blow the bitch Metra's brains out as soon as he got a chance. Mann and Dre tried to talk him out of it, telling him that now wasn't the time and that he could take care of it as soon as everything cooled down. Black wasn't trying to hear any of that. His mind was made up and Mann and Dre both knew that when he got like that it was no stopping him.

Mann, Dre, and Black walked into Mann's apartment and saw Lando and Quick laying on the floor smoking weed and playing Techmo Bowl on Mann's huge TV. They were surprised to see Black. Walking up to Black, they both gave him "5" and showed their love.

"What's up nigga?" Quick asked.

"Ain't shit young nigga," Black said as he went on to tell the young dudes what he had been up to over the jail.

"I thought you was goin' to have to wait to go to trial," Lando said.

"Na, they dropped da shit," Black said. Mann and Dre walked back into the bedroom and left Black in the living room with Lando and Quick.

"So what da fuck is up wit y'all? I hear y'all got the National Guards and shit round da way," Black said as he flopped down on the sofa behind the two younger dudes. Quick got up to get a light for the blunt while Lando began to tell Black how things were going around the way. Where Mann would always give him the rules of the game, Black would sometimes encourage him to use the "fuck the world" outlook, without knowing. Quick came back with a fat blunt of skunk weed and passed it to Black while Lando was proudly telling Black how him, Quick, Baby-D, and Lil' Garvin had slaughtered shit when Mann got shot.

"No Bullshit!" Quick said as he sat down on the floor with Lando, "we went up dat joint and sprayed shit."

Black let out a cloud of weed smoke as he laughed a little bit saying, "Oh yeah, y'all put dat work in huh? Dat's right, fuck dem niggaz. They better be glad I wasn't home."

Back in the bedroom, Mann and Dre were talking about how Dre was going to get some money with the Feds being all over the place now. Opening a safe and pulling four zip lock bags out, Mann laid the bricks of coke down on the dresser and said, "Dis what I'ma do. I'ma give you two and a half of dese joints and we gon go half on ten of 'em when you done. Silk only want $80,000 for five, so when you done we can both put up 80 and we'll be set. The only thing is dat you can't push dis shit around the way."

Confused, Dre said, "Where you think I'm supposed to push two and a half joints at if I don't push 'em around da way?" Mann let Dre know that right out side of his apartment was a strip that was pumpin' from sun up to sun down and that he would put him down with the two dudes that had shit locked out there, which was Da-Da and LeRon.

"Cool," Dre said, "I'm wit dat, but what we gon do 'bout Black?" Mann knew he had to find something for Black to do that would stop him from robbing when he didn't have to, but that was so hard to do. Many, many times before, Mann had tried to get Black to slow down and just make some money but Black loved to run the streets and live from caper to caper. It was something that he did well.

"I'ma see if I can give 'em a brick of dis shit, he might be ready to slow down," Mann said. He also told Dre that he knew Black couldn't hustle out Maryland because he would try to take the dudes that he was dealing with bad, therefore he would have to find a spot for him, but until then he would make sure he was taken care of. At the present time Lando and Quick was his biggest worries.

It was snowing very hard in the city today. Mann had given Black a brick of coke and talked him in to trying to hustle for a while and Black was doing just that since he gave Mann his word that he would chill for awhile. Slowly riding down Rittenhouse Street in the snow Black saw Kisha walking up the street to her mother's car. Blowing the horn of his Acura Legend, Black got Kisha's attention. Looking over at the tinted window car that Lando had been driving, Kisha thought it was Lando blowing the horn as she walked over to the car. The driver side window came down slowly and Kisha screamed when she saw that Black was home.

"Shh," Black said as he put one finger over his lips, "stop making all that noise." Kisha ran around the car and jumped in the passenger seat.

Shutting the door as Black pulled off, Kisha said, "When did you get out boy?"

Black was amused by Kisha's excitement to see that he was home. Smiling at Kisha as he turned up 5th Street, Black said, "I been home for 'bout a week."

Smacking Black on the arm, Kisha said, "You been home a week and I'm just seeing you." Black let Kisha know that things were too hot around the way for him to come through, he told her that the detective that had the case that he just came home on was the same one that had been riding around the neighborhood with the hot dude Hall, whom everybody in the neighborhood knew.

"So you ain't got to go back to court or nothing? You out to stay?" Kisha asked.

"Yeah," Black said as he went on to ask her about Onion.

"So what's up wit your sucka ass boyfriend?"

"Ain't nothing up wit him. Don't even start dat shit Black!" Kisha said. Kisha wanted to give Black the pussy bad, but she felt that he would tell somebody. Black somewhat sensed that in her and came right out with it.

Reaching over and rubbing Kisha's thick thigh, Black said, "You know I done wanted you for a long ass time, why you keep actin' like you ain't tryin to fuck wit a nigga?" Looking down at Black's hand that was creeping up her leg, Kisha was forced to say something.

"You talk too much Black. If I give you some pussy you gon let everybody know and its gon get back to Onion." Black assured Kisha that he would say nothing if she let him hit the pussy. Kisha thought about it for a minute. She had wanted to fuck Black for a long time and now was her chance.

Smiling at Black, Kisha said, "Fuck it, let's do it." Black took her straight to the hotel and Kisha welcomed him home in a way that he could get use to.

Ten

Onion picked a fine time to get locked up for Carrying a Pistol Without a License. Hall was the first officer to talk to him after he got booked at the 4th District Police Station. Hall knew that Onion had a drug case pending in court and if he was to come back in front of the judge with a gun beef he was sure to lay down for awhile. Onion couldn't see himself going back over the jail when he had information that he knew would set him free. He told Hall and the homicide detective Brown all about the shooting that they were trying to solve. Lando and Quick were now officially wanted for Murder and Assault With Intent to Kill.

It had been three weeks since Lando and Quick had killed the stick up boy and shot at the police. They were feeling a bit more comfortable now. Being as though Black was home now he was driving his car and they were rolling in Quick's huge Cadillac. Even though they weren't hiding out at Mann's apartment anymore, they still didn't feel safe going around Rittenhouse Street. The National Guards still had the spot under siege, so Lando and Quick were basically living off of Mann at the time. They felt as though things were too hot for them to be riding around robbing niggaz at the time so they just laid back and waited for things to cool off even though it seemed like they were only getting hotter.

Kelley was sitting at the dining room table studying for a big test that she had to take at school tomorrow when she heard a loud knock at the door that scared her.

"Open up it's the police!" a loud voice said from the other side. Pamila came running down the steps when she heard that it was the police. Opening the front door and looking outside from behind the thick steel door, Pamila saw at least ten police standing on her porch, five of which were in all black with helmets on. Taking a closer look, Pamila saw that they were A.T.F. agents. The sight of force that the police presented, standing on her porch with their guns out put fear in Pamila's heart.

"What do you want and why do you have those damn guns out on my fuckin porch!" Pamila yelled.

Eyone Williams

"Sorry miss," a small white   A.T.F. agent said to Pamila as he let her know that they had a warrant for the arrest of a Mr. Orlando Mills. Pamila's heart dropped. She knew this day was coming and she knew that it was because of the shooting that she had been hearing about on the news a few weeks ago.

"Do you have a search warrant?" Pamila asked, knowing that just because they had a warrant for Lando's arrest didn't mean that they had a warrant to search her house for him.

"No ma'am, we don't but it would be best for you to help us take Mr. Mills into custody safely so that nothing happens to him. If he's caught on the streets he might be shot. He's wanted for Murder and Assault With Intent to Kill a police officer," the small white man said. Pamila let him know that Lando wasn't in her house and that he hadn't been there in the last three weeks, then she shut the door on the Feds and went to beep Mann.

"Hold up, hold up. What you just say?" Mann said into the phone as he sat on the sofa in the living room of his apartment with Black and Dre. Pamila was hysterical and talking 100 miles a minute.

"Find Lando damnit!" She screamed at Mann, "Find him and take his lil' ass somewhere safe until I can send him to Ohio with Grandma Doris. You gotta find him before the cops do. They are going to shoot 'em!" Mann tried to calm Pamila down but she snapped at him, "Don't try to calm me down damnit! Find that boy!" she said as she hung up the phone.

Turning to Black and Dre, Mann said, "We gotta find Lando and Quick before the Feds do!"

Lando and Quick were watching Nakia and Trina walk into Nakia's house when Lando's beeper went off. Mann was beeping him *911.

"Who dat young?" Quick asked.

"Mann hittin' me 911," Lando said. "It's too hot out here, I'ma hit him back soon as we cross da line." Quick pulled off and headed for the DC line.

Carefully driving down Georgia Avenue they pulled up at a gas station right across the DC line. Lando hopped out and jogged to the pay phone leaving Quick in the car. Still very paranoid to be out in the open,

Quick watched his back vigorously. From behind the tinted windows of the huge Cadillac Fleetwood, Quick looked up and down Georgia Avenue with a queasy feeling in his gut. Quick didn't like when he got this way. He became very impatient and started looking over at Lando to see what was taking so long. Lando stood over at the pay phone with a numb look on his face. Quick could tell something was wrong.

The "jump outs" were riding around looking for a group of young black males to jump out on, but the still, cold weather had everybody inside today. "Jump out" Speedie, a short slim white dude with outstanding speed, sat in the passenger seat of the 1990 Nissan Pathfinder that the "jump outs" were using. His three "road dogs" Big Al, who was driving, along with Pac-Man and Officer Hall, who had been reassigned to the vice cop squad. The four door Pathfinder that the "jump outs" were rolling in today had just been seized on a drug bust downtown therefore no one knew who was behind the tinted windows of the truck as it prowled the city streets.

Speeding down Blair Road, Big Al made a left turn onto Georgia Avenue.

"Don't nobody seem to be outside today," Hall said from the back of the truck.

The three other "jump outs" laughed as Speedie said, "You gotta take it easy Hall. This shit is just like fishing, something's gonna bite in a minute." He couldn't have spoken sooner. Riding by the gas station on Georgia Avenue, Hall saw Lando jogging back to Quick's Cadillac. Hall couldn't control his excitement.

"There he is!" Hall yelled, "That's that little motherfucker right there!" Everyone turned to see what Hall was so excited about and saw Lando hopping into the huge car. Wasting no time, Big Al made a quick U-Turn as the Cadillac pulled off.

"What da fuck did Mann want?" Quick asked, as he watched the black tinted window Nissan Pathfinder buck a quick U-turn and get behind him.

"Slim!" Lando said with a no non-sense tone, "We on da run for real now young! Mann say da A.T.F. and shit been over my house looking for me. Mann want us to go out his apartment until he get there."

Making a right turn down Blair Road to see if the black Pathfinder would follow, Quick said, "Dat ain't no problem, but dis black Pathfinder behind us made a U-turn on da Ave. and been on our back since."

Eyone Williams

Lando pulled a small black .380 out the pocket of his over-sized Eddie Bauer and said, "You seen dat joint before?"

Turning off into an alley, Quick said, "Na, I ain't never seen dat joint before, but let's see if da joint follow us through dis alley." Slamming his foot down on the gas, the huge Cadillac picked up speed as it flew through the alley. The Pathfinder was right behind them now, picking up speed as well.

"Dis niggaz on our back young!" Quick said as he swung the big car out of the alley and fish tailing into the traffic on Georgia Avenue. Looking over his shoulder, Lando saw the Pathfinder swing out onto Georgia Avenue right behind them. Police sirens hit the air somewhere close as Quick whipped the big Cadillac in and out of traffic.

"Dat's da mothafuckin bodeans!" Lando said, sounding worried. Quick dangerously swung the big car down a side street with the Pathfinder close behind. Flying through a stop sign at the end of the block Quick looked back at the Pathfinder through the rear view mirror and saw police car after police car swinging out onto the side street behind the Pathfinder. A helicopter grew close in the air. Police sirens became louder and louder. Quick and Lando could both feel their blood pressure rising. Flying through stop sign after stop sign, they kept looking back at all of the police cars behind them. A police helicopter was now hovered right above them. Quick bent the corner and took the huge car flying and fish tailing out into 5th Street with a trail of police following. Smashing into a passing van, the huge Cadillac pushed it across the street into the parked cars as Quick took it full speed ahead like a raging war tank. The police cars and helicopter had Quick and Lando on the run with nowhere to go, yet they kept pushing. Flying up 5th Street and pass Pamila's house, the Cadillac went into the air at the top of the hill and came slamming back down hard sending flaming sparks flying from under the car. Coming down the street Quick rolled down his window and threw his 10mm out into the street while he tried to control the big car. Lando rolled down his window and threw his .380 as well. Slamming on the brakes, Quick tried to slow the car down as a police patty wagon shot out in front of them but it did no good. The huge Cadillac smashed straight into the patty wagon and spun out of control as it flipped over and slid onto the sidewalk knocking Quick and Lando unconscious.

Hours later, Quick woke up chained to a bed in DC General Hospital. Rubbing his head, Quick tried to shake off the pain. Amazingly, him and Lando only suffered a few scratches in the terrible crash.

Painfully, Quick looked over at Lando who was chained to the bed beside him.

Slowly Lando opened his eyes as well. "Lando." Quick called out in a low voice. Lando slowly looked over at Quick as if he was lost somewhere.

"What's up young?" Lando said in a low and weak voice.

"You okay young?" Quick asked.

Lando slowly raised up and said, "Yeah."

Looking at the cuffs on his hand, Lando said, "We gotta find away to get da fuck outta here!"

"How da fuck we gon do dat?" Quick said, not seeing any sense in what Lando was saying. They both looked over at the door to the room as it slowly opened.

Smiling, Hall and Detective Brown came into the room. "Well, well, well," Hall said. "That was some real brave driving that you boys did. You almost killed yourself. Even so, the party is over. We know that you two little bad motherfuckers killed that guy on Rittenhouse Street. Y'all going down for it too! The only thing about it is that we can't charge you little motherfuckers as adults." Brown cut in and began to tell the two co-defendants that they were under arrest for murder and that they would be in court in the morning.

The next morning, Pamila, Mann, and Black sat in the court room of the Honorable Judge Queen. Pamila was still shook up about not being able to see Lando and Quick last night. Judge Queen was not playing with the juveniles that were coming in front of her this morning. She was sending each one of them down to Oak Hill's Juvenile Detention Center. Pamila knew that Lando and Quick were not coming home, they had no chance. She only came down to support them and to see when they would go back to court again.

The side door to the court room opened, a big dark skinned Marshal came out behind Quick and Lando. They walked up to the thick wooden table where their public defender stood. The crazy looking dark skinned man told them to sit down while the prosecutor began to talk.

"Your Honor, these two juveniles are charged with Murder and Assault With Intent to Kill. I asked that they be detained until their next court date." Judge Queen, an older brown skinned woman with gray hair, looked down from her high seat at the two little juveniles.

Eyone Williams

Raising her glasses to get an up close look at the two murderers, Judge Queen said, "These two little babies are charged with murder?"

"Yes ma'am your Honor," the white female prosecutor said.

Looking over to the crazy looking white man that Quick and Lando had for a lawyer, Judge Queen said, "What do you have to say Mr. Shwortz?"

"Your Honor, I ask that my clients be released to the custody of Ms. Mills." Mr. Shwortz said.

Judge Queen laughed and said, "You can't be serious. I don't think so. The two juveniles will be detained at Oak Hill until their trial date. Ms. Prosecutor, what is a good date for the city?"

Looking through a folder in front of her the prosecutor said, "Your Honor, May 11th will be great."

"May 11th it is. Next case," Judge Queen said. As the Marshal walked Quick and Lando back to the bullpen, Lando looked back at Pamila who was crying. They caught eye contact as Lando walked through the door, Lando felt her pain for the first time but there was nothing he could do to stop it now. He was now in something Pamila could not get him out of no matter what she did. Lando and Quick were on their own for the next three months.

All the lights were out when Lando and Quick walked into Unit 10A. A big black counselor took them to their cells after letting them take a shower. Standing at the door of his cell in a dark red institution shirt and blue institution jeans, Lando looked through the small glass window over at Quick, who was right across from him, and said, "We gon be down young!"

Quick flashed a smile and said, "No bullshit! We ain't gon beat dis shit joe. Everybody on the block probably saw us kill dat nigga, plus the police gon come in there and swear dat he remember us."

Lando looked around his small cell, letting out a sigh as he said, "Fuck it young, we gotta go wit da flow!"

"You right, fuck dat shit. I'm bout to go to sleep. I'ma see you in da morning joe," Quick said as he stepped away from his window. Lando did the same.

Lando laid in the bed with all of his clothes on for hours thinking about the way Pamila had looked at him when he was leaving out of the courtroom. He couldn't get it off of his mind. He knew that he had fucked up big this time. He didn't really care about the little two years that he could get at the time, he had Quick with him and he knew whatever he needed, Mann would get for him. What had him so upset was that he knew how Pamila felt this time around. He saw the pain in her eyes as he walked away and no matter what happened with the case he knew that he had to slow down, even though he had no plans to stop running the streets, he promised himself that he would stop all the wild shit.

A week had passed. Lando and Quick had both been transferred to Unit 7A where all the juveniles that were waiting to go to trial were. They were now in cells that were side by side. Quick had met a little brown skinned dude named Freeway, who had all of the Newports in the unit. Freeway had shown Quick how to knock the wall out between his cell and Lando's cell, so that him and Lando could talk all night while they passed Newports back and forth.

Freeway was from SE. He was cool. Quick had become close to him almost over night. Lando had taken a liking to him as well, but he stayed into so much shit that Lando would only play him close when Quick was with him. Freeway had all the dudes in Unit 7A scared of him before Quick and Lando got there, he had tried Quick the first day he came in the unit but he quickly saw that Quick was ready to go all the way with whatever so he began to like Quick himself, which brought Lando into the picture.

Quick and Freeway were robbing everybody for their canteen and even taking their shoes when either one of them needed shoes. This had Quick into some kind of beef everyday. A big black dude named Big Youngin' had a fresh pair of Air Jordans that were Quick's size. Quick and Freeway had taken the shoes and now Big Youngin' had worked up the heart to do something about it.

Lando was sitting in back of the TV room playing cards with Short Dogg, a short brown skinned dude that Lando had taken a liking too. Lando looked up at the TV and saw Big Youngin' with a pool stick in his hand about to smack Quick in the back of the head. Lando jumped up and ran over to Big Youngin' with the hard wooden chair that he was sitting in, in his hands and smacked Big Youngin' to the floor. Quick and Freeway turned around and saw what was going on and got with it, stomping Big Youngin' out on the ground. Short Dogg came running over with another wooden chair and broke it across Big Youngin's head. Blood was everywhere. Counselors flooded the TV room causing everyone to scatter. Big Youngin' was knocked out on the floor when the crowd was gone.

Eyone Williams

After locking the unit down and taking Big Youngin' to the infirmary, the counselors came back to get Freeway and Short Dogg being as though they were the only faces that they recognized. Quick and Lando got away with everything and it was known that they were going to roll together with whatever.

Early the next morning, Unit 7A was walking to the chow hall dressed in their light blue institution sweat shirts and blue institution jeans. With his Oak Hill hat cocked to the back, Quick was at the front of the line with his partner Lando right beside him. Walking across the compound they heard somebody calling them from 10A's window. Looking to see where the counselors were, Quick and Lando ran over to see who was calling them from the lock down unit.

"What's up wit y'all niggaz young?" Freeway said with a smile. Quick and Lando let him know that everything was cool, even though Big Youngin's older homies that were in Unit 8B were acting like they wanted to do something about the situation.

"So where Short Dogg at?" Lando asked. Freeway let him know that he was down the hall.

"When y'all get out?" Quick asked. Freeway let him know that him and Short Dogg would be out in 10 days.

"Check dis out joe," Lando said. "My brother suppose to come down here today. He gon bring some smoke. When we come out later on, I'ma get you." Freeway was cool with that and let Lando and Quick know that he would make sure that Short Dogg got some. Lando and Quick then caught up with the rest of the unit and went into the chow hall.

Pamila and Mann pulled up outside of Oak Hill's Juvenile Detention Center just as the compound was clearing. Pamila watched as the basketball court full of young kids emptied. She shook her head. Lando was actually locked up for murder and this was a fact that she just could not come to grips with. Sitting behind the wheel of her Volkswagen Rabbit, Pamila stared at the tall razor wire fence. To Pamila, Oak Hill reminded her of going to see Mann and Lando's father down Lorton's Maximum Security Prison. The sight itself filled Pamila's heart with sorrow for the bad situation that Lando and Quick had put themselves into this time.

Lando came into the small visiting area with his Oak Hill hat cocked to the side. Pamila sat at a table with her arms folded. Mann was leaning back in a chair playing with an ink pen; he was the first to see Lando.

"What's up shorty?" Mann said. Pamila looked up when she heard Mann speak. Before Lando even said anything to Mann he looked at Pamila, wondering how she would act. This was the first time that she had been to see him since he had been down Oak Hill.

Slowly walking over to the table, still watching Pamila's every expression, Lando said, "What's up Mann?" Sitting down across from Pamila beside Mann, Lando looked at Pamila and tried to break the ice. "What's up Pamila?" Lando said very cautiously.

Unfolding her arms and putting her hands together in front of her face with her elbows placed on the wooden table in a serious thinking posture, Pamila said, "What's up?" and looked around the room as if to say how can you ask me something like that. "This is what's up," Pamila said. "I shouldn't be here, that's what's up Lando. You don't have no business being locked up. What is on your mind these days?" Lando knew that Pamila wasn't going to just accept the present situation without trying to understand what was on his mind.

For the next 30 minutes, Pamila scolded and even tried to reason with Lando about the way him and Quick were living. Lando looked over at Mann like, "Damn do something joe." Mann knew it was nothing that he could do or say that would make Pamila lighten up on Lando, besides that, Mann knew that everything Pamila was saying were things that she had deep within her heart that she had to get out of her system.

After Pamila felt as though she had chastised Lando long enough, she said, "Come here boy." Lando got up and walked around the table. Pamila stood up and hugged him tightly, full of emotions of love, care, and concern. "Boy I love you so much," Pamila said, as she held Lando in her arms. "I'll always be here for you, but I just want you to wake up and see that the streets ain't got no love for you. The system is just waiting to take you away from me. I can't lose you to the streets!" Lando felt every word that Pamila said.

"I know, I'ma slow down. I promise," Lando said. Pamila let him go and he sat back down.

"Where is the restroom?" Pamila asked. Lando walked her to the door and pointed her to the bathroom.

Walking back into the room with Mann, Lando smiled and said, "What's up joe?" as he sat back down beside his brother.

Mann reached over and rubbed his little brother on the top of the head as he said, "Ain't shit shorty. How you doing down here?"

"I'm chillin. Dis shit ain't shit."

"What's up wit Quick lil' ass?"

"Slim chillin'. He down here takin' dese niggaz bad," Lando said as Mann laughed. He had a feeling that is how Quick would be down Oak Hill. Mann always thought that Quick would be another Black when he got older and it sure looked like he was going in that direction.

"So what's up," Lando said. "You bring dat?" Mann looked around and pulled a sandwich bag of weed out of his black Polo jacket.

"How you gon get dis shit back to your unit?" Mann asked. Lando let Mann know that he knew what he was doing and then they began talking about the case that Lando and Quick had.

"So what your lawyer talking 'bout shorty?" Mann asked. Lando looked away as if to say that he wasn't even thinking about what his lawyer had to say. He knew in his heart that he wasn't going to come home. Lando and Quick both knew they would be gone for at least the next two years of their young lives, which to them seemed like a lifetime.

Looking back at Mann, Lando said, "It really ain't shit dat he can say joe. Me and Quick smashed dat nigga right on da sidewalk joe. It ain't no telling who seen us. Besides dat, we shot at the bodeans dat night and I know they gon swear they remember us." Mann shook his head.

He had never did any time before. He felt sorry for his little brother. Mann had a feeling that Lando and Quick were going to do some time himself, but he was going to do whatever he could to get them off on the beef.

Rubbing his hand on his chin Mann said, "Just take it easy down here. I'ma make sure you and Quick stay tight while y'all down here and I'ma do all I can to get y'all out as soon as possible. Dese juvenile peoples play a lot different then da adult system." Lando knew Mann was right. Pamila walked in the room while they were still talking.

"They say it's time for us to go Lando," Pamila said as she walked over and hugged him. "You take care of yourself down here. Don't trust nobody but Quick. These boys down here know more about doing time then y'all, so y'all stick together. I'ma pray that the Lord looks over y'all" Lando looked over at Mann as he hugged Pamila, and smiled at him. He knew Mann knew that him and Quick would be able to hold their own, but to Pamila they would always be babies. Lando kissed Pamila and let her know that he would be fine.

Walking back to his unit with Counselor Mr. Roy, Lando thought more and more about all that Pamila had said to him about slowing down. She was right Lando thought. He began to think about all of the money that him and Quick had been making in the streets at their age. He felt that they could have been much smoother with what they were doing. He began to think about his brother and how Mann had been making money in the streets for the longest and never went to jail for anything. No matter what the outcome of his stay down Oak Hill, Lando swore that he was going to get back to the streets and get money just like Mann, even if he had to murder for it.

Mr. Roy, a big light skinned man that stood at least 6 feet, let Lando in the unit and said, "Stay out of trouble shorty. Your lil' name is kickin round here and you ain't even been down here a whole month yet."

Lando looked at Mr. Roy, waving his statement off with his hand as he said, "Whatever nigga." Lando walked on down the hall to Quick's cell never looking back at the counselor as the door shut behind him.

Quick had a full house when Lando walked in the small cell. Mann had taught him about crowds long ago and Lando didn't trust a lot of new faces, which could be seen by the look on his face. Laying on his bed, surrounded by Demo, Hub, and Monkey-D, Quick saw that Lando wanted to say something to him about all the niggaz he had in the cell. Before Quick could say anything, Lando said, "Let me holla at you slim." Quick got up and walked next door to Lando's cell.

Lando sat on the bed and told Quick to shut the door and put some paper over the window. Quick took care of that and turned around asking Lando why he was acting like he had a problem with the dudes in his cell.

"You know I don't fuck wit a rack of new niggaz young. I don't know dem niggaz!" Lando said as he pulled the weed out of his drawers.

Looking down at the weed with a smile on his face, Quick said, "Look joe, I dig dem niggaz. They cool as shit, you ain't gotta fuck wit dem slim." Walking over and sitting down beside Lando, Quick went on to tell him that he was smoking with the new dudes that were in his cell.

"You put dem niggaz in our business young?" Lando asked.

"Yeah, I told dem we were getting some bud, stop trippin' nigga," Quick said.

Lando looked at Quick for a minute thinking about the whole situation and then said, "If you say dem niggaz cool like dat then I'ma go wit dat joe. Let's go put dis shit in da air."

On the bricks, days seemed to go slow for Mann. His money was still coming like he wanted it to. Black was laid back for a minute. Dre was moving coke like it was legal out Maryland. Kelley was beginning to mean more and more to Mann by her display of trust, love, and loyalty. Silk was giving Mann deal after deal now that him and Supreme were getting to know each other better. Things were smooth, but without Lando running around getting into shit, life was not the same and would not be the same until shorty was back on the streets. Mann knew that Lando would be down for awhile and he could tell that he would miss his little brother everyday that he was gone.

Mann stood in front of the oven in his small apartment out Maryland cooking up a brick of coke for Da-Da, who had beeped him 30 minutes ago saying that he had $25,000 right now and needed to cop a brick quick because he had sold out early this week.

Dre walked in the kitchen with the cordless phone in his hand and said, "Lando on da phone slim." Mann told Dre to watch over the coke while he went to talk to Lando in the living room.

"What's up shorty?" Mann said as he sat down on the sofa in the living room, turning the TV on with the remote control.

"Ain't shit joe. What's up wit you slim?"

"Some lil' girl call da house for you 'bout two days ago," Mann said as he tried to recall her name.

"Was it Nakia?." Lando asked. He had told her to call Pamila and ask her if she could bring her to see Lando the next time she went.

"Na, it began wit a J.... Dat's it! Jazmin, she called asking for your address. Lil' Garvin told her you were locked up. I gave her your address and all dat good shit. She act like she want to come see you..."

"You tell her you gon bring her to see me?" Lando said. Mann laughed at the excitement in his little brother's voice. He could tell that shorty had feelings for Jazmin.

"I thought you were in love wit da young girl Nakia?" Mann said.

"Yeah, Nakia my folks, she pose to be comin' down to see me dis weekend wit Pamila. Jazmin my lil buddy, I digs her and everything but she got me on big brother shit," Lando said. As the conversation went on Mann asked Lando about Quick.

"Quick chillin," Lando said. "Hold on, I'ma call him for you joe." Lando ran down the hall and got Quick who was in Freeway's cell shooting dice with him, Short Dogg, Demo, Hub, and Monkey D.

Quick ran back to the little room where the phone was and picked it up as he sat down on the wooden chair looking out into the hallway.

"What's up nigga?" Quick said. Mann laughed out loud. Quick sounded like he had grew years in just a few weeks.

"What's up wit you shorty?" Mann responded.

"I'm chillin. Dis Oak Hill shit ain't shit joe. I'm down here takin' dese suckas bad young."

"Shorty, you can't keep thinking everybody a sucka joe. You gon sleep on da wrong nigga."

"Yeah, yeah, I know you right but dese niggaz punks. Anyway, you seen Baby-D and Lil'Garvin?"

"Yeah, I saw dem young niggaz down 14th Street bout two days ago. They jive getting a lil' money too. Lil' Garvin want me to do something wit 'em."

"Oh yeah?" Quick said sounding happy that his niggaz was doing something for themselves on the streets.

"Check dis out Mann, tell dem me and Lando tryin' to catch up wit dem and we need a number where they be at so we can holla at dem."

"I got dat shorty, I'ma do dat for you when I go back around da way."

"Cool, I'ma put Lando back on da phone," Quick said. Lando got back on the phone and let Mann know that it was time for him to roll and that he would call back later on in the week.

"Take care of yourself shorty, I'ma see if I can get Pamila to bring da lil' girl Jazmin down to see you," Mann said. Lando hung up the phone and went back down the hall to shoot dice with everybody else.

Metra had been hanging across town with a few of her buddies for the last few months. She knew she wasn't welcomed around the way being as though she had turned Dre into the Feds. Now that nothing had happened to her since Dre and Black had been home she began to feel too comfortable.

Black was sitting in his Acura Legend with the driver side door wide open. Now that Mann and Dre were doing their thing out Maryland, Rittenhouse Street was his. Smoke and Serge were sitting in the back of the car counting money while Black rolled a blunt of weed up front.

"Y'all ready to roll out?" Black asked as he shut the door of the Acura.

"Yeah, lets' get da fuck out of here," Smoke said. He really didn't like being around the way longer than he had to be these days. Things were just too hot. The Feds were coming through in every kind of way that you could think of. Black, Smoke, and Serge had cut themselves off from everybody else. They were doing their own thing and didn't care who didn't like it.

As Black started the car he saw a black BMW 325i bend the corner and pull up in front of Metra's house. Black watched as Metra ran out of her house and jumped in the BMW.

"I thought dat bitch lived over SE somewhere now," Black said as he pulled off behind the BMW, headed up Rittenhouse Street.

Smoke raised up and saw the car that Metra had just got in and said, "I been seein' dat joint right there around a lot lately joe." As Black drove up the street behind the car he thought about how Metra had turned Dre in. All of his anger came back.

"I'ma smash dis hot bitch!" Black said as he pulled out onto Georgia Avenue behind the BMW. His two partners in crime were always ready for drama, they didn't object at all. As far as they were concerned it was Blacks' call.

The BMW pulled over in the McDonald's parking lot and a slim brown skinned dude got out and jogged inside. Black pulled up at the end of the parking lot and told Serge to stay behind the wheel while he took care of business. Smoke wanted to roll with Black even though Black wanted to put the work in solo. Black agreed to let his man roll. They slid on ski masks that Black had on stand-by in the glove compartment and whipped out their pistols.

Creeping through the parking lot unseen on this cool spring night, Black and Smoke slid up on the passenger side of the BMW with the speed of professional hitmen. Metra turned to look out of the window and screamed when she saw the two killers in black pointing pistols right at her face. She covered up her head and jumped over into the driver seat. Her actions were of no use. Smoke and Black pumped the whole car full of hollow point slugs from their .45 automatics. Gunfire exploded into the air. Metra laid in the driver seat lifeless, but is wasn't enough for Black. Pulling his sweat shirt sleeve over his hand, he opened the passenger side door and stuck his pistol inside and hit Metra in the head two more times. In seconds, Black and Smoke were back in the Acura Legend with Serge flying down 14th Street smoking weed. Once they were downtown, Black told Serge to pull the car into an alley where him and Smoke wiped their fingers prints off of their pistols and threw them down a sewer hole.

It was 12:00pm the next day when Kelley came home for lunch. She walked downstairs to the basement and saw Mann laying on the bed. She walked over and laid down beside him asking, "Why you ain't in school?"

"I ain't gotta go 'til 2 today."

"Oh yeah, well guess what happened yesterday," Kelley said in a way that got Mann's attention quickly.

"What's up?" Mann asked sounding very concerned. Kelley had just seen Kisha, who had gotten back in school and she had told her about Metra getting shot in the McDonald's parking lot. Kelley gave Mann the whole run down just as Kisha had given it to her and she had the facts as far as the killing went. Metra had been shot 19 times and never had a chance.

"Who killed her?" Mann asked.

"Don't nobody know. Some nigga she was wit told da police dat two dudes in ski masks ran up on his car while he was ordering food and started shooting," Kelley said. She told Mann a little more of what Kisha had told her about the shooting and then she had to go pick Pamila's work clothes up from the cleaners.

Mann got up and got ready for school himself. All he could think about was Black, it was no doubt in his mind that Black killed Metra. Mann hoped that Black left no loose ends. He would have to check on Black as soon as he got a chance. Grabbing his car keys, Mann hit the streets.

Eyone Williams

Eleven

Mann never got the chance to check up on Black. Officer Hall and the "jump-outs" caught up with him first.

Black was high as a kite standing in the alley slangin' rocks like it was legal. Hall and the "jump-outs" sat in a new Chevy Blazer, with dark tinted windows, watching him. Black had sold just over an ounce when somebody beeped him. As he began to walk through Kisha's yard, Hall and the rest of the "jump-outs" ran up to Black and slammed him to the ground. Black was caught and he knew it. Hall pulled a bag of 50 rocks out of Black's Polo jacket and placed him under arrest. On the way to the police station, Black thought he was going down for Metra's murder. He couldn't believe he was out there on the strip slippin'; just two days after killing the hot bitch.

Hall made Black's day when he came to the holding cell and told Black he was going down to Central Cell Block for distribution of crack.

Black smiled at Hall and said, "You happy as shit dat you done locked me up for something."

Hall put Black against the wall placing the handcuffs on him while he said, "Yeah, I'm happy motherfucker."

"I ain't nothin' but 16. I ain't goin nowhere but down Oak Hill for a few months. Dat ain't shit!"

"Yeah, well tell your lil' cousin Lando I said hi and I'll be at his up coming trial," Hall said with a laugh as he walked Black to the police car.

Down Oak Hill two days later, every unit was out on the compound for their outside recreation. Lando, Quick, Freeway, Short Dogg, and Demo were sitting behind the gym smoking weed when Monkey D ran over and said, "Lando, some new nigga up 10A say he want you to come to his window." Lando passed the jay of weed to Demo and walked across the compound like he had a .44 magnum tucked in his waistband wondering who could want him that was up 10A. Maybe Lil' Garvin or Baby-D could have caught a case or something.

"Lando!" an excited voice called from the same window that Freeway was in a few weeks ago. Lando recognized the voice off the top and ran over to the window to see what his cousin Black was doing locked up.

"What's up young?" Lando said in an excited voice. "What da fuck you doing locked up joe?"

"I let dat hot nigga Hall catch me slippin' around the way. I jive got caught with 'bout an ounce in back of Kisha's house."

"Yeah, when you go back to court?"

"I gotta status hearing in 'bout a month."

"You think they gon let you go?"

"I ain't sure, if they don't it ain't shit. Where da fuck Quick at?"

"He over there smoking behind da gym."

"Y'all got bud?"

"Yeah, I'ma run over to da unit and get some for you. I got dis nigga holding it for me, I'ma tell Quick you over here too," Lando said before he ran across the compound to get Quick and some weed for Black.

In less then 5 minutes, Lando and Quick were back at Black's window with 3 fat jays already rolled up. Lando slid them through a hole in Black's window. Black got the jays and told Lando that he needed a light.

"You think I'ma forget da cow?" Lando asked as if Black had said something stupid. They all started laughing as Lando slid a lighter through the window.

"So what's up with y'all niggaz?" Black asked.

"Ain't shit," Quick said. "We chillin like shit just waitin' to go to trial."

"Y'all know who telling on y'all?" Black asked.

"We don't know slim," Lando said. "Mann asked me da same thing last week. It was a rack-a-niggaz outside dat night young."

"No bullshit," Quick said, "pipeheads and all. We won't know who tellin' on us til we get to trial joe."

"So what's goin on round da way." Lando asked. Black let them know that he had the block locked down now that Mann and Dre were both doing their thing out Maryland. He told them how he ain't fuck with Onion and Corey no more because they had been acting funny now that Mann and Dre weren't around. Black was getting the feeling that they really didn't want him around the way now that he was hustlin' and not just robbing niggaz.

"What you mean they actin' funny?" Lando asked.

"They be rollin out when me, Smoke, and Serge be comin' around. Fuck dem niggaz for real, Smoke and Serge tryin' to rob dem niggaz anyway."

"I heard da bitch Metra got her head hit up da Ave bout 3 or 4 days ago," Lando said.

Black smiled and said, "Me and Smoke caught dat hot ass bitch up da Ave in some nigga's BMW and aired da joint out."

"Damn young! Y'all put dat work in right in front of da police station?" Quick said sounding surprised. Black went on to tell them how him and Smoke killed Metra and before they knew it, it was time for the compound to clear. Black told Quick and Lando to call Mann and tell him to send him some money. They told him that they would get right on top of that and they were waiting for him to get out of 10A, so that he could get in the same unit with them. When they were done talking, they ran across the compound and into Unit 7A for the night.

Mann, Dre, and Silk were in Pamila's basement watching UNLV play Duke on Mann's huge color TV. Dre had bet Silk $500 that UNLV would pull the game off. Dre was a die-hard fan. While Silk and Dre sat on the sofa, Mann sat on his bed with a cup of soda in his hand.

"You know Baby-D fight out Maryland University this weekend," Dre said to Mann.

"Oh yeah, shorty stickin' wit dat shit huh?" Mann said. Dre let him know that he saw Baby-D when he was on his way home earlier and that he asked him if he was coming to see him fight. Dre let him know that he would be there. Silk was a big fight fan himself, he knew Baby-D but he didn't know he could box. Asking Dre about Baby-D, Silk and him got into a conversation about his fight game. Pamila called Mann from the top of the steps and told him to pick up the phone.

Rolling over on his bed, Mann picked up the phone and said, "Hello?"

"What's up joe?" Lando said into the phone.

"What's up young nigga?" Mann said. Lando began to talk and let Mann know that Black was down Oak Hill with him, which took a load off of Mann's back because he was worried that Black might have gotten charged with killing Metra. He could deal with him being down Oak Hill. One thing was for sure, he wouldn't have to worry about Lando and Quick with Black down there with them.

"So what Black locked up for?" Mann asked.

"Slim gotta punk ass coke beef," Lando said as he went on to tell Mann that Black wanted him to send him some money. Mann told Lando that he was going to send all of them some money in the morning and that he would be up to see him sometime within the next two weeks. After talking to his little brother for a few more minutes, Mann got off the phone and told Silk and Dre that Black was cool and he was only down Oak Hill on a coke beef.

With Lando, Quick, and Black down Oak Hill, Mann only had two dudes on the street that he had any trust in and that was Dre and Silk. This made Mann begin to think more and more about getting out of the game. His money was growing like never before with him and Dre going half on 10 bricks of coke every week. As the weeks turned into months, Mann had been riding by an old Subway fast food joint that was for sale. Everyday that he rode by it, he kept thinking of what him and Silk had always talked about. Suddenly, he made his mind up one day as he passed by the Subway and it was no longer for sale. He was going to buy a small store of some kind and he knew where he was going to do it. All he needed to do was find out whose name he was going to get it in. The place was no problem, there was an old corner store owned by an old black couple that sat on Georgia Avenue right by the Maryland line. Mann told himself that it was going to be his as soon as he saw the for-sale sign go up. His next move was to pull up on Silk, he knew Silk would help him get the store the right way because his sister named Pam has good credit. His goal was set.

Oak Hill wasn't the same for the last 3 months with Black on the compound. As soon as he was moved from Unit 10A to Unit 7A with Lando and Quick, the corruption started. Black had the Oak Hill counselors bringing in weed, pizza, beer, and just about everything else you could think of that wasn't suppose to be on the compound. Freeway, Demo, and Short Dogg had been found guilty of their charges and were now in Unit 8B, but they still ran the compound with Quick and Lando during school and at rec. time. Monkey-D and Hub went home two weeks ago, both of them had juvenile murder charges. By being found not guilty, Quick and

Lando began to believe that they could actually beat their murder case when they went to trial in two days.

Quick had grown a love for basketball over the past 3 months and played everyday after school, no questions asked. He was running late today and was in a rush to get his rec. shoes before they locked the door to the compound. Running down the hall to his cell, he saw that his door was locked. "Damn!" he said out loud as he ran up the hall to Black's cell to get his Air Jordans.

Black was lying on his bed reading Sun Tzu's The Art of War, a book that Mann had sent him in the mail and Black had read it every day like a Bible since. Seeing Quick at his door in a rush, Black thought that something was wrong.

"What da fuck is up shorty?" Black asked rising up off the bed with his war face on.

"Ain't shit joe. Let me see your shoes, I'm 'bout to go shoot some ball," Quick said. Black got the shoes from under the bed and gave them to Quick asking him if the mail had been passed out yet. Quick kicked his Oak Hill boots off and slid into the Jordan's telling Black that the mail hadn't come yet as he took off running down the hall.

Almost out the door, Quick ran by the back room where the phone was.

"Quick!" a voice yelled out. Quick knew it was Lando and if it was anyone else he would have kept on going because he knew that the teams would already be picked by the time he got outside.

"What's up young?" Quick said in a voice that displayed his hurry as he stepped in the phone room where Lando was.

Lando covered the phone so that Nakia could not hear what he was talking about and said, "Our lawyer suppose to come see us at 6:00 tonight so don't get rapped up out there." Quick let Lando know that he would be ready for their legal visit and ran out the door and onto the basketball court where Freeway, Short Dogg, and Demo were waiting to run a whole court.

"Yeah, I'm back boo," crooned Lando in his smooth 'I'm like that with the ladies' voice that had grown a little deeper over the last 3 months.

"So are you coming home or not Lando?" Nakia asked. She had been growing very impatient with Lando's stay down Oak Hill. Lando kept telling her that he would be home in May and now May was here and Nakia wanted Lando home. He was her first love and the only person she had ever been with sexually. The things Lando did with her and showed her made her love him, so she thought at her young age.

"Look, I can't tell you what the future holds. All I can tell you is that I should be home after my trial."

"You gotta come home Lando. You ain't kill dat boy, so they gotta let you and Quick go right?"

"Nakia, I told you, they gon do what they want to do. Somebody telling them that they saw me and Quick kill da nigga so they gonna try to make us do some time."

"Why Lando?" Nakia said as she began to cry like she did very often. "Why they won't just let y'all go?" Lando hated when Nakia cried about the situation and he spent the rest of his time on the phone trying to make her believe that things would be fine.

The court bus was packed leaving Oak Hill this bright spring morning. Shackled and handcuffed on their way to court were 30 of DC's most out of control youths. Seven of which were some of the most vicious teenage killers of the 90's. Quick, Lando, and Short Dogg, being an outstanding 3 in the bunch due to their names floating around the streets at such a young age.

Chained together at the waist, Lando and Quick sat behind Short Dogg who was going to court for his disposition hearing for a murder that he had been found guilty of. Short Dogg was telling Quick and Lando how the Feds were going to have someone that they least expected to pop up at court and say that they saw everything go down. Short Dogg wasn't guessing either. His partner in crime on the murder, an old childhood friend, came to court and told everything so Short Dogg knew what he was talking about.

"Yeah, your man told on you huh, young?" Quick asked, he was disgusted at how Short Dogg told him and Lando about his man telling on him. Quick couldn't think of telling on Lando about anything, he was going to go all the way with him.

"Yeah slim," Short Dogg said, "They gon play real dirty in there." Lando sat back listening to everything that Short Dogg was saying, he tried to come up with the person that the Feds could have telling on him besides the police that him and Quick shot at that night and the only person he could come up with was pipehead Sheila being as though she put him and

Quick on point about the robbery that was taking place. Other than that, Lando couldn't think of anyone else. He sat on the court bus kicking it with Short Dogg and Quick for the rest of the ride to the Receiving Home where the U.S. Marshals would later pick all of the juveniles up and take them to the Superior Court of the District of Columbia.

Sitting in a holding cell behind the courtroom of the Honorable Judge Queen, Lando and Quick talked about their feelings toward the case as well as their feelings toward their weird ass lawyer. Quick didn't like Mr. Shwortz at all and had cursed him out every time he went on a legal visit. Quick's whole outlook on the case was one that he had got from Black and that was to let nature take its course. Quick felt that whatever was going to go down, was going to go down and that he would deal with whatever came his way. Lando on the other hand felt that if his lawyer could just do a half way decent job at defending them that all they would have to worry about was the statement that the two police would give. As they sat and talked a Marshal came back into the bullpen to get them for trial. "It's time to go," the Marshal said as he opened up the door to the holding cell and escorted the two young killers into the courtroom.

Walking into the court and seeing his grandmother sitting in the back of the courtroom next to Pamila and Mann, Quick waved at them as if there was nothing wrong at all. You would've never guessed that the young dude was on trial for murder, he showed no signs of worry at all as he sat down beside Mr. Shwortz and folded his hands on the long wooden table. Lando was a little more concerned than Quick and you could see it in his face as he looked back at Pamila and Mann. Lando slowly walked over to the table where Quick had already taken a seat beside their lawyer. Lando paid attention to everything in the courtroom as he sat down. Sitting across the aisle from Pamila, Mann, and Quick's grandmother there was a cute light skinned young girl with a baby in her arms. Lando kept looking back at her to see if he could recognize her face from somewhere. The young girl had a very angry look on her face, which led Lando to believe that she had to be some kin to the dude that got killed that night on Rittenhouse Street. Judge Queen came out of her chambers and snapped Lando out of his thoughts by calling the court to attention.

With no jury in juvenile trials, all arguments were directed to Judge Queen. The government marched in witness after witness into the courtroom and onto the witness stand to report their professional opinion of the way the victim was slain. A doctor reported how the victim was brought to the hospital already dead, then a coroner got on the witness stand to report to Judge Queen how many wounds the victim sustained on the night of the murder. Mr. Shwortz put up minimal fight against these witnesses because they could not point the finger of guilt at his two clients.

The slim white lady that was the prosecutor for the government called one of the officers that Lando and Quick had shot at on the night of the murder to the stand. Officer Wilson, a short brown skinned young man, was the officer driving the police car that came flying around the corner on the night of the murder. After being sworn in under oath, Officer Wilson was directed by Prosecutor Jamerson to tell Judge Queen what he witnessed as he and his fellow partner ran across the shooting. Officer Wilson told the judge everything that he had seen that night and he told the whole truth. Lando cracked a slight smile as the officer wrapped up his story by saying that it was no way that he could say for sure that the two juveniles that were on trial were the same two that shot at him and his partner.

"No further questions!" Ms. Jamerson snapped with anger in her voice. Mr. Shwortz stood up and began to reinforce the fact that Officer Wilson could not identify Quick nor Lando as the shooters. Making sure he didn't go overboard, he wrapped up his cross-examination with speed and allowed the government to try their hand again.

"I call Officer Halkins to the stand your Honor," Prosecutor Jamerson said. The double doors that led out of the courtroom opened and Officer Halkins walked in, causing everyone to turn their heads his way. A sick feeling went through Lando's body as he caught eye contact with the officer. Lando remembered looking him right in the face as he shot at him that night and by the way the officer looked at him, Lando knew that he remembered as well.

"So tell us what happened on the night of January 19th," Ms. Jamerson said to the officer. He told the story exactly how he remembered it up until where his partner had said that he couldn't identify the shooters.

When he got to that point he looked over at Lando and said, "I know for certain that the little light skinned kid right there was one of the kids doing the shooting that night."

Prosecutor Jamerson stood up smiling as she walked over to the table where Lando was sitting and while pointing right at him, she said,

"You are sure that this is the child that you saw shooting at you and your partner?"

"I'm sure. He looked me right in the face while he was shooting at us that night. I can't believe he's just a child."

"Well what about this one?" Prosecutor Jamerson asked as she pointed at Quick.

"I can't say. The other shooter was further away and it was very dark that night," Officer Halkins said. Ms. Jamerson led him on for awhile trying to make him say more than he wanted to say about the shooting but Judge Queen put an end to the legal games that she was trying to play and allowed Mr. Shwortz a chance to defend his clients.

As it stood now, Lando was the only client in danger as far as Mr. Shwortz was concerned. Quick couldn't be identified by either officer that had been on the stand. Therefore, Mr. Shwortz tried to save Lando as best as he could by bringing everybody back around to the matter at hand, which was murder.

"So Officer Hawkins," the crazy looking white lawyer said. "You say you know that one of my clients shot at you, but Ms. Jamerson so conveniently forgot that these two kids are charged with 1st Degree Murder. Did you or your partner see them kill this guy uh...Ramen Biggs?" The officer told the judge that he had seen no such thing that night. Mr. Shwortz had done what he intended to do, he made sure that everybody in the courtroom still felt that there was a chance that Lando and Quick might be innocent of murder. Officer Hawkins was dismissed and Judge Queen asked Ms. Jamerson if she had any other witness before she passed her judgment. Looking through her folder, the prosecutor said, "As a matter of fact I do Your Honor."

As it stood now the government had only succeeded in proving that Lando had shot at a police officer that was far from the attempted murder of a police officer that the government was saying took place. Lando was cool with that; he would take Assault With a Deadly Weapon any day over a Murder.

Leaning over and whispering into Quick's ear, Lando said, "Looks like you gone beat dis shit young."

Quick turned to Lando and said, "Dis shit ain't over yet."

"I call Mr. Kareen Swan to the stand," Ms. Jamerson said.

Looking at Lando, Quick said, "Who da fuck is dat?"

"I don't know, young," Lando said as he looked back at the double doors that led out of the courtroom. Slowly the doors opened and a U.S. Marshal came through. Mann looked at the look on Lando's face as he looked back at the doors and turned to see what had his little brother looking so confused. As Mann turned to look at the double doors himself, he was fucked up to see Onion coming through the doors behind the Marshal.

"You bitch ass nigga!" Mann said out loud as Onion walked by him on his way to the witness stand. Pamila saw the anger in Mann's dark face and tried to calm him down.

She grabbed his arm and said, "You can't be mad. I've always told you and Lando that y'all can't trust them boys around there, they ain't no good."

"You right," Mann said as he got himself together and made up his mind that Onion was a dead man.

Dressed in all black with a black bandanna around his neck, Onion looked like a model thug nigga straight out of a 'how to be a gangsta' handbook. His face showed no sign of shame about what he was doing. He looked over at Lando and Quick, then back at Mann as the prosecutor walked up to the stand and asked her first question.

"Mr. Swan," she said, "would you tell the judge what you witnessed on the night of January 19th." Onion turned and looked at Judge Queen with a look of a man that had no regard for the side of the game that he came from.

"Yeah, I'll tell her what I saw dat night," he said in a smooth voice. "Me and my niggaz Smoke, Serge, Corey, and Kevin were hustlin' and smokin' weed up by the crack house when some niggaz tried to rob us..."

"Your Honor, I object," Mr. Shwortz said, cutting Onion off. "This man is a street thug and a confessed drug dealer. Ms. Jamerson can't truly expect this honorable court to allow him to come in here and tell the truth."

"Objection overruled. You may go on Mr. Swan," Judge Queen said. Onion went on to tell her how the stick up boys had robbed him and everyone else outside that night. He said that when they were done, they ran out onto Rittenhouse Street.

"Is that when the shooting started?" Ms. Jamerson asked.

"Yeah dem young niggaz put dat work in dat night," Onion said. "They shot one of the dudes as soon as he came outta da yard where we was."

"Who shot the dude?" Ms. Jamerson asked.

"Lando and Quick. Dem two young niggaz right there," Onion said as he pointed the finger at them.

"No further questions Your Honor," Ms. Jamerson said as she sat down.

"Your witness Mr. Shwortz," Judge Queen said.

Nothing seemed to surprise Mann these days, but seeing Onion get up on that witness stand truly puzzled him. He didn't understand how Onion thought he was going to get away with something like this. Mann looked up at Lando who had turned to look at him as Mr. Shwortz got up to question Onion. Looking in his little brother's eyes, all Mann could do was shake his head. He knew Lando and Quick were gone for the next two or more years of their life.

Mr. Shwortz's cross-examination didn't last long at all. The case was over when Onion got on the stand. All of Mr. Shwortz's efforts to discredit Onion fell on deaf ears. Judge Queen passed her judgment. Lando and Quick were guilty of Murder in the 1st Degree. They were to come back to court for disposition in one month.

Lando and Quick looked back at Pamila, Quick's grandmother, and Mann as they walked back into the bullpen with the Marshal. They saw the way their loved ones looked at Onion as he walked by, but Mann caught their attention the most. They knew Mann was going to do something about Onion getting on the witness stand.

"I'ma kill dat bitch ass nigga when we get out young!" Quick said to Short Dogg on the court bus on their way back down Oak Hill.

"You ain't gon get a chance young," Lando said as he looked out the window into the night in a daze. "Dat nigga gon be dead long before we hit da bricks again joe." Short Dogg had heard a lot about Mann over the past few months that he had been locked up with Quick and Lando, he felt like he knew him.

In fact, he felt so strong about the way he thought of Lando's older brother who made sure they all always had weed to smoke, that he said, "Your brother gon smash dat nigga joe. He ain't gon let 'em get away wit no shit like dat." They all agreed that Short Dogg was right, they knew Mann was going to do something about the hot nigga Onion.

Fast Lane

Black was in front of the TV watching the Chicago Bulls go after a win against the Detroit Pistons. Air Jordan himself had just hit a big three pointer late in the 3rd to put the Bulls on top. The TV room went off. Quick and Lando bent the corner and walked to the back of the room and sat at the card table by themselves. Black knew that things didn't go well at court, but he would never guess what they would have to tell him. Black got up and walked to the back of the TV room where they were.

"What's up wit y'all?" he said as he rubbed Lando on the top of the head.

Lando looked at Quick and said, "Tell 'em young."

Looking up at Black with a look of defeat on his face, Quick said, "Dat bitch ass nigga Onion came to court and told dem peoples dat he seen everything young."

"What?" Black said, his anger already boiling. Lando and Quick could see the all too familiar look of murder in Black's eyes as they told him how things went at court. When they were done, Black said, "Oh dat nigga dying first thing in da morning!" Black walked off headed for the phone room.

"Hello can I speak to Smoke?" Black said into the phone. Smoke's mother knew Black's voice well and she knew when he was upset.

"What's wrong wit you boy?" She said in a motherly tone. Black told her that he had just got some bad news and that he was okay. Smoke's mother then went and got him.

"What's up nigga?" Smoke said into the phone. It was clear that he was glad to hear from his man. "Me and Serge just sent you some money young. You should get it in a few days."

"Dat's a bet but check dis out. Dat nigga Onion....."

"Yeah?"

"He came to court on my lil' cousin and Quick today. He got 'em found guilty on dat body."

"He did what?" Smoke said, not believing Black had said what he thought he said.

"Yeah, dat's right. Dat nigga told like da bitch he is. I want you to smash dat nigga!"

"I got dat for you joe, believe dat. Dat nigga good as got!" Smoke said. His word was good as gold to Black. Black knew Onion was a dead man. Black hung up the phone and called Mann to see what he had to say, as well as to let him know that he didn't have to kill Onion because Smoke was already on top of it.

The next afternoon, Smoke and his cousin Serge sat in a dark blue Thunderbird on Rittenhouse Street waiting for Onion to come out of his house. They had already got word that he had been on the block earlier that morning. It was just a matter of time now and the beautiful day was sure to bring their prey out.

Sitting in the tinted window Thunderbird smoking weed, Smoke and Serge were somewhat unseen. The car was new with paper tags on it and no one would know who got out of it shooting when Onion walked out of his front door at the end of the block. The loud sound of a powerful motorcycle hit the air and Smoke and Serge turned to look back up the street to see where the loud bike was coming from.

Dressed in all black on a 900 Ninja, Wee-Wee, Quick's older cousin, pulled up and parked his bike right in front of Kisha's house. He had got the news that Onion had told on Quick and was coming up Rittenhouse Street to take care of the situation. Getting off of his bike, on point, he looked up and down the street noticing the dark blue-tinted window Thunderbird on the other side of the street. He gave the car a quick second look and then went into Kisha's house to find out where Onion was since he knew that Kisha was fucking with him and that Kisha would not play games with him being as though she had known him since she use to live down V Street where he was from.

"Ain't dat Wee?" Smoke asked as he took a deep pull of weed into his lungs.

"Yeah, dat's him. He must have heard about Onion too, he don't pop up unless something wrong," Serge said. Tapping Serge on the leg to get his attention while pulling his .40 cal pistol from under the seat, Smoke pointed down the street towards Onion's house. He was coming out of his front door with a brown paper bag in his hand.

"Let's get dis nigga and jump right out on 'em," Smoke said as he began to pull off.

Seconds after Smoke and Serge pulled off in the Thunderbird, Wee-Wee came out of Kisha's house. Standing on her porch, he adjusted his Glock 17 on his waistband. Putting his hand over his eyes to block the sun, he looked down the street towards Onion's house and saw him walking down the steps. "Shit!" he yelled out.

Slowly crossing 5th Street in the Thunderbird, Smoke and Serge could taste death. Coming to a stop, Smoke grabbed the handle to the door and was about to jump out when he stopped suddenly and watched.

As Onion walked down the long steps that led from his porch to the sidewalk on Rittenhouse Street, two little dudes in ski masks popped from out of the bushes beside his house. Gunshots hit the air. Bullets slammed into Onion's back, knocking him down the rest of the steps and flat onto the sidewalk. Smoke slammed his door back shut and smashed the gas. Him and Serge didn't know what was going on. Flying down the street, they looked over their shoulders and saw the two little dudes in ski masks standing over top of Onion with gunfire jumping out of their hands.

Later on, as the sun started to go down, Mann was just coming back in the house from taking his G.E.D. test. For eight hours he sat behind a desk, taking test after test, and it was worth it because he felt that he had passed it. Walking down the basement steps, Mann heard the sobs of a female crying. He thought that Kelley was downstairs crying so he hurried down his steps to see what was up. When he got to the bottom of the steps, he saw Kisha sitting on his bed crying her heart out into her hands with Kelley hugging her telling her to be strong. Mann knew what was up without asking, but he thought that Smoke was the reason.

"What's wrong?" Mann said as he walked over to Kisha and showed his concern.

Looking up at Mann, Kisha managed to say through her sobs, "They killed my baby!"

Grabbing Mann with her tear soaked hands Kisha said, "Why Mann? Why?"

Looking at Kelley as he sat down beside Kisha rubbing her head Mann said, "They killed who?" as if he knew nothing. Kisha got herself together enough to tell Mann that two young dudes had shot Onion to death on his front steps and that nobody knew who did it. Mann was puzzled, he couldn't think of who would have killed Onion before Smoke. He sat and talked to Kisha for a while to calm her down then he left her and Kelley alone so that Kisha could get the rest of her hurt and pain out.

Mann had to meet Silk at a night club called Takoma Station so that they could put the plan together for Mann to buy the store that he wanted because Silk's sister had already agreed to put it in her name.

Eyone Williams

Pulling up outside of the nightclub in his 300ZX, Mann parked and dug into his pocket to get his beeper that was going off. A set of headlights hit Mann in the eyes as a car pulled up behind him. Not being able to see who was behind him due to the bright lights, Mann got a little uncomfortable and pulled a 10mm from under his seat. The car door of the car behind him opened and a short dude got out of the car and began walking toward Mann's car. The passenger side door of the car opened and another little dude got out of the car and started walking up to Mann's car on the other side.

"What's up nigga?" Baby-D said as he tapped on Mann's window.

Rolling his window down and sliding his pistol between his waistband, Mann said, "What's up shorty?" as Lil' Garvin walked up and stood beside Baby-D.

"What y'all niggaz been up to?" Mann asked.

"We chillin out here, you know how we do it slim," Baby-D said.

"We heard about Onion telling on Lando and Quick yesterday," Lil Garvin said.

"Yeah somebody smashed da nigga earlier today," Mann said.

"We smashed dat bitch ass nigga. Young! Fuck dat nigga. Lando told us what happened on da phone last night," Baby-D said. Mann looked at the two younger dudes standing outside of his car and smiled, he couldn't believe how fast all of them had grown up.

"Oh yeah," Mann said, "y'all put dat work in huh?"

Baby-D and Lil' Garvin went on to tell Mann how they had hid in the bushes beside Onion's house for 30 minutes waiting for him to come outside. They told Mann how they were fucked up about him getting Lando and Quick found guilty so they killed him. As they told Mann about the whole situation, he knew in his heart that the two young dudes knew what loyalty was all about. Their partners from childhood were locked up for murder and somebody around their way told on them and that was all that needed to be said for them to fill Onion with hollow point slugs. After they were finished telling Mann about the killing, Mann told them not to tell anybody about what they had done hours ago. He told them that he wanted them to come over Pamila's house tomorrow so that he could talk to them about something important and then they got back in their car and left.

Sitting in his car thinking about what Lil' Garvin and Baby-D had just told him, Mann decided that he was going to make sure that he did something big with the two young dudes so that they would be set for awhile. He felt that they deserved a shot at some bigger money than they were making and he was going to give it to them for what they did for his little brother and Quick. Looking out of his window, Mann saw Silk pulling up across the street in his Ferrari. Mann cut his car off and got out to go talk to Silk.

A week later, Lando was coming back off of A visit with a big smile on his face. Pamila brought Nakia down Oak Hill to see him and Mann brought him a 50 bag of weed, along with the news of how Baby-D and Lil' Garvin had killed Onion the very next day after he had testified against him and Quick.

Black and Quick were playing a game of chess in the TV room when Lando came walking down the hall and past them with a smile on his face. They knew what time it was and they both got up and walked down the hall to Lando's cell together.

"What up joe?" Black asked as he walked in Lando's cell and sat on the bed.

"Y'all ain't gon believe dis shit here joe," Lando said, as Quick walked by him and sat in a chair in the corner of the cell. "Y'all know Lil' Garvin and da Baby smashed da nigga Onion," Lando said as he began to tell Black and Quick how they had killed him while dumping the weed that Mann had brought him on a piece of paper on the bed beside Black.

Grabbing a big bud of weed and putting it into a split blunt, Black said, "Dem young niggaz ain't playin' out there joe." Quick shut the door of the cell and put a piece of paper over the window while Lando lit an incense, hanging it by the door while Black lit the blunt of weed that he had just rolled.

Blowing a cloud of weed smoke out of his mouth and passing the blunt to Lando, Black said, "Dat's how shit pose to be done. Dem young niggaz ain't do no fakin!" Black was impressed to say the least. He didn't know who could have killed Onion. Smoke told him how he was in the car with Serge and they were about to smash Onion when two little dudes jumped out of the bushes and gunned Onion down right in front of his house. Black's first thought was that Onion had tried to take some young niggaz bad and they killed him. Now that he knew that Onion got killed for telling on Lando and Quick, he felt a lot better.

After smoking another blunt with Quick and Black, Lando went to get on the phone. He called a pay phone number that Lil'Garvin had given to Mann for him to reach him at. Without saying the wrong thing on the phone, Lando let Lil' Garvin know that he knew what was up and that he respected the move. "You know how we roll slim, dat ain't shit joe," Lil' Garvin said.

"Where Baby–D at?" Lando asked, sounding high as ever.

"Hold on. He in da alley," Lil' Garvin said as he called up the alley for Baby-D.

"Hello?" Baby-D said as he got on the phone breathing hard from running down the block.

"Yeah slim, I was telling Lil' Garvin dat y'all real as shit. Y'all keep it in the family you know," Lando said.

Baby-D knew exactly what he was talking about and said, "You my nigga from jump street, you know dat slim. But check dis out, da "jump-outs" at da top of da block joe, I gotta roll. I got a joint on me. Call me over Lil' Garvin's house later on," Baby-D said as he hung up the phone. Lando missed Baby-D and Lil' Garvin, but he knew that no matter how long he was locked up, they would be there for him and Quick and that was all that he could ask of a partner.

High as a kite and thinking about Jazmin, Lando called her house. "Hello?" a young dude said into the phone.

Surprised, Lando put some bass in his voice and said, "Jazmin there?"

"Who dis?" the dude asked, as if he had a problem with a dude calling Jazmin's house.

Lando laughed a little and said, "Can I speak to Jazmin or not slim?"

"Who da fuck is dis?" the dude said, as he got angry. Lando could hear that Jazmin must have just walked in the room because the dude was saying that somebody was on the phone and wouldn't say who it was.

"Hello?" Jazmin said, sounding sexy as always.

"What's up joe?" Lando said.

"What's up boy?" Jazmin said sounding excited when she heard that it was Lando on the phone. He hadn't called her in about 3 weeks, but he could hear in her voice that things hadn't changed between them except for the dude answering the phone.

"So you gotta man now?" Lando said without the least bit of jealousy in his voice.

"Yeah, dat's my boyfriend," Jazmin said. Lando could hear him complaining in the background about him calling her house. "Look this is my friend and he can call here anytime he want, dis is my house!" Jazmin snapped at her boyfriend.

"You want me to call you later?" Lando asked, feeling like he was causing a problem between her and her man.

"No you don't gotta call me later. We always gon be tight and anybody dat's in my life gon have to accept that or they really don't want to be in my life." Lando respected what Jazmin said and took it to heart. If there were a way to finalize a bond, it would have been that very statement. Lando began to tell Jazmin that him and Quick had been found guilty on their case and that they would most likely be down Oak Hill for the next two years. "Dat's a long time," Jazmin said.

"Yeah, you right. It feel like it's the rest of my life, but I gotta do it the best way dat I can."

"You strong boo. I know you can make it. I asked your brother could I come see you, he told me dat I gotta holla at your mother," Jazmin said. Lando explained to her that Pamila was cool and that she would dig her. Jazmin agreed to call her and ask if she could go see Lando with her. Lando let Jazmin know that he would be writing her a letter and sending her some pictures soon and then got off the phone.

Lando walked back down the hall to his cell where Black and Quick were talking about different ways to make money when they were back on the streets. Lando thought that it was cool for Black to be thinking like that, he might be out within the next month or so, but Lando knew that him and Quick would be spending the next 2 years down Oak Hill. That was enough to make him think of other things at the time, he would deal with the streets when he got there again.

Twelve

With the summer now here and his G.E.D. behind him, Mann had two goals for the summer. The first one was to get his store, which he had decided would be called Mann's World and his second goal was to pay the rest of Kelley's way through college. His money was right and his mind was set, it was all about putting his plan into effect. Silk's sister had already gotten a loan from the bank and spoken to the old couple that owned the store that Mann was going to buy. To make Pam feel a little safer about her decision to put the store in her name, Mann gave her the whole loan of $150,000 up front so that she was already out of the hole. On top of that, he gave her an extra $5,000 just for her trouble. After Mann spoke to a friend of Silk's named Rick, who had a degree in business management, Mann's World would be open for business.

After Kelley graduated from Coolidge High School, Mann took her on the best trip of her young life. They spent 7 long and beautiful days and nights in Barbados, along with Dre, Tina, and their son. The trip did a lot for them all, but more so for Dre and Mann because it showed them that the world was bigger than the small city of Washington, DC and its money, drugs, and murder.

Kelley woke up early in the morning and began rubbing on Mann's chest to wake him up. She knew that he had plenty of reason to be dead tired after the love making that they did last night, but she knew that Mann had to meet Silk's sister Pam downtown at the law office of Mr. Larry A. Williams, Sr., who was the father of Silk's old friend Rick.

Rolling over on his side to face Kelley, Mann began to rub his hand through her beautiful hair and said, "I dreamed about last night all night."

"Is that right?" Kelley said, clearly turned on by Mann's straightforward approach. Mann began to get closer and closer to Kelley until she had to remind him of his meeting with Pam and Rick.

"You know you gotta make sure everything is right so you can get da store dis week," Kelley said. Thinking of the store and how it would be his way out of the game, Mann began to tell Kelley how this was the beginning of something that may become as big as Bloomingdales or a store of that nature. Mann explained to Kelley that all big things start out small and that as long as he was alive, he would always think big. Kelley was amazed by Mann's belief in himself. That was one of the reasons that she wanted to be his woman for the rest of her life.

Pulling up behind Pam's silver BMW 850i, Mann parked right in front of the law office of Mr. Williams. Getting out of his Nissan 300ZX, Mann walked up to Pam's window and tapped it with his car keys.

"You ready beautiful?" Mann said with a smile. Pam found Mann very attractive since the first time she laid eyes on the dark skinned young man. Stepping out of her car into the hot summer sun, Pam drew all the attention of the busy downtown street and 16th Street was very busy during the working hours of the day.

Short and brown skinned with long jet black hair, not to mention a body that could cause a car crash, Pam hugged Mann after shutting her car door. Mann had to take in the sight of such a beautiful woman. In her tight Guess jean shorts with her hairy legs shining in the summer sun, Mann thought about shooting his shot at Pam being as though he knew that she had a thing for him for the longest, but that would take away from what they came downtown to do. Mann and Pam talked for a minute and then went inside to get down to business.

Eight days before his 13th birthday, Lando and his partner, Quick, were committed to 2 years at the Oak Hill Juvenile Detention Center. Now that they had time, they were transferred from Unit 7A to Unit 8b where Freeway, Demo, and Short Dogg were doing their 2 year commitments as well.

The sun was in full blast today and while everybody was out for rec, Lando stayed inside to use the phone. Nakia was starting to grow further and further away from him as the days started to turn into weeks now that Lando had 2 years to do. Pamila had told him that the girl was too young to stay put for 2 years and Lando had accepted the fact that Pamila was right as always. Out of the feelings that he had for Nakia, Lando talked her into being his friend while he was locked up because he felt that she would somehow cross him if they played any kind of love games while he was locked up. After awhile and a lot of protest, Nakia agreed with Lando's plan when she began to see how hard it was for her not to deal with other dudes that were after her now that she was becoming more and more of a young lady everyday. Lando made sure that he stayed in touch with her and Jazmin, but did his time playing sports and lifting iron, not to mention using the phone, which is exactly where he was today when Short Dogg came running inside the unit looking for him.

"Lando," Short Dogg said, as he stepped into the small phone room. Lando put Nakia on hold to find out what he wanted. Black had sent Short Dogg to get Lando so that he could see him before he went to the group home today. Black had pleaded guilty to his drug charge in order to get out on probation for the summer. They had just called him for the group home about 15 minutes ago and Short Dogg told Lando that he had to hurry up. Lando told Nakia that he had to call her back and then hung up the phone to run over to Unit 7A to see Black before he hit the streets, again.

Short Dogg and Lando walked into Black's cell while he was throwing away all of his mail. Quick was already in the cell along with Freeway, who Black had taken a liking to as well.

"What's up joe? You know I'm outta here young!" Black said as he walked over and hugged his little cousin.

"I know, take care of yourself out there young," Lando said as he walked over and sat on the bed along with Quick and Freeway. Lando was happy to see Black leave, but at the same time Black was taking a part of Lando to the streets with him and Lando felt it. Black started giving away his name brand shorts and T-shirts as well as his fleet of $100 tennis shoes.

"I'ma miss y'all niggaz young," Black said as he began to tell everybody how he was about to hit the streets and take shit bad.

"You betta get you some money," Quick said. Everybody started laughing, they all knew Black well enough to know that he didn't care about anything but some trouble. Black went under his bed and pulled out a plastic bag. Opening it, he pulled out a knot of cash, $2,000 exactly. Black gave all of the younger dudes $500 each. A counselor came to the door and told Black that if he wanted to stay he could but his ride was leaving with or without him. Black hugged everybody and hit the road leaving only his love behind.

Mann wasn't the only one making plans for the legit world. Silk had already bought a barbershop on Minnesota Avenue. He had kept it from him until it was open and today he picked Mann up and took him to Silky's Barber Shop for it's grand opening which was a get together of old buddies and the three barbers that he had given jobs too. There was music, weed, and drinks in the back, while it was free haircuts going on for all who wanted one. The whole place was live, but most of all, Silk's plan to inspire Mann worked well.

"Yeah dat was big shit joe," Mann said, as he sat in the passenger seat of Silk's Ferrari 355 Spyder while they flew through the 9th Street tunnel on their way back uptown. Mann was impressed by the way Silk had kept everything to himself about the barbershop.

"Yeah, dat was just somethin' I wanted to try before I try dis other move out Maryland wit a car lot," Silk said as he slid a Sade CD in his disk player, "Pam signed da papers for the store today, so Mann's World is on the move now. I talked to dis dude dat work wit my uncle, he gon do all of da remodlin' for me. Da place in good shape."

"After your man Rick give me all da paper work, I'm in business joe."

"How long you think dat's gon take."

"I give it 'bout 3 weeks at the most. I got da legal shit and da insurance shit done already, thanks to Pam," Mann said.

Silk looked over at Mann with a brotherly love in his eyes and said, "You know how to get dat cash young nigga, dat's one thing I respect about you. So what da fuck Dre gon do?"

"Dre ain't made up his mind yet. He say he gon put some of his money into my store and see what he get back. On da real, he think dis shit ain't gon work, but I know it is so I'ma kick him a little extra cash back like money coming from everywhere so he'll think it's something to take serious. He'll get da idea and try da same thing, he been like dat since we was kids." Silk really respected the fact that Mann always took Dre along for the ride. Silk could remember when Dre was wild and running the streets gunning everything down with Black. It was Silk that encouraged Mann to get Dre to get some money that would last.

When they pulled up in front of Pamila's house it was like a block party. Pamila had the front door open with two big stereo speakers out on the porch. The front yard was packed with neighbors and their little kids. Pamila was on the grill. Kelley, Kisha, and Tina were sitting on the front steps, while Lil' Garvin, Baby-D, and Dre were sitting on the hood of

Dre's ZR1. Tyesha was playing catch with Dre's son and two other little kids on the side of the house. You could feel the summer time spirit in the hot evening air.

Everybody paid close attention to Mann and Silk as they got out of the Ferrari, it drew a lot of that and Mann could see that it may have drawn a little too much attention by the way Pamila looked at it.

Silk stepped to Dre and the two younger dudes that sat on the hood of his car with him. They all showed much love to Silk, he was somewhat a ghetto icon to say the least. Mann walked by and said what's up to everybody, but Pamila had given him an eye like she wanted to speak to him so he told everyone that he would be right back. Walking by Kelley, Kisha and Tina, Mann hugged and kissed Kelley, asking all the ladies how they were doing and then walked over to the grill where Pamila was standing over the food talking to an old lady from her church named Mrs. Gather.

Tyesha was very excited to see Mann. As he spoke to Mrs. Gather, Tyesha ran and jumped into his arms.

Catching his balance, Mann said, "You gettin' big shorty." Tyesha smiled and kissed Mann on the cheek as she broke loose from his hug and ran back over to the crowd of kids to play catch.

"What's up Pamila?" Mann said. Pamila closed the grill and led Mann away from Mrs. Gather so that she couldn't overhear the conversation and take it back to church and put it on the grapevine.

"Mann you know I don't like you bringing your friends over here showing off all that drug money. It ain't right. You do what you want to with your life, but don't bring it around here," Pamila said. And it was nothing Mann could tell her about Silk not being involved with drug money, Pamila was too bright for that. Mann just agreed and went on with the program. "You know your bad ass cousin is out of jail. He called here looking for you."

"Where is he?"

"He's in some group home. He said he gets to come out on the weekend. Ask Kelley where he is?" Pamila said, "While you at it, try to keep that boy out of trouble!" Mann hugged Pamila and told her that he would do just that, then walked back over to Dre's car.

"Y'all know dat nigga Black home," Mann said to the group of dudes standing in front of Dre's car.

"Yeah, Kelley was telling me," Dre said. It was news to Baby-D, Lil' Garvin, and Silk, but they were all happy to hear that Black was home.

"Where he at?" Baby-D asked. Mann let everybody know that he was in a group home and that he would be out for a home visit on the weekend. They all sat and talked, just kicking it about what was going on around the way, how Lando and Quick were doing, and about Mann's store. Mann enjoyed times like these, times where everybody was just laid back, yet even at times like these he was always thinking and Black was who he was thinking about. Mann wondered if Black would chill this time. Only time would tell.

Black was awakened by the loud sound of the group home counselor screaming, "Wake up! It's breakfast time!" Black rolled over in his bed still wearing Oak Hill drawers and saw the small dark skinned man coming into the room that he shared with two other juveniles that he knew from down Oak Hill. The counselor kicked the bed of one of the young men to wake him up. The whole sight reminded Black of being locked up. He sat up on his bed trying to rub the sleep out of his eyes so that he could get up before the counselor came at him with the same bullshit. Trouble was truly the last thing Black wanted for once in his life.

"Mr. Mills. Do you think the rules don't apply to you?" The counselor asked, as he kicked the bed and snapped Black out of his sleep. In a flash, Black shot to his feet and knocked the counselor onto the floor. The counselor was out cold. Black looked around the room as if he was unsure of what he had just did.

"Shit!" Black said out loud as he reached for his clothes. He had fucked up. His anger had gotten him into another bad situation and he now had only two choices to make. One was wait until the head counselor came upstairs to see what was going on and which would surely lead Black right back down Oak Hill not even 24 hours after he left or he could go on the run.

Black decided to run. Throwing his clothes on with lightning speed while the other two juveniles watched in amazement, he shot down the steps knocking the head counselor down as he hit the door and sprinted down Harvard Street.

Pamila sat at the dining room table opening bills this evening after a long day at work. She came across a letter with Kelley's name on it from the University of Ohio. Pamila called Kelley downstairs to open her mail. Kelley came downstairs with Tyesha in her arms. Walking over to the table Kelley began to smile, she knew what was in the envelope. As Kelley began to open her mail the phone began to ring.

"Hello?" Pamila said as she answered the phone.

"What's up girl?" Her sister said.

"What's up V?"

"You seen my bad ass son?"

"No, he called here yesterday looking for Mann. Why?"

"Girl, da police is looking for him. He done beat up a counselor at his group home and ran away from the place. He just won't do right," Black's mother said. Pamila wasn't surprised at all. Black was always in trouble. Pamila talked to her sister for a few more minutes and let her know that she would get Mann to find Black and then they hung up the phone.

After getting off of the phone, Pamila said a short prayer for her sister and her son, and then asked Kelley what kind of news she got. Kelley let her know that she had been accepted to the University of Ohio on a partial scholarship.

"That's still good girl. It's so good that you will have the chance to go away to school. The city ain't no good for you," Pamila said. Kelley felt as though she was right and she knew that going away to school was what she wanted to do. All that was left to do now was to get Mann to pay the rest of the way through school which was nearly a given.

Mann had got a beep from Da-Da on his way home from doing the last of the paperwork for his store. Da-Da wanted a brick and he needed it tonight so Mann shot out White Oak to get the coke for him. That was an easy $25,000 and Mann knew he had to grind up some money now that he had put so much cash into Mann's World. Things were going to be okay, Mann thought to himself during the ride to his apartment. With Pam on paper as the owner and himself on paper as a supervisor, Mann still called all the shots. Legally he would run the store for Pam, but they knew who was in charge.

Mann pulled up in front of his building, parked his car, and got out into the cool summer night wearing an all black Polo short set with a .40 magnum 13 shot strapped under his shirt. Walking up to his door,

Mann noticed that someone had been inside of his apartment due to the top lock not being on when he stuck his key in to unlock it. Looking over his shoulder to see if anyone was looking, Mann pulled his pistol from under his shirt and let himself in the door with it pointed in front of him, ready to blast the first thing moving.

Once inside, Mann hit the lights and saw Black lying on the sofa sleep. "Black!" Mann yelled, "Wake da fuck up!" Mann put his pistol up and walked over to the sofa and started shaking Black who was dead sleep still wearing his Oak Hill clothes and smelling like a pound of weed. Black opened his eyes and sat straight up when he saw Mann.

"What's up young?" Black asked as he sat back on the sofa.

"What da fuck is up wit you? Why you ain't in da group home, it ain't Friday yet." Mann asked.

"I fucked up joe. I knocked a counselor out dis morning and had to roll out da joint slim."

"You did what?"

"Yeah joe, I'm on da run," Black said as he shook his head truly not pleased with his own situation. Mann sat down beside his younger cousin and began to scratch his head. Mann didn't understand how Black always put himself in such fucked up positions.

"So what you gon do now Black?" Mann asked, knowing that Black had some extra go hard plan of how he was going to stay on the run for the rest of his life.

"Slim, I don't even know dis time. I ain't gon turn myself in, dat's out joe. I'ma lay low here for a few days until I come up wit something."

"I'm cool wit dat, just don't let nobody know where dis spot at," Mann said as he got up to get the brick of coke that he had came to get. Once back in the room with Black, Mann began to get on him about how he was still doing the same dumb shit that he was doing when he was Lando's age and that now was a new day in time, he was older now and couldn't make those same mistakes. Mann gave Black the little bit of money that he had in his pocket, which was close to $300 and then left to go serve Da-Da the brick of coke that he wanted.

Days later it was sweep time in the neighborhood. Hall and the rest of the "jump-outs" were floating through all drug spots uptown just waiting to catch somebody in the wrong, but nobody was dumb enough to be on the block until later on.

Eyone Williams

Riding through Rittenhouse Street in a new Isuzu Trooper, Hall turned to one of the four vice cops in the truck with him and said, "Al, did you hear anything about the killing of the guy Onion?"

"Who is that?" Big Al asked, not remembering the rat off hand.

Speedie cut in from the back seat and said, "You know the guy he's talking about, the snitch that got wacked about a month or two ago."

"Oh, yeah, I remember the dirt bag. Two little gangsters gunned him down like a day or two after he told on the two little guys that shot at Wilson and his partner," Big Al said. Hall went on to ask if anyone had heard anything about the situation. No one had any information about that, but Speedie told Hall that his favorite thug was home and on the run.

"Who is that?" Hall asked.

"Black!" Big Al said with a little laugh behind it knowing that Hall took every case that he put on Black to heart. Hall had anger written across his face.

"They let that motherfucker get away with murder. We'll catch his ass wrong. It's summer time, he'll pop up and kill somebody before September," Hall said as he turned up 5th Street with his mind set on sending Black to jail before the summer was out.

Pamila decided to pop up and surprise Lando and Quick by bringing Jazmin and Quick's grandmother down Oak Hill to see them. They all walked into the chow hall where the rest of the visits were and waited for Lando and Quick to come out. Pamila could tell that the place made Quick's grandmother very uncomfortable, she was like that the last few times that she brought her down to see him. Pamila also saw how all the boys in the visiting area were looking at Jazmin. She was a very cute young girl, Pamila thought. After bringing her to see Lando a few times, she had learned that the child had something on her mind. Pamila was really impressed by the fact that Jazmin had plans for the future at such a young age. She could really get used to dealing with Jazmin.

Lando and Quick walked into the visiting area only expecting to see Pamila and Quick's grandmother. They were both surprised to see Jazmin.

Quick looked at Lando and said, "Damn joe, your folks lookin' good as shit." Lando responded with only a headshake as they both walked over to their visits. Quick hugged his grandmother as Lando did the same to Pamila. Jazmin watched as Quick and Lando embraced their loved ones.

Quick turned to hug Pamila as Lando hugged and kissed his grandmother. Lando turned to Jazmin and just looked at her for a second. She was growing more and more attractive as the year went on.

Quick's grandmother, Mrs. Jones said, "Go ahead and hug the young lady, she ain't gon bite you boy." Pamila and Quick laughed at the old woman's statement. Jazmin stood up with her hair pulled back into a beautiful ponytail and opened her arms to hug Lando.

As they hugged, Lando said, "I'm glad you came to see me. I been thinkin' 'bout you a lot."

"I been thinking bout you too boy," Jazmin said before they sat back down and began to talk with Pamila and Quick's grandmother for the rest of the visit.

Slapping a 90 shot clip into an AK-47, Black sat on the sofa in Smoke's apartment and aimed it at the wall. "Dis ah work!" Black said to Smoke and Serge, who sat at the dining room table loading clips to their Mac-11. Black had been on the run for a week and was ready to hit a quick caper. Smoke and Serge, who were not doing too good money wise, were both more than willing to go on the move. They both knew what to do to get money and had the balls to carry it out but for some reason they needed the quick aggressiveness of Black to push them into bigger caper situations and Black came up with just the caper that they were looking for this time.

It was a jewelry store ran by two Chinese dudes right across the Maryland line in Silver Spring. Black had been inside already and he had put the plan together for them to hit the joint. He knew how much money was in there and he knew when and how they moved the money. He began to tell his crime partners that they would hit the store from the back as the Chinese dudes tried to move their money at 7:00pm this evening.

"So what y'all think?" Black asked. Smoke and Serge were ready for the move. "Let's roll then," Black said as he led the way to the car they were going to use for the move.

Mann was sitting on a bucket of paint watching the remodelers put the last touches on the wall. They had transformed the old store into an up-to-date urban version in only 2 weeks. Mann had been making calls to all big wholesale stores in New York all week and his first shipment of

Polo, Nautica, and Eddie Bauer clothes would be in Mann's World and on the racks no later than the end of the week. The word was out on the street that the store would be making its grand opening on the 4th of July. Pam had gotten a radio commercial on the top radio station in the DC area to promote the grand opening. Mann couldn't wait. He had food, drinks, live music, fireworks and he was giving away a free Polo short set along with a pair of new Air Jordan's to the first 10 people to show up in front of Mann's World where everything was to go down.

Pam was on the phone behind the computer making phone calls to a few wholesale companies when Dre and Tina eased their way through the fleet of working men. As they both spoke to Pam, Tina stopped to talk for a minute, while Dre walked over to talk to Mann.

"What's up joe?" Mann said to Dre as he waved at Tina. Tina smiled and waved back at Mann, while Mann responded by throwing his hands up in the air and looking around the almost complete store like 'look at what I got here'. Dre laughed at Mann's gesture. He knew Mann had the right to play big for a second, he put his plan into effect from scratch and it was now ready for take off.

"So what's up wit you joe?" Mann said to Dre, noticing a slight worry in the face of his partner.

Dre let out a small sigh and said, "Joe, da Feds raided da White Oak spot." Mann rubbed his chin as he stood up and told Dre to follow him into the back office that he had made strictly for himself. Mann sat on a new sofa as they walked through the door. Dre sat across from him in a padded leather office chair and looked at Mann who was still thinking about what Dre had just told him.

"So what went down?" Mann asked. Dre began to tell him that some young dude that was buying coke from Da-Da and LeRon had been selling coke to an undercover. They raided the strip early in the morning and locked the young dude up along with his little crew. "Did they get Da-Da and dem?" Mann asked. Dre let him know that the Feds only locked the young dude up and that everybody else was okay.

"What can da young dude tell'em?" Mann asked wanting to know whose names could be given up.

"He only knew Da-Da and some other lil' dude dat be hustlin' for 'em," Dre said.

"So we jive cool then," Mann began to say, "We gotta lay low for awhile, dat's all."

"I'm cool wit dat slim, I'ma go back around the way for a minute while shit cool down out Maryland," Dre said. Mann didn't agree with him going back around Rittenhouse Street because things stayed so hot around there, but he knew Dre lived for the cash of the fast lane.

Sitting in his black Impala outside of the Coolidge High School Gym, Lil' Garvin smoked a blunt of weed with a cute young girl named Imani that he had met downtown. As people came out of the gym and went their own ways, Lil'Garvin waited patiently for his man Baby-D to come out of the doors. As Imani leaned over to pass Lil' Garvin the blunt of weed, Baby-D crept up on the side of the car and jumped at the window scaring the two of them. Lil'Garvin jumped out of shock, dropping the lit blunt of weed on his black Polo shorts as he quickly reached for his Glock .40. Baby-D burst out laughing as he hopped in the backseat. Lil'Garvin saw nothing funny as he smacked the burning blunt on to the car floor to stop it from burning his leg. Leaning over to pick it up, he said, "Ain't shit funny nigga! Dat's a good way to get shot!" Imani began to laugh at the scene.

Lil' Garvin looked over at the cute brown skinned girl and said, "What da fuck is so funny?"

Still giggling, Imani said, "You was scared as shit!"

"You was scared as shit bitch! Matter fact, get da fuck out my car," Lil' Garvin said, becoming dead serious.

Imani gave up a sad face and said, "I'm sorry...."

"Fuck dat. Get the fuck out bitch!" Lil' Garvin said as he started up the car. Imani began to cry as she got out of the car into the dark summer night while Lil' Garvin pulled off with Baby-D in the backseat laughing at the top of his lungs.

Corey, Keith, and a few younger dudes from the neighborhood were in front of Kisha's house pushing rocks when Lil' Garvin and Baby-D pulled up and parked. The two younger dudes got out and spread their love as they walked up and leaned on the fence with everyone else that was out for the dollars. Lil' Garvin, still upset at Baby-D for making him burn his leg with the blunt, was in no mood for anybody's funny style ways tonight and he noticed Corey looking at him and Baby-D in a strange way. Lil' Garvin had been picking up vibes from Corey ever since Onion got killed. Lil' Garvin decided to say something about it.

Eyone Williams

With his hand inside his shorts on the pistol that he had tucked between his waistband, Lil' Garvin said to Corey, "What da fuck you keep starin' at me for nigga?" Tension hit the air, as things were about to come to a head and everybody outside waited to see the explosion.

"Who da fuck you think you talkin' to young nigga?" Corey snapped.

"You know what da fuck is up bitch nigga. You think I had something to do wit your hot ass man gettin' smashed. If you fuck wit 'em so much do somethin' bout it!" Lil' Garvin said, full of anger. He knew that Corey thought that him and Baby-D had killed Onion and he was tired of him acting like he wanted to do something about it. As Corey began to walk up on Lil' Garvin, Black bent the corner in the red Oldsmobile that him, Smoke, and Serge had just robbed the jewelry store in no more then 30 minutes ago.

Seeing the conflict, Black slammed on brakes and got out of the car leaving it in the middle of the street with Smoke and Serge still inside while he walked over to the sidewalk.

"What da fuck is up?" Black said with a murderous frown on his face, as he looked Corey's way. Keith began to take the whole situation much more serious now that Black was on the scene, he walked up beside Corey in clear support of his man.

"You ain't got shit to do wit dis Black!" Corey said, appearing a little worried now that Black had popped up.

Stepping between Corey and Lil' Garvin, Black got up in Corey's face and began to tap his finger on Corey's forehead while he said, "Bitch nigga! Anything dat got something to do wit dese young niggaz got somethin' to do wit me!"

Keith began to step around Corey as he said, "Black, man you need to mind your....." BOOM! Two gunshots rang out and Keith's words were cut short as he fell to the ground holding his chest. The gunshots scared everybody. They all turned to see who had fired the shots and saw Baby-D with a smoking .45 automatic in his hand.

Baby-D began to walk toward Keith to finish him off as Corey ran through the cut beside Kisha's house. Two more gunshots put Keith to rest.

"What da fuck you do dat for?" Black said as he looked down at the body.

"Dat nigga was reaching for a joint!" Baby-D said as he began to run towards Lil' Garvin's car followed by Lil' Garvin. The few other younger dudes that had just watched their first murder all ran as Black leaned over to see if Keith was really reaching for a pistol. With Smoke and Serge screaming for Black to hurry up and get in the car, Black bent over and pulled a 9mm from Keith's waistband. With the pistol in his hand, Black ran to his car leaving the dead body on the sidewalk as he jumped in and pulled off followed by Lil' Garvin's Impala.

Keith's murder changed Rittenhouse Street for good. In the weeks that followed, a new breed of young dudes seem to come out of nowhere and take over the abandoned drug strip. Corey hadn't been seen since and Baby-D and Lil' Garvin had shot to the status of shot callers on the block now that they had the most years in the fast lane out of the new young dudes on the block and they loved the ghetto fame.

Things didn't look as good for Black. Whoever witnessed Keith's murder had the facts mixed up. They told Homicide Detective Brown that Black was the person that they saw shoot Keith that day. Now Black was no longer on the run from the juvenile system alone, he was now wanted for a murder that he would be charged as an adult for. Once again, Black would be facing life in prison if the police caught him and Officer Hall was so happy to be on the hunt for Black.

Mann was not happy with the events that had turned the whole neighborhood upside down, but he had learned a long time ago that some things were just meant to be and this had to be one of those things as far as he was concerned. Even so he stuck by Black and made sure that Black always had a place to lay his head and anything else that he needed. Mann had got Tina to get an apartment outside of DC in her name for Black to stay in while he was on the run. While Black turned the apartment to a headquarters for his nightly capers, Mann went on with his plan of getting out of the drug game.

The local sounds of Rare Essence, a DC go-go band, filled the air at 12 noon on the 4th of July. The crowd already filled the whole block of Georgia Avenue between Eastern Avenue and Fern Place. Little kids ran up and down the block. Mann stood at the front door of Mann's World passing out free shoes and short sets. Silk, Dre, Pam, Tina, and Kelley enjoyed the music in the hot summer sun as well. Mann felt a sense of pride for himself looking at the huge crowd of people that he had brought together for his grand opening. It was a sight to see.

Pamila and Tyesha decided to drop through to see what Mann had going on. Pamila had said that she wanted nothing to do with the store since she knew Mann had put it together with drug money, but the more she thought about what Mann was trying to do, she had to show her face in the place.

Mann was standing beside a rack of T-shirts that he was giving away when he saw Pamila. He couldn't believe his eyes, he told Dre to pass out the rest of the shirts while he walked over to Pamila and Tyesha and wrapped his arms around them both.

"I'm glad to see you, you know dis means a lot to me. I'm tryin' to leave da streets alone. Dis is bigger than me. Dis for me, dis is for Lando, Dre and everybody else Pamila! If I can just get dis store off da ground, da streets will be history. By da time Lando come home, everything should be up and rollin' and he will see dat he can make it wit out da streets. Feel me?" Pamila smiled as Mann talked. As much as she hated how he started his store, she knew that his intentions were good and for that she had to agree with his dream of getting out of a life of drug selling.

"You right Mann. Do what you have to do to make this thing work, maybe you will wake Lando and Black up," Pamila said. Mann was pleased with Pamila's slight approval. He told her to enjoy herself as he got back to making sure that things were running smoothly with the festivities. Pamila walked around for a while, spoke to Kelley about her SAT's, and then went back home.

Inside of Mann's World, hid away from the public in the office hideout, Black, Lil' Garvin, and Baby-D sat in front of the huge 60" color TV playing John Madden's Football on Sega while they smoked blunt after blunt. Mann walked inside of the office and smelled nothing but weed smoke in the air. "Damn!" he said out loud as he sat down and got on the phone. Lil' Garvin, who was not playing the videogame at the time, walked over and sat down beside Mann who was just hanging up the phone with a New York retailer that he was trying to do some business with.

"What's up shorty?" Mann asked Lil' Garvin.

"Ain't shit slim, I just wanted to tell you dat I digs dis shit here joe. You be thinkin' big as shit young," Lil' Garvin said. Mann smiled at the younger dude. He knew that Lil' Garvin could see what he was putting together and he liked the fact that he called himself commending him on his actions.

"You gon have all dis shit too shorty. All you gotta do is want it joe," Mann said.

Silk walked into the office and said, "Y'all niggaz 'bout to miss the fireworks."

Everybody hit the door and followed Silk out front.

Mann and Black were side-by-side when they walked out into the crowd of people. Black had been inside all day and didn't know how many people had shown up to support Mann's World.

"Damn slim, everybody and they momma out here, dis big shit joe," Black said as the first rocket exploded into the night air. Mann smiled as the five TNT rockets hit the air right behind the first one.

"I just want dis shit to work out joe. If all goes well dis is just the beginning," Mann said as he looked down at his beeper.

Silk had overheard Mann's statement as he was walking over, and placed his arm around Mann's shoulder and said, "All is going to work out slim. Dis is just the beginning. Ain't dat right?"

Looking over at Silk with a smile, Mann said, "Yeah, dat's right. Dis is just da beginning." Things would never be the same, and it was no looking back for Mann. He had his mind set on making Mann's World a success and that is just what he set out to do as he put all of his energy into it.

Part II

13

By early 1992, Mann was already an 18-year old entrepreneur that had his business in order. Mann's World was now in his name and paid for legally. He also owned a recording studio in Silver Spring, Maryland that he was in the process of putting together for business. His goal was to have it up and running by the summer time so that he could start renting out studio time. Mann had hired Dre as the manager of Mann's World just to put him on the payroll. Kisha worked as a cashier along with a new cute light skinned girl that she had introduced to Dre by the name of Naomi. Mann's World was now up and running, not to mention producing enough revenue weekly for Mann and Dre to live off of, but they still flipped bricks of coke on the side to keep their money stacking until they were sure that they could hang with the big dogs in the corporate world.

Kelley was in her second year of college at the University of Ohio studying criminal law, thanks to the deep pockets of her true love Mann. She called DC every night of the week to talk to Mann, who never missed a call from her no matter what he was doing and Kelley wanted for nothing while she was away at school. Mann made her feel as if he was around the corner by popping up out of the blue to visit her and bring her small gifts every now and then. As long as Mann had something to do with Kelley's future, it would be a success as far as he was concerned and she felt the support by the minute.

Black's constant run-ins with the law never stopped. By late 1990, he was spotted by Officer Hall and his gang of vice cops. Black took the cops on a wild car chase that extended all the way into Fort Washington, Maryland. He was caught with a .50 Caliber Desert Eagle and sent to DC Jail to await trial for Keith's murder which Baby-D committed. Black played by the rules of the game and told the Feds nothing about Baby-D. Mann got Black a top notch lawyer and Black beat the murder charge but was found guilty of an armed robbery that he committed in late 1990. He was sentenced to a 3 year youth act in the adult system and was now waiting to see the parole board at Lorton's Youth Center.

It had been 2 years since Lando and Quick went down Oak Hill for murder. Despite how long 2 years seemed to them in 1990, by now it only seemed like weeks. They were now eligible for weekend home visits and could probably be coming home on an after care program by the summer time if they did good on their home visits. They were a lot bigger now and eager to hit the streets after all that they had been hearing about Lil' Garvin and Baby-D running things around the way now. Quick was now much more aggressive at 15. Lando began to see more and more of Black in Quick everyday now. Lando on the other hand was still a little wild, but at 15 he was more focused than he had ever been which had a lot to do with the many visits Mann had paid him over the last 2 years, soaking up the knowledge from each visit like a sponge. As Mann spit the game to his little brother, Lando listened to every word and was ready for the streets now that they were so close that he could taste them.

Pamila stuck by Lando and Quick every step of the way while they were locked up. Pamila had even gotten legal custody of Quick now that his grandmother had passed away. Quick loved Pamila for that and he truly looked at her as his mother now. The only guidance that he got these days was from her. Pamila couldn't wait for her two boys to come home on their first home visit.

At 5 years old Tyesha was growing by the hour. The cute little girl was almost 4 feet tall already. She had grown very close to Lando while he was locked up being as though she saw him more now. She had been talking about seeing Lando ever since Pamila had told her that he would be coming home for the weekend, she couldn't wait to see him.

Mann walked in the front door and saw Tyesha sitting at the dining room table drawing on a big drawing pad. Seeing Mann, she jumped down from the table and ran into his open arms.

"What's up shorty?" Mann asked as he laughed at the child's joy of seeing him. Tyesha kissed Mann and led him over to the table to show him her picture.

Pointing at the colorful drawing, Tyesha said, "Look dat's Lando when he come home dis weekend." Mann smiled at Tyesha as he picked her up and looked at the picture she had drew of her, Pamila, Mann, and Lando. Mann could tell that the love that the little girl felt for Lando was more than just a love from cousin to cousin, it was a love from sister to brother and Mann was pleased by the whole situation.

Pamila came down stairs to see who had come in the house and saw Mann holding Tyesha in his arms.

"Black called here for you a few minutes ago. He wants to know if you gave something to his girl for him," Pamila said.

"Yeah I did dat already," Mann said. Walking over to the table to look at the picture that Tyesha had been working on since she had been home from school, Pamila told her that it was lovely and that Lando was going to love it.

Looking at Mann, Pamila said, "You know Lando and Quick are coming home for a weekend visit this Friday. I won't be home from work by the time they are supposed to be picked up from the Receiving Home so you gotta do it." Mann had no problem with that. In fact, he couldn't wait to see his brother and Quick himself. Pamila told Mann to talk to the two younger boys and to encourage them to do right. Mann told her that he would do just that and then went downstairs to call Black's girlfriend.

Black had met a beautiful young lady named Mia while he was locked up this time around. Mia was a 19-year old law student at Georgetown University. Black had been trying to get legal advice about an issue on his armed robbery case and had written a letter to the legal department at the school. Mia saw legal errors in Black's case and decided to help him. She began to go see him on legal visits in order to get a better understanding of the case and quickly became infatuated with Black's style. After Black's appeal for a new trial was denied, Mia was already in love with Black and began to come see him every visiting day down Youth Center and was now talking about marriage.

"Hello?" Mia said into the phone in her tiny voice.

"What's up Mia? Dis Mann."

"Hi Mann."

"What's up, did Black see da board today?"

"Yeah he did. He said he should know what they gonna do in about a month or so. I pray that they let him go, I want him here with me," Mia said full of warmth. Mann thought of how he knew Black would act when he hit the streets and wondered if Mia would be able to deal with his madness, even so Mann knew that Black thought that he was in love as well so however things went would be up to him.

"Check dis out Mia," Mann said, "tell Black I'll be down there to see 'em first thing next week...."

"I'm suppose to go down there next week," Mia said feeling like Mann was taking her time away from seeing her man. Mann laughed, he understood what was up with Mia so he told her that they could go together, he just wanted her to tell Black that he had the new shoes that he wanted and that he would wear them down Youth Center when he came. Mia was cool with that arrangement and told Mann that she would tell Black what he said tonight when she went to see him. Mann got off the phone thinking about the sweet girl that Black had in his corner as he went to pick some coke up from Silk.

Sitting around the conference table in the back office of Mann's World, Silk, Rick, Mann, and Dre worked on the taxes for Mann's World and Silky's Barber Shop. Rick was a financial genius, he made sure that Mann and Silk had the revenue books straight, while showing them how to pull all of their drug money into play with their business money.

After they had taken care of all business, Mann leaned back in his chair and stretched saying, "Another day at the office." Everybody laughed.

"I see you like the business world, huh?" Silk said to Mann.

"It's more like I like working for myself," Mann said.

Dre looked at his watch and said, "It's almost time to go get Lando and Quick, ain't it?" Mann slid his chair back and told everybody that he had to leave to go get Lando. Silk asked Mann to bring Lando and Quick to see him before they went back down Oak Hill. Mann told him that he would try, but he didn't think that Pamila would let them out of her sight. Silk understood. Mann and Dre shook Rick's hand and hit the streets to go get Lando and Quick.

Impatiently waiting for Mann to show up with Lando and Quick, Pamila stood at the living room window talking to Kelley on the cordless phone.

"I know you can't wait to see dem two little rough necks."

"I'm standing here looking out of the window right now waiting for them to pull up. I just pray that they stay out of trouble this time," Pamila said. It was nothing more she wanted than for Lando and Quick to just live their young lives outside of a detention center. She stressed this over and over in many conversations with Kelley and Kelley could feel her pain every step of the way. As they talked for a few more minutes, Pamila saw Mann's gold Range Rover pulling up with Lando and Quick in the backseat.

"They outside right now!" Pamila said, full of excitement.

Pamila passed Mann the phone as she stepped around Dre and opened up her arms to hug Lando and Quick. She couldn't believe that they were standing inside the living room.

"I don't want no shit outta y'all, you hear me," Pamila said.

"You ain't gon have no problems out of us," Lando said as he smiled at Pamila. "Dat goes for your little behind too!" Pamila said as she looked at Quick.

"You ain't gotta worry about me Pamila, I'm chillin'," Quick said.

Tyesha heard all of the excitement going on downstairs and came running down the steps to see if Lando was home. At the bottom of the steps she saw Lando and Quick standing in front of Pamila.

With her drawing, she ran over to Lando and said, "I made dis for you." Lando picked Tyesha up in his arms and began to look at the picture asking Tyesha who was who. She told Lando who was in the picture and Lando began to tell her that Quick would be living with them from now on. The loving child told Lando put her down so she could go and put Quick into her drawing. As Tyesha ran up the steps to fix her family picture, Lando and Quick sat down on the sofa beside Dre and Mann and listened to Pamila talk about how they didn't have to sell drugs and run the streets anymore. They assured Pamila that she didn't have to worry about them at all.

By 11:00am the next day, Mann had taken Lando and Quick shopping and they were now fresh again. They had grown a lot while they were locked up. Quick had gotten tall and slim while Lando had gotten just a little taller and very thick from weight lifting. They both had let their hair grow long and they kept it in cornrows. Over all, they were no longer little boys anymore, they were now young men.

After talking Dre into letting him keep his Corvette for the night, Lando was flying down Georgia Avenue with Quick in the passenger seat on their way over Jazmin's house. Quick leaned over and picked up a Geto Boys CD and slapped it into the CD player. Lando rolled down the window to let the cool night air into the car as the music began to blast through the speeding car.

"It feel good as shit to be back on da streets young," Lando said to Quick as he pulled up in front of Jazmin's apartment building.

"No bullshit!" Quick said as Lando cut the car off and got out.

Lando kept his home visit a secret from Jazmin in order to catch her off guard. Standing at her door in a grey Polo sweatshirt, Lando couldn't wait for her to open the door. He wanted her to see how serious he was about her being the first female to see him when he hit the streets. Even though he still had deep feelings for Nakia being as though she played fair with him while he was locked up, Jazmin still lived inside of his heart one way or another.

"Lando!" Jazmin screamed as she hugged him tightly after opening her door. "When did you get out?" Taking a step back from Jazmin, while still holding her in his arms, Lando took in the beautiful sight of the young woman.

"I'm on a home visit. I gotta go back down Oak Hill Sunday night," Lando said as he smiled uncontrollably.

Hugging Lando again, Jazmin said, "I can't believe you home, boy!" Lando was pleased that Jazmin was so happy to see him. They stood out in the hallway and talked for about 15 minutes before Quick popped up.

Walking up on Lando and Jazmin, Quick couldn't believe how much of a woman Jazmin had grown into while he and Lando were gone. In a pair of tight blue jeans and a Madness T-shirt standing in the hallway with no shoes on, Jazmin looked beautiful.

"What's up Jazmin?" Quick said.

Jazmin looked at him and said, "Hi Quick." She walked over and hugged him saying, "Are you 2 going to stay out of trouble now dat y'all coming home on home visits?" Quick laughed and let Jazmin know that he planned on staying home, but that he was going to be himself, which worried her a little but she knew that Quick was always going to be himself. She then asked Lando the same question.

Thinking about what the truth was and what Jazmin wanted to hear, Lando said, "I'ma do my best to stay out. I ain't as wild as I was 2 years ago. You ain't gotta worry about me." Jazmin was pleased with the way Lando had responded to her. She could tell that he had grown up a lot while he was gone. Jazmin stayed in the hallway talking to Lando and Quick for about an hour before telling them that she had to go out of town for the weekend with her mother but she would be able to hang out with them next time they came home on the weekend. Lando hugged Jazmin and kissed her on the cheek before he headed back to the Corvette with Quick.

Their next stop was Rittenhouse Street. They had to roll through the hood to see how Lil' Garvin and Baby-D were doing since they had been hearing so much about them.

Pulling up in front of Old Tima's house in Dre's turquoise, tinted-window convertible ZR1, Lando and Quick were taken off guard by the crew of new young dudes that were pushing coke on the block, but they were even more bothered by the way they ran up to the car thinking Dre was in it. A tall new young dude walked up and tapped on the passenger side window.

Quick rolled the window down and said, "Da fuck is up shorty?" The young dude was a little shook when he saw Quick because he didn't know his face.

"Where Dre at?" the young dude asked, becoming very uneasy now. The rest of his little crew began to walk up to stand beside him. Lando had flashbacks of when he and Quick were just like them.

One of the young dudes that had walked up with the crowd said to the taller one who had tapped on the window, "Ah Tank, who da fuck is dem niggaz?" Tank said over his shoulder without taking his eyes off of the car, "I don't know young." As the scene became more and more heated, Lando tried to take control of the situation by telling the young dudes who he was and that he was looking for Lil' Garvin and Baby-D.

"Oh, you Lando?" Tank said, "So you must be Quick then," he said as he looked at Quick. Rubbed the wrong way and feeling a little forgotten, Quick shook his head yeah. Tank reached out to give Quick five as he told everyone to back up. Quick gave him five as Tank told them that Lil' Garvin and Baby-D were up Georgia Avenue.

On their way up Georgia Avenue, Quick expressed his displeasure with the whole situation that had just took place. "You can't be fucked up at dem young niggaz joe. We was just like dat when we was they age," Lando said as he laughed at the whole situation.

"Fuck dat! You see how dem young punk ass niggaz walked up on us when we was talkin' to da young dude Tank," Quick said. Lando saw the anger in Quick's face and knew where his mind was already. Lando began to remind Quick of all the wild shit that they had done coming up and what they would have done if some niggaz had pulled up on them like that.

"Look joe!" Lando said." Dem young niggaz most likely hustle for Dre or Lil' Garvin and dem. Don't trip off dat shit joe. We just hit da streets." Quick thought about what Lando had said and took it to heart, he knew that Lando was starting to become more of a thinker now.

Georgia Avenue was packed tonight; people were everywhere and doing everything from shooting dice to pushing crack rock. Quick spotted Baby-D standing by a group of young females and told Lando to pull up and park in the parking lot.

Baby-D spotted Dre's Corvette pulling into the parking lot and began walking over to it as it parked. The driver side door flew open and he saw Lando step out looking like a running back for a NFL Team. Baby-D couldn't believe his eyes. Quick added to his excitement by getting out of the car on the other side.

"I can't believe y'all niggaz out joe," Baby-D said as he sat on the hood of Dre's car with Lando and Quick, after showing his love.

"Yeah, we only out for the weekend," Lando said as he began to explain how he and Quick had to do a few home visits before they were done with their juvenile commitments.

"Damn young, y'all 'bout to come home, Black 'bout to come home. Everybody gon be out by da summer," Baby-D said full of excitement.

"So where Lil' Garvin at?" Lando asked, as he looked over at the young females that were sitting on the black BMW 850i that Baby D was standing by.

"He went to get some Backwoods so we can smoke weed wit dese bitches we met earlier," Baby-D said.

"Dem bitches right there?" Quick said as he pointed to the crowd of females. Baby-D told them they were all trying to go to the hotel and that he and Lil' Garvin were going to take their little man Tank and some of his little men with them, but now that they were on the scene it was only right that they go.

Dressed in an all black Versace sweat suit, Lil' Garvin walked up on the three of them talking. "What da fuck is going on out here?" Lil' Garvin said out loud as he smacked hands with Lando and Quick. They got up off the hood of the car and hugged him, they could tell that Lil' Garvin and Baby-D missed them. After talking for a little while Lil Garvin asked his two partners if they had been high since they had been out. They told him that they were trying to do that now. Lil' Garvin told them to follow him down 5th Street where his van was and that they would hit the hotel from there.

Starting up the Corvette, Lando saw Lil' Garvin, Baby-D, and three of the young females get into the black BMW 850i.

"Damn, I know dat ain't slim's joint," Lando said as he pulled off behind it.

"Shit!" Quick said, "they say him and da Baby gettin' dat cash. It might be his." Shaking his head in approval, Lando said, "We gotta get out here and get dis cash joe."

"You right," Quick said as they followed behind the BMW down Rittenhouse Street.

Once inside Lil' Garvin's huge family size van with Baby-D and the three females, Baby-D began to light Backwoods and pass them around while Lil' Garvin began to put Lando and Quick down with the way things were going around the way.

"Shit ain't da same no more young," Lil' Garvin said as he took a deep pull on the Backwood and told the females to go sit in the back of the van for a minute.

"Me and da Baby got shit locked out here. We getting 6 to 7 bricks a week from Dre. Shit is pumpin' around da way. We got da young dude Tank and his lil' crew flippin' da shit like hotcakes left and right..."

"Yeah joe dat ain't shit, Baby-D got da twin turbo joint, we doing da muthafucka out here. We just waitin' for y'all and Black to come home," Lil' Garvin said as they pulled up in front of the Super 8 Motel.

As they all got out and went into the hotel, all Lando could think about was coming home to get him some cash. He was ready and had his mind right, but right now he was trying to get him some pussy.

At 12:00pm the next day, the phone rang in the hotel room and woke Lando up. Lil' Garvin woke up and answered the phone. Looking over at Lando after a long night of fucking, Lil' Garvin said, "It's check out time joe." Lando looked around at the room of sexy naked young females and all he could think about was how Pamila was going to be beefin' about how he and Quick didn't call home last night. He decided that he would deal with it when he got home. Meanwhile he woke Quick and Baby-D up so they could smoke an early mid-day Backwood of weed before they dropped the females off.

Pamila was flaming with anger when Lando and Quick walked in the house at 4:00pm that afternoon. She wasn't really upset that they had been running the streets all night, she was more upset that they didn't call and let her know that they wouldn't be coming home. She hated worrying and that is just what she had been doing all night. She began scolding them as soon as they walked in the door.

"What kind of camp do you muthafuckas think I'm running here? I'ma let you little muthafuckas know this right now. If y'all think y'all gonna come back out here with that same wild shit y'all were doing two years ago, y'all asses won't be staying in my house!" Lando and Quick sat on the sofa and listened to Pamila vent her anger without saying word. After about 20 minutes, Pamila cooled down a little bit. She told the two young men, that she knew that they were older now, but as long as they lived in her house they would have to play by her rules and there were no exceptions to that at all. When she was done talking, she told them to go take a shower so that she could take them out to eat with her and Tyesha.

Later on that night, Lando decided that he had to go see Nakia. This time he got Mann's 1992 Nissan 300ZX Twin Turbo. After dropping Quick off downtown over his cousin Wee-Wee's house, Lando shot out Silver Spring, Maryland to see what was up with Nakia.

Stepping out of the shiny silver car, Lando not only felt like a big boy, but he felt free. Waiting for Nakia to open the door all he could think about was how he was going to get rich as soon as he was done with his juvenile commitment.

Nakia opened the door as her mouth fell to the ground when she saw Lando in a slick Hugo Boss leather jacket with his hair in fresh cornrows that he had gotten one of the females to do last night. Rubbing her hand over Lando's silky hair, still in shock, Nakia said, "Boy you look so good. Come in."

Upstairs in Nakia bedroom, they talked for a while about how things could, should, and would be now that he was going to be home in a few weeks. The more Lando looked at Nakia in her nightgown, he could see how much he had been missing while he was locked up. Even though she came to see him at least 2 or 3 times a month, it was always with Pamila. He hadn't been this close to her alone since he was on the run two years ago. He was still in love with her after all of that time. Lando's mind was made up; he wanted his childhood love back.

Eyone Williams

"Lando," Nakia said, "I still want you. I prayed that you would come home every night while you were gone and you're here. I want you all to myself." Lando thought about where Nakia wanted to take their relationship and he had no problem with it but he learned to leave a little up to the imagination while he was away.

Grabbing her into his arms, while not playing too big, Lando said, "Let's see where things take us. You know how much I love you boo." Lando leaned over and kissed Nakia in the mouth while laying her back on her bed. Nakia could feel her whole body heat up as she thought of what was about to take place.

"I waited for this for so long," she said as she began to let Lando pull her nightgown up. In seconds, they were deeply intertwined in a heap of love making that neither one would ever be able to forget.

Just after 2:00am Lando was back in Mann's Twin Turbo on his car phone with Pamila telling her that he was going to be in the house late tonight because he was going to the Black Hole with Quick. She told him to make sure that he and Quick didn't get into any trouble and that she would see them in the morning. It felt good to be on good terms with Pamila for once, Lando thought as he began to dial Wee-Wee's car phone number to see if he and Quick were going to meet him at the go-go.

"Hello?" Wee-Wee said in his little kid voice, with Rare Essence blasting out of his car speakers. Lando could tell by his voice that he was smoking weed.

"What's up joe? I'm on my way down da Hole. Y'all gon meet me there?" Lando said as he flew down Georgia Avenue at 60mph.

"Yeah shorty, we on our way up there now joe," Wee-Wee said. Lando told Wee-Wee that he would see him down there and told him to put Quick on the phone.

"What's up nigga?" Quick said sounding like he was having the time of his life hanging out with his big cousin Wee-Wee while he was on his home visit. Lando told him that he talked to Pamila and that she was cool with them hanging out for the night and that he would talk to him when he got down the Black Hole. Lando hung up the phone and began thinking about Nakia as he continued racing down the Avenue in the Twin Turbo.

Coming through the door of the Black Hole dressed to impress, Lando saw people from all over town, some he knew from down Oak Hill and some from the streets. Making his way through the crowd, he was already feeling the loud music of the Back Yard Band and you could see it in his step. Looking over to his right, Lando saw Mann, Dre, Silk, and the New York dude Supreme that he had heard about a few times. Lando made his way over to the group of older dudes as they all embraced him as if he was a movie star of some kind.

"You stayin' outta trouble shorty?" Silk asked as he pulled out a knot of $100 dollar bills and gave Lando a few. Lando told him that he was just having a little fun for the weekend and that he didn't plan on getting into any shit while he was out. Everybody laughed at how much he had grown up while he was gone. Dre pulled out a knot of cash and handed it to Lando as he hugged him and told him to stay cool. Mann told everybody that he would be right back as he walked away from the table with his little brother.

Standing by the restroom, Mann told Lando that he was fucked up that he had been home all weekend and that they ain't even hang out together yet.

"It ain't like dat joe. You my nigga slim. I just been gettin' some fresh air Mann. We gon hang out all day tomorrow. Okay?" Lando asked as he smiled at Mann.

"I'ma hold you to that," Mann said, "Go ahead and have some fun shorty. I saw Lil' Garvin and dem young niggaz come in a while ago, they in here somewhere."

"You seen Quick and dem."

"Yeah, he came in wit Wee-Wee and dem a while ago too," Mann said.

Giving Mann five, Lando said, "I'ma see you in da morning, pick me up over Pamila's house."

"Cool, I'll call you before I come, and don't let nothin' happen to my car," Mann said.

Lando made his way to the dance floor, bobbing his head to the thumping music. All the way up front by the stage he saw Wee-Wee, Quick, and about 30 V Street niggaz, Quick was right in the mix with them. Spotting Lil' Garvin and Baby-D leaning against the wall with Tank and his crew of young niggaz, Lando walked over.

"What's up nigga?" Baby-D said as he puffed on a blunt.

Looking around at all of the young dudes that they had with them, Lando said, "Ain't shit joe. Let me hit dat smoke." As Lando began to hit the blunt Lil' Garvin introduced a few of the young dudes to him, Tank being the first.

"Dese my niggaz right here Lando," Lil' Garvin said as he pointed at the crew of five.

"I met shorty right there already, I like 'em," Lando said as he looked at the tall brown skinned one they called Tank. Not getting too friendly with the young dudes, Lando got to know them and then made his way up front.

A group of healthy body young women caught Lando's eye, as he made his way up front to where Quick and Wee-Wee were. "Hey boo!" A female voice said as someone hugged Lando from behind. Not knowing whom it was, Lando snatched away and quickly turned around to see Kisha and a group of new broads.

"I heard you was home, why you ain't let me know?" Kisha said. Seeing Kisha's face made Lando think about Onion and he had to hide his feelings.

"I jive been on the move," He said, as he looked at how good Kisha was looking.

"Well go ahead and do your thing," Kisha said as she licked her thick shiny lips, "I might have a welcome home present for you." Lando smiled as he continued on his way up front.

"What's up joe?" Lando said to Quick once he made it up front. The music of the go-go band was so loud now that Quick really couldn't hear him.

"I said what's up?" Lando screamed. Quick told him that he was chillin' and that he was high as shit. "Me too," Lando said as he smiled at his partner.

"Check dis out," Quick said as he told Lando that he had ran into Ant's brother Jammie while he was downtown.

"Oh, yeah?" Lando said. Quick said that he was hanging down by 7th and N Street now and that when he saw him he started acting scared as shit.

"Fuck dat nigga!" Lando said, not even thinking about the punk. While they were talking, Lando noticed Wee-Wee and a big fat dude in each other's face. "What's up wit Wee?" Lando asked. By the time Quick turned around it was a circle forming around the two dudes. Everybody that was with Wee-Wee was getting behind him and everybody that was with the fat dude was getting behind him. Suddenly, the music stopped playing and Big G from the Back Yard Band was calling for security to clear the floor.

Wee-Wee whipped a long shiny butterfly knife out and started swinging at the fat dude, stabbing him in the neck. The two different crowds of dudes charged each other. Lando and Quick went with the flow and started swinging punches. In seconds, the floor was covered with blood and everyone was running for the doors.

Outside it was complete pandemonium; people running and screaming, police everywhere, car tires screaming. Lando made sure that he ran to Mann's Twin Turbo with his head low, he knew gunfire was about to hit the late night air. Unlocking the car door, Lando quickly looked around for anybody he knew, but with people running every which way he couldn't make anyone out. Starting up the car and shooting out on to Georgia Avenue, Lando heard the inevitable. Automatic gunfire hit the air in three quick successions followed by the sound of breaking glass and a loud car crash. Somebody was dead for sure and Lando knew it as he went flying uptown in a flash of light.

Rolling over on the sofa in Pamila's basement the next morning, Lando saw Quick stretched out on the floor knocked out. He was glad to see him. Walking over to Quick, Lando began to shake him.

Wiping the sleep out of his eyes, Quick said, "What's up joe?" Lando asked him when did he come in the house. Quick told him that Wee-Wee dropped him off about 4:45am. Lando then asked if anybody they knew got shot last night. Rolling over to sit straight up, Quick told Lando that Wee-Wee and two other dudes that were in the truck with them had pulled up beside the dudes car that they were beefin' with last night and unloaded on it with an AK-47.

"Dem niggaz smashed right into the wall of the Black!" Quick said. Quick finished telling Lando about the shooting and who got shot.

While they were talking, Tyesha came downstairs with her drawing and ran over to Quick saying, "I got you in da picture now." Quick smiled and hugged Tyesha asking her if he could have the picture. She told him yes as she laughed.

Turning to Lando, Tyesha said, "Mann called here a few minutes ago. He said he on his way to get you and Quick." As Tyesha went back upstairs with Pamila, Lando and Quick got themselves together.

Shit gon be sweet for y'all joe," Mann said as he talked to Lando and Quick while they sat in the back of his Range Rover on their way out Silver Spring to see his recording studio. "I'ma make sure y'all be okay as long as I live joe, y'all know what's mines is yours," Mann said as he pulled up in front of what looked like a garage.

After walking around to the back they went inside and things looked much different. Lando and Quick saw that Mann wasn't bullshitting at all. The studio was more put together than they thought. Mann had 4 different recording studios full of equipment and padded walls.

Taking them upstairs into an already furnished office that over looked all four studios, Mann said, "Dis shit here gon make money and y'all gon be a part of it." Lando and Quick listened as Mann gave them the run down on his plan for the recording studio. He told them how he had gotten the idea from Supreme and ran with it and that the studio would be open by the summer time. He already had two white boys that knew how to work all of the equipment that would be running things when the spot first opened for business. Quick and Lando were amazed once again by Mann's ability to think his way through the streets.

After Mann gave them a tour of the studio, he took them shopping again and then they went to the movies. The whole time Mann had the two younger dudes with him, he was telling them how things would be as long as they stayed out of trouble when they came home. He knew they were not going to stop running the streets, but he wanted them to at least think for the future. They seemed to take everything to heart.

When the movie let out Mann took them way out Maryland over Silk's house. They had never been there before and the sight of the huge gate that they had to go through to get to the main house was something they had only seen on TV.

"You see dis shit here?" Mann said as he drove up to the house, "All dis kinda shit gon be y'alls when da time is right joe, but you gotta want it and the only way to get it is with clean money." Quick was really feeling Mann's big money talk but he couldn't see how he and Lando were going to do it.

"How we suppose to get money like dis joe," Quick asked. Mann laughed and told him that he was going to show him.

A maid opened the door and led them back to the entertainment room where Silk was playing video games with his son. "Well, well, look what we have here," he said as he offered them a seat. Mann, Lando, and Quick sat down while the maid brought them all something to drink. Silk began to talk to Lando and Quick about what they planned to do when they were out. They really had no plan. They just wanted to get out first. Silk could feel where they were coming from. They all sat down and listened to Silk talk for a while before leaving. It was the first time Lando and Quick had ever felt close to Silk, being as though he always played things by ear and never on the scene.

As the time grew near for Lando and Quick to go back down Oak Hill, they sat in Mann's Range Rover laughing and joking in front of Pamila's house. Everybody seemed to be out front as the nightfall grew over the DC streets. Dre, his son, Mann, Tina, Kisha, Lil' Garvin, and Baby-D all stood around the truck spending the last little bit of time with Lando and Quick before they had to leave. A gray Volvo pulled up beside Mann's truck. Lando looked over to see who it was. A huge smile grew across his face when he saw Jazmin in the passenger seat of her mother's car.

As Lando walked down the street alone with Jazmin, leaving the crowd of people behind, they spent his last few free minutes talking about how their friendship was something that was very important. Jazmin expressed her feelings for Lando. She was attracted to him, but she felt that if they took their friendship to another level that it may hurt it if their relationship didn't work out. Lando grabbed Jazmin's hand and looked her in the eyes as they stopped walking. Lando felt nothing but love for the extremely beautiful young woman as he said, "Your friendship means more to me then anything boo. I love what we have just as it is, and I'm cool with us being friends." Lando's words hit Jazmin in the heart and she knew that she would always have a friend in Lando. She kissed him on the lips and told him that she wanted to hang out with him when he came home next weekend. Lando hugged her and let her go as she ran back up the street and got in her mother's car.

By the time Lando walked back up the street, Pamila was outside running everybody away for making too much noise. "It's time to go," Pamila said, standing on the porch beside Tyesha. Lando and Quick spread their love as they told everybody that they would see them next week. Dre passed Quick a sandwich bag of weed, making sure Pamila didn't see him, while Baby-D passed Lando one as well. Their first home visit had now first home visit had now come to an end and they reluctantly told everybody that they would see them next week.

14

Black was now in the 1010 halfway house downtown. Mann had him on paper as having a job at Mann's World so that he could get out from 8:00am until 8:00pm, Monday through Friday. Black actually did a little bit of work while he was in the store. All he had to do was keep a job for 30 days and he was good to go as long as he checked in with his parole officer once a week. Black felt as though he could deal with that.

Lando and Quick were home now as well. They were trying their best to get back on their feet. Mann gave Lando and Quick a brick each when they first hit the streets for good a month ago after weeks of successful home visits. They were now buying 2 bricks each and stacking cash like they had never been gone. Mann gave Lando his 1992 Nissan 300 ZX Twin Turbo. Quick hustled up a 1992 red Chevy Suburban and put shiny chrome Hammer rims on it along with huge tires. They were right back in the fast lane with no problem and living in Pamila's basement on good terms with her. Things were smooth for them by far.

Kelley was now home for the summer and staying with Mann at his new apartment in Landover, Maryland. Mann gave her a job working with Kisha and Naomi. She didn't need to work, but she felt better about herself by doing so.

Smoke and Serge were starting to come back around the way now that Black was back on the streets, but they were still up to their same old ways just looking for a caper here and there but not making any real cash. Lando was selling them quarter bricks for $5,000. They were trying their best but it just wasn't in the script for them to be paid unless they robbed for it so that's what they did.

The bright summer sun was shining off of Lando's silver Twin Turbo as he slowed down in front of Old Tima's house to talk to Tank for a second. Lando was trying to find a little dude that ran with Tank that owed him some money. Because Lando had taken a liking to all of the younger dudes, he dealt with them more. Quick, on the other hand, still had a hard time dealing with them, though he was getting better.

"What's up joe?" Tank said as he walked up on Lando's car while keeping his eye on everything moving since he and the rest of the younger dudes were beefin' with some young dudes from across town.

Smoking a fat blunt of weed, Lando turned down his blasting Geto Boys CD and said, "Where Lil' Mo at?"

"I ain't seen him since last night." Tank told Lando as he began to tell him that the little dude had lost all of the coke Lando had gave him running from the police about a week ago.

"Tell shorty, I ain't fucked up at him. Tell 'em I said holla at me, he ain't gotta duck me," Lando said.

Mann and Dre pulled up beside Lando in Dre's Corvette ZR1. "What's up shorty?" Mann said sitting in the passenger seat.

Lando reached over and gave his brother "5" as he said, "Where y'all on y'all way to?" Mann told Lando that he and Dre were on their way out to the studio to see how a female singing group sounded.

"I'ma be out there later," Lando said. Dre told Lando to stay out of trouble as he pulled off.

"You tryin' to roll wit me?" Lando asked Tank.

Tank got in the car and said, "Where we going joe?"

As Lando passed the young dude the blunt that he was smoking, he said, "We going horseback riding." Lando pulled off and headed for Nakia's house to pick her and her buddy Trina up.

Mann's World was busy. Young people came in and out buying clothes and tennis shoes all day while they shook their heads to the music that played throughout the store. Black sat in the back office on the phone with Mia who was fussing about him not coming to see her yesterday before he went back to the halfway house.

"I told you I got caught up boo. Why we gotta keep going through the same ole shit?" Black said into the phone while he watched Rap City on BET.

"I love you, that's why Black. Why can't you understand that?" Mia said in her sweet voice. She always got Black with it. He couldn't see himself taking her for bad after she had done time with him.

"I'll be over your house before I go back to the halfway house," Black said. Mia was happy, she didn't ask for much. Hanging up the phone with her, Black leaned back in his chair. Kisha came into the office and said, "Quick and dem out front waiting for you." Black got up and went outside.

Jumping into the huge Suburban with Quick, Baby-D, and Lil' Garvin, Black felt at home as they pulled off.

"You still ain't smoking no weed?" Quick said from behind the wheel of the big truck. Black let them know that he wasn't smoking until he was out of the halfway house. Baby-D laughed as he took a deep pull of the weed and blew it into the air.

"We bout to go shoot some ball joe," Quick said as he flew down Georgia Avenue.

"I need y'all to take me down Mia's house joe," Black said. Quick headed in that direction.

Black knocked on Mia's door as Quick took his huge truck roaring down the street. Mia opened the door and jumped into Black's arms.

"What's up boo?" Black said as he carried her into the house, kicking the door shut behind him. Sitting down on the sofa with Mia, Black asked her where her father was. Black couldn't stand him and Black knew the feelings were mutual. Mia's father always tried to come between the two of them, he swore Black was a street thug and would never be anything. Mia didn't give a damn what he thought and her actions showed it.

"My father ain't here boo. Let's go upstairs," she said as she took Black's hand and led the way to her bedroom.

Black watched as Mia slowly and seductively undressed in front of him. "Good girl gone bad!" Black said as he licked his lips and rubbed his hands up and down Mia's smooth body.

"Who said I was ever a good girl?" The beautiful dark skinned girl said as she pushed Black down on the bed and jumped on top of him with no clothes on.

Undressing her man, Mia said, "I got you all to myself now boo. I'ma enjoy myself today, I deserve it." Throwing Black's clothes to the floor, Mia raised up and sat right on top of Black as she slid him inside of her thin but sexy body. She began to slowly slide up and down while scratching Black's chest with her nails and swinging her long hair into the air like a wild woman.

Mann, Dre, and Silk sat in the office of Mann's studio that overlooked the four studios. Through the tinted window, they looked down on the three beautiful young girls that were paying $80 an hour for studio time. The girls called themselves PASSION, which is just what they filled anyone with that listened to them sing their songs of love and heartbreak. Cherry, the lead singer of the group, had been putting up the money for their studio time. Mann took a liking to anyone who followed their dreams, so he gave her the $80 deal while everyone else paid $100 to $120 for studio time. The other two girls, Chocolate and Caramel were both committed to one day finding a record deal somewhere. All of their talks about a big record deal, made Mann think of bigger and better things as he faithfully came to hear their studio sessions.

"Dem girls sound good as shit slim," Mann said as he shook his head to the sound of one of PASSION's better songs. Silk was feeling the song as well. He began to tell Mann how Supreme kept telling him how he had a record label in New York that he was trying to get started. Right now, he had a few rap groups that he was trying to put out, but so many people thought that they could rap these days that it made it hard to put them out.

"Dese broads can get a deal from one of dem big labels if somebody get behind dem," Dre said. Mann had an idea now.

Cherry took off her headphones and told the recording engineer to kill the beat when she saw Mann waving at her through the door. Dressed in a black Versace body suit that showed off every inch of her thick body, Cherry walked out into the hallway to see what Mann wanted. Mann smiled at the cute light skinned, almost pink young woman as she shut the studio door behind her.

"What's up Mann?" Cherry asked. She knew it had to be important because Mann never came down to the studio while people were recording on their own money.

"What kind of moves are y'all making with your music?" Mann asked sounding inspired. Cherry let him know that her and the other girls were just making tapes and sending them out to big record labels but none of them had got back at them yet and lately they were just doing it because they loved it.

"What would you think about me managing your group?" Mann asked. Cherry smiled, she loved the idea but she had no idea what kind of money Mann had and what he could do when he put his mind to it. Everybody that had ever heard her group sing had stepped to her with the same idea but nothing had ever happened and her and the girls really didn't believe in the manager thing anymore.

"I gotta ask the others and see what they have to say," Cherry said.

"Well let's call them out here and see what they have to say," Mann said. His mind was made up and it was no way that a person could turn him down when he got this way.

Cherry called Chocolate and Caramel out into the hallway and gave them the run down on the deal Mann had just offered her. Caramel, a light brown skinned cute young woman who was tall and thick in the thighs, was all for the idea. In fact, she was for just about anything that Mann had to offer. Chocolate on the other hand respected Mann a lot and would have even given him some play if he would have ever tried his hand, but she was no nonsense when it came to her music.

She crossed her arms and said, "I'm cool wit dat Mann, but what's in it for us. Everybody always step to us wit dese great ideas but we always end up right where we started, right here in da city singing to ourselves." Mann respected where she was coming from and was ready for her reaction. He knew she was the only one that would have any real questions. Mann let her know that he would set aside a studio just for them that they would use for free everyday of the week, he would also begin working on getting them a few shows somewhere. The girls were pleased with the sound of things, but Chocolate thought that things sounded a little too good.

"What's in it for you?" she asked sounding very suspicious. Mann rubbed his hand on her shoulder and smiled while letting her know that all he wanted was a little money on the side, which he would put in writing for them later. Right now everything would be free and if they didn't like the way things played out in the end then they would owe nothing because they won't have to sign anything until they see some kind of money. In the end, if it were all a waste of time they would have had their chance to show the music world that they could sing. The young women agreed and went back into the studio very excited.

Days later in the alley behind Old Tima's house, Smoke and Serge were in the shadows of darkness wearing ski masks with their pistols in their hands, creeping through the cut. Looking out onto Rittenhouse Street they could see all of the younger dudes standing on the sidewalk. They were easy prey as long as they never saw what was coming.

In a flash, Smoke and Serge shot out of the shadows and laid everybody down. Tank acted like he wanted to buck, but Smoke put his .357 magnum to the back of his head and said, "Act like you want it!"

Eyone Williams

Taking money, drugs, jewelry, and 4 pistols, Smoke and Serge ran off into the night. They were too slick for the younger dudes. Even though they had gotten away with the robbery, Smoke and Serge knew that they couldn't let anyone know about it, not even Black. They would have to keep this one under their hat.

Lando and Quick pulled up in Quick's big red Suburban blasting N.W.A.'s 'Niggaz 4 Life' just a few minutes after the robbery. They could tell something was wrong so they got out and walked over where the younger dudes were. They were talking about who could have robbed them when Lando and Quick walked up.

"What da fuck is up?" Lando said to Tank who looked like his face was on fire. Tank told him that they had just been robbed.

Lando looked around as if to see if there was any trace of the recent stick up boys as he said, "Y'all don't know who it was?" Tank shook his head no. All he could think about was the $5000 that he lost in the robbery, his mind was set on getting it back tonight one way or another.

"I ain't gon sit around here and look stupid, fuck dat. Let's roll out," Tank said to his little crew as they all got up.

"What you 'bout to do?" Lando asked with a little smirk on his face.

"We going on a caper," Tank said as he and the rest of the young dudes jumped into Lil' Garvin's huge van, that Tank was driving.

Standing in front of the drugstore on Georgia Avenue, along with Lil' Garvin, Baby-D, Quick, and a few other dudes that all slung coke on the Ave., Lando carefully served a pipehead four 50 rocks for $150.

Walking back over to the phone booth where everybody was, Lando said to Quick, "Light some of dat shit up." Quick took a fat blunt from behind his ear and lit it while Lando began talking to Lil' Garvin about the robbery that had just taken place down 5th Street.

"Dem young niggaz gon kill some shit if they find out who did dat shit," Baby-D said as he opened the door to his red 1992 Twin Turbo that was parked right in front of them. Sliding his pistol and his bag of 50 rocks under the seat, he shut the door just in time.

Hall and his gang of vice cops came flying around the corner and into the mini mall parking lot. Quick threw the blunt that he had in his mouth and took off running. He was too fast. The "jump-outs" didn't even bother to chase him. They jumped out and put Lando, Baby-D, Lil' Garvin, and the rest of the dudes against the wall.

While the other vice cops were searching everybody else, Hall took pleasure in harassing Lando.

"Well, I guess you are the big boy on the block," Hall said. Lando knew Hall had only gotten hotter with time. He didn't even respond to his statement, Lando knew that his coke was stashed away in his car. He just waited for Hall to finish doing his thing so that he could go ahead and finish pushing the rest of his coke for the night.

When Hall and the "jump-outs" were done shaking them down, Hall leaned over and whispered in Lando's ear, "I'm watchin' you. Let me catch you wrong and it's no more Oak Hill for you. No more 2 years. Kill somebody now and your lil' ass is going to the big house."

As Hall and his gang of vice cops left, Lando thought about what he had said to him. Lando hadn't shot a pistol in over 2 years. He wasn't even thinking about killing anything. It was all about the money now. Lando had no plans of running wild anymore. If he was to blast a nigga nowadays, it would be because somebody jumped way out of bounds.

A pipehead walked up on Lando while he was still in a daze of thought and said, "I got a ball, let me get two of dem 50's." Lando walked him to his car and served him. Dollars made sense now.

Quick had a .44 magnum on him along with a half of brick of coke that he was about to serve when the jump-outs came through. With his Olympic speed, he ran all the way down 5th Street to Pamila's house in less than 5 minutes. Walking in the house out of breath, he saw Tyesha and Kelley sitting in the living room watching TV.

"Who you running from boy?" Kelley said as Quick walked by her and Tyesha on his way to his room in the basement which he shared with Lando.

"The bodeans just jumped out up da Ave., I had to get ghost," Quick said on his way down the steps to the basement.

Pamila was in the back room washing clothes when Quick came downstairs.

"Where is Lando?" she asked.

"He still up da Ave. chillin'," Quick said. Pamila had been getting on them about hanging out on Georgia Avenue. She didn't like it because she knew that it was only a matter of time before they got in trouble with the law again.

"I keep telling you about hangin' out on Georgia Avenue, find somewhere else to spend your time," Pamila said as she walked by Quick and headed up the steps.

As Quick began to lie back on his bed, Lando, Black, and Lil' Garvin came through the basement door bringing the smell of weed smoke with them. Lil' Garvin and Black came over and sat on the bed with Quick while Lando ran upstairs for a minute. Black started wrestling with Quick while Lil' Garvin grabbed the remote and turned the huge color TV on that sat in the corner. Rap videos were on. Black stopped playing for a minute to see what video of N.W.A.'s was coming on next.

"I fucks wit dem niggaz joe," Black said, "Dem niggaz puttin' they lil' city on da map. You got niggaz dat don't even know where Compton is, screaming Compton. Dat's how niggaz suppose to be screaming DC joe." Lando came back downstairs with a rack of money in his hand and cut into the conversation,

"Mann 'bout to try to put some singing broads out on dat New York nigga's record label."

"We need some street niggaz outta DC to come through," Black said.

Lil' Garvin was feeling him, he said, "You know Lil' Tank and dem young niggaz think they can rap and shit joe. You wanna take dem young niggaz out to da studio and see what they sound like?"

"Yeah, let's do dat. I'll pay for the time, cause Mann ain't gon let us go in there for free," Black said. The idea was a good one and worth a try as far as they were concerned.

Flying down the beltway on their way to Wild World's waterpark was damn near the whole neighborhood. Racing through the beltway traffic and leading the fleet of vehicles, Lando and Baby-D put their Twin Turbos to the test. Lando had Nakia in his passenger seat scared to death while he flew from left to right at top speed. Baby-D wouldn't be outdone at all. With Tank in his passenger seat, he made move for move right with Lando. Mann, Kelley, Kisha, and Naomi moved at a much safer speed in Mann's Range Rover while they watched the two sports cars put on a show in front of them.

"Lando shouldn't be drivin' like dat without no license," Kelley said as she saw Lando dangerously swerve across the beltway followed by Baby-D, Quick, Black, Lil' Garvin, and Lil' Dee-Dee who were in Quick's big Suburban smoking weed and playing this crankin Essence tape from da

Black Hole. Dre, Tina, and their son were in Dre's Corvette ZR1 right behind Quick's truck. Today was going to be one of those good ole summer days.

Once inside the water park, the females split up from the dudes and went on their own way. They were all supposed to meet back up at the Wild Wave sight at 2:00pm. Dre took his son with him as the dudes went to have a little fun. Dressed in all top flight swim wear from Polo to Madness, the dudes roamed the park in the blazing hot sun as if they owned it. Dre's little son had the time of his life watching Black almost drown at the bottom of a water slide. Walking around to get back in line for the water slide, Lil' Garvin saw a beautiful brown skinned girl in a two-piece Gucci bikini. In his black Polo swimming trunks and colorful Nike aqua shoes, Lil' Garvin tightened his stomach muscles to flex his 6 pack and stepped up to bat.

"Hi you doin?" Lil' Garvin asked the beautiful girl that was standing alone, licking on an ice cream cone.

Lil' Garvin saw the girl's eyes drop down to look at his stomach as she said, "I'm doin okay, it's just hot as shit out here."

"You out here by yourself?"

"Me and a few of my girl friends," The girl said as she began to play with her licks on the ice cream.

"What's your name beautiful?" Lil' Garvin asked as he stepped closer to her.

"Yummie," she said. Lil' Garvin smiled when he heard her name, it fit her, he thought.

"Yummie says a lot," Lil' Garvin said as he began to shoot his spill at Yummie. She was all smiles before Lil' Garvin left with her number.

Across the park by the eating area, the girls were getting their fair share of play too, but all of them had a man and were not giving up any rhythm. Kelley had her hands full with a dude that just wouldn't take no nicely.

"Look nigga! I told you I gotta man!" Kelley snapped as she walked away in her pink two-piece. The dude and all of his buddies couldn't help watching Kelley's behind shake every which way as she walked over to the water fountain. The dude walked up behind Kelley who was bending over getting a drink of water. Pointing at Kelley's ass and smiling back at his men, the dude squeezed Kelley's ass. Kelley turned around in a flash and smacked the taste out of his mouth. His friends burst out laughing as he pushed Kelley against the water fountain and raised his hand to smack her. Kisha, Tina, Naomi, and Nakia walked up just in time, they all got up in the dudes face and caused a big scene. The dude's friends came over to cool the situation off before it got out of hand, but it was too late. The girls went looking for Mann and everybody else.

Why on Earth did they run into Black before Mann? After they told Black what had went down and how the dudes looked, he went looking for them by himself not thinking about Mann, the halfway house, or the law. After Black stepped off to run the dudes down alone, Kisha realized that they had made a mistake by telling Black before they saw Mann. Worried about what Black might do out of his anger, they began to frantically look for Mann.

About 10 minutes later, Kelley and the rest of the girls ran into Mann and everybody else. Mann almost lost his cool when he found out what had happened, but when he thought about Black running around the park in a rage, he got himself together as everybody began looking for Black. As they walked back toward the eating area, Mann knew that he was too late. 10 park security guards came running by them on their way towards the eating area. Mann, followed by everyone else, ran behind the guards.

Once at the eating area the guards rushed a crowd of people. Dre, being a little over 6 feet tall, could see over the crowd. Black had the dude that had felt Kelley's ass on the ground punching him in the face thunderously. As the guards broke up the fight, the dude got off of the ground and ran for the parking lot with his men. Black and everybody else ran too.

Black ran straight for Lando's Twin Turbo knowing that he kept some kind of pistol under the dashboard just like Mann. Mann ran up behind Black, followed by Lando.

Grabbing Black, who was flaming with rage, Mann said, "Hold on joe! You can't smash dese niggaz right out here in da parking lot." Holding Lando's .45 automatic in his hand, Black tried to think about what his older cousin was telling him. The sound of screaming car tires hit the air as a black Nissan Pathfinder went flying out of the parking lot. Standing up with the pistol in his hand, Black could see the dudes in the truck. Mann felt relieved that they had gotten away because he knew what state of mind Black had slid into.

Mann was back to his old tricks. He had pulled A few strings and got PASSION a spot on Amateur Night at the Apollo. Chocolate was won over by the move and couldn't stop thinking of how things might turn out if they won. They were all over Cherry's house packing their things for the trip to New York. Mann let them know that he would pick them up at 9:00pm tonight.

Trying on different clothes to see what she would wear, Caramel stood in the mirror talking about how excited she was to have a chance to sing on live TV. She couldn't get over it.

"Who knows, I might even have a shot at Mann when this is over," she said.

Chocolate, being the backbone of the group, checked her quick, calling her by her real name, "Look Tracy, we got other shit to think about right now. Worry about Mann later." The girls went on preparing for their big night while waiting for Mann.

Meanwhile, Mann had rented two huge mobile homes to ride everybody to New York in. He wanted it to be fun for the whole neighborhood. He would drive one and let Dre drive the other. Everybody seemed excited about the trip, which made Mann feel as if he was really doing something that everybody could get something out of.

Pulling up outside of Caramel's apartment in a huge mobile home with Dre right behind him, Mann blew the horn for PASSION to come out. It was already a full house in the mobile home that Mann was driving with Kelley, Tyesha, Lando, Black, Quick, Baby-D, and Lil' Garvin inside. The three young singers would have to ride with Dre.

Coming downstairs quickly with their luggage, Cherry, Chocolate, and Caramel jumped in the mobile home that Dre was driving along with Tina, Lil' Dre, Kisha, and Naomi. Once inside, Dre pulled off behind Mann and headed for the interstate.

The trip to New York was fun from the start. In Mann's mobile home, Baby-D and Black had everybody laughing as they tried to sing and began joning on one another's voice.

Laughing at Black, Baby-D said, "Your black ass sound like you just got shot in da neck and you talkin' 'bout you gon get on stage at da Apollo. Sandman gon run down on you wit dogs and beat your ass!" Everybody burst out laughing, even Black himself. Mann almost spit his soda out when he heard what Baby-D said. Their whole ride was live.

Eyone Williams

PASSION entertained everybody in Dre's mobile home. They even made Tina a believer in them and that was hard because if you weren't some big singer with a record deal already, she wouldn't even hear you out.

"Y'all really sound good," Tina said.

Kisha cut in and said, "Yeah, y'all think I could do a song wit y'all."

Dre laughed when he heard Kisha trying to cut into the girls deal and said, "Don't fuck up they program, you know you can't sing." Kisha began singing an old Anita Baker song and made everybody laugh as they rolled along up the highway.

While Mann had everybody on their way to New York, it was business as usual for the young dudes around Rittenhouse Street. Tank and the rest of the young dudes had the strip pumping with 50 rocks left and right. Smoke, a snake in the grass, was out on the strip with them and the sad thing about it was that the young dudes not only knew nothing about him and his cousin Serge robbing them a while ago, but they really fucked with the two cruddy niggaz.

Walking down Rittenhouse Street on his way down 5th Street to push a little coke, Serge thought deeply about his status in the game. He had been in the streets just as long as Mann and Dre and he remembered when he was on the same level with them. They seemed to blow up, and he wondered why his luck wasn't as good as theirs. He was tired of nickel and dime capers. He wanted a big fish now.

Walking up on the group of dudes that were pushing coke in front of Old Tima's house, Serge gave them all five and didn't think twice about how he had laid them down at gunpoint and took all of their money and coke not too long ago.

"You tryin' to smoke wit us joe?" A little dude named Lil' Dee-Dee said to Serge as he and rest of the young dudes began walking into the dark cut beside Old Tima's house.

"I'm on my way shorty," Serge said as he pulled Smoke to the side.

"What's up slim?" Smoke asked, knowing Serge had something up his sleeve. Serge knew Smoke wouldn't go for his snake ass plan up front so he beat around the bush and appealed to Smoke's pockets by telling him how this caper would put them on for good.

In the restaurant of the Marriot Hotel in New York, Mann and everyone else acted as if they were right at home. Black always acted straight ghetto and Quick, Lando, Baby-D, and Lil' Garvin went right along with it. They ran all of the white people out of the cafeteria when Black started throwing food and getting loud.

Shaking his head at the foolishness, Mann looked over at the table where they were making a mess and said, "Black!" Black looked over at Mann with the look of a child caught in the wrong and smiled. "Stop actin' like a bamma, nigga," Mann said as he finished eating.

When they were done eating, they all went upstairs to the hotel rooms that Mann and Dre had paid for. Lando, Quick, Black, Lil' Garvin and Baby-D shared a room together. They had the room lit up with weed smoke in no time. Stretched out on the bed, Black blew weed smoke into the air as Lando stepped over Quick to get on the phone. After calling Nakia to let her know that he was already in New York, Lando called Jazmin to see if she had finished a design that she had shown Lando that he thought would be slick for a T-shirt.

"Yeah, I finished it. I don't know why you like that one so much, it's just like some Madness shit. I only finished it because you was talkin' 'bout you liked it," Jazmin said, talking about a design of what looked like a solar system of all the things you could think of in the streets revolving around a dollar sign instead of the sun. Lando thought that it was a big statement for those that could understand that the design was saying that all of the things revolving around the dollar came with money in the streets. He wanted to show it to Mann when it was done and see if he would get the design put on a T-shirt and manufactured so that he could sell them out of Mann's World.

"I told you I'ma get my brother to get some shirts made wit dat design on it and sell 'em out his store," Lando said. Jazmin knew Lando always did what he said he would but she didn't think Mann would like the design so she really didn't have her hopes up about what Lando was telling her.

"Yeah, whatever you say," she said.

"I'm tellin' you, dat joint like dat. Niggaz gon dig some shirts like dat. Watch, my brother gon give you some money for dat joint," Lando said. Lando and Jazmin talked for a while, but the room started to get loud now that everybody was high and playing around. Lando told Jazmin that he would see her when he was back in town and hung up the phone.

12:00pm the next day, Kisha was helping Cherry pick out an outfit from the many that she had brought with her.

"Un Unh, dat's some plain jane shit. Let me see how you look in dis," Kisha said as she pulled out a DKNY skirt out of Cherry's suitcase. As Cherry slid her thick body into the outfit, Kisha gave her the much needed approval that Cherry needed to kill the butterflies in her gut. Chocolate and Caramel came into the hotel room dressed to impress as well, but Caramel stole the show with Baby-D walking with her resting his arm around her shoulder. Kisha's mouth dropped to the floor. Caramel was 20 years old with Baby-D looking as if he had played his cards right at 16 years old.

Kissing Caramel on the lips, Baby-D said, "I'll see you at the Apollo," as he left out of the door.

"Oooooh, what's that all about?" Cherry asked Caramel with a sly smile on her face. Kisha couldn't even get her words out of her mouth.

Caramel smiled as she pulled a white Prada body suit out of her suitcase and walked to the bathroom saying, "I like shorty, he got style."

Chocolate, being no nonsense, shook her head and grabbed her suitcase saying, "She don't know what she want to do. First she want a man and now she want a boy."

Later on everybody was walking down the crowded street that led to the Apollo as if they were from New York and everybody else was out-of-towners. Holding Kelley's hand with Tyesha riding on his shoulders, Mann gave PASSION some comforting advice.

"Just be yourself. Take it easy, act like y'all act when y'all in da studio. We gon support y'all no matter what nobody say," Mann said. Cherry felt better already, she smiled at Mann brightly.

Chocolate was a little over confident, "We gon do fine Mann, watch. You gon be glad you put your time into us," she said.

Mann laughed and said, "We gon see," as he looked over at Caramel who was walking hand and hand with Baby-D.

"What you want me to say?" Caramel asked Mann.

"I don't want you to say nothin', I just want you to do your best. Dat's all," Mann said, as they all walked into the Apollo behind the huge crowd that had shown up for the taping of the live event.

Inside of the world famous Apollo Theater, Mann and everyone else made their way to the front where their seats were. Black immediately got his face on camera. The crowd began to applaud as Sinbad came out on stage and welcomed them to the Apollo.

"We have a wonderful show for you tonight. Special guests BBD will be with us tonight," he said. The crowd went off again. Sinbad cracked a few jokes and let the show begin.

BBD came on stage and performed their hit single Poison. The crowd went off, the women went extra crazy. Kisha ran up front along with Naomi and Kelley. As BBD took control of the crowd, they began throwing roses out into the crowd. Kisha caught one and started yelling and screaming as if she had just hit the lotto. As BBD brought their song and superstar performances to an end, everybody went back to their seats.

Sinbad came out again and said, "I wish I could make da ladies yell and scream like dat. I might have a lil' more fun in the bed." The crowd exploded with laughter as Sinbad called out the first amateur guest. A tall white man came out talking about he was going to play his guitar and sing a country song he wrote. He was on stage no longer than 30 seconds before the crowd ate him up and forced Sandman to run down on him.

Sinbad quickly snatched the attention of the crowd by saying, "Ole Uncle Sam need to take his tired behind back down Texas where he from." The crowd burst into laughter once more as the next guest came out for amateur night. A slim, sexy brown skinned young sister came out saying that she was from Arizona and that she would be singing an old Teena Marie song called 'Cassanova Brown'. The sister had a beautiful voice and sang the song as well as Teena herself. The crowd applauded her great performance as she left the stage.

"Mary Williams from Arizona. I guess they ain't got no lotion out there cause dat's sister's arms were ashy as beat up knuckles!" The crowd began to boo loudly as Sinbad called for the next guest.

"Okay, okay, I take it back but it's gonna be your fault for her going through life ashy as hell," Sinbad said with a laugh. "Our next guests is all the way from Dodge City. Give up a big round of applause for PASSION!" Sinbad said as he dragged their name out adding a little essence to it. Cherry, Chocolate, and Caramel came out looking like runway models. Sinbad asked them all their names and what they did for a living. Cherry told him that they all worked at Bloomingdales and that she wanted to thank the person that made it possible for them to be at the Apollo.

"Thank you Mann, I knew you would make something happen for us. I love you DC," she said.

"What about you, you pretty thing you?" Sinbad said as he looked at the thick tall, sexy, brown skinned Caramel. She was a little shy. All she said was that she wanted to win tonight and that the song that they were going to sing was one that she had wrote for the group, called 'Destiny'. Sinbad said a few lasts words and sent them on stage.

Cherry walked up to her microphone in her tight white DKNY skirt and kicked the show off. The first note to the song, which began with the pleasant sound of Cherry's beautiful voice singing "Destiny!!" Chocolate and Caramel quickly came in backing her up as the song went into telling the world how much of a role destiny played in a relationship. The ladies in the crowd went off. The dudes had to bob their heads as well, as Chocolate walked to the edge of the stage in her black Fendi outfit singing a part of the song that was all hers.

"Dat's right!" Black yelled, supporting PASSION. The whole section where Mann and everybody else was sitting made sure that everybody in the building knew that they were there to support PASSION. Lando was so high that all he could do was bob his head to the music. He felt if he was to get up and clap his hands like everybody else that he would fall out.

As PASSION finished their song, they walked off stage, feeling the love of the crowd. They just knew that they had won. They could feel it in the air.

Sinbad felt PASSION's song so much that he just watched the bodies of the healthy young women as they walked by saying, "Dat's a whole lot of lovin' there. Too much for one man." Moving right along, Sinbad called the next guest out. Two brown skinned dudes came out on stage and said that they were from Brooklyn. The crowd automatically went off and accepted them as their own.

"So what y'all gone do for us tonight?" Sinbad asked.

"We gon represent for BK wit some hip hop. Big up Brooklyn!" the taller of the two dudes said. The crowd went off again, barking and screaming BK. The two dudes walked up to the microphones and did their thing, sending the Apollo into an uproar. Black, Lando, and everybody else from DC had to bob their heads to the New York dudes that called themselves 'Double Barrel'. They electrified the Apollo and walked off stage like "What?"

Sinbad watched them leave the stage and didn't dare to say anything about them.

"I ain't gon get on your homeboys cause I might not be able to come back next week if I do," he said to the crowd of mostly New Yorkers. Sinbad then called out two more guests that were quickly booed and ran off stage by Sandman.

The moment of truth was now at hand. All amateur guests were called back out onto the stage. The lovely Kee-Kee Shepard marched out onto the stage showing off one of her many beautiful gowns and the decision-making began. Kee-Kee walked behind Mary Williams of Arizona and placed her hand over her head and waited for the crowd's response. They showed a little love but everyone knew that it wasn't enough to win. She then did the same to PASSION. The crowd went crazy, sending chills through the bodies of the three young women. They couldn't control their smiles as they heard Mann and everybody else supporting them. Kee-Kee then went over to Double Barrel. The Apollo was on it's feet yelling and screaming for the New York rap group.

"Looks like we have a winner..." Sinbad said. "Double Barrel!!" PASSION and Mary Williams walked off of the stage in defeat. Chocolate showed no signs of anger, she felt that life always went the way that it was suppose to go; she took the defeat in stride. Cherry walked away with her head down, she couldn't believe that they didn't win. Caramel's eyes began to water as she followed her two buddies off the stage. She thought they had lost because their song wasn't good enough, however, Chocolate later assured her that her song was great and that it just wasn't meant for them to win.

"Fuck dat!" Black said as he stood up and looked at Mann in disbelief.

Mann shook his head and said, "Dat's how shit go slim. We in New York, they gon support they own joe."

"Fuck dat! I'm gone slim. I'll see you back at the hotel," Black said as he headed for the door with Lando, Quick, Baby-D, and Lil' Garvin.

"Fuck dese New York niggaz!" Black said out loud as he walked to the exit. A group of New York dudes sitting right behind him overheard what he said.

They gave Black a funny look and Black snapped, "You don't like what I said, bitch ass nigga?" Black asked the dudes out of his with a bad attitude. Bammas was mumblin', but didn't want mess with the crazy ass DC nigga.

Mann sat through the rest of the show not upset in the least bit. He knew in his heart that the three young women had done their best and that someone else would see the same thing he saw soon enough.

15

A week after the trip to the Apollo, Mann and Silk were walking in the door of Mann's studio talking about how Mann thought the girls were a little discouraged with their singing after not winning. Silk was listening carefully and saw that Mann had really taken a liking to PASSION.

While they walked up the steps to the office, Jimmy, one of the white boys that ran the studio for Mann, walked up and said, "Mann I need to talk to you when you get a chance." Mann told Silk to go ahead upstairs while he talked to Jimmy.

"What's up?" Mann said as he leaned against the wall in a grey Hugo Boss sweat suit. Jimmy began to tell him that the studio was getting a lot of business lately and that with him and Todd running all of the recording equipment, he felt that Mann needed to hire someone to keep up with all of the paperwork now that the studio was actually serving its purpose. Mann thought about what Jimmy was saying and told him that he would get right on top of the situation.

Walking into the office, Mann saw Silk looking down on a group of young white boys that had been renting studio time for the last few days.

Looking over at Mann, who was sitting down behind the desk full of paperwork, Silk said, "What da fuck is up wit dese white boys?"

Mann laughed while putting all of the paperwork into one stack and said, "You know they do dat heavy metal shit joe." Silk had his face balled up as he looked and listened to what the white boys were playing down in the studio.

"They look like they playing some Satanic shit!" Silk said before walking over and sitting down on the other side of Mann's desk.

"So when was the last time the girls were in here?" Silk asked Mann.

Typing some financial figures into his computer, Mann said, "They only been out here once since we been back from New York. I talked to Cherry yesterday and asked her what was up, she didn't sound interested in coming. She talkin' 'bout she got   bills to pay and dat she was on her way to work."

"So what you gon do? You gon let dem give up on themselves?" Silk asked. Mann let him know that he had no plans on letting them give up on themselves. Mann was going to go over Chocolate's house himself and see where her heart was and see what would be next for PASSION.

Mann was getting out of his Range Rover outside of Chocolate's apartment at 11:00pm. Walking up to her building's door, Mann kept his eyes on the group of young dudes at the end of the parking lot. He knew he was an outsider in their neighborhood after dark and he wasn't about to sleep on the local's deep in the heart of SE Washington DC.

Chocolate heard a knock at the door as she sat on the sofa in her living room looking through the paper for a better job. Putting down the paper she walked over to the door and opened it with the chain on it. Looking through the crack of the door, she saw Mann and quickly let him in.

"Have a seat," Chocolate said as she moved the newspaper out of Mann's way so that he could sit down. "What you doing out dis part of town dis late at night?" Chocolate asked as she sat down beside Mann.

"I'm out here to talk to you," Mann said as he got straight to the point as he always did. He let Chocolate know that he could tell that her and the other girls were discouraged after not winning at the Apollo and that he wanted them to put their hearts back into their music.

"Mann," Chocolate said, "I got a son I gotta look out for. I can't keep pretending that I'ma be a big superstar. I gotta think about bills and shit like dat." Mann could feel her pain and it was only one thing he could think of to restore their drive.

"Check dis out. I'ma turn my studio business into a record label myself," Mann said.

Chocolate smiled and said, "I love the way you believe in yourself and I love the way you believe in us, but dat kinda shit will take forever. What am I supposed to do until all of dis stuff come through?"

Quick on his feet, Mann said, "How much do you make an hour at Bloomingdales?"

"I make $6.50 an hour."

"Check dis out. I'll pay you, Cherry, and Caramel, $10.00 an hour to work at da studio."

"Doing what?"

"Paperwork, answering phones, and scheduling people for studio time. If everyone else likes the offer, y'all all show up Monday morning and y'all gotta job," Mann said.

He knew he had victory in his hands once more in life. By the way Chocolate's face lit up, he knew he had put the drive and desire back into her heart to sing.

Standing up and walking for the door, Mann said, "Part of y'all job is to work on y'all music, so make sure you let the other girls know." Chocolate understood what Mann had just done. She wished all men could be as much a man as Mann was. Walking towards Mann, she passionately hugged and kissed him on the cheek before he stepped out into the nightfall.

The next morning Mann walked into Mann's World just to see how things were running. As the glass door shut behind him, he could hear the music of Anita Baker in the air.

"What's up Mann?" Kisha said from behind the counter as Mann walked up.

"Ain't shit, what's up? Shit don't look busy in dis joint today," Mann said. Kisha let him know that it was too early and that in another hour or so a rack of young people would be in the store buying the latest outfits, tennis shoes, or tapes. Mann liked the sound of that.

"Keep up da good work," Mann said as he began to walk toward the back office, laughing at his businessman like statement.

"Whatever nigga!" Kisha said, catching on quick.

"What's up Mann?" Naomi said, as she walked by Mann with an arm full of brand new Polo shirts. Mann spoke to her and went into the office where Dre was standing in front of a pile of boxes writing down what was there on a pad.

"I see you hard at work joe," Mann said to his partner.

Dre turned around and said, "Ain't shit joe. Just makin' sure all dis shit here."

"Where dat nigga Black at?" Mann said.

Dre walked over to the desk and sat on top of it as he said, "Black took da day off so he could move in wit Mia." As Mann began to think of what the future would hold now that Black didn't have to check in with the halfway house people anymore, he asked Dre what he had planned for the day. Pulling out a box of price tags for Naomi to put on the new clothes, Dre told Mann that he was going to take Tina and his son out to the Baltimore Harbor for the day after he served Da-Da 2 bricks of coke. Mann told Dre to come by his apartment later on as they headed out into the store area.

Walking up to the counter, where Naomi was ringing up a pair of Jordans and a few CDs for a young dude in a Fila short set, Mann looked out of the glass door onto Georgia Avenue and saw Lando pulling up in his silver Twin Turbo with his long hair out and a black bandanna around his head. Mann smiled and began to think of how much his little brother had grown up over the last two years as Lando came pimping into Mann's World with a folder in his hand.

"What's up joe?" Lando said as he walked up on Mann and gave him five.

"Ain't shit shorty, what's up," Mann said as he looked down at his beeper. Lando told him that he had the design that Jazmin made and that he wanted Mann to look at it to see if he could do something with it for him. Mann told him to come back into the office so that he could look at it. They both started walking toward the back as Lando spoke to Dre and Kisha who were going over what needed to be put on the store floor.

Once in the back office, Mann jumped on the phone real quick as he sat on top of his desk. Naomi was pulling Hugo Boss T-shirts out of a well-taped box from New York.

"What's up cute thing?" Lando said as he smiled at her and flopped down on the leather sofa while turning on the TV. Naomi found Lando smooth for his age and came over to enjoy a quick conversation with him while Mann was on the phone.

Mann hung up the phone and walked over to sit down beside Lando, who was laying his lick to take Naomi out to eat. Naomi, being about 4 years older than Lando, was trying to play big but walked away telling the young dude to call her. Mann laughed a little bit as he asked Lando for the folder with the design in it. As Mann laid eyes on the creative design, he was all for it.

Lando's face lit up as he said, "So you can get some shirts made like dat for da summer?"

Mann smiled and said, "Slow down young nigga, shit don't happen overnight." Mann began to explain to his little brother how he had to do all of the paperwork and get the design sent to a company that he worked with that made Mann's World T-shirts for him. It would be early September before the shirts would be on the rack in Mann's World, Mann told Lando, which meant that they would have to be sweatshirts instead of T-shirts. Lando was cool with that. He had accomplished his goal and he felt good about being able to tell Jazmin that her design would be on a sweatshirt by this fall. Lando gave his brother five and told him that he would catch him later and walked out of the office on his way up Rittenhouse to serve a nigga a half a brick.

Walking out into the store area, Lando saw Short Dogg trying on a pair of new Air Jordans. Lando hadn't seen Short Dogg since he had gotten sent out of town to a residential program from down Oak Hill. Lando walked up behind Short Dogg and put his hand against his back like a gun and said, "You slippin' nigga." Short Dogg spun around and saw Lando.

Standing up to hug Lando, Short Dogg said, "What's up nigga?" Short Dogg was excited to run into Lando.

"What you doing up dis part of town?" Lando asked. Short Dogg told him that he was staying uptown with an aunt of his. Now that he was home, he was trying to buy himself a little gear for the summer.

"You gettin' you some money?" Lando asked as he sat down beside Short Dogg. Short Dogg began telling Lando that he had only been home for a week and that he hadn't even tried to get himself any money yet. Being well off in the fast lane, Lando gave Short Dogg his beeper number and told him to beep him later on so that he could do something with him to welcome him home. Short Dogg was happy to see that Lando was real as he claimed to be when they were locked up.

"You know dis my brother's store?" Lando said, as he began telling Short Dogg about how he and Quick were getting money nowadays. "You gon see joe. Hit me," Lando said as he stood up to leave. Short Dogg told Lando that he would beep him later on. Lando gave him five and then ran outside. Short Dogg watched as Lando jumped into his Twin Turbo and took off flying down Georgia Avenue.

Across town in Silky's Barbershop, Lil' Garvin and Tank just finished getting their hair cut while Quick stood in the side door talking to Silk about how all the young dudes were going to go to Mann's studio and make a tape.

"Yeah, y'all should do dat shorty. Y'all livin' dat for real, while dem bammas niggaz rappin' 'bout it. You know Mann bout to get da rights to the name of a record label for PASSION, he might be able to do something wit y'all," Silk said. The words inspired Quick to really try to rap. Quick gave Silk five and told him that he would see him later.

Hopping into Quick's huge Chevy Suburban, Tank and Lil' Garvin got on the phone that was recently installed in the consol. Quick lit a fat blunt of weed as he pulled off into the thick Minnesota Avenue traffic.

"Can y'all young niggaz rap for real or what?" Quick asked Tank as he passed the blunt back to him. Tank grabbed the blunt and began free styling for Quick.

"Nine millimeter, nickel plated..." Tank started to rap. Quick and Lil' Garvin felt him off the top.

"Shorty like dat!" Lil' Garvin said as he began to hit the blunt. Quick turned onto 37th Street behind a black Nissan Pathfinder.

Tank rose up and said, "Dat's dem bitch ass niggaz Black was beefin' wit down Wild World joe," Quick and Lil' Garvin leaned up to look at the truck full of niggaz. Sure enough it was them.

"What you trying to do young?" Tank said as he pulled a .45 automatic out of his waistband that looked bigger than he did.

"Hold up shorty," Lil' Garvin said as he pushed Tank's hand down.

"Let's follow dese niggaz and see where they go," Quick said as he began to follow the Pathfinder.

Unnoticed and creeping behind the Pathfinder, Quick followed it all the way to East Gate Gardens. The Pathfinder pulled over and parked on Drake Place. Passing by and stopping at a stop sign at the end of the block, Quick, Lil' Garvin, and Tank looked back and saw the dudes get out and start mixing with the dudes out on the drug strip.

"Let's hit dem niggaz up joe!" Tank said, ready for whatever.

Quick, now older and wiser, said, "Naa, we gon holla at Black and Lando first. If they still tryin' to see dese niggaz, we'll come back at night and light dis muthafucka up!" Lil' Garvin agreed as Quick pulled off and headed back uptown.

In the dark, broken glass littered the trash-filled alley behind Sam's Liquor Store on Georgia Avenue, Quick stood to the side telling Lando how he, Tank, and Lil' Garvin had ran into the niggaz that were driving the black Pathfinder down Wild World.

Watching Short Dogg shoot the dice in the crap game that was going on in front of them, Lando said, "Fuck dem niggaz joe dat's old news now."

Quick shook his head in agreement with Lando as he said, "What you think Black gon have to say about it?"

Pulling some cash out of the pocket of his Guess jean shorts, Lando said, "Don't tell 'em 'bout dem niggaz." Quick felt it was best to leave the situation alone as well. Walking up behind Baby-D and Lil' Garvin, Lando and Quick got right into the crap game along with the crowd of young niggaz that were letting the dice roll to see who would walk away a winner tonight.

By Monday, Chocolate, Cherry, and Caramel had quit their jobs at Bloomingdales to work at Mann's studio. The girls naturally found their places. Chocolate took on the responsibility of booking who would get studio time and when, along with filing the fees for the studio time. Cherry had a thing for computers and went into the File Manager of Mann's computer and reorganized everything in a very easy to use way. Caramel got the easy end of the deal. When there was nothing more to really do, Mann told her to answer the phones at the front desk, which turned out to be good for her anyway because she was the songwriter of the group. In only her first two hours at work, she had written a beautiful song called 'Sun Rise' and was already humming a beat for it.

Mann and Rick sat on the black leather sofa inside the office of the studio, while Cherry sat at the computer working on different ways to name files. Filling out the paperwork that would turn the studio into a record label, Mann sat back with his hand on his chin thinking of what the name should be when Pamila walked in the door.

Mann got up and introduced Pamila to Cherry and Rick as he pulled a chair out for her to sit in. Pamila shook hands with them and began to tell Mann how professional the studio seemed as she came through the front door.

"You got somebody at the door answering the phone, all the studios downstairs have people in them, you're up here working. This looks like a real place of business," Pamila said, as she looked over Cherry's shoulder to see what she was doing.

Sitting back down on the sofa with Rick, Mann said to Pamila, "What you think the name of my record label should be?" Pamila laughed not knowing where to begin.

"Give me anything," Mann said. Pamila thought for a minute.

She began to think of how Mann got the money to do all of the things that he was now doing and she said, "You should call it Fast Lane Records, cause you got everything in the fast lane." Mann liked the sound of that.

Looking at Rick with a smile, he said, "Look like it's Fast Lane Records."

Back around 5th and Rittenhouse Street, Black was jumping out of a cab in front of Kisha's house where Smoke, Serge, and a few young dudes were leaning on the fence, smoking weed in the early morning summer sun. Walking up on the small crowd, Black showed his love and grabbed the blunt from Lil' Moe.

"What's up wit y'all niggaz?" Black said to Smoke and Serge. Breaking away from the younger dudes, they began to walk up the street as Serge told Black about a caper that he had his eyes on for the last two weeks.

"Who is da nigga?" Black asked as he blew a cloud of smoke into the air. Serge began telling Black about the move and that it was at least 2 bricks and about $60,000 in the house. "Who is it joe?" Black asked again.

Serge said, "Lil' Tim."

Looking at Smoke to see if he agreed with the move Serge was talking about, Black said, "Fuck naw!" Smoke already knew Black wasn't going to be with the move due to the fact that they all went to school with Lil' Tim when they were younger. Black had no picks in the game, but he did have principles and never went against the grain.

"Da money got you fucked up like dat joe?" Black asked Serge, looking at him in a way that showed his disgust.

Looking over at Smoke, Black said, "I know you ain't wit no shit like dat!" Smoke knew in his heart that the move was a snake move, but he felt as though Serge would find a way to get Lil' Tim one way or another. Black was against the move whole- heartedly and let it be known.

"I ain't wit dat shit. If y'all hit slim, I ain't got nothin' to do wit it," Black said.

While Black was still venting his disgust about Lil' Tim, the "jump-outs" bent the corner at top speed, slammed on brakes and jumped out. All of the young dudes broke through the cut beside Kisha's house. Smoke threw the blunt he was smoking as he, Black, and Serge just waited for the "jump-outs" to put them against the fence.

Two "jump-outs" ran after the young dudes while Hall and Big Al walked up on Black.

"You know what the deal is Black. Get against the fence," Hall said. Black smiled and sighed as he turned around and got on the fence. Big Al made Smoke and Serge do the same while Hall began to harass Black.

This was the first time that Hall had the pleasure of running into Black in almost 2 years and he was happy to catch him on the drug strip, even though he knew Black wasn't dirty but he knew it would only be a minute before he would be.

"So you finally worked your way out of the system again," Hall said as he patted Black down.

"Well I want you to know that I'm still around. I ain't gon no where. I know all about your little cousin, Lando being the big dope boy now. I guess crime runs in the family," Hall said as he went on and on about how he was going to find a way to bring their whole neighborhood down.

"Are you finished?" Black asked becoming fed up with the bullshit.

"Yeah, I'm finished for right now," Hall said, "but don't let me catch you slippin'."

Sitting in Quick's big Suburban outside of what was now "FAST LANE RECORDS", Quick, Lando, Lil' Garvin, Short Dogg, Tank, and Lil' Moe smoked a bag of weed before going into the studio to see how the two younger dudes would sound. Short Dogg let everybody know that he could play all instruments and that he would make a hittin' beat for the young dudes to rap to.

"Don't be bullshittin'," Quick said with a little laugh. Short Dogg assured him that he was good at making real tracks.

"Let's see then," Lando said as they all got out and headed for the studio.

Lando was the last to walk in the door when he heard a car pulling up behind him. Looking over his shoulder he saw Baby-D parking his red Twin Turbo behind Quick's Suburban with Caramel in the passenger seat. Lando smiled and went on into the studio.

At the front desk, Chocolate had the whole mob on hold giving them instructions that Mann had left.

Eyone Williams

"Ain't gon be no playing and all dat shit in da studio. Mann said he don't want no shit!" She said as she led the mob into studio B.

Once inside the studio, Chocolate called White Boy Jimmy, into the studio to show Lando how to work everything. While everybody touched and turned this and that in the studio, Lando listened to everything Jimmy had to say. Like magic, Lando caught on in seconds and knew how to load the disk into the digital mixer and make it a record.

"I got it from here," Lando said as he grabbed a pair of headphones. Getting everybody's attention, Lando took control like a real producer. Jimmy sat back and watched as Short Dogg went from the drums, to the keyboard, to the bass guitar. In less than 30 minutes, Short Dogg had a deep bass track blasting in everyone's headphones.

Looking around at all of the nodding heads in the room, Short Dogg said, "Y'all like dis?"

Standing up and walking over to an open mic, Quick said into everybody's headphones, "Let's light some smoke up and see what dese young niggaz sound like." Lando knew Mann wasn't going for weed smoking in the studio, so he quickly killed the idea telling everybody that they had to see what Mann thought about it. Out of respect for Mann, they all agreed. Tank and Lil' Moe jumped on the mic and put the tales of the bloody DC streets into rhymes like it was nothing.

Baby-D walked up to the studio door and looked through the window, seeing everybody nodding their heads back and forth, he could tell that Tank and Lil' Moe had the spot "rockin". Walking in and grabbing a pair of headphones, Baby-D listened to Tank and Lil' Moe go back and forth free styling.

"Damn! Dese young niggaz like dat!" he said, looking at Lil' Garvin who was smiling as he shook his head to the beat.

Mann and Dre were just coming to the studio this morning after buying some more recording equipment for PASSION. Walking upstairs into the office, Mann looked down through the window over top of the studio that Lando and everybody else was in and could tell that something was going on that had to be worth listening to.

Calling Dre over to the window, Mann said, "Look at dis joe."

Dre walked over to the window and saw everybody into what was going on and said, "Ain't no way we can hear what's going on down there?" Mann looked over at Cherry, who was doing some work on the computer and told her to get the headphones out the desk drawer. Cherry brought the headphones over to Mann and hit a switch on the wall that allowed him to hear what was going on downstairs in any studio from A to D.

"Dese young niggaz sound good as shit joe," Mann said as he shook his head to the beat.

Handing Dre the headphones, Mann said, "Listen to the beat too." Dre agreed, Tank and Lil' Moe sounded like they could be on a tape in the record store somewhere.

"Who made dis beat?" Dre asked.

Mann threw his hands up in the air as if to say he didn't know as he looked at Cherry and said, "You know who made dis beat?" Cherry got up from the computer and walked over to the window.

Looking down into the studio, she pointed at Short Dogg and said, "See da short one wit da black bandanna on his head?" Mann shook his head yeah. "He made it," Cherry said.

Mann and Dre went downstairs to see what was up with Lando and everybody else and to see who the young dude was that had made the beat that they were rapping to. Lando introduced Mann and Dre to Short Dogg and told them that Short Dogg was a good nigga that he and Quick had met down Oak Hill.

Mann looked at Short Dogg, thinking about what Lando had just told him, Lando didn't call everybody a good nigga so it must be something good in Short Dogg, Mann thought. "Let me holla at you real quick shorty," Mann said to Short Dogg as he walked for the door.

Outside in the hallway, Mann gave Short Dogg the run down on how he had just started a record label and that he had a female group on the label already. He also let him know that he was looking for someone that could make R & B tracks.

"I can do it all slim," Short Dogg said, looking up at Mann.

"Good then, I need to see what you can do for dis song that they workin' on now," Mann said, "I'ma pay you for it too." Short Dogg smiled, Mann was talking his kind of talk.

"So when you want me to do dis?" Short Dogg asked. Mann told him to come back up to the studio about 9pm and then they could talk some more. Short Dogg was all for the plan and was waiting to see what would manifest.

Later on as the night began to grow dark, Quick, Black, Lando, and Short Dogg were on their way back to the studio. Quick had the tape of Tank and Lil' Moe free styling in the tape deck blasting.

"I ain't know you knew how to make beats joe," Black said to Short Dogg, "When we was down Oak Hill all you wanted to do was smoke weed and shit." Short Dogg began to tell Black how he used to play drums and stuff when he was small at his grandmother's church.

"I can't see you in church wit a ski mask on shorty," Black said.

Pulling up in front of the studio, Quick said, "Well, we gon be up da Ave joe. Beep me when you done slim." Short Dogg showed his love and jumped out of the truck into the darkness of the Silver Spring side street.

Flying down Wisconsin Avenue early in the morning, on his way to pick Black up from his apartment down Georgetown, Quick spotted a group of young girls in catholic school uniforms. Something about the uniforms told Quick that he wasn't suppose to be able to pull one of the girls, which made him want to try his hand even more. Riding by the young girls, who had to be on their way to some kind of summer camp, Quick looked over his shoulder with a blunt hanging out of his mouth and saw a cute brown skinned girl in the group of white girls. Quick put the blunt in the ashtray and pulled over at the end of the block waiting for the girls to walk by.

Dressed in all black with his hair in cornrows, Quick leaned against his truck as the girls walked by smiling in their green and yellow uniforms. Looking at the black girl, Quick noticed the white girls smiling his way too.

Walking up on the side of the girls, Quick went straight to work. Addressing all of the girls, Quick said, "Do y'all mind if I have a word wit ya friend?"

The white girls laughed as the one who seemed to be the oldest said, "No, go ahead."

Looking at the cute brown skinned girl with pretty eyes, Quick said, "Can I have a minute of your time?"

A little scared of Quick's thugged out look, the girl said in a real soft voice, "Yeah."

Stepping off to the side by his truck, Quick asked her what her name was. Not able to look Quick in the eyes, the girl said, "Amber."

Smiling at the girl, Quick stepped closer to her grabbing her hand, and said, "Well Amber, they call me Quick." Amber felt a sudden ease when Quick grabbed her hand and worked up enough courage to look him in the face.

"Why do they call you Quick?" she asked. Quick told her that he has always been quick to go after what he wants and that's how he got the name. Amber giggled a little bit and Quick knew he had the little catholic schoolgirl. In less than 2 minutes, Quick had her deeply interested in him and the side of the world he was from. After getting Amber 's phone number, Quick let her know that he would be calling her tonight. She was so excited. Quick gave her and her friends a ride down the street to St. Albans Catholic School and went down Georgetown to pick Black up.

As Quick blew the horn outside, Mia was beefin' with Black about how he had been running the streets all night now that he was out of the halfway house.

"You don't never be in the house!" Mia said. Black turned and put his hands on Mia's shoulders as he comforted her knowing that was all she ever wanted.

"Look boo, you know I love you, but you also know that I'ma street nigga. I'ma run da streets, yet and still you gon wake up beside me every morning. Okay?" Black said as he kissed Mia. She wanted to melt in his arms, Black knew what made her tick and he gave her what she wanted every time being as though he could never forget the loyalty that she showed him out of nowhere when he was locked up. Mia hugged Black, smiling brightly as Black walked out of the door.

On the way uptown, Quick put Black on point about the news that he had heard last night.

"You know a nigga robbed and killed Lil' Tim 'bout two nights ago slim," Quick said as he slid a Spice 1 CD in the disc player. Black shook his head. He knew Smoke and Serge had to have been the ones behind the caper. Some niggaz just had no cut cards in the game. Black thought that Smoke and Serge would leave the situation alone after the way he reacted a couple of days ago, but now Black began to think that the "keep it real" shit didn't apply to them at all.

Standing in the bedroom doorway of his two-bedroom apartment with a smile on his face, Mann watched Kelley put her clothes on as he asked her what she wanted to do for the day. Looking out of the bedroom window in the bright beautiful sunlight of the late summer day, Kelley thought that it would be good to just go downtown and go pedal boat riding. Having only one day left with Mann before going back to school for the fall, she wanted to go somewhere that none of his friends or partners from the hood would be able to steal her time.

"I was thinking of pedal boating or something, I don't care. I just want to be with you alone boo," Kelley said as she got up and hugged Mann. Thinking of what he could do to bring her wish to life, Mann's mind quickly went to work.

"I got an idea," Mann said, "Get a change of clothes and some swim gear." Kelley backed away from Mann smiling, she knew Mann could come up with anything at the drop of a dime and she wanted to know what he was thinking at this time.

"Where we going boo?" Kelley asked full of excitement. Walking out into the living room to use the phone, Mann told her she would see when they got there.

"What's up CEO?" Silk said in a joking way. Mann laughed, even though it was a true statement, Mann wasn't used to the realness of it at only 18 years old. Getting straight to the point, Mann told Silk that he was trying to use his beach house along with the yacht that he had down Virginia Beach to show Kelley a good time before she went back to school.

"I like your style young nigga," Silk said with the sound of admiration in his voice, "Come get da keys and shit. I'ma be here till bout 12." Mann told Silk that he was on his way and hung up the phone.

Mann wasted no time getting to Silk's huge house out Maryland. Pulling through the huge gates up front, Mann looked at his watch. It was only 10:15am. He had good time, from here it would only take about 3 hours at the most to get to the beach house. Looking over at Kelley who was still intrigued about their secret destination, Mann kissed her and told her that he would take her inside but he was on a clock.

Once inside, Silk's beautiful baby mother led Mann back to the pool where Silk and his son were playing out in the sun. Seeing Mann, Silk got out of the pool with his son and walked over to Mann dripping wet.

Giving Mann five with his son in his arms, Silk said, "Have fun," as he handed Mann the keys to everything he needed.

Putting the keys into his pocket while giving Silk's son some candy, Mann said, "I hate to stick and move but I'm trying to catch a lot of day light." Silk laughed, he understood, walking back toward the pool Silk told Mann to call him later as he jumped into the water with his son in his arms.

Mann had to do everything but lie to Kelley about where they were going. Just when it seemed that she was going to guess where they were going Mann pulled in front of Silk's beach house.

Pointing to the house as he cut his Range Rover off, Mann said, "We staying here for the night boo."

Kelley's face lit up with joy as she said, "Come on, let's go in."

Silk had the place decked out as if he really lived in the house. As soon as they walked in the door, Mann noticed all of the new furniture that wasn't there the last time. Mann himself was impressed. Dropping her bags to the floor, Kelley dived on a big black leather sofa in the living room.

"You really know how to treat a woman," Kelley said to Mann, who was walking around the huge house looking all around.

"I gotta get us one of dese joints boo. Maybe next summer da record label thing will make enough cash for some shit like dis," Mann said as he dove on top of Kelley.

"I don't put nothing pass you boo," she said as she kissed Mann passionately in the mouth. "Let's see what upstairs looks like," Kelly said.

Walking into the main bedroom, things only got bigger and better. Silk had a king size waterbed already made up with silk Versace sheets. Right in front of the bed was a mini movie screen that hung from the ceiling. Kelley looked around amazed at the show of class along with money. Looking to her right, Kelley could see the ocean through the balcony window. Walking over and pulling back the curtains, Kelley opened the door letting the cool air and the smell of the ocean water breeze into the house. As Kelley took a deep breath of luxury, Mann walked up behind her and wrapped his arms around her.

Rubbing his dark arms, Kelley said, "This is much more than I could think of."

Leading Kelley to the bed, Mann said, "Da day is just beginning." They both sunk down into the waterbed and began to make love.

Hours later they were just getting out of the shower. Getting dressed in the bedroom, Kelley told Mann how good he made her feel and that she wanted to make love to him again. Grabbing the keys to his truck, Mann told her that they would do everything that she wanted to do before the sun came up.

"I'm bout to go get us something to eat down da street. I'll be right back. Be out front in 15 minutes," Mann said as he walked out of the room.

Kelley laid back on the bed and gazed out at the ocean. Mann had made her dreams come true once again. He was all that she had ever wanted. She loved him with all of her heart. Rolling over on the waterbed, she felt as if she was floating as she grabbed one of the fluffy pillows and closed her eyes thinking of the beautiful love making that she and Mann had just enjoyed. She couldn't keep it to herself. She grabbed the phone and called Kisha to tell her all about her day at the beach.

Kelley was standing out front with a beach towel around her, hiding her bikini when Mann pulled up with a bushel of crabs in the back of his truck.

As Kelley jumped in, Mann said, "I got one more surprise for you," as he pulled off.

"You got us some crabs?" Kelley asked as soon as she jumped in. Mann knew she loved them and he had his mind set on making this her day.

"Today is your day, boo," Mann said.

About a mile down the road, Mann pulled up and parked across the road from a small port of anchored boats. Some of which were just small fishing boats, but two beautiful yachts sat at the end of the pier. As Mann and Kelley walked across the road, Kelley couldn't take her eyes off of the huge white yacht with the two jet-skis on the back.

"I know we ain't 'bout to get on one of dese boats," Kelley said as she and Mann walked up to the gate of the port.

Flashing a members-only card to the young white dude at the gate, Mann grabbed Kelley's hand leading her down to the yacht that she had been looking at while saying, "We 'bout to get on dis one right here." Kelley hugged Mann tightly before they stepped over onto the yacht.

Walking around the deck behind Mann, Kelley asked if he knew how to drive the yacht. Mann let her know that Silk had shown him how to drive a long time ago. Walking up behind the wheel, Mann cranked the beautiful boat up and slowly pulled out into the setting sun.

30 minutes later, Mann and Kelley where so far out into the Atlantic Ocean that is seemed as if they were the only two people in the world.

The sun had just set, leaving a beautiful bluish orange haze in the sky. Looking out at the horizon, Kelley sat on Mann's lap telling him how much this day meant to her. Mann was pleased to hear that Kelley was enjoying herself, but he wanted to add more to the day.

"Come on," Mann said as he jogged to the back of the boat.

"Where we goin boy?" Kelley asked as she jogged behind him. At the back of the boat, Mann hit a switch that lowered one of the jet-skis into the ocean.

"I ain't getting on dat thing," Kelley said, standing behind Mann in her bikini.

"Yes, you is!" Mann said as he grabbed Kelley and jumped into the water beside the jet-ski.

Soaking wet, they both climbed on the jet-ski as Mann started it up. As they took off flying, water shot way up into the air behind them. Kelley yelled and screamed for Mann to slow down as she held on for her life. Looking over her shoulder, Kelley saw that the yacht was growing further and further out of sight.

"Let's turn around before we get lost out here Mann!" Kelley said. Spinning the jet-ski around like some kind of dirt bike, Mann looked back at the yacht which now looked like a white dot on the horizon.

"We cool. We got 'bout 10 or 15 more minutes of light left," Mann said as he took off flying through the water again. As the jet-ski soared through the waves, the sound of a racing boat began to grow near. Slowing down, Mann looked over his shoulder and saw a Coast Guard boat speeding their way. About 100 yards from where they were, a uniformed Coast Guard officer came out onto the deck of the boat and said into the bullhorn, "You are in international waters. Please turn around!" Mann wanted no problems with the law and quickly turned around and headed for the yacht as the Coast Guard went on their way.

Back on the yacht, Mann and Kelley went downstairs and laid out on the bed.

"I'm tired as shit joe," Mann said as he grabbed the remote and cut the TV on.

Lying beside Mann in only a towel, Kelley rolled over on top of him and said, "You ain't going to sleep on me." Wrapping his arms around Kelley, Mann looked her in the eyes and thought of how bad he used to want her years ago. Now he had her and so many other things that he

Eyone Williams

had set out to get. As Kelley sat straight up on top of Mann and threw her towel to the floor, all he could think of was making love to her. After taking a shower and getting dressed all over again, Mann and Kelley went up on deck and sat at the edge of the yacht looking up into the sky.

Pointing at the stars, Mann said, "Its gotta be a Creator out there somewhere. No one can put something together like dat." Kelley looked up into the dark sky and listened as Mann began telling her that someone or something was in control of everything that goes on in the world and that whoever that someone was knew what they were doing because all things in life worked itself out if a person just played by the rules of the game of life.

"I did a little wrong, but I don't always play by the rules," Mann said as he went off into deep thought about what the future would and could hold. "We gon be alright, me, you, Lando, and everybody else. Watch," Mann said as he laid down on the deck beside Kelley. Kelley cuddled up tightly beside Mann and they both fell asleep.

As the early morning sun began to cross the horizon, Mann opened his eyes and looked over at Kelley who was still fast asleep on his chest. He had out done himself. Life wasn't as bad as people made it out to be, Mann thought.

Waking Kelley up, Mann said "Well, was dis what you call havin' me all to yourself?" Kelley sat up and looked out at the endless water. She got all that she wanted yesterday and had more fun in one night than she had all summer.

16

September opened up a lot of doors for Mann and Fast Lane Records. Mann decided to manufacture PASSION's first album himself and then find a distribution deal with the final product in hand when the time was right. Spending over $10,000 on duplicating equipment along with bulk boxes of over 500,000 blank tapes, Mann was set to put PASSION out. No one could tell him that his plan of having PASSION's debut album out by the first months of 1993 was a fluke.

Mann had paid Short Dogg $300 a track for every track that he had made for PASSION. Mann thought they all had what it takes to be a hit. Mann's next move was to launch an all out promotion campaign to prepare the world for PASSION by putting out their first single that would drop at the end of the month if all went well. A small distribution company by the name of Cross Country Distribution had agreed to distribute the single for Fast Lane Records for 15% of all sales generated. Mann had worked hard using everything the streets had taught him to secure the distribution deal and PASSION was very pleased with the turn of events in only a couple of months.

The start of school in the city was right around the corner and Lando decided to spread some love by taking Nakia and Tyesha shopping. They had spent the day out White Flint Mall buying everything from book bags to boots. Lando enjoyed being able to buy Nakia and little Tyesha anything they wanted.

On their way back to town, Lando thought that it would only be right for him to spend some money in Mann's World. Besides that, Nakia wanted a Mann's World sweatshirt to go with the rest of the fresh gear that she had to wear to school.

Walking into Mann's World with Nakia and Tyesha, Lando walked over to talk to Kisha for a minute while Nakia and Tyesha looked around for what they wanted.

"What's up bad ass?" Kisha said as she sat behind the counter eating some fried chicken.

"Ain't shit," Lando said as he hopped up on the counter telling Kisha how he had heard the single that PASSION was about to put out. Kisha was still impressed by the fact that Mann actually had a record label. She began talking of videos and concerts around the country. Lando laughed as he watched Tyesha run around the store dancing to the music that was coming through the speakers.

Looking at Kisha, Lando said, "Yeah, Mann 'bout to put DC on da map joe. Slim ain't bullshittin'." Naomi walked out of the back office with some Polo sweat shirts thrown over her shoulders and saw Nakia and Tyesha picking out clothes. She knew Tyesha through Mann. She also knew Nakia, but she thought Nakia was just some young girl Lando was having sex with. She had no idea how serious the two were.

Walking up behind the counter where Kisha was sitting, Naomi looked at Lando with a crazy look on her face and asked if Nakia was his girl now or just another broad he was fucking. Firmly, yet still smooth, Lando told her that Nakia was his "folks". He gave her a look that told her that she better not start no shit. Naomi was very jealous of the younger girl, but it had only begun to show the last few times that she had saw Lando and Nakia together. Naomi's feelings for Lando were starting to show in her actions. She had slept with Lando a few times during the past summer and she was on him harder than she even knew. Annoyed and hurt, Naomi walked off and went into the back office so she could get away from everyone and get her emotions together. Older and much smoother than he used to be, Lando noticed that Naomi's feelings were hurt so he went into the back to make her feel better, without letting Nakia see what was going on.

Lando walked into the office and saw Naomi sitting on the sofa pouting like a child. Lando walked over to the sofa and sat down beside her, putting his arm around her neck saying, "I know you ain't fucked up 'bout me bringin' my folks to da store."

Looking over at Lando, the older girl said, "You know how I feel about you." Lando thought back to the first night he had sex with Naomi and how she told him how she hoped he knew what he was doing and that she didn't want him to get hooked. Now it seemed as if she was the one hooked on Lando. Even so, Lando didn't rub that in.

Instead, he played his cards right saying, "Naomi" as he put his hand on her chin turning her face towards him, "I ain't did nothin' to hurt you. I done played everythin' like you asked. You said you ain't want me actin' like you my woman so dat's how I been carryin' shit. You know we still tight." Naomi's face lit up with a bright smile, and no matter how much she tried to make herself believe that Lando was a little boy, he always showed her that he was very much a young man.

After making Naomi feel better, Lando stood up and walked over to some boxes sitting over in the back of Mann's office.

"What's dis?" Lando asked. Walking over to the boxes, Naomi told Lando that they were some sweatshirts that Mann had been waiting for. Against Naomi's protest, Lando ripped one of the boxes open thinking that the shirts with Jazmin's design on them were inside. Lando was right. Pulling out one of the thick cotton sweatshirts with the heavy sewed design, Lando said, "Dis joint like dat!" Naomi was still upset that Lando had went inside the boxes without Mann being around, but she still had to agree that Mann had the shirt made as a top quality shirt. To Lando, the shirt looked like a Hugo Boss sweatshirt, only with a hood. He had to take one to Jazmin's house tonight. Lando kissed Naomi on the cheek and left out of the office to pay for the clothes that Tyesha and Nakia wanted before dropping them off for the day.

Lando wasted no time dropping Nakia and Tyesha off. In less than 30 minutes, he was knocking on Jazmin's door wearing the sweatshirt with her design on it. Opening the door, Jazmin didn't even look at the shirt, instead she invited Lando in and led him back to her room where she was drawing another design.

Lando walked over and sat on Jazmin's bed while she sat down at the little desk she was working at in her room. After adding a few lines to a sketch that she had been working on, she turned around to Lando and laid eyes on the design that was sewed into the thick grey shirt. "Ohmi God!" she screamed as she jumped out of her chair. She couldn't believe that one of her designs was actually on a shirt that looked so good. Lando stood up to calm her down.

As he hugged her, she said, "I don't believe you pulled it off." Lando laughed a little as he told her how it was boxes of the shirts in Mann's store. "When is he going to start sellin' 'em?" Jazmin asked.

"He gotta put 'em on the rack before school start cause dat's when the most business gon come through da store," Lando said as he began to explain that the shirts were in all colors and that Mann would be in to check them out tomorrow.

Eyone Williams

"How much they gon cost?" Jazmin asked as she stepped back and began rubbing her hands over the thick stitching in the shirt. Lando didn't know how much the shirt would go for, but he knew that Mann would give Jazmin some of the money he made off of them; he was that kind of nigga.

Crime paid, and Black had been on leave for too long. Two nights later in the darkness of an alley behind an apartment across town, Black, Smoke, and Serge ran back to an old Chevy Impala dressed in black. Black had 4 bricks of coke and $80,000 in a book bag on his back as he led the pack. Once again, Black had led Smoke and Serge on a caper that produced more than $30,000 which is all they got when they robbed and killed Lil' Tim.

As Smoke jumped behind the wheel of the car, Black and Serge ran around to the other side. Serge blatantly by-passed the front seat and jumped in the back seat as Smoke started the car. Black's danger alarms quickly went off. He had seen Serge trick niggaz into the front seat after capers and blown their brains all over the windshield. As Black hesitated to get in the car, Smoke became impatient knowing that someone had heard the shots that had just went off inside the building. Black put his paranoia to the side and jumped in the car as Smoke took them flying down the alley.

Black had been robbing niggaz and going on capers with Smoke and Serge since he was 12 years old and had never felt like he needed to watch them, but for the first time he began to doubt Serge. Even though he didn't respect that Smoke and Serge had robbed and killed Lil' Tim, a nigga that they all grew up with, Black never thought that they would try him in the least, but now he believed that Lil' Tim's murder affected him more than he had first thought.

Downstairs in the basement, Lando and Quick broke bricks of coke down to ounces like they had been doing all summer. Together, they were moving 5 bricks a week. What Lil' Garvin and Baby-D didn't have locked down, Lando and Quick quickly snatched up and were moving coke from the city all the way out to Maryland. Slowly but surely, they were learning what it took to be money makers.

"Weigh dat shit right there," Lando said to Quick as he ran across the room to answer the phone. "Hello?" Lando said as he sat down on his bed and turned the TV down. All he could hear on the other end were soft sobs. "Who da fuck is dis?" Lando said as he listened closely. It sounded like someone was outside in the rain crying.

"Who is dis?" Lando asked again, sounding concerned.

"Lando...." a female voice said through small sobs, "I'm pregnant."

Lando thought it was Nakia for a minute and then thought otherwise and said, "Who is dis?"

Nakia cleared her voice and said, "It's me."

"Why you cryin'?" Lando asked. Nakia began to tell him that she told her mother that she was pregnant and that her mother went off and put her out. She was now at the gas station down the street from her house standing out in the rain. Lando cut her off and told her he was on his way to get her and that she could tell him the rest when he got there. Hanging up the phone with Nakia, Lando told Quick to bag all the coke up for him because he had to roll out and that he would be right back.

Flying through the evening rain in his Twin Turbo, Lando began to think of the situation at hand. He knew that he had been making love to Nakia all summer without a rubber, but he thought that he always was on time when it was time to release his load. He didn't doubt that the baby was his for a second and he knew that no matter what came about in the end that he would be there for his child and his child's mother.

Slowly Lando pulled into the gas station and saw Nakia sitting on top of her suitcase beside the pay phone in the rain. Despite her tear stained face, Nakia managed to smile when she saw Lando getting out of the car.

Walking over to Nakia as she stood up, Lando hugged her and kissed her.

"You okay?" he asked as he picked up her suitcase and led her to the car.

"Yeah, I am now dat you here," Nakia said.

Walking around to the driver's seat, Lando said, "I'm always here for you boo." Pulling out of the gas station onto Georgia Avenue, Lando said, "Tell me what's up." as he rubbed Nakia's thick thighs.

Nakia began telling Lando that she had been pregnant by him since his first home visit from Oak Hill. She didn't know how or when to tell him, but her mother had found out about her pregnancy a month ago. Her mother told her to get Lando to pay for an abortion or get out. Nakia had stalled for awhile, but today her mother drew the line and told her to pack her bags and leave. She could only come back home if she was to get rid of the child, which she was not going to do even if it killed her.

Lando listened to her every word and felt her pain. He was doing well enough in the streets to take care of him, her, and a child. He took her home with him and put her to bed in Tyesha's room so that she could calm down. They would talk to Pamila in the morning.

Outside of Fast Lane Records, Baby-D sat in his red Twin Turbo waiting for Caramel to finish her studio session. As the sound of Tank and Lil' Moe's free stylin' tape blasted through the JVC system that Baby-D had just put in the car, he lit a blunt of weed as he looked up and down the dark side street. Baby-D looked over at the bright lights that read Fast Lane Records. Mann had done it again, Baby-D thought. To see Mann go from neighborhood street hustler to C.E.O. of a record label gave Baby-D the hope and inspiration he needed to look past the street life of the fast lane. The sound of talking and laughter hit the air and snapped Baby-D out of his moment of thought as he saw Mann, PASSION, and Silk's sister, Pam, coming out of the double doors.

Caramel told everyone that she would see them at the studio in the morning as she jumped in the car with Baby-D and kissed him on the cheek saying, "What's up boo?" Starting up his car, Baby-D looked over at Mann and waved as he pulled off. Shooting by Mann, Baby-D saw Mann giving him a look that said, 'Dat's right shorty'. Baby-D knew Mann was impressed by the way he had pulled Caramel, being as though she was much older than him.

Flying across town through the empty DC streets, Baby-D asked Caramel what was going on with the PASSION single.

Turning the loud music down, Caramel said, "We finished wit da single. We workin' on da album now." Pulling out a CD, Caramel cut the tape deck off and threw a copy of PASSION's single in the disc player. "Listen to dis," Caramel said, as the booming sound of the song 'Destiny' filled the car.

"Short Dogg made dat beat?" Baby-D asked. Caramel told him that Short Dogg had made all the beats that they were going to use on the tape. Feeling the R&B song more than he thought he would, Baby-D turned it up and said, "Y'all ain't bullshitin', huh?" Caramel began telling him how Mann made moves so quick and so precisely that she couldn't believe that he hadn't ran a record label before.

In what seemed to be overnight to Caramel, Mann had turned the studio into a record label. He had gotten a distribution deal for the single and was working on another one for the album. Through Silk's partner Rick, Mann had secured a publishing deal that would get PASSION paid years after their single was old news, if it did well. Within the upcoming week, Mann had two interviews set up for PASSION. One was with BET and another on WPGC 95.5, the local DC radio station. A week after that, Mann had a crew of Howard University filming students coming in to shoot a video to promote the upcoming single.

"Damn, Mann ain't bullshitin'," Baby-D said as he pulled up outside of Caramel's apartment on Martin Luther King Avenue.

"You done known Mann longer than me. You know how he carry shit," Caramel said as she and Baby-D got out of the car and headed for her house.

After parking his truck around the corner, Quick walked around to the drug strip on Georgia Avenue and ran into Lil' Garvin, Short Dogg, and a few older dudes that used Georgia Avenue to pay the bills.

"What's up joe?" Quick said to Lil' Garvin, after speaking to everyone else.

"Ain't shit joe. Where Lando at? He ain't tryin' to get none of dis money?" Lil' Garvin asked. Quick told him that Lando's girl had just got put out of her mother's house because she was pregnant by him and that he was staying in the house for the night. Short Dogg lit up a blunt of weed as he walked over and passed it to Quick. Quick took the blunt and leaned against the wall as he watched the Avenue like a moving snake that was sliding into striking distance.

Money had been coming through without a rest for the last half hour as Quick and everyone else got what was theirs. Running across the street to serve a pipehead, an older dude named Lip saw an old Dodge sitting in the alley down the hill from the Ave. Serving the pipehead quickly without taking his eyes off of the out of place Dodge, Lip ran back across the street to get his pistol. Grabbing his pistol form under the parked car, he put Quick and the rest of the younger dudes on point about the Dodge in the alley.

Just as everybody started walking towards Rittenhouse Street so they could see what was up with the Dodge that was in the alley, three niggaz

Eyone Williams

in ski masks dressed in all black   bent the corner and opened fire on the mini mall parking lot. Lip started emptying his pistol at the gunmen. Quick and Lil' Garvin did the same, while running behind a parked car. Short Dogg knew more than the rest about the gunmen, which drove him to run right in their direction fearlessly as he spit round after round out of the Mac-11 that he was carrying. The three gunmen came to do the shooting, not to get shot at. Short Dogg's rampage shooting caused them to run for their car. Followed by everyone else, Short Dogg ran behind the gunmen with the Mac-11 blazing causing the three gunmen to abandon their car and disappear into the darkness of the early morning hours.

As the night grew old, Nakia laid asleep on the extra bed in Tyesha's room dreaming about having Lando's baby. Waking up in the middle of the night, she couldn't stand being upstairs without him, knowing that they were in the same house. She got out of the bed and went downstairs with Lando, unnoticed as well as unheard. Looking at Lando laying asleep on his bed with the TV still on, Nakia laid down beside him and fell asleep as well.

Pamila woke up bright and early in the morning to get Tyesha ready for her first day of school. Pamila had been on Quick and Lando's back about getting into school or at least taking a G.E.D. class like Mann had done. They gave her their word that they would do it when school started for everyone else and Pamila was going to make sure they kept their word.

Going downstairs to wake Lando and Quick up so that they could go sign up for G.E.D. classes, Pamila saw that Quick wasn't in the house, but she was more surprised to see Nakia in the bed with Lando because she was asleep when Lando brought Nakia in the house last night. She never knew the girl was there. Walking over to Lando's bed, Pamila shook him. Lando and Nakia both woke up looking confused. Lando didn't even know Nakia had come downstairs last night.

"What da hell is going on down here, Lando?" Pamila asked, she didn't like people in her house when she didn't know it. Wiping the sleep out of his eyes, Lando sat up on the bed and looked over at Nakia, who looked scared.

"Pamila," Lando said, as he began to explain what was going on, "You know dis my girl."

Pamila shook her head yes and said, "And...." Lando told her that Nakia's mother had put her out and she had nowhere to go, so he let her stay over for the night.

"What did your mother put you out for?" Pamila asked Nakia. Full of fear and embarrassment, Nakia looked at Lando for help. "Cat gotcha tongue?" Pamila asked. Lando knew Pamila was too aggressive for Nakia.

Cutting in Lando said, "Her mother put her out because she's pregnant by me." The whole room went silent. Pamila just stared at Nakia for a second not saying anything.

Suddenly, Pamila looked over at Lando and said, "So what you gon do mister?" Lando began to tell Pamila that he was going to take care of the baby.

"How you think you gon do that?" Pamila asked. Lando knew he had enough money to do it, but he didn't know how to tell Pamila that he did.

"I'll find a way. You know dat," Lando said. Knowing more than he thought, Pamila began to tell him that if he thought he was going to take care of Nakia and the baby by selling drugs all night, that he would be hurting all three of them more than he would be helping. She suggested that Lando get a job and get into a G.E.D. class like he said he was going to do. She told him that she would get Mann to give him a job if she had to but she wanted him to get one somewhere.

"Okay, I'll work on dat," Lando said.

"And for you, miss hot drawers. You can stay here until everything works itself out, but you gon have to let me talk to your mother. I can't have you in here without your family knowing where you are." Nakia was pleased that Pamila was so understanding and quickly agreed to giving Pamila her mother's number. Pamila told Lando that she would talk to him later on when she got home from work.

"Behave yourselves," Pamila said to the two young people as she left to take Tyesha to school.

Wondering why Quick hadn't come home last night, Lando stood up and looked at Nakia, who seemed to be pleased by the way things went with Pamila.

"What's up?" Lando said with a smile as he stretched.

"I didn't know your peoples were going to be so understanding," Nakia said.

Laughing a little bit, Lando said, "Yeah, Pamila real peoples. She go hard, but she mean good." Lando began to explain to Nakia that she would grow to love her like a mother as time went on. Their relationship would be way more than rides down Oak Hill now.

"Shit gon be cool boo, watch," Lando said as he leaned over and kissed Nakia.

After taking a shower, Lando was coming back downstairs when he heard the door open behind him. Mann was coming in the door wearing one of the sweatshirts with Jazmin's design on it.

"What's up joe?" Lando said as he turned and walked over to Mann.

Giving Mann five, Lando said, "I got some shit to tell you joe."

Mann walked over to the sofa and sat down saying, "I got something to tell you too. You want da good news or da bad news first?" Lando quickly became alert wondering what the bad news could be.

"Fuck it," Lando said as he sat down beside Mann in his towel, "Give me da good news first joe." Mann pulled a knot of money out of his pocket and gave Lando $500 telling him that Jazmin's design was selling like hot cakes and that he wanted Lando to give her $200 for coming up with the design.

"For every shirt I sell, I'ma give her $15," Mann said.

Smiling, Lando said, "She gon love dis here slim."

Bracing himself for whatever the bad news could be, Lando said, "So what's da bad news."

Growing up with all of the older dudes on Georgia Avenue, where Lando and all of the young niggaz now sold coke, Mann knew Lip from back in the day. They were close. After the shooting on the Ave., Lip took Short Dogg, Quick, and Lil' Garvin to the hospital. Short Dogg had gotten shot in the leg as he ran toward the shooters. Coming back uptown, Lip beeped Pat-Pat to tell him what had happened and to see if he knew what was going on. Pat-Pat didn't know of anyone who would want to come up the Ave. shooting at the time, but did know that Quick and Lando were Mann's peoples so he beeped Mann and put him on point with everything that Lip had told him.

"So Short Dogg da only one dat got hit last night?" Lando asked, as his anger grew a little bit.

"Yeah shorty da only one dat got hit out there," Mann said, "but I think shorty may know why dem niggaz came up da Ave. bustin'. When you catch up with 'em, find out." Lando thought about what Mann said and was surely going to see if he could find out who shot his man.

"I got dat slim, don't worry about dat," Lando said as he stood up with the $200 in his hand.

"So what you got to tell me joe?" Mann asked. Lando began telling Mann about how he was about to be a father and how Pamila was going to let Nakia stay over the house until he decided what he was going to do. Mann smiled. He could see that Lando was already looking forward to having the baby. But Mann knew that he couldn't live in the basement with Nakia while Quick stayed down there.

"I'm happy for you shorty," Mann said as he stood up, "but now you gon have to think for three people. It ain't no more ride or die shit, you got a youngin' on da way." Mann told Lando that he felt that it would be best for him to get a little apartment for him and Nakia.

"I like dat idea. I'ma need somebody to put da joint in their name for me though," Lando said. Mann told him not to worry about it, and that he would have an apartment for Lando by the end of the week. Before leaving the house, Mann reminded Lando to find out if Short Dogg knew who had come up the Ave. shooting.

"I got dat joe. I'ma catch you later." Lando said.

Downstairs in the basement, Lando got dressed while he told Nakia that he was going to get them an apartment by the end of the week.

"So if your mother still act like she don't want you to come back home, we'll go ahead and live together. I know you'll like dat," Lando said smiling at Nakia. She was excited by the sound of having Lando all to herself.

"What you think Pamila gon say?" she asked. Lando told her that he would make Pamila understand what he was doing. While they talked, the phone rang. Quick was calling from Short Dogg's aunt's house around the corner. Quick told Lando to come over as soon as he could. Lando hung up the phone and told Nakia that he would be back later.

"Where you going?" she asked as she stood up and hugged Lando.

"I gotta take care of something," Lando said. He kissed Nakia and hit the door.

Walking in the basement door of Short Dogg's aunt's house, Lando saw Short Dogg lying on a pullout bed with his thigh wrapped up in bandages. Quick, Lil' Garvin, Baby-D, and Tank all sat around him talking about what needed to be done about the three gunmen that had came up the Ave. shooting.

"Hold up! Hold up!" Lando said as he walked over and sat down beside Short Dogg. He just knew that he was missing too much of the story if they were already talking about what needed to be done. "Y'all already know who did da busin'?" Lando asked the room as he looked around.

"Yeah, some niggaz from around my mother's way out SE did it," Short Dogg said.

Two years ago, Short Dogg killed an older dude around his way along with an old partner of his who later testified on him in juvenile court which is how he got sent down Oak Hill and met Lando and Quick. The older dude that he killed had two little brothers that were Short Dogg's age. Short Dogg knew that they were looking for him, along with an older cousin of theirs but he thought he could take care of the beef himself without bringing Lando and everyone else into it.

"We in it now joe!" Lando said as he looked around the room once again. "We ain't no fuck wit you halfway niggaz. If we fuck wit you we fuck wit you joe!" Lando made it clear that he was with whatever Short Dogg was trying to do and Short Dogg felt the realness in the room.

"So where dese niggaz be at?" Lando asked. Short Dogg told him where the dudes could be found. Lando shook his head and said, "We gon see what dem niggaz really 'bout." Standing up, Lando told everybody to meet him at Pamila's house later on so they could take a ride out SE.

"I gotta go sign up for dis G.E.D. class; I'ma holla at Black on my way down there. We gon get dat "K" he got and tear shit up," Lando said as he left the house.

School was letting out as Lando was coming back from signing up for the G.E.D. class. He decided to stop in front of the High School to see if he could catch Jazmin.

Sitting in his Twin Turbo with Tupac blasting out of the speakers, Lando watched all of the young people go back and forth in all of their new school gear. Lando was surprised to see five sweatshirts with Jazmin's design on them, he felt good that he played a part of the whole thing. Seeing all of the high school kids getting on the bus, Lando thought back to when he was a regular kid. The fast lane had forced him to grow up and he was now knee deep in it. It was no turning back for him.

Jazmin saw Lando's car as she walked up the hill on Georgia Avenue with a few friends. Breaking off from the crowd, she walked up and got in Lando's car.

"What's up boy?" Jazmin said with an excited smile as she leaned over and kissed Lando on the cheek.

Starting the car up and whipping it into a U-turn across to the other side of Georgia Avenue through the traffic, Lando said, "I got a surprise for you," as he pulled out the money Mann had given him for Jazmin.

"My brother wants you to have dis for your shirts. Dem joints must be sellin'." With a bright smile on her face, Jazmin took the money and thanked Lando for getting her shirt made.

"I seen a rack of people at school wit my shirt on." Jazmin said. She couldn't believe it. Not only had her respect for Lando grown, but her respect for Mann was starting to develop. Lando encouraged her to keep on working on her designs as he drove her home.

As the night grew dark, Lando made his way to Mann's old apartment out White Oak to pick up a few bricks. Walking in the door he saw Black and Dre sitting on the sofa talking about some young dude that had disrespected Dre earlier.

Dre had given an old female friend a ride home after leaving Mann's World. When he dropped her off at her house, her baby's father was out front with a few other young dudes. Seeing his baby's mother get out of Dre's ZR1, the young dude smacked her and started talking shit to Dre. Dre got out of the car and stepped to the young dude telling him that he wasn't messing with his baby's mother but the young dude wasn't trying to hear anything, he pulled a pistol out on Dre and told him he better get to stepping.

"Who da fuck is dis young nigga?" Black asked, not liking the way things had went down.

"Some lil' nigga name Shawn," Dre said.

Lando cut in, "You talking 'bout Lil' Mousy from around 21st Street." Dre didn't know the young dude but he knew he was from around 21st Street. Lando knew Lil' Mousy from junior high school. The young dude was known amongst Lando's generation for being a quick killer. Lando told Black and Dre about Lil' Mousy and how long he'd known him. Dre really wasn't even tripping off the young dude, but was fucked up that he pulled a gun on him.

"We should go around there and air dat joint out!" Black said. Dre didn't agree. He felt that everybody would point the finger at him.

"Naa, let's let da shit ride for awhile joe," Dre said.

Switching the subject, Lando   told them about the dudes that had shot at Short Dogg and that he planned to go around SE tonight with everybody else and catch the niggaz slippin'. One way or another, Black was going to get some gunplay tonight.

"When y'all rollin'?" Black asked. Lando told him that everybody would be over Pamila's house in a little while. "I'll be over there in a half hour," Black said as he left.

Mann walked out into the living room after talking to Kelly for an hour.

"What's up shorty?" Mann said as he handed Lando a Foot Locker bag with 2 bricks in it.

"Ain't shit joe," Lando said before putting Mann down with who shot Short Dogg and why. Mann knew his little brother well. He knew Lando was going to roll with Short Dogg on the sole strength that he had love for the young dude. Not wanting Lando and the rest of the young dudes around the way to get into another long drawn out beef, Mann asked Lando to take care of the situation as quick as he could and to leave no one that could tell on him.

"Watch yourself shorty. Stick and move," Mann said. Lando took the advice his brother had given him and left. Mann thought about what the night would hold and didn't feel good about any of it, but knew that some things had to be done.

Heavily armed, sitting in Lil' Garvin's van at the top of 30th Street SE, Black, Lando, Short Dogg, Quick, Baby-D, and Lil' Garvin looked down the street and quietly watched the three dudes that they were after. Timing was everything and Lando wanted to get everything over with at one time.

"Let's roll up and jump out on dem niggaz!" Quick said as he sat on the floor spinning a chrome .45 on his finger.

"Naa, it ain't no telling what might go wrong like dat," Lando said as he explained that they only wanted the three dudes that had done the shooting. They all knew that they couldn't walk up on the crowd of dudes at the bottom of the hill as deep as they were.

"Fuck it!" Black said, "we gotta separate dem niggaz somehow if we only want dem three."

15 minutes later, Lando gave up on waiting for the three dudes to leave the drug strip so they could follow them to their death spot.

"We gotta pull up on dem niggaz joe," Lando said, "let's roll." Lil Garvin wasted no time. He started up the van and started slowly rolling down the hill. "Clear everything out and then we gon run da niggaz down," Lando said to Black since he had an AK-47 that was just right for the job.

Creeping at a deadly pace 20 feet away from life or death, Black sat right in front of the sliding side door of the van with his hands wrapped tightly around his AK-47 just waiting for Baby-D to open the door so he could start spraying.

Behind Black on the floor talking to Short Dogg, Lando said, "You ready?" Short Dogg laughed, he wanted to get this over with more than anyone.

"Watch me work!" he said with a little smirk.

"Here we go!" Lil' Garvin said from behind the wheel, letting everybody know that it was game time.

Baby-D yanked the side door open and Black jumped out with the AK-47 firing murderously. Black went crazy waving the AK-47 from side to side causing the crowd to run different ways. As automatic gunfire ripped through the late night air, Lando and Baby-D ran after two of the dudes that had done the shooting on the Ave. Quick and Short Dogg ran after the other one while shooting at everything moving. Short Dogg, still in pain from his gunshot wounds, seemed like his adrenaline was taking over. Waiting for everyone to get back to the van, Lil' Garvin sat behind the wheel firing his Glock in all directions out the window.

After Short Dogg and Quick had put slugs in one of the two dudes that they had went after, they had to shoot their way back to the van, allowing one of the dudes that had done the shooting on the Ave. to get away. Lando and Baby-D came running back to the van shooting back into the cut that they had just killed one of the 30th Street niggaz in. He was one of the shooters that hit Short Dogg up the Ave. Allowing everybody to jump into the van, Black made sure no one would even think about running out into the street shooting by the way he backed into the van spraying in all directions. Still spraying, Black jumped backwards into the van, as Lil' Garvin took them all flying out of sight with the tires screaming.

Mann woke up the next morning and looked at his radio clock, it was 7:30am and he had to be at the studio in 30 minutes. Wasting no time, Mann got up and jumped into the shower. In the shower, he could hear the local radio station playing all of the new music that was out at the time. A lot of West Coast music was playing.

Jumping out of the shower, Mann heard the DJ say, "We got something new from a group of bad sistas outta DC called PASSION." Mann couldn't help it. He was excited. He had waited for the day when he would hear PASSION on the radio. He sat on his bed drying off as he shook his head to 'Destiny,' PASSION's soon to drop single, da joint straight rocked.

"That was PASSION, their first single will be in stores September 30th. Go pick it up," the DJ said. Mann's morning was starting off on the right foot. After the next song went off, the DJ came back on with the morning news.

"There was a terrible shooting on 30th Street SE last night that left 4 dead and 6 wounded," the DJ said, "police said it was a gangland shooting." Mann shook his head. He knew that Lando and the rest of the dudes from around the way were responsible. Mann got dressed and beeped Lando before leaving for the studio.

Mann had only been behind the track board for 30 minutes when Lando and Quick walked into the studio. Mann took his headphones off as they sat down behind him.

While PASSION kept going over their song, Mann turned around and said, "So what went down last night?" Lando began to tell Mann how they ended up spraying everything and one of the dudes still got away. Mann had a feeling that was going to happen, he never handled business like that, but he knew that he and his little brother were two different people.

In deep thought about the whole situation, Mann looked at Quick then back to Lando and said, "So what y'all gon do now?" Quick felt as though there was only one thing to do at the time.

"We gon ride til dis shit over. You know how we do it Mann," Quick said, looking over at Lando to make sure that he shared his feelings.

"Yeah," Lando said, "we gon ride da shit out. We ain't young and wild no more. We gon be alright joe." Mann thought about that for a second. They had slowed down a lot and they could hold their own in the streets. Mann told them to watch their steps and to try their best to get the beef over with as quick as they could. If they had to, keep a vest wit dem at all times.

Black didn't feel safe trying to make it all the way back to Georgetown late at night with an AK-47. He got Lil' Garvin to drop him off over his mother's house in NE DC. Black had given his mother hell his whole life, but she still loved him and kept a room for him all the time.

"Richard," Black's mother said, "I got something for you to eat boy." Black woke up smiling. His mother always had breakfast made at 8:00am in the morning, her style never changed. The tall dark skinned woman sat on the bed beside Black and tried to enjoy a minute with her only son.

"When you gon slow down boy? Dem streets gon kill you one of dese days," she said. Black laughed as he bit into the egg and cheese sandwich that she had made for him.

"Ma, I'm chillin'. I got a job at Mann's store and everything," Black said as he tried to make his mother believe that he was leaving the streets alone.

"You can't fool me boy. I been around too long. I'm hip to your lil' bad ass, you can tell dat to da cops next time they get on ya ass, but I know betta," his mother said. Black sat back and listened to his mother talk about life and how things go, then she popped up with some news.

"You know your friend Smoke called here from jail yesterday," she said. Black had just seen Smoke and Serge two days ago.

"Did you give him my number?" Black asked. His mother didn't give Smoke the number because she didn't know if Black wanted him to have it, so she told him to call back in a day or two. "Give 'em my number whenever he calls back," Black said as he got up to take a shower.

Tank and the rest of the young dudes on 5th AND Rittenhouse all sat in the alley pushing coke in the late night darkness. Lil' Garvin had warned them that some dudes might come through looking for Short Dogg and everybody else, but Tank and his little men thought they were ready for whatever and went on with their everyday money making.

As the pipeheads started coming from every direction, the night began to move faster on 5th and Rittenhouse Street. The young dudes were making as much money as possible now that they had the 5th Street strip to themselves since Lando and everybody else were all getting money on the Ave. With every second that passed, death grew closer tonight for the young dudes. Chip, one of the dudes from 30th Street SE that had gotten away last night, was on the move with payback on his mind. Not only had Short Dogg been responsible for the deaths of three of his cousins, but he was responsible for the death of one of his partners as well.

Rolling through Georgia Avenue along with two younger dudes from 30th Street, Chip could find no one. He had heard that some of the dudes that Short Dogg was now hanging with sold coke on 5th and Rittenhouse Street so he decided to ride through and see what he could find because somebody had to pay for what happened last night.

Chip came rolling through Rittenhouse Street slowly and saw Kisha getting out of a blue Pathfinder.

"What's up wit da niggaz in dat Path?" One of the young dudes in the back seat of the old Chevy station wagon asked.

As the Pathfinder pulled off, Chip said, "We ain't looking for dem niggaz." Chip then pulled up to the corner of 5th Street ready to head back for SE when he saw Tank and the four other young dudes come out of the alley behind Kisha's house. Chip had what he wanted now. He didn't care if Short Dogg wasn't outside or not. He just wanted some kind of payback.

Chip circled the block and came back down the street slowly. Tank and everyone else spotted the car and posted up to see if trouble was on the horizon. Sure enough, Chip smashed on the gas and came flying down the street. The two younger dudes leaned out the window firing their automatic weapons at the group of young dudes in front of Old Tima's house. Tank and Lil' Moe were on the front line, they stood behind a parked car shooting at the speeding station wagon. Dee-Dee, Tank's little cousin stood right behind Lil' Moe shooting at the car as well while everyone else with them did the same. As car windows broke and bullets slammed into bricks and metal, no one knew if they were hit or not, it was all or nothing.

Seconds later the station wagon was bending the corner at the end of the block as the sound of gunfire died out. Tank ran into the street and spit a few more rounds as the station wagon bent the corner. When he looked back over to the sidewalk, he saw Lil' Moe standing over his cousin Dee-Dee. Tank knew he was dead. Tears began to gather in his eyes. Dee-Dee laid in Lil' Moe's arms with a chunk of his young head blown off. At only 12 years old, his young life was over before it even started in the fast lane.

Fast Lane

17

Every single night after Dee-Dee's funeral, Tank, Lil' Moe, and the rest of the 5th Street youngins made it their business to ride across town to 30th Street, get out, and spray anything that looked like it could be affiliated with the beef.

At first Tank held a grudge against Short Dogg for Dee-Dee's death, but Lando explained to him that Short Dogg never meant for any of his beef to affect 5th Street. Tank had grown to respect Lando and tried to understand what he had said, but it was Short Dogg that eventually won Tank over by riding around 30th Street with him and killing one of the young dudes that had killed Dee-Dee after they had gotten word who they were.

The beef was in full swing with nightly shootings uptown and over SE. Homicide Detectives were lost. They couldn't understand what had sparked such a war. Vice Cop Hall on the other hand knew everything about the beef, but kept it to himself so that he could crack the thing wide open as soon as someone left a loose end. Hall checked his traps on a regular basis and it was amazing how much information he got off the streets from pipeheads and dope fiends. Hall already knew that the whole beef was over a murder that Short Dogg committed 2 years ago. He also knew that Lando and the uptown dudes now played a major part in the beef because of the first Georgia Avenue shooting. It was all a matter of time before Hall would have an arrest for someone's murder and he didn't care who it was as long as they went to jail for the rest of their young life.

For Lando and the rest of his childhood partners, this was the first time they were involved in a beef with dudes that were bringing the heat back their way. Short Dogg, on the other hand, was used to it and really wasn't trippin' one way or another. Now that he was hanging uptown, he still hung on the strip pushing coke when he wasn't riding with Lando and everyone else looking for Chip, who had been laying low until he could pop up and kill one of the uptown dudes or Short Dogg.

Now that Lando had moved into the apartment that Mann got for him and Nakia, he could really feel the strain that the beef was putting on his pockets. Most of his money came from selling weight to the young dudes on 5th and Rittenhouse, but with them going on nightly manhunts, they weren't moving as much coke as they use to which caused Lando to hit the block more to cover the difference. The extra stress of wearing a bulletproof vest everywhere he went, having a baby on the way, and not knowing if he would see tomorrow had Lando and everyone else desperately trying to hit the head of the problem so that the body would fall, which in this case the head was Chip and the body was the ruthless young killers of 30th Street.

At a rented mansion in Bowie, Maryland, Mann SAT behind the director of PASSION's first video shoot talking to Black about how wild the beef was getting between 30th Street and the hood. Sipping on his drink in the cool fall wind, Black watched PASSION give the camera their best looks out back while the music of their first single blasted through the air.

"You gettin' too old for dat beefin' shit," Mann said to Black, "you done done your dirt, you gotta get some money now." Mann knew that Black loved everything about the streets. He lived for it. But Mann also felt the peace of mind that he now got from not being on the block and he wanted Black and everyone else to feel it as well. With Mann's World doing well business wise and PASSION's first single, which had been pushed back a month, looking promising, Mann was ready to give the game up all the way.

"I feel ya," Black said, "but I gotta ride wit Lando and dem. It's me joe." Mann could understand where Black was coming from. At the same time, Mann knew that Lando and the rest of the young dudes could hold their own. He wished that his cousin could see it that way too. Instead of pulling himself back into the streets that he had worked so hard to get out of, Mann focused on making his business hustles work so that he could pull everyone else out of the fast lane. Black had to respect Mann's point of view.

As PASSION's video shoot came to a close, Black got ready to leave.

Giving Mann five as he hugged him, Black said, "I gotta go over da jail to see Smoke and Serge. They want me to take care of some BI for dem about they case." Mann smiled, as much dirt as Black did, he was real to his niggaz. Mann respected that more than anything about his younger cousin, even though he didn't respect the dudes Black was fucking with. Mann knew Lil' Tim as well and when he found out that Smoke and

Serge had killed him, Mann just added that to his dislike and lack of trust for them.

"Come by da studio later on and holla at me," Mann said as Black left.

18

Despite all of the madness of the streets, BABY-D's love for boxing never went away. Fish Bone, his trainer, knew that Baby-D was deep into the streets, but he managed to get him in the gym a few nights a week. Even with Baby-D's lack of consistent training, his natural skills kept him above the rest, which is what placed him in the position to fight for the Golden Glove middle weight championship along with another DC boxer by the name of Robert Lane who was going after the Golden Glove feather weight championship. The event had the whole city ampted up at the possibility of the DC fighters bringing home the belts and being as though the fights were being held in the Howard University gym, it seemed as though the fights were world title fights. People from all parts of town flooded into the gym to see their homies fight. Lando and his whole mob came out to see Baby-D and Robert Lane fight. Ever mindful of the beef, Baby-D took 3 pistols in the gym for Lando to come get from his locker room once he and everybody else were inside.

Music was blasting inside the big gym as Lando and everyone else walked in. Lando told everybody that he was going to go get the pistols and that he would meet them back at their seats in about 5 minutes.

Lando made his way through the huge crowd and back to Baby-D's locker room. Fish Bone had Baby-D warming up for the fight while he gave him instructions.

"I'm tryin' to see a knock out joe," Lando said as he walked over and grabbed the book bag with the pistols in it.

"Fuck dat shit!" Fish Bone said as he held his mitted hands up for Baby-D to throw his combination into. "I want a smart fight youngsta," Fish Bone said as he looked over at Lando with a look that told him to mind his business right now. Lando took the hint and made his way back out to his ringside seats.

Silk, Mann, and Black were already inside by the time Lando got back. Walking up and sitting down beside Mann with the book bag of guns, Lando began talking to Mann about how Short Dogg had gotten word where the dude Chip was staying and that once they hit his head the beef would eventually die down.

Through all of the noise, Mann managed to say, "When y'all going to take care of dat business?" Lando told him that they planned to put the work in tonight if they could catch up with the dude. Mann told Lando that he really needed to get the beef over with because the longer he let it ride, the better his chances were to get himself killed.

While Lando and Mann talked, the ring announcer began to introduce Baby-D. You could tell that it was a DC thing by the way the gym went off as Baby-D and his entourage led by Fish Bone marched out to the sounds of Maze's 'Back in Stride Again'. Baby-D could feel the love as he walked to the ring in a zone. As he walked by Mann and the rest of the dudes from the neighborhood, deep inside he told himself that he had to win. Just as he stepped into the ring, Baby-D looked up at the top seats and saw PASSION, Caramel was screaming his name out, which meant not only did he have to win, but he had to look good while he did it.

The Golden Glove middle weight champion was then announced as he and his Philadelphia entourage made their way to the ring with the sounds of N.W.A.'s 'Niggaz 4 Life' playing.

Dre stood at the front door looking around for any sign of Mann or Lando. As the bell for the first round rung, Dre knew where to find his homies by the way they went off cheering Baby-D on. Walking down to the ringside seats, Dre looked on as the thicker champion slowly walked around Baby-D sizing him up. Dre could see that Baby-D was his same old self. Just as Dre was about to say something to Silk, the first punches exploded.

Baby-D stood with his chin safely tucked behind his shoulder, right hand waiting to fire and his left hand dropped to the side as he weaved the champs 6 punch combination. Looking back up in the ring after hearing the sound of smacking leather, Dre saw Baby-D catch the last punch thrown by the champ as he quickly rocked away and slammed a punishing straight right hand hard down the pipe splitting the champs mouth wide open.

Eyone Williams

"Damn young nigga!" Dre said as the whole gym flew to their feet screaming. The champ fell straight into Baby-D's chest getting blood all on him as he went out. Hardly sweating, Baby-D turned and began walking to his corner as the champ fell hard to the canvas.

Caramel went crazy in the stands when she saw Baby-D smoothly step back to his corner. She felt herself getting wet in the pants as she screamed out Baby-D's name in the same way she did when they made love. She had a right to be excited. Her man was now the Golden Glove champion and it only took him 49 seconds to do it.

While Baby-D received his belt and was declared champ, Dre sat in between Mann and Lando telling them that he had just saw the 30th Street niggaz at the front door. Lando wanted to head for the door so that he could catch them coming out. Quick, Lil' Garvin, and Short Dogg felt the same way, but Mann thought different.

"Fuck dat," Mann said, "wait til dis is over. If opportunity presents itself, follow 'em to a nice spot and air they ass out. Don't just run out into the streets shooting with no plan." Silk watched Mann at work, he liked how the younger dude passed the game on to his little brother and was even more impressed by the respect they had for Mann's advice.

While Mann was somewhat schooling Lando and the rest of the younger dudes, the ring announcer began to introduce Robert Lane. The noise in the gym grew so loud that Mann had to wrap up what he was saying as Robert Lane and his entourage flooded the gym floor on their way to the ring, led by the Golden Glove champion Vernon Boykin who had won his title in the same building. Local go-go band Rare Essence blasted through the speakers as Robert "Fighter" Lane climbed into the ring. By the time the announcer was introducing the champion, the gym was so loud you would have thought Robert Lane was already the champion.

Two minutes into the first round, the taller and more experienced New York City Golden Glove Champion looked real good. He knew he had the belt and despite the DC crowd, he knew he was the champ. For the next round, the champ played it smart and stayed away from the lightening speed of 'Fighter'. Halfway through the 3rd round, Fighter knew he had to make something happen if he wanted to be champ. Fighter rushed the champ forcing him to throw jabs. Fighter put his speed to work and slipped under one of the taller fighter's jabs digging three sharp uppercuts to the body, one to the bottom of the gut and another two to the right side under the heart causing the champ to take a knee in the middle of the ring. It seemed as if the whole city came alive in the gym as the noise factor shot to a whole new level. Fighter could taste the championship. After the champ got up, Fighter rushed him throwing everything he had. A powerful overhand landed right on the champ's chin. As he began to fall, Fighter followed up with a quick uppercut. The referee stepped in waving his hands as the champ fell to the canvas. Fighter was disqualified. The whole gym went off while the champ's corner rushed the ring with smelling salt.

Quick and Black weren't pleased at all. They stood up and threw their large sodas in the ring. The police rushed the ring while most people tried to find the door. Lando reached for the pistol that he had in his waistband and began watching his back amongst all of the confusion. The angry mob grew so out-of-control that Mann had to get everybody's attention so that they could safely slide out of the locker room door.

Once outside in the darkness of the night, Lando and Short Dogg broke off and ran for Lando's Twin Turbo.

Running behind Lando in the middle of the street, Short Dogg said, "I just seen dem niggaz going down the street." As they ran up on the car, Lando looked back down the street to see if he could see the 30th Street dudes.

"It's too much shit going on out here slim. We gon go ahead and slide out Maryland and lay on dat nigga Chip," Lando said, as they jumped in the car. What Mann had said to Lando about ending the beef as soon as he could, had hit Lando hard. Lando had his mind made up that he would be putting a stop to Chip tonight, even if it took all night.

The late night hours were hours only meant for those that worked the graveyard shift or those up to no good. Tonight, Lando and Short Dogg laid in the dark woods across the street from Chip's apartment in Burtonsville, Maryland waiting for him to come home and walk into the arms of death.

At 4:45am, Lando and Short Dogg had been laying in the woods for over 3 hours. The sun would be up in about 15 minutes and Lando was becoming impatient. Short Dogg had laid on niggaz for nights on end and knew that it was all a matter of time.

"Dis nigga ain't comin' home tonight joe. Let's roll, I'm tired as shit," Lando said.

Short Dogg smiled and said, "I know for a fact he gon be comin' home tonight. Just lay joe."

Fate wasn't with Chip tonight. He had made sure no one followed him home and had made it all the way home with no signs of trouble. As he pulled up in his building parking lot, he looked all around to make sure it was no one around. After checking out the scenery, Chip got out and began walking to the front door, which faced the woods that his young killers laid in, watching him unnoticed. Sliding his key into the front door, Chip heard slow moving footsteps behind him. Turning the key, he looked back and saw death coming his way. Quickly he snatched the door open as the first sounds of automatic gunfire tore through the Pamila hour air. Short Dogg and Lando ran up on Chip's body as it fell to the ground and filled it full of lead before running back into the woods unseen.

A week later, Lando woke up to the sound of Nakia laughing in the living room. Walking out into the living room, Lando saw PASSION on BET talking about their video that had just went off.

Nakia, who was really beginning to look pregnant, said, "They was just on TV talking about Mann and his record label. Mann suppose to come on after dis video go off." Still half sleep, Lando told Nakia to call him when Mann came on TV as he walked to the kitchen in his boxers to get something to eat.

Two minutes later Lando came back into the living room and sat down on the soft black leather sofa with Nakia. Mann was just walking out to talk to Donnie Simpson about his record label. Lando put his arm around Nakia and watched as Mann did his thing.

Donnie Simpson asked Mann all about PASSION and what the world could expect from them and the city of DC.

Looking into the camera, Mann smiled and said, "Well, first the world can expect to see a whole new side of DC. Fast Lane Records is going to be a way out of the streets for a lot of people, but right now it's going to be the way out for my family and friends, then we move on to the rest of da city and even da world." Donnie Simpson was impressed by the way Mann carried himself, he wanted him to tell the viewers how a young man like himself was able to escape the fast lane. Being very careful, Mann told him about some of the things he faced coming up and how he worked for

Pam at Mann's World store and eventually bought it with money loaned from the bank.

"Overall," Mann said, "anybody can make it if they put they heart into it."

Lando watched as Mann finished his interview, he was always impressed with his bigger brother and he knew that one day he would be able to lay back and wash his hands of the streets as soon as he had enough money to do it. Now that Chip was dead, he could put his mind back on money making, even though Tank and the 5th Street youngins had their mind set on riding things out until there was no more 30th Street.

Laid back in the passenger seat of Quick's truck, Lando told Quick how Mann had carried things on BET.

Pulling up in front of St. Albans High School to pick up Amber, who he had been seeing for a while, Quick said, "Mann always makin' something happen. I respect dat about da nigga."

Looking out of the window at the school kids that were his age, Lando said, "Dat ain't all slim." As he began to tell Quick how Mann was going to wash his hands of the coke game and stick with his store and record label.

Not really believing what Lando had said, Quick responded "So Mann just gon give up all dat money on da streets?" Lando explained to him that Mann didn't care about the streets anymore now that he had made his way out. Mann was now going to turn Lando on to his coke connect so that he wouldn't have to deal with someone he didn't know.

"So what, Mann gon put you down wit Silk?" Quick asked.

As Amber walked up to the truck with her books in hand, Lando said, "Yeah, we 'bout to be on for real slim."

Feeding $100 dollar bills into a money counter, Mann and Silk sat in the dining room of Mann's apartment.

"So you out? No more hustlin' no more streets or nothing?" Silk asked Mann after Mann finished telling him that he was through with the coke game.

"I'm done slim. I got what I came for," Mann said as he pulled one stack of money out of the machine and placed another into it. With $957,000 counted on the dining room table, Mann told Silk how he wanted him to deal with Lando so that he didn't have to deal with just anybody on the streets.

"We gon see where Lando's head at," Silk said. "If shorty want to make some cash I got 'em, but if he still wanna be some Wild West gun slinger, I can't fuck wit 'em." Mann had to respect where Silk was coming from and now it was all on how Lando carried things when he came over tonight.

Lando walked into Mann's apartment minutes later and saw all the money that Mann was stacking into a big safe.

"What's up shorty?" Mann said as he shut the safe and sat back down at the table. "Sit down joe. We got to holla at you," Mann said. Lando walked over, gave Silk five, and sat down. Mann began telling Lando that Silk was willing to fuck with him as long as his mind was right. Lando understood just where everything was going.

"I feel y'all slim," Lando said as he looked at Silk. "Man, I got a baby on da way now. I ain't trying to be stuck in da streets forever." Mann and Silk could see that Lando was serious about getting some paper.

"Look here," Silk said, "I'ma make sure you get what you got comin', but you gotta understand a few things." As Silk told Lando that he would only be dealing with him and none of his little buddies, Lando listened and took everything to heart.

"Our business is our business," Silk said.

Mann looked at Lando and said, "You dig what he sayin shorty?" Lando understood very well. Standing up, Lando reached across the table and gave Silk five again, before leaving to take Nakia out to eat.

Down Georgia Avenue on Morton Street, Black sat on top of his new Nissan Pathfinder talking to one of his old buddies about where to find a witness that was telling on Smoke and Serge. Will, a dark skinned slick young nigga that had been around a long time, began telling Black that he knew the witness whose name was Kindle.

"Dat bitch ass nigga just asked me to drop him off down da court building to take a UA. Dat nigga probably goin' down da grand jury," Will said, becoming upset that he could have even indirectly played a role in some "hot shit."

"So when you think da nigga gon be back around here?" Black asked as he watched the non-stop traffic of money and coke being exchanged from hand to hand.

Turning around to serve a pipehead, Will said, "Dat nigga should be back around here 'bout 10." Black jumped down off of the hood and told Will that he would be back later on tonight.

Tank and his little crew all stood on Rittenhouse Street pushing coke from hand to hand when Lil' Garvin came through in his 850.

Rolling down the window as he stopped in front of Old Tima's house, Tank walked up to the car and said, "What's up young?" as he jumped in. Backing into a parking space, Lil' Garvin handed Tank two bricks of coke while looking around to make sure no unwanted eyes looked on.

Tank tucked the bricks under his sweatshirt and handed Lil' Garvin a brown paper bag with $19,000 in it and said, "I'ma have da rest of dat tonight."

Lil' Garvin had grown a lot of love for Tank and he knew that Dee-Dee's death was still bothering him deep down inside, but Lil' Garvin also knew that if Tank kept taking his little crew on murder moves over 30th Street almost every other night, that shorty would eventually get them all killed or locked up. Lil' Garvin had to say something to Tank about the way he was carrying things.

"Look here joe," Lil' Garvin said as he looked up the street through his rear view mirror, "I know you still fucked up about Dee-Dee, but da niggaz dat did dat shit dead now. You can't keep ridin to be ridin. No matter how many niggaz you kill, you can't bring shorty back." Tank could feel Lil' Garvin and he had felt a lot better when he found out that someone had killed Chip, but he just couldn't stop beefin' with the dudes that were rolling with Chip when he was alive.

Tank looked at Lil' Garvin as he opened up the door and said, "I gotta finish what they started slim."

Pulling off, Lil' Garvin thought about how Tank might end up being one of the dudes that just never get out of the fast lane. Some people just couldn't think outside of the streets. Stopping at the stop sign, Lil' Garvin saw Baby-D flying around the corner in his red Twin Turbo. Baby-D started blowing his horn for Lil' Garvin to pull over as he passed by him and stopped in front of Kisha's house.

Lil' Garvin parked and got out to talk to Baby-D who was now sitting on Kisha's porch. The nighttime fall air was blowing hard as Lil'

Garvin walked up on the porch and sat down beside Kisha, who had just came outside to see who was on her porch.

"Hey boo," she said to Baby-D as she hugged him. She then turned around and hugged Lil' Garvin before going back in the house swinging her behind from side to side.

"What's up joe?" Lil' Garvin asked as he looked down at his beeper.

Baby-D began telling Lil' Garvin how some people had saw him fight for the Golden Glove title and that they got in touch with Fish Bone to tell him that they wanted to work with Baby-D to train him for pro fighting. Lil' Garvin couldn't understand what the problem could be.

Confused, he said, "So what's da problem?" Baby-D told him that he would have to leave town and move up to Philadelphia for a while to stay at the camp of Bernard Hopkins so that he could start his training.

Lil' Garvin sighed and said, "Man, you better jump on dat shit. Ain't shit around here but da streets joe. Fuck dis shit! Dis shit gon be here young." Baby-D was glad his partner understood where he was coming from.

Smiling, Baby-D stood up excited, he gave Lil' Garvin five and said, "You right joe. I'ma try dis boxing shit."

Black was twisting a silencer on to a 9mm in the front seat of Will's BMW as they pulled into an alley down the street from Morton Street.

"I'ma go get dis nigga out his girl house and act like we 'bout to go get some smoke," Will said as he got out of the car and walked down the dark alley. Black was cool with the plan Will had given him. Will was supposed to lure Kindle out into the dark alley while Black was waiting in the darkness of the cool night.

Hiding behind a huge dumpster, Black waited to hear the back door of the old apartment building to open so he could get rid of another rat. As Black began to think how easy it was to kill a witness that really felt safe after coming home from the grand jury, the old wooden door opened. Black stood still and listened to the first footsteps that began to quickly move down the alley. While Black eased out behind Will and Kindle, he could hear Will telling Kindle how he had some bitches back at his house. Black smiled under the ski mask as he began to raise his 9mm in the air. Kindle heard someone behind him and Will as they walked. As soon as he turned to see what was behind them, Black placed two hollow point slugs into his forehead without a blink.

At noon on September 30th, people flooded Mann's World and many other record stores in the city and across the country to buy PASSION's first single. Dre couldn't believe how much business the single had brought Mann's World. Standing in the back of the store in front of a huge poster of the three beautiful young women known as PASSION, Dre smiled as three young girls left the store after buying three different color sweatshirts with Jazmin's design on it along with a copy of the soon to be a hit single 'Destiny'.

Dre walked by the counter and told Naomi and Kisha that he had to go take care of some business and that he had to leave early tonight. Stepping out on to Georgia Avenue into the cool fall evening air, Dre thought of how Mann's plan worked not only with the store, but it looked as if the record label thing was going to work as well. Dre had his doubts at first, but Mann had made him and Black believers in no time.

Walking around the corner to his car, Dre zipped up his new Hugo Boss leather as he adjusted his .40 caliber that was in the inside pocket. Watching his back as he walked up Georgia Avenue, Dre saw an old blue Ford LTD at the corner with tinted windows. As the car slowly pulled up beside Dre, Dre made sure to get close to a parked car until he could tell what was going on. The LTD stopped and the passenger side window dropped. Dre saw the young dude Lil' Mousy in the passenger seat. Before Dre even thought about pulling his pistol, Lil' Mousy fired several rounds at him. Dre ducked behind the car as bullets crashed into the brick wall behind him. Dre pulled his pistol out quickly as he heard the car tires screaming down the street. Standing up to look over the car he was kneeling behind, Dre emptied his clip at the speeding LTD before running to his car.

"I told you to take dat lil' nigga serious!" Black said to Dre as they sat in the stands inside of Coolidge High School gym watching Baby-D spar. Dre knew Black was right and by not taking Lil' Mousy serious it could have cost him his life. Dre told Black how he had went looking for the young dude all last night. He had even gone over his baby's mother's house, but he was nowhere to be found.

"I'ma catch his lil' ass. Believe dat," Dre said.

Word was out that Baby-D was leaving town to go box in Philly. The whole neighborhood seemed to pop up at the gym tonight to say their goodbyes. Lil' Garvin, Lando, Quick, and Tank walked in and sat down beside Black and Dre. While they watched Baby-D do his thing in the ring, Dre told the younger dudes about the situation with Lil' Mousy in hopes of being able to track him down. Lando sighed when he heard what had went down, if it wasn't one thing it was another. Quick knew that Lil' Mousy had a cousin that lived on 13th and Kennedy Streets. Lil Mousy used to live on 13th Street too when he went to junior high with Lando. Dre decided he would take a ride up 13th Street to see if he could find his man and Black took the ride with him.

Waiting outside of the gym for Baby-D to come out so they all could hang out before he left for Philly, Lando and everybody else shot dice in the darkness behind Coolidge High School. Quick looked across the parking lot as he shot the dice and noticed a set of headlights coming in. Even though Chip was dead and the 30th Street beef was dying out, everybody was still on point and wearing bulletproof vests under their coats. As Quick stopped to see who was pulling up, Tank slowly pulled a .45 out of his big Eddie Bauer. As the money green 240 SX pulled up they saw that it was Caramel in the car with Cherry. Everybody laughed as the two beautiful young women got out of the car looking like the up and coming recording artist that they were.

"Where Baby-D at?" Caramel asked as she and Cherry walked over to the crap game in their tight blue jeans and black leather jackets. Lil' Garvin, who had started liking Cherry, told Caramel that Baby-D was inside getting dressed. Smiling because she understood that Lil' Garvin wanted her to go inside by herself so that he could rap to Cherry, Caramel went on in after showing her love to the rest of her somewhat new extended family.

Baby-D was just getting out of the shower when Caramel walked into the locker room. Standing in only a towel, Baby-D laughed a little and said, "I knew you were going to show up before I came over your house tonight." Caramel walked up and hugged her man.

"I was just in the neighborhood and I wanted to stop by before going out to the studio," she said as she kissed Baby-D in the mouth. Sitting down on the bench to put his clothes on, Baby-D asked Caramel what she thought about him going up to Philly to train.

"I'm all for you gettin' out da streets. We can both do something with our life. We 'bout to be on da road to promote our album too. We still gon see each other," Caramel said. She wanted to go after her dreams as well so she understood where Baby-D's heart was. They talked for a while about how things would be and agreed to finish their conversation later at her house. Standing up to leave out with her, Baby-D kissed her as they headed for the door.

Mann and Silk sat in the office of Fast Lane Records talking about how Lil' Mousy had shot at Dre yesterday while Mann read over a copy of the contracts that Rick had drew up for PASSION which would give them their first royalty checks for the single 'Destiny' as soon as the first Sound Scan numbers came through.

"You gotta think ahead of dis shit Mann," Silk said. "Dre your man and all dat joe, but you got too much to lose now. Dre and dem can take care of dat shit. I'm sure they ain't gon even want you to get caught up in nothin' dat's gon fuck all dis up." Mann shook his head in agreement; he knew that everyone knew that he was trying to make a way out of the streets for not only himself, but for everyone close to him.

Signing his name on the contracts, Mann leaned back in his chair and said, "You right slim. I'm not looking back at all."

Nakia was sitting on the living room of the apartment that she shared with Lando getting her hair done by Trina when the doorbell rang. Trina went to answer the door and came back into the room with Pamila.

Nakia, now 5 months pregnant, stood up and hugged Pamila saying, "Hi, how you doing?" Pamila had made it her business to come check on Nakia every now and then just to make sure that Lando was doing what he was supposed to do.

Sitting down on the sofa behind Nakia, Pamila asked her where Lando was. Like always, Lando was running the streets with his men at the time. Pamila shook her head. Lando just wasn't going to slow down at all.

Eyone Williams

"So what you going to do about school Miss Thing?" Pamila asked. Nakia told her that she was going to wait until she had the baby in March of 1993.

"I trust that you mean that because you can't do nothing in this world without an education. The little bit of money Lando call himself makin' up there on Georgia Avenue ain't gon last forever," Pamila said. She had started to like Nakia and didn't want the young girl to mess her life up. As much as Pamila loved Lando, she knew that selling drugs only led to one of two things, either he was going to go to prison or someone would end up trying to kill him.

"Well I just dropped by to see how you were doing. Tell Lando I came by," Pamila said as she left.

A few days later, Silk had Lando riding around with him in his new black Land Cruiser. Silk had decided to give Lando the ropes just as he had done for Mann a few years back. Rolling through the city protected from the cold weather inside the truck, with PASSION's single playing, Silk said, "Shorty dis coke shit ain't meant to be something you do to pass time. You get in and get out. Dat's why I respect your brother so much. Slim got in and got out faster than most people get in and out of their pants." Silk could tell how much Lando looked up to Mann. He could see the drive to get money in his eyes, the same drive Mann had years ago.

"You gotta think bigger than your lil' block. Your brother made moves all over the city," Silk said, as he told Lando that he would be able to lock things down if he played his cards right. Almost every single young dude he went to school with when he was coming up was knee deep into the drug game now. Lando could see the picture that Silk was painting and it looked so good. He began to think of all the dudes he knew downtown, all he would have to do was talk to Quick and they both could talk to his cousin Wee-Wee about moving a lot of coke downtown.

Inspired and ready to take his shot at being the man, Lando said, "I dig what you sayin' joe. I'ma get dat cash."

Mann had been on the highway for 6 hours on his way to see Kelley at the University of Ohio. Mann had so much time to think on the road by himself. It felt good to get out of the city and to leave all of the madness behind him. He had waited for the day when he no longer had to hustle this and that to get things he wanted in life and it was now here. He knew it would be a while before Lando was ready to give up the streets, but as soon as he was ready, Mann was going to make sure he had a way for him to step into the corporate world.

Mann parked his truck outside of Kelley's dorm and got out to surprise her. Every female in sight seemed to be watching the dark skinned new man on campus as Mann walked into the dorm. Mann laughed to himself as he walked by a group of good-looking women sitting on the sofa in the front of the dorm.

"Y'all know where Kelley's room is?" Mann asked the girls.

A cute brown skinned tall young woman smiled and said, "You talkin' 'bout light skinned Kelley?" Mann shook his head yes trying to hurry up and get on his way. The young woman directed him straight to Kelley's room and Mann was off with all eyes on him.

Kelley was sitting at the desk in her room when she heard a knock at the door. Letting out a deep sigh, she asked who it was. When she heard no one answer, she became frustrated because she had been studying all day and it was less than 24 hours before she had to take a final exam in computer science.

"Who is it?" Kelley snapped as she walked to the door.

"Open da door and see," Mann said. Kelley knew his voice very well. She snatched the door open and jumped into Mann's arms.

"What you doing up here?" she asked as she led him into her room.

Mann sat down on her bed smiling, sitting down on the bed with Mann she said, "I heard your group on the radio up here. I got all my lil' buddies to go buy it." Mann laughed as he grabbed Kelley and rolled over on top of her.

"Things 'bout to get real big. By da time you come home for Christmas break, Fast Lane gon be what everybody gon be talking 'bout."

The first snowfall of the year hit the city as soon as November rolled in and everybody was in the back of Mann's World at Baby-D's going away get together. Mann had ordered drinks and all the food you could eat. With the music pumping through the speakers and everybody having fun, Mann sat behind his desk looking on at one of the few times when there was nothing to fear, no danger, everyone was family and it felt good to be a part of something that he could say that he put together from the floor up. As the phone rang, Mann snapped out of his moment of thought and answered it as he kicked his feet up on the desk.

While Lando and Lil'Garvin played football on Sega, Baby-D and Quick slap boxed in the middle of the room. Kisha, Tina, Naomi, and Nakia sat on the sofa talking about girl stuff and who they thought had the most brains out of everybody in the hood.

"If you talkin' 'bout brains, you gotta count Black out," Naomi said as she laughed. Everyone else laughed trying not to let Black and Dre hear what was being said being as though they were sitting only a few feet away talking about more serious things.

"My man gotta be the smartest," Tina said. "He ain't never into shit and his name don't be kickin in da streets."

Kisha cut right in and said, "Shit we all know without Mann, everybody around da way would be locked up or broke. Y'all know dat."

"Da lil' nigga can't hide forever," Black said to Dre. They had been hot on the trail of Lil' Mousy for about two weeks now and had came up with nothing at all.

"We might have to snatch dat bitch he gotta baby by," Black said. Dre felt that she had nothing to do with the whole thing and wanted to leave her out of it.

"We gon have to do somethin', da lil' nigga fuck around and be looking for us now dat he know we came by his people's house," Black said.

"One way or another we gon catch his lil ass real soon," Dre said as he looked over at the door and saw PASSION walking in.

Mann was just getting off the phone with Cross Country Distribution when PASSION walked in the door. Mann waved his hand for them to come over to his desk.

"What's up CEO?" Chocolate said as she and the other two girls walked over to talk to Mann. Mann smiled. He was too down to earth to separate himself from others that had came up in the streets.

"I just talked to our distribution company. They say dat da single is selling well and dat they gon be sending us our first check next week," Mann said as he stood to walk over and talk to Black and Dre. Chocolate grabbed Mann as he tried to walk by and hugged him.

"I knew you was going to make shit happen," Chocolate said as she kissed him on the cheek.

Patting her on the back, Mann looked at Cherry and Caramel and said, "We all made it happen and shit ain't even hit da fans yet."

19

"**I knew you was** gon take care of business," SMOKE said to Black as he and Serge rode in Black's truck to PASSION's video shoot in downtown DC. In no time, Smoke and Serge were back on the streets thanks to Black killing their witness.

"We only been gon 4 months and shit done changed like dis joe," Serge asked. Black let them know that Mann had the drive of a speeding train when he had his mind set to do something.

"So what's up wit you, you getting some paper?" Smoke asked.

"I'm jive layin' on dis Maryland nigga dat suppose to be getting bricks from some down south nigga," Black said as he put his partners down with his upcoming caper.

As the New Year came in, Lando had more time to spend at home with Nakia since he and Quick had found a way to move all of the coke Lando was now getting from Silk. Quick had worked out a move with his cousin Wee-Wee from V Street that had allowed him and Lando to flood downtown with coke and to help Wee-Wee fatten his own pockets. With not much to do on the block now, Lando and Quick both spent a lot of time hanging out at the Fast Lane Studios or at Lando's apartment.

Laying in the bed with his soon to be baby's mother early in the morning, Lando reached over and rubbed Nakia on her round stomach.

Watching videos on BET, Nakia put her hand on top of Lando's and said, "Can you feel her kickin'?"

Wanting a boy with all of his heart, Lando said, "Yeah, I feel him kickin'." Lando had grown more and more fonder of becoming a father, while Nakia at the same time was thinking about becoming a mother and had started pressing Lando to get a job at Mann's record label so that he could get out of the streets.

Thinking about what Pamila had been putting into her ear every time she came over, Nakia turned to Lando and softly said, "We really got to think about what we gon do when our baby get here. You not gon be able to run da streets and shit like you want to." Lando assured her that he was ready to be a father and that he was going to slow down, but in the meantime he had to stack his paper up so that they could be set in the long run.

Leaning over to kiss Nakia, Lando said, "We gon be fine boo. Don't worry."

An hour later Quick let himself into Lando's apartment with Amber. Nakia came out of the bedroom and spoke to the couple as she walked up and hugged Amber, who she had began to grow close to since Quick would drop her off over Lando's apartment to hang out with Nakia when he wanted to run the streets with Lando.

While Nakia and Amber sat in the living room talking about their two men, Quick walked into Lando's room and dived into the bed with his big down coat on.

"What's up nigga?" Quick said as he looked back at Lando who was looking at his fresh cornrows in the mirror.

"Wee-Wee beeped me dis morning. He got a move out VA for 5 bricks," Lando said.

"For how much?" Quick asked as he sat up on the bed to listen carefully. Wee-Wee wanted 5 bricks for $85,000 which he would sell and make $40,000 off of after he sold the bricks to the Virginia dudes for $25,000. Quick smiled, he loved how Lando had things going with Silk.

"We gon lock da whole city down!" Quick said, excited about the whole idea of being one of the big niggaz at last. Shaking his head in disagreement, Lando thought of all the things that Silk had been dropping in his ear for the last few months.

"Fuck da city joe. We gon do dis shit for a hot second just like Mann did. Once we got enough to get outta dis coke game we gon joe. Feel me?" Lando said. Quick thought about what Lando said, he didn't want to be trapped in the streets for the rest of his life, he wanted a way out as long as it left him well off.

Mann was hard at work trying his best to make Fast Lane Records a force to be reckoned with in the music world. Mann wanted Lando to witness how it was done, from start to finish. He told Lando to meet him at his apartment so they both could have dinner together with an executive from Priority Records. The whole dinner would be business and a bigger distribution deal is what Mann was after.

Walking up to Mann's apartment, Lando had a lot on his mind. He was really starting to become a thinker. He had just left Quick over Pamila's house and ran into Pamila at the door. Pamila had been looking for Lando to scold him about not going to his G.E.D. classes. Pamila had a way with words and when she was done talking to Lando, she really had him second guessing all the things that he thought meant so much to him as far as the streets were concerned.

Walking into Mann's apartment, Lando spoke to Dre and Black who were smoking weed while they played video games on Mann's huge TV. Walking into Mann's bedroom, Lando saw Mann on the phone. It was clear as day that Mann had something weighing heavy on his mind. Lando walked over and sat on the bed while he waited for Mann to get off of the phone. With all of the stuff that Mann had going on, Lando could understand why his brother would have a lot on his mind, after all Mann was carrying a lot of people on his back and he wasn't even 20 years old yet.

Upset and not in a good mood at all, Mann got off the phone and said, "Let's roll shorty." Lando wasted no time as he walked with Mann out into the front room and out the door into the cold night time air.

Once inside the warmth of Mann's Range Rover, Mann finally opened up some as they cruised along the highway on their way to meet the executive in Georgetown.

"Dat nigga Black just won't grow up shorty," Mann said. "He still doin da same shit he was doing when we was growing up. I'm gettin' sick of dat bullshit." Mann had just had a big argument with Black about the way he was carrying things in the streets these days. It was time to slow down and get some money without drawing too much attention, Mann was telling Black, but Black wanted to get his money the way he had been getting it all his life. Mann expressed his disgust with the way Black chose to·live life all the way down Georgetown.

Houston's restaurant was packed tonight. Mann and Lando walked in and saw a tall white man sitting all the way in the back smiling at them waving his hand for them to join him. Following behind Mann, Lando thought that the white man looked like he was eager to beat Mann out of something and it would be interesting to see how things went tonight.

After a little small talk, they all ordered their food and got down to business.

"So Mr. Ferry," Mann said as he folded his hands on the table. "I really don't need a record deal as I told you on da phone earlier. What I need is nation wide distribution." Mann had no intention on throwing away what he had worked for just because Priority Records had ran across some sound scan information saying that Fast Lane Records had sole 75,000 copies of PASSION's single without a major distribution deal.

"Mr. Mills you have to think about the future of your record label," Mr. Ferry said as he explained that with his label as a part of Priority Records that he would be sure to see money without worrying about anything but making music.

"Na, I ain't movin' dat fast. I'ma maintain control of Fast Lane no matter what you can offer me. I know we gon sell records," Mann said.

As Mann and Mr. Ferry went back and forth about what they could do together to help make each other money, Lando watched Mann handle himself as if he had been in the music business for years. Finally, Mann got what he wanted after breaking down a few numbers.

"Dis is all dat I can give you Mr. Ferry," Mann said, telling the man that he would only make an 85/15 deal or it was nothing in it for him. "It's about makin' money, not givin it away. You can make some money wit me, but you ain't gon sit back and make no money off me," Mann said as he got up to leave.

As Lando stood up beside his brother, Mann turned and said, "Holla at your peoples, tell 'em I'm tryin' to make some money wit 'em, they'll understand. I'm sure I'll be hearing from you." Shaking Mr. Ferry's hand, Mann winked his eye at the man as he left the restaurant with Lando.

Broke and looking for some quick cash while they waited for Black to take them on a move with him, Smoke and Serge hid in the darkness of some bushes across the street from Lil' Garvin's house on Kennedy Street waiting for their chance to break into the basement.

"Dis our move right here," Smoke said as Lil' Garvin's older brother Dex walked out of his front door along with two other dudes. In the January nighttime air, Smoke and Serge jogged across the street and into Lil' Garvin's back yard. Looking around to make sure no one was around. Serge kicked the back door in as he and Smoke went inside with their pistols drawn. Once inside, they looked all around the basement room that Lil' Garvin shared with his brother.

"Damn!" Serge said after about 10 minutes of searching.

"Let's get da fuck outta here, joe," Serge said as he began walking for the door.

"Na, hold on," Smoke said as he stared at the ceiling, "we might got somethin' slim." Grabbing a chair, Smoke stood up and stuck his hand into a hole in the ceiling that use to hold an old ceiling fan. The block of the ceiling that held that part of the ceiling fell down making a lot of noise. Three plastic bags of coke fell on the floor as someone came to the top of the basement steps to see what the noise was. Smoke and Serge took the three bricks of coke and ran out of the door into the night.

Early the next morning everybody from the neighborhood met up at Fast Lane Records to be a part of an interview for MTV about inner city independent record labels. While Mann, PASSION, and Lando were sitting on the sofa talking about how things seemed to happen overnight for Fast Lane, Lil' Garvin was telling Quick and Black how somebody had broken into his house last night.

"I'm fucked up 'bout dis shit joe," Lil' Garvin said as he expressed his anger. "I owe Dre some money for dat shit too," Lil' Garvin said. Quick told Lil' Garvin not to worry about owing Dre money because they all knew that Dre wouldn't be tripping off of some money that Lil' Garvin owed him.

"Who you think coulda did some shit like dat?" Black asked as Dre walked up on the conversation. Lil' Garvin began to tell Dre how his house had gotten broken into last night. Dre told Lil' Garvin not to worry about the money that he owed him before asking Black to take him over his house so that he could get a bulletproof vest that Black had been trying to sell.

"So what's up wit da lil' nigga Mousy?" Black asked as he and Dre pulled up at the gas station on Georgia Avenue just across the DC line. Dre hadn't seen the little dude since the night he had shot at Dre.

"I don't know where dat lil' nigga hidin' at, I'ma catch his lil' ass sooner or later," Dre said, as he got out to pump the gas.

While Dre walked over to pay for the gas, Black sat in the car thinking about how upset Mann was after their last conversation. Mann was right Black thought, it was time to slow down. He knew he couldn't keep running wild nowadays.

"I gotta do something wit myself," Black said to himself as he looked out the window into the clear winter day.

As car after car pulled into the gas station while Dre was caught up talking to a beautiful young woman that worked behind the glass at the gas station, Black noticed a big brown Cadillac pull up with dark tinted windows. Black watched the car carefully as Dre walked back to the car to pump the gas. The driver side door popped open and Black saw Mousy getting out of the car with a pistol in his hand.

In a flash, Black pulled his .40 caliber, jumped out of the car, and pushed Dre to the ground as he and Mousy opened fire at each other in broad day light. Shocked and confused while the gunfire tore through the air right above his head, Dre covered his head as glass broke and car tires began screaming while people ran for their lives crying out in fear. Mousy ran out of bullets and began to run across the street with bullets from Black's .40 caliber flying in his direction. Hearing only one set of gunshots going off, Dre uncovered his head and saw Black bleeding from the chest as he fired his pistol. Dre got up and saw everybody who was still around laying on the ground. When Black's pistol ran out of bullets, he turned around out of breath and said, "Get me outta here joe, I'm hit." Dre and Black jumped inside of Dre's Corvette and shot down Georgia Avenue just as the sound of police sirens hit the air.

"Time is money and I couldn't wait any longer MR. Ferry. Maybe next time," Mann said to Mr. Ferry when he finally called back willing to do business. He was too late; Mann had already made another deal with Cross Country Distribution for PASSION's album that would be out by the end of the week.

Hanging up the phone and spinning around in his chair to see who was winning the football game between Quick and Lando, "Who winnin' over there?" Mann asked.

"I'm blowin' dis nigga out Mann," Quick said while he threw another touchdown with the Washington Redskins.

"Fuck dis shit, let's start over," Lando said as he cut the game off. Mann laughed and spun around to his desk to check on the numbers and locations of PASSION's sells from their single.

Cherry walked into the office and tapped Mann on the shoulder saying, "Dre on line 3." As Cherry went back down to the studio with the other girls, Mann picked the phone up.

"What's up?" Mann said as he picked the phone up.

Dre said, "I got some bad news slim."

Eyone Williams

Letting out a deep sigh, Mann said, "What's up? Put me down." Dre told Mann that Black had been shot in the chest during the shoot out at the gas station with Lil' Mousy.

"Where he at now?" Mann asked becoming frustrated with all of the madness.

"We both over his house with Mia," Dre said, "but I think we on da run slim."

While Mousy was shooting at Black and Dre, he shot an old lady in the back that was sitting in the car across from Dre's. Eyewitnesses took Dre's tags down as he and Black went flying away. Dre had called Tina, whose father worked for the 4th District Police Station, she had told him that she thought he and Black were on the run because her father called her and asked her had Dre let someone drive his car because a Corvette like his was involved in a murder.

"Shit!" Mann said, just when shit started to take off for him, things seemed to get worst. "I'm on my way over there!" Mann said as he hung up the phone.

20 minutes later, Mann walked into Black's apartment with Quick and Lando. Mia led them into the bedroom where Black was laying in the bed with towels wrapped around him soaked with blood. Mann saw that Black was sweating all over.

"How you feel slim?" Mann asked. Black wasn't feeling good at all. He dug the .45 slug out of his chest himself with a knife, but he could tell that he was losing too much blood.

"I'm gettin' cold slim," Black said to Mann. Looking back at Lando, Mann told him to go pull his truck up to the backdoor of the apartment complex. As Lando and Quick left, Mia asked Mann what he was going to do; she knew Black needed to see a doctor but she couldn't get him to go to the hospital.

"I'ma get him to a doctor," Mann said. Dre and Black looked at each other with a worried look on their faces when Mann spoke of a doctor.

Knowing what they were thinking, Mann said, "I'ma take Black out my apartment and get a doctor to come over. I want you to come too; y'all might be on the run."

The next morning the news was out. Dre and Black's faces were flashed all over the news. They were wanted for murder once again. Dre had stayed with Black over Mann's apartment after the doctor that Mann got to come over had worked on Black. Not letting anything get in the way of his progress, Mann still went to the studio first thing in the morning, leaving Black and Dre in his apartment.

"We gotta get outta town," Dre said as he watched the news.

Black looked over at the TV and shook his head in agreement, "Yeah joe, you right. We can't stay around here."

On 5th and Rittenhouse, Lando sat on the steps in front of Kisha's house talking to Smoke and Serge while he waited for Kisha to come out so he could give her a ride to Mann's World.

" I seen dat shit on da news dis morning shorty," Serge said as he looked back and forth up and down the street watching his back for the crud that lurked in his past.

Rubbing his hands together to warm them up, Smoke said, "Where do da lil' nigga dat shot Black be at?" Lando told him that he knew Lil' Mousy and that he was from around 21st Street NE, but he stayed on Kennedy Street.

"We gone see da lil' nigga. Don't worry bout dat," Lando said as Kisha came out the front door.

Later on Pamila paged Mann and told him that she needed to see him as soon as he could find the time. Like always, Mann put everything on hold and went straight over to see what could be so important. When Mann got over Pamila's house, she was in the living room corn rowing Tyesha's hair with her thinking cap on. Mann could tell Pamila had seen the news and knew that Black and Dre were wanted for murder.

Shaking her head in disgust, Pamila got straight to the point.

"Mann," she said in a very concerned voice, "you have come a long way. You have gotten your shit together and got out of the streets." Mann knew where the conversation was going and he felt as though he had to listen to what Pamila had to say even though he had already had the conversation with himself. Pamila told Mann that she was convinced that Black was never going to do the right thing and that even though he was blood she didn't want Mann to let him or the madness that he stayed in cause him to lose focus of all the things he was now doing.

Eyone Williams

Standing up to hug Pamila, Mann said, "You don't gotta worry about me champ. I gave Black some money earlier so that him and Dre could go down Georgia to Dre's aunt's house." Mann had thought long and hard about what would come behind the latest heat and he knew that the feds would be looking all over for Dre and Black. Therefore he couldn't have them around while he was trying to take care of business.

"My group's album drops in two days," Mann said as he gave Tyesha $50.00, "and ain't nothin' gon get in the way of that."

After losing 3 bricks of coke, Lil' Garvin was back on the block serving rocks hand to hand. Lando had given him a brick to get back on his feet and Lil' Garvin had decided that he was going to push the whole thing, rock for rock, until he was done and in only a day he was halfway finished.

Tank pulled up in Lil' Garvin's van and parked on Georgia Avenue. Jumping out in his huge coat, Tank walked up on Lil' Garvin and Short Dogg who were both serving pipeheads with their backs turned to the street as they stood in the alley.

"What's up shorty?" Short Dogg said as he stuffed some balled up cash into his coat pocket. Tank had just seen Lil' Mousy in Johnney's carry out on 5th and Kennedy Street and he wanted to know what they were trying to do about him shooting Black.

"It ain't in da talk," Lil' Garvin said as he zipped up his coat, "let's roll."

Lil' Mousy was still sitting in the carry out with two other dudes from around his way. Pulling a ski mask over his face, Lil' Garvin thought back to how Black always rolled with him about anything when he was coming up which added to his drive to finish Lil' Mousy.

"Circle da block," Lil' Garvin said to Short Dogg, as he and Tank jumped out in broad daylight with two .45 automatics.

Without a second guess, Lil' Garvin and Tank went inside the carryout and unloaded on the group of three, leaving no one breathing as they hit the door and ran to the van that was sitting right out front.

Once inside, Short Dogg said, "Did y'all get 'em?"

Laughing, Tank said "We smashed everything in dat joint." Lil' Garvin wasn't as excited about the killing. He knew Lil' Mousy since they were 8 years old, but he also knew that sometimes things went that way and this was just one of those times. Black was like blood and in Lil' Garvin's world, blood was thicker than water.

Days later, the warrant squad was kicking in Mia's door looking for Black. Armed officers burst into her apartment at 6am and woke her out her sleep by slamming her to the floor.

"Where is Mr. Mills?" one officer yelled while he pointed a Glock at Mia. She swore that she didn't know where Black was and after tearing up the whole apartment they left.

Drying the tears from her face while trying to calm her nerves, Mia began straightening up the place. The phone began to ring while she picked up a picture of her and Black, ice-skating downtown. Tears flooded out of her eyes again as she looked at the picture, she didn't know if she would ever be able to enjoy life with the man she loved.

"Hello?" Mia said as she answered the phone. On the other end a female sounded as if she was crying as well as she asked to speak to Mia.

"This is Mia. Who is this?" Mia asked. Tina's apartment had just been raided as well and she was calling to see if the same thing had happened to Mia. Both women sat and talked about how much trouble their men seemed to be in while they tried to come up with what they could do to help them, but the only thing they could come up with was to turn to Mann.

On a payphone just outside of DC, Mann spoke to Black, who was also on a payphone down the road from Dre's aunt house at a local gas station.

"I can't stay down here slim," Black said to Mann as he expressed his dislike of the country, "I gotta come back up top." Knowing how the feds were looking for Black and Dre, Mann tried to talk Black into staying down south, but he had a feeling that he would be seeing him soon.

"What Dre gon do?" Mann asked as he looked over his shoulder. Dre had no plans on coming back home anytime soon. In fact, he was making plans to get Tina and his son to come down.

"Look here Black," Mann said in a no nonsense voice, "you need to stay your ass down there wit Dre, it's too much shit going on up here and I don't need you up here getting in no shit. I'ma send y'all some money down there in Dre's aunt name. Don't make no calls up here and don't tell nobody where y'all at." Mann hung up the phone and headed to the studio to put PASSION's album release party together for the up coming week now that their album was out and selling well according to the Sound Scan.

When Mann got to the studio, Lando, Short Dogg and Quick were in Studio D with PASSION nodding their heads with the headphones on. Mann walked in and saw Silk sitting in the back smiling.

Sitting down beside Silk, Mann said, "What's up?" Silk pointed to Lando and gave Mann his headphones. PASSION's hit single was going off and only the beat that Short Dogg had made was playing, Lando began to rap something he had wrote while he was high last night. It sounded good, Mann thought.

Looking over at Lando, Mann said "You think you could write some shit like dat about what they talking 'bout in da song?" Lando laughed and told Mann he would try. Mann got a great idea, he would remix PASSION's hit single and if Lando could write something that went along with it, Mann was going to put him on the song.

Talking about how he might be on PASSION's remix, Lando told Nakia that if he could write something that was good enough for the song that Mann was going to put it out with him on it.

Nakia laughed, as she and Amber went through a book of baby names, "Now you want to be a rapper. Boy you too many things."

Quick walked into the room with Tank and Lil' Garvin saying, "Dat shit gon work joe. Watch." Tank already knew he could rap, as well as everybody else. When the news of Lando trying to write something for PASSION's remix was out, Tank asked if he could go back into the studio to record a song he wrote about his little cousin Dee-Dee. Quick supported the idea and he had heard Tank rap the song outside last night. He felt that the song was good.

Lando stood up and said, "Dat's what we gon do slim. I'ma try to write dis shit for da remix and if it work, we gon get Mann to put out a rap group on his label." Everybody agreed with the idea, they only had to run it by Mann and get Tank, Short Dogg and Lil' Moe to stay out of trouble long enough to get into the studio.

"So what you be doing wit da money Mann be giving you for dem sweatshirts with your design on 'em?" Lando asked Jazmin as he pulled up in front of Takoma Subway Station. Jazmin smiled as she grabbed her pocketbook and told Lando that she was saving all of her money for college.

"You need to think about something more than da streets Lando. Dis shit ain't gon last forever," Jazmin said as she got out of the car.

Rolling down the passenger window, Lando leaned over and looked Jazmin in the eyes as the cold evening wind blew into his face and said, "I got something in the making now, you gon be fucked up at dis shit here too." Blowing Jazmin a kiss, Lando took his Z flying up the street on his way to PASSION's album release party.

Lil' Garvin had been walking up and down Georgia Avenue all day exchanging crack rocks for money trying his best to recover from the three bricks that he had lost. After serving his last $50 rock, Lil' Garvin looked at his watch and saw that it was almost 9pm and PASSION's album release party was starting in 30 minutes. Sliding his hands inside the warm pockets of his huge coat, Lil' Garvin walked across the street to his BMW.

Just as Lil' Garvin stashed his pistol under the dashboard, Hall and the "jump-outs" pulled up behind him, jumping out with their Glocks drawn.

"Freeze!" Hall said as he snatched the driver side door open, pulling Lil' Garvin out of the car slamming him to the ground.

"Get da fuck off me!" Lil' Garvin yelled as he tried to get up. Hall wrestled him back to the ground while the other officers tore the car up looking for anything that would give them the pleasure of locking someone up for the night.

"I know you killed the sorry sack of shit on 5th and Kennedy!" Hall said as he whispered into Lil' Garvin's ear telling him that nothing went on uptown without him knowing it. Lil' Garvin felt his heart drop as Hall told him everything about Lil' Mousy's killing and why it happened. Things just weren't going Lil' Garvin's way this year at all and a murder charge would just add to his troubles.

"You know what though?" Hall said as his trained hounds told him that the BMW was clean, "I don't even want you. You are not the big dog. I want Black. This murder is on me this time." Hall got up and walked back to the car with the rest of the vice cops while Lil' Garvin dusted himself off thinking about what Hall had just told him. Thinking about Black and Dre, Lil' Garvin shook his head and jumped into his car, he still could make it to the album release party in time.

Eyone Williams

Downtown on the 9th floor of a K Street office building that Mann had rented, PASSION's album release party was already in full swing with drinks, food, and a paid DJ. Lil' Garvin walked in the door smiling at the scene, Baby-D was the first person he ran into.

Standing against the wall with his arms wrapped around Caramel, Baby-D said, "What's up slim?"

Lil' Garvin caught up on a few things with Baby-D, but he couldn't really say too much in front of Caramel so he hugged his partner and said, "I'll catch up with you before you leave joe."

"Shorty got big as shit," Silk said as he and Lando talked about Baby-D.

"I hope slim do something wit dat boxing shit cause he got what it takes," Lando said as Lil' Garvin walked up on the scene. After showing his love, Lil' Garvin told Silk and Lando what had just took place between him and officer Hall on Georgia Avenue.

Silk shook his head in disgust, he had counted Black out long ago, "Slim stay in some shit," Silk said as he walked across the room to talk to Mann.

Alone with Lando, Lil' Garvin asked his man what he thought would come of the whole situation with Black and Dre.

Sipping a cup of soda Lando said, "I really don't know but da feds know too much so we gotta lay low. Dis music shit Mann got going look real good, I gotta feeling we can go along for da ride and say fuck dem streets so we ain't gotta worry 'bout what da feds gon do." Quick walked up and sat down with Lando and Lil' Garvin.

Playfully punching Lando to the body Quick said, "What's going on?" Lando told Quick what he and Lil' Garvin were just talking about with a serious look on his face.

"I'm wit dat slim. I told you dat already, it's on y'all," Quick said as he voiced his approval with the music idea.

Waving his hand for the DJ to kill the music, Mann got on the microphone and said, "Dis next song is from Fast Lane Records first album and I'd like to thank the three beautiful young women called PASSION for believing in the whole Fast Lane idea." As Mann spoke, the whole room began to clap in approval of his words.

"Second of all, I wanna thank all of you dat came out to support dis album. You can expect much more from us," Mann said as PASSION's single began to pump throughout the room.

Sitting back down with Silk and Supreme, Mann gave Silk 5 and said, "I knew dis shit would work slim." Silk smiled as he began to tell Mann how he couldn't stop attacking the music business with all of his heart now that he had a group out with an album.

Looking from Supreme back to Mann, Silk said, "Supreme can tell you, now you gotta find some more talent to put out if dis music shit gon be how you make your livin'." Mann could feel where Silk was coming from, he was already thinking of how he was going to try to make something out of Lando and his desire to rap.

Supreme cut in and said, "Son, you got a gold mine in all dem young niggaz your lil' brother be wit god. Just think, you can come right back at da music world wit a group of real street niggaz and they gon love 'em."

As Supreme told Mann how his rap group didn't work out because they were just rappers, Mann began to think about the idea Lando had been pushing him about letting him and the rest of the younger dudes record an album.

Shaking his head in agreement with Supreme, Mann said, "You might be right slim."

Getting up to go use the phone, Supreme looked back at Mann and said, "I know I'm right god, don't miss your move son."

Sunday night, just before Baby-D was supposed to leave to go back to Philly, he stopped by Lando's apartment on his way from Caramel's house. Sitting in Lando's empty second bedroom, Baby-D listened as Lando told him all about all of the stuff that was going on around the way while he was gone. Quick being excited about Lando's plan to get Mann to put a rap group out with them as a part of it, had started writing raps in his free time and was thinking big already.

"Fuck dis shit joe," Quick said, "we gon be able to make millions like dem muthafuckas on TV." Lando was thinking more realistic. He told Quick and Baby-D how they would still push coke while they tried the rap thing, but if it didn't work they would open up another Mann's World that they would run themselves. Baby-D had to respect how his men were thinking while he was gone and he felt that everybody just might turn out okay after all. As the night began to grow old, Baby-D had to be on his way.

Leaving his men with his love, he said, "I'ma be callin' from up Philly joe. Stay on top of da rap shit. We all fuck around and get rich one way or another."

After a few days of thought, Mann got Lando to bring Tank, Lil' Moe, Quick, Short Dogg, and Lil' Garvin to the studio to sit them down while he gave them the run down on how things would go now that he was going to give them a shot at recording a record.

Sitting inside Studio C, Mann said, "Dis how shit gon go. If y'all serious we can make some money. If y'all just gon waste my time, we can go ahead and cut dis shit right now." Everybody was in accord with Mann's request. "Dis how we gon do dis," Mann said as he put Lando in charge of the project.

"Y'all got studio time in Studio C for 4 hours in da morning and 4 hours after 6 at night." Mann told Short Dogg he didn't want anyone messing with the recording equipment but him and that if he needed anything other than what was in the room to let him know. After the plan was laid down, Mann left everything up to Lando and Short Dogg.

While Short Dogg was downstairs in the studio with everyone else working on their first track, Lando was upstairs talking to Mann about his chances of really being on PASSION's remix of their first single.

"Let me hear what you wrote for da song," Mann said. Lando stood up and beat on his chest as he began to rap his 16 bars for the remix. Mann smiled as he leaned back in his thick leather chair with his feet kicked up on his desk. Lando sounded good.

"I'll tell you what shorty," Mann said as he popped a track tape into the stereo that sat on the side of his desk, "rap to dis beat here." As the track began to pump through the speakers that surrounded the office, Lando rapped his verse again sounding even better with the beat.

"We gon start on da remix tonight," Mann said. Smiling, Lando gave his big brother 5 and went back downstairs with everyone else.

Mann picked up a book of dates that sat on his desk to see where he could book PASSION for a few shows to promote their album now that it had been out for two weeks and selling pretty well. On a Sound Scan listing, Mann saw that most of PASSION's album sells were along the east coast, New York, New Jersey, Philly, Virginia, and few in the south. Mann decided to build on the biggest crowd of fans and made a few calls to places in New York to book PASSION a few gigs. At the least, he would up their sales.

Caramel came walking into Mann's office while he was at work trying to put his plan together. Walking up behind Mann and rubbing his shoulders, Caramel shook a set of car keys in Mann's ear. Mann turned around and saw Caramel in a black Mann's World sweatshirt and tight pair of blue jeans smiling at him with a set of BMW keys in her hand.

Mann stood up, put his hand out to see the keys and said, "I thought we talked about all dis spending money." Mann had to have a long talk with Caramel the last time he gave her a royalty check for their first single when she had spent over $10,000 on clothes.

"You ain't made enough money to be out here just throwing money away," Mann said as he went into explaining to Caramel that she needed to save her money for other things just in case the album didn't do well. Mann knew that the music business was just like any other hustle. You had to stick and move because it was no telling when you would go broke. Mann put Caramel back on track, telling her to concentrate on making music and not on spending money. Once he felt that he had made his point, Mann gave Caramel the run down on how he wanted to work on the Destiny remix with Lando tonight. All for the idea, Caramel went downstairs to get Chocolate and Cherry ready for their session.

A day after recording the first take of the Destiny remix, Lando was in the back office of Mann's World talking to Silk after getting 10 bricks to move.

"Shit gon be big slim," Lando said to Silk as he gave him a book bag containing $160,000. Silk was pleased with the way Lando was putting his heart into the project that he was working on and he really wanted it to work for the young dude.

As Lando and Silk walked out into the store floor, Silk told Lando that he needed to start thinking about what he was going to do if the music thing paid off for him, "Hustlin' and rappin' ain't gon mix. You should have you a nice stash by now, you been movin' 10 joints a week. It might be time for you to throw your hand in." Silk gave Lando 5 as he left him with that thought on his mind knowing that Lando would think about the statement for the rest of the night.

Leaning against the counter still thinking about what Silk had dropped on him, Lando could see himself and the rest of his crew all over the TV making money, going here and going there and he believed that he wanted to shoot for it. Kisha, who was running Mann's World now that Dre wasn't around, came out of the storage room and gave Lando a copy of the inventory list to take to Mann. Seeing him in deep thought, Kisha asked him what was on his mind. Lando simply told her "Money" as he left the store with Naomi.

Making music wasn't as easy as everyone thought it was. Lil' Garvin had called it quits after two days; coming to the studio at 8am in the morning was too much for him. Quick couldn't make it to the studio on time either. He also lost interest in making music and decided to stick to the coke game. Tank and Lil' Moe would have fell off as well but Lando knew that they were the only one's that could really rap so he went to pick them up everyday for the last week and took them to the studio with him.

Lando had been working on the remix of the Destiny single for the last week and he was now also starting to get tired of getting up to go to the studio. It was 7:30am when the phone rung in his bedroom. Nakia rolled over and answered it. Tank was on the phone wanting to know if Lando was going to the studio. Nakia woke Lando up and gave him the phone.

Half sleep Lando said, "What's up?" Tank was up and ready to hit the studio.

"You comin' to da studio dis morning?" Tank asked. Wiping the sleep out of his eyes, Lando rolled over and looked at the clock; it was too early for him to make it to the studio. Lando had been up all night smoking weed with Quick and couldn't find the energy to make it out of the bed.

"You talked to Short Dogg?" Lando asked. Tank said that he, Short Dogg, and Lil' Moe were all on Georgia Avenue catching the early morning crack sells. That was Lando's way out. He knew how much Short Dogg loved making music so he told Tank to go ahead to the studio with him so that they could finish the song they were working on together. Tank went on to the studio after telling Lando that he would catch him later.

Lando hung up the phone and laid back down staring at the ceiling.

"You ain't goin to da studio dis morning?" Nakia asked.

Fast Lane

Lando rolled over and said, "I'm tired of dat shit, dis rappin' shit ain't for me. It was good for a minute, but I got shit to do later on so I gotta get some rest." Lando didn't feel like he was giving up, he just felt that it was easier to move coke by the bricks than it was to get up early in the morning and go to the studio. Nakia took Lando's reasons for not going to the studio and went back to sleep herself.

Sitting behind the huge track board in Studio C, Mann listened to Tank and Lil' Moe rap a song about growing up in DC. They had a sound that was real and everything they said went right along with the deep bass track that Short Dogg had made for them.

Shaking his head to the whole song, Mann turned to Chocolate who was sitting right next to him and said, "Dese three young niggaz gon be Fast Lane's first rap group." Feeling the rap song herself, Chocolate asked Mann what he was going to do about Lando. Mann had a feeling that the excitement of rapping would wear out for Lando, he was just glad that Lando laid down his verse for the Destiny remix before he lost interest.

"Lando doin' too much shit out there in da streets, dis music shit take time and he too use to fast money and getting everything when he want it," Mann said as he let Chocolate know that he was going to put it out after he gave the PASSION album a few more weeks to sell, but in the meantime Fast Lane would be working on Tank, Lil' Moe, and Short Dogg.

20

Taking advantage of the warmer weather, Pamila was outside washing her car in a pair of gray sweatpants and a Mann's World T-shirt. PASSION's Destiny remix with Lando rapping on it was on the radio and pumping through the speakers of her Volvo 740. The sound of laughter and kids playing smoothly floated through the early spring air as Tyesha and a few other kids from the block ran back and forth playing hide and seek. Pamila had heard the Destiny remix over and over since it first hit the air waves two weeks ago, but every time Lando's part came on she would stop what she was doing and just smile.

Looking over her shoulder, Pamila saw Black's Pathfinder coming up the street. As he pulled up and parked behind her car, Pamila shook her head and wondered if Black really knew how much trouble he was in or if he even cared.

Carefully looking around, Black got out and walked up to Pamila saying, "What's up?" Black hugged Pamila and waited for her response, which he already knew would be about him being wanted by the police. Black and Dre had been on the run for two months now, but despite Mann's advice, Black got tired of the country and came back to DC two weeks ago and was roaming the streets like nothing had ever happened. After warning Black of how much trouble he was in, Pamila told Black that he needed to be trying to find himself a lawyer while he was still on the streets so that he could work on clearing himself of a murder that he didn't commit.

"You right," Black said, "I'ma get on top of dat."

As Black began to walk in the house to get Quick, Pamila said, "Pull your damn pants up before you take your black ass in my house." Black smiled and pulled his Mann's World jeans up as he went inside.

Downstairs in Pamila's basement, Quick and his big cousin Wee-Wee were sitting on the sofa playing video games while Spice 1 blasted through the speakers on the wall. Wee-Wee looked up at Black with a smirk on his face, he knew Black was wanted by the feds, he had also seen his face all over the news for weeks after the gas station shooting.

Reaching out his hand to give Black five, Wee-Wee said, "You bold as shit walking around town like you ain't wanted." Black flashed a Desert Eagle 50 and told Wee-Wee that he wasn't going back to jail alive as he walked over to the bed and got on the phone to call Lando's apartment. Ring after ring, Black didn't get an answer. Hanging up the phone, Black went and sat on the sofa to watch Quick and Wee-Wee play John Madden football.

A few hours later, Pamila sat on her front porch reading the paper as the sun began to set. She loved this time of the year. The cordless phone beside her began to ring. Pamila answered the phone finding out that it was Nakia. Breathing hard and out of breath, Nakia told Pamila that she was having back-to-back contractions and that she thought that she was about to have her baby.

Excited and on her feet, Pamila said, "Where is Lando?" Nakia had been beeping him for the last 15 minutes and hadn't heard from him yet. Calling for Tyesha to come in the house, Pamila told Nakia that she would be right over.

Speeding around the beltway in his Twin Turbo with Short Dogg, Lando made his way back to DC after spending a few hours at the gun range.

"Somethin' must be up wit Nakia," Lando said as he looked down at his beeper.

Short Dogg puffed a blunt of weed as he slapped a Tupac CD into the disc player saying, "You gon stop and call her?" Lando looked down at his watch and told Short Dogg that he would just fly over to his apartment.

In less than 10 minutes Lando was pulling up in front of his apartment. Just as he parked his car his beeper went off again, this time it was Pamila's code followed by 911. Lando and Short Dogg got out the car and quickly walked up to the apartment.

Once inside they saw that Nakia wasn't in the apartment, but all of the lights and TV was still on. Short Dogg grew suspicious and pulled his .40 caliber from his waistband. Lando looked through all of the rooms and then jumped on the phone to call Pamila back at the number she had paged him from.

Eyone Williams

"Where your little ass been?" Pamila snapped from the other end of the phone. Lando told her that he had been taking care of some business out Maryland.

"I'm at the hospital with Nakia. She's in labor right now. We're down Howard so get your ass down here," Pamila said before hanging up the phone. Lando looked over at Short Dogg and told him what was going on.

"We gotta get down Howard Hospital, Nakia down dat joint havin' my baby," Lando said as he and Short Dogg shot out the door.

Mann was the first person Lando saw as he and Short Dogg walked down the hall of the hospital. Dressed in a tan Armani linen outfit, Mann stood outside of Nakia's room playing with Dre's son.

"What's up?" Lando said as he walked up on Mann.

Mann smiled and shook his head saying, "You five minutes too late shorty, you already a father."

At 9:57pm on March 17th, Nakia gave birth to a 10 pound 8 ounce baby boy that already looked just like Lando.

"Where da baby at?" Lando asked. Mann told him that the doctor had taken the baby down the hall to run some test on him and that he would be able to see him whenever the doctor was finished. Lando tried to walk by Mann and go in the room to see Nakia but Mann put his hand out telling him that he had to get a hospital gown before he went in so that he didn't take any germs in the room with him, Lando looked down at his all black outfit and smiled, he could still smell gunpowder on himself. Looking over at Short Dogg, Lando told him that he was going to be staying at the hospital for awhile and that he could take his car and leave if he wanted to. Short Dogg gave Lando five and told him that he would ride back uptown with Mann.

"I'ma see you tomorrow or somethin' joe," Lando said as he went down the hall to get a gown.

Nakia was lying in the bed almost sleep when Lando walked in the room in the light green gown. Pamila turned and looked at him placing her finger over her lips telling him to be quiet so that he wouldn't wake the exhausted girl. Lando sat down beside Pamila and smiled like the young 15 year old that he truly was at heart.

"How does he look?" Lando asked. Pamila assured him that the baby looked just like him.

Nakia slowly turned her head over towards Pamila and Lando, opening her eyes halfway she said in a tired voice, "I was waiting for you to come down here so that you could name our son." Just the thought of a son somehow made life a much bigger blessing in Lando's mind as he began to think of what he could name his son. Sliding up to the side of the bed, Lando softly grabbed Nakia's hand looking her in the eyes and said "Shit gon be like it supposed to be."

Late night on Georgia Avenue, the talk of the town was that Lando had a son.

"I'ma uncle nigga!" Quick said as he leaned against a fence in the darkness of the alley behind Sam's liquor store smoking weed with niggaz from the hood.

"What Lando name shorty?" Black asked while lighting another blunt of weed.

Quick looked around for Short Dogg and said, "You gotta ask Short Dogg, I think he said Eion, Eyone, or some shit like dat."

Just as Black turned to see where Short Dogg had went, the short young teen came jogging down the alley looking over his shoulder and said, "Black! You gotta get da fuck outta here! Da warrant squad and a white van just parked across da street!" Black pulled his pistol and jumped the fence that led to 13th Street leaving only the smell of weed smoke behind.

Fast Lane Records was quickly becoming a respected name by PASSION's aggressive climb of the Billboard charts, but Mann didn't let that go to his head. He saw something big in Tank, Lil' Moe, and Short Dogg. He named them 'Da Youngins' and was devoting a lot of time to their soon to drop album which Mann wanted out by the summer if he could get a good single out by May. This seemed very much in reach at the time. With the release of the PASSION album and the follow up remix featuring a young street nigga that sounded like a 15 year old Q-Tip, Fast Lane Records was what everybody swore it could never be, a real record label.

Sitting behind a huge mixing board looking through the window at Da Youngins, Mann talked to Tina about what he was trying to do for Dre and Black.

"I done been to see a good lawyer by the name of Mr. Williams, he's the best in the city," Mann said, "for $20,000 he say he can clear Dre and

Black, but they gotta turn they self in." Tina thought about what Mann had just told her, it was a little light upon what had become a dark nightmare for her and her son, but could it really work is what she wanted to know.

"Do both of them gotta turn their selves in?" she asked. Mann had never looked at it in a one or the other situation, he was trying to get both of them off of the hook.

"I never thought about it like dat, but I'm sure dat if Dre turned himself in the lawyer dude could still work his magic." Mann knew what Tina was thinking and she was right. If anyone was going to turn their selves in, it wouldn't be Black in a hundred years.

Sitting on the edge of his bed, Lando watched Nakia breast feed their son Eyone. Lando hadn't even left the house in the last two days since Nakia was released from the hospital. Everything that he needed or wanted was brought to him by someone.

"Don't dat shit hurt?" Lando asked. Nakia laughed at him, Lando knew nothing about babies.

Reaching over to rub his son's head, Lando said, "Shorty ain't gon ever want for shit." One thing Lando promised himself on the way home from the hospital was that his son would be protected from the fast lane and no matter what he grew up to be, he would know that the streets weren't a friendly place. Lando knew he had made a big mistake by forcing his way into the game when he never had to, but he was going to try with his heart and soul to keep Eyone away from the same fate.

At about 4pm, Quick and Lil' Garvin came over to see Lando's son for the first time. Sitting in the living room looking at Eyone like a new car, they all wondered how the little boy would grow up.

"Shorty ain't gon be like us!" Lando said as he fed Eyone a bottle.

After Lando had finished showing off his son, Nakia came and got him, taking him back into the bedroom leaving Lando with his partners for awhile.

"Joe, I gotta sale for 3 bricks over SE!" Quick said, "I need you to get dat for me from over Naomi's apartment, I ain't got no more stashed over Amber's house." Lando shook his head and laughed. When Quick met Amber, she was a quiet school girl and in only a few months he had her holding bricks of coke and automatic weapons in her mother's house in Rock Creek Park.

"I'ma slide over Naomi's house and get dat sometime tonight, but it's gon take a minute cause I'ma have to stroke her a lil' bit cause we gon be beefin about da news of me havin' a baby," Lando said. Quick and Lil' Garvin laughed, Lando always had to run some kind of game on Naomi to keep her holding his coke in her apartment, but he got the job done.

On the side of an old country road outside a gas station, Dre carefully watched his back as he spoke to Mann on the phone about the lawyer.

"I don't know about turning myself in joe," Dre said. He was sick of the country, but would take it over a dirty cell in the DC Jail any day of the week.

"You said something to Black 'bout dat shit?" Dre asked.

"You know Black, he ain't tryin to hear dat shit," Mann said.

"Yeah, I know, but we gon have to do something. I miss my son and I'm sick of being down here hidin out."

"Slim I feel ya," Mann said, "shit ain't' da same up here wit out you but it ain't too much I can do. It's your call, I'm down for whatever. You my nigga." Dre thought about his options for a minute and told Mann that he would get back with him after he gave the situation a little more thought.

"I'ma let you know something, but I need to hear from Black before I make up my mind," Dre said before hanging up the phone. He was truly stuck between a rock and hard space, shit was starting to hit home now.

Since the feds had kicked her door in looking for Black, Mia had moved back in with her father. She still loved Black and didn't care what her father thought about it. Even with Black wanted by the FBI, she still made sure she hooked up with him a few times a week in a spot that they would put together just to make sure that the feds weren't watching her. Tonight, their spot was just outside of the National Airport where Black loved watching the huge planes take off with effortless grace and freedom.

Sitting in a rented black Ford Explorer, Black kept his eyes on the road with his hand on his pistol, he swore that the feds wouldn't take him alive this time around and he meant it with all of his heart. Looking in his rear view mirror, Black saw a set of head lights at the end of the road. As the car got closer, he could see that it was a cab. Stopping a few feet behind him, he could see Mia's sexy, tall, and dark frame walking up on him. If Black had felt anything close to love for any woman in his whole life, it was her.

Kissing Black on the lips, Mia said, "I missed you boo." Black let her know how much he had missed her as well while he pulled off. Mann had pitched the idea of Black and Dre turning themselves in to them both. As expected, Black wouldn't even think about it, but now once again the idea came at him again from Mia.

"Black you know how well I know the law and I've studied cases like yours everyday since the police came looking for you. I, along with the help of the lawyer that Mann spoke of can beat this case for you and Dre, but y'all gotta turn y'all self in," Mia said. Black laughed as he pulled into a hotel parking lot in Falls Church, Virginia.

"Mia," Black said as he cut the truck off, "I ain't turning myself in. Fuck dat. An old lady got killed dat day. Somebody gon pay for it and it ain't gon be me. It ain't a lawyer around dat can get me off dis beef here."

The FBI knew that if you wanted to turn a neighborhood against a person, all you had to do was make it hard for the people in the neighborhood to make money and that is just what the FBI and the U.S. Marshals were doing after they had gotten word that Black was back in the DC area. Lil' Garvin and the rest of the young dudes that used Georgia Avenue to make a living were having a bad week. The feds were coming through 4 to 5 times a day flashing pictures of Black and they said that they would be bringing the heat down everyday until they caught up with him or Dre.

Lil' Garvin had only made $600 before he got fed up with the heat the feds were bringing down on the avenue. He followed his gut feeling and called it a day early. Jumping into his BMW he decided to shoot out to Fast Lane Records and see what Da Youngins were working on for the day.

Cherry was the first person Lil' Garvin ran into when he walked into the studio. Standing to the right of the front desk, in front of a gold album of PASSION's first single, Cherry was conversing with White Boy Jimmy who did all of the technical work for the record label. Lil' Garvin had tried his hand with Cherry a few times but she always played hard to get, but now that she was making more money then she had ever made before in her life, she was really caught up on herself.

With a black Mann's World baseball cap cocked to the side, Lil' Garvin cracked a smile and spit a little game at Cherry once again. As White Boy Jimmy walked off, Cherry smiled at Lil' Garvin and said, "You don't give up huh?"

"You gotta work hard for what you want and you just happen to be somethin' I want." Cherry was in the middle of recording a new song that PASSION was asked to do for a Universal Studio's soundtrack.

Kissing Lil' Garvin on the cheek she said, "We gon get together," as she walked down the hallway in her skin tight black jeans.

Walking into studio C, Lil' Garvin saw Mann sitting behind the mixing board with White Boy Todd while Da Youngins recorded a song for their upcoming album. Sitting in the back of the small room, Lando and Quick were shaking their heads to the thumping song. Lil' Garvin showed his love and grabbed a pair of headphones so that he could see what the song sounded like.

Turning around to the younger dudes, Mann said, "Dis da next big hustle, dis rappin' shit. Anybody can do it. Y'all better think about dis shit. Tank and dem gon get rich off dis shit." Mann sounded as if there was no doubt about Da Youngins becoming big in the music business, but Mann always sounded that way when his hand was involved in something.

In yet another hotel just outside of DC, Black spoke to Dre on the phone for the first time since Mann had given them both the idea that the lawyer said would work. Black had no problem with Dre turning himself in and he would take care of any business for him from the outside but he wasn't turning himself in for anyone, not even his pleading mother.

"Do what you feel is right slim. I'ma try my hand out here on da run. I may find a way to leave da country or something, but I ain't turning myself in," Black said. After talking to Dre for a few more minutes, Dre told Black that he was going to turn himself in.

"Cool slim. I'm here for you," Black said as he got off the phone and headed for the city.

Flying down Georgia Avenue, Black saw Mann's Range Rover sitting in front of Mann's World. Slowing down, Black pulled up and parked behind Mann's truck. Just as Black got out, Mann was walking out of the front door with Kisha and Naomi. While they locked the store up for the night, Mann walked over and hugged Black.

"What's up nigga?" Mann said. Black told him about the conversation that he and Dre had just had. Placing his hand on his chin, Mann thought that Tina must have talked Dre into turning himself in. "So what you gon do?" Mann asked. Black lit a Newport and smiled at Mann as if Mann should have known better than to ask him such a question.

Laughing, Mann said, "My bad, I shouldn't have even asked you no shit like dat." Black explained to Mann that no matter how much people wanted him to turn himself in, that he was going to be Black even if it cost him his life. This Mann already knew, but he wished he could change it.

"Well slim," Mann said with a sigh, "I guess you gon be Black, but Black gotta come up with something to do about dis mess. I done tried my hand and it wasn't good enough for you."

Walking up to Black and hugging him, Kisha said, "Where you been hidin' boy?" Black laughed and told Kisha that he was just laying low for a minute.

"Well can I get a ride home wit you?" Kisha said with a look of seduction in her eyes. As much as Black wanted some pussy at the time he turned her down on the offer.

"I jive got something to do tonight, but you think I could stop by your house later on to see how you doing?" Black said. Kisha could read between the lines very well and told Black that he was always welcome to drop by. Kissing Black again, Kisha and Naomi walked over to Mann's truck and got in to wait for Mann to drop them off at home.

"I'm 'bout to roll joe," Mann said, "watch your step out here. Life is short."

Black parked in the alley right behind Kisha's house and walked around front to where everybody was. Smoke and Serge were sitting across the street on someone's front steps. Tank, Lil' Moe, and the rest of the 5th Street youngins were sitting on Old Tima's porch catching the few crack sells that were coming through. Nighttime was the time when Black could roam the streets and not feel too jumpy, so he made most of his moves at night.

"Y'all ready?" Black asked Smoke and Serge. They were supposed to go on a caper tonight for $75,000. The move was sweet for the taking Black told them, all they had to do was snatch the dudes baby's mother and make her take them to the money. Smoke and Serge had been waiting for this move since Black had told them about it a week ago.

"We ready slim," Smoke said as he stood up and dusted himself off.

Just as they began to cross the street the 2moment of truth sprung itself upon Black. Hall and the vice cops slowly bent the corner in a dark green Buick. Hall knew Black's walk, talk, and anything else that could identify a man. Stopping in the middle of the street, Black looked Hall right in the eyes. Time seemed to stand still as the Buick slammed on the brakes. Mortal enemies were about to face off. Smoke and Serge had left their pistols in the alley and as the Buick's doors started to fly open they both shot across the street and ran through Kisha' yard into the alley. Black never moved. Just before the four vice cops stuck their feet outside of the door, Black sent two 50 caliber slugs flying through the windshield, one of which hit Hall right in the middle of his bullet proof vest and the other hitting him in the neck, snapping his neck. As the sound of gunshots hit the air, Black felt a bullet slam into his leg, then another into his back as he tried to jump behind a car. In minutes gunfire had numbed his hearing. Falling to the ground on the sidewalk, Black thought he was dying, but at least he went out like he had planned.

Black found out that life had a way of doing what it wanted to do, and things didn't always go as planned. Next he found himself waking up at Washington Hospital Center late the next day chained to the bed being watched by an armed police officer. Not only had he gotten arrested again, but he also succeeded in making his bed a lot harder to lie in. Hall died from the gunshots he suffered which now meant that Black was not only charged with one count of murder, but two and one was the murder of a police officer.

Black was painfully sore when he woke up. He had been shot five times, the worst shot being the one he took in the chest. Even so, Black was alive and would have to face the music and that was far more painful than any gunshot wound when he began to think that he would never be free again.

When Black opened his eyes the tall white police officer that stood at the door broke the news to him.

"Well, Mr. Cop Killer, you finally woke up," the police said to him with a smirk on his face. Black listened as the officer told him what happened after the shooting stopped last night. Black would have been a dead man if Kisha's mother and many other neighbors didn't come outside to see what was going on after Black fell to the ground.

"You might as well get ready to take your ride down Central Cell," the officer said, "You'll be in court in the morning."

Mann was hurt when he heard that Black had gotten shot on Rittenhouse Street, but some of his pain went away when Black's mother called to let Pamila know all that she had found out the next day. Mann had feared that the police would end up killing Black and sure enough they ended up shooting it out which is how Black said it would go. Now with the stakes higher and the situation much worst, Mann knew that he was the only person that could help Black in any way, so two days after Black was sent to the DC Jail to await trial, Mann made it his business to go see him.

Many times over the years Mann had sat in the DC Jail visiting area waiting to see his little cousin, but the stakes were never as high as they were now. Mann didn't know how Black would work his way out of this jam or if he truly could work his way out of such a jam.

Walking into the visiting area with the look of a man with a lot on his mind, Black sat down behind the glass and picked up the phone.

"What's up cuz?" Black said. Shaking his head in sorrow and pity Mann asked Black how he felt.

"I'm cool, a little gunshot ain't da least of my worries," Black said. For the first time ever Mann could see real fear in Black's eyes and he knew it wasn't a fear of being in jail or a fear of facing a dark situation, but a fear of the thought of spending the rest of his life in a tiny, dark, and dirty prison cell somewhere not even known at the time.

"Shit don't look good for da ole boy dis time," Black said as he and Mann began talking about the case at hand.

"Slim, I'ma do all I can to get you out," Mann said. "Money ain't shit, you gon have da best lawyer money can buy."

Smiling at Mann, Black shook his head and said, "We both know money can't buy my way outta dis one here joe. I'm through. All you can do now is make sure I'm okay in here and make sure my mother is takin' care of out there." The stinging truth of the words that Black spoke with the utmost authority hit Mann right in the heart. Deep down inside, Mann felt the same way but would never allow himself to believe such a thing. Looking at reality from Black's point of view, Mann accepted the situation at hand in the way that Black gave it to him. As their visit came to an end, Mann felt his heart drop when he had to tell Black he would see him later.

Mann knew that later would be behind a glass or in a prison visiting hall for a long time, but he had to wrestle with reality.

Black's present situation was weighing deeper on Mann's mind than he cared to admit, but nothing got by Pamila. As Mann dropped by to bring Tyesha a few outfits from his store, Pamila noticed a look of worry on his face.

"You still bothered about that situation with Black ain't you?" Pamila asked from the dining room table. Sitting a brown Mann's World bag on the sofa, Mann walked over and sat down at the table with Pamila.

"Yeah, I been thinking about Black every single day since he got locked up," Mann said, "Life got a way of taking a turn for the worst when you least expect it."

Stopping what she was doing Pamila looked across the table at Mann and said "Life doesn't take a turn for the worst, people take their own turns. The Creator doesn't place a burden on a person that is too great for them to bear. We as people bring forth just about every single misfortune in our lives." Mann listened as Pamila spoke her words of wisdom. She told Mann that just as he worked hard to get out of the streets, Black had worked hard to stay in the streets.

"You both got what you worked for," Pamila said, "I love Black just as much as you, he's family, but he's also a grown man. We can't think for him as much as we would like to. If the Creator sees fit for him to come out of this situation without spending the rest of his life in jail, then that is what will happen. All we can do is stand by him at the time, but life goes on." Pamila had a way with putting things into the proper perspective and she had surely done just that.

Just then Kelley called him breaking his train of thought.

"Yeah, besides da situation wit Black, shit goin smooth down here. I'm just fucked up they got my man boxed up like dat," Mann said to Kelley.

"So what you gotta tell me?" Mann asked.

Kelley laughed and said, "I told you dat I would tell you when I came home dis weekend. Just wait." Mann tried to talk Kelley into telling him what her surprise was, but she stuck to her guns and ended her conversation by telling Mann that she loved him and would see him Friday when she came back home for the weekend.

Smoke and Serge had been lying low as they could for three weeks after Black killed Hall and they were now desperately looking for a quick caper. Down to $1,000 between the two of them, it was time for another taking.

"We gotta find a move quick," Serge said. As he and Smoke rode down Rittenhouse Street in Black's Pathfinder.

"One way or another we gon come off," Smoke said, "All dese niggaz getting all dis money out here, it's only right dat we get some of it."

Tank and Lil' Moe were sitting on top of a sky blue 1990 300 ZX when Smoke and Serge pulled up and parked in front of Old Tima's house. Walking up on the two younger dudes, Smoke and Serge looked at the fresh paper tags on the car.

"Who joint is dis?" Serge asked. Tank said that he had bought the car with the signing bonus that he got for signing a contract with Fast Lane Records.

"Mann just givin money away like dat huh?" Serge asked.

"Nah, it ain't like dat," Lil' Moe said. "We be in da studio workin' hard as shit. Mann just gave us a lil' bit of money up front cause he think our album gon sell." Smoke and Serge found it hard to believe that the two little young dudes were real artist on a record label.

"So you mean to tell me dat y'all gon have a real album out in da stores and shit." Serge asked. Tank told him that they would have much more than that if Mann was right about them being what the rap world was missing.

Quickly changing the subject, Tank pulled a bag of weed out of his shorts and said, "Y'all tryin to smoke wit us?"

Lando sat in Naomi's living room with Silk and Quick, weighing bricks of coke while they talked about Black's situation. Lando was fucked up about Black getting locked up and even more worried about the extra murder he picked up when he got locked up, but Black had always found a way to get out of fucked up situations. Lando truly thought that with Mann on Black's team that they would find a way for Black to beat yet another case. Silk on the other hand knew much better.

"Shorty, I hate to tell you dis, but Black got his hands full dis time around," Silk said, "he charged wit killing a police. It's a whole new set of rules." Quick took in Silk's words, he had started to respect Silk in the same way as he had always respected Mann and when Silk spoke Quick tried to pay close attention.

"Black made a name for his self long ago," Silk said as he looked at the two younger dudes. "Even if he didn't kill dat jump out, they still want him to go down for something because he done beat murder after murder since he was what, 13 or 14." Lando began to think of all the times Black had gotten away red handed with things from Armed Robbery all the way down to Murder. As much as he didn't want Silk to be right this time, Lando started to see Black's situation for the big mess that it truly was.

Just as Silk was about to leave he turned to Lando and Quick and said, "Don't get me wrong. I don't want Black to go down on a beef like dat, I just want y'all to look at da situation for what it's worth."

Mia was going to stick by Black for as long as he needed her. She not only put her education on hold to work on his case, but had talked her old law professor at Georgetown into taking Black's case for only $10,000 which Mann had put up without delay. Mia was sure that she would help Black and Dre both win their freedom.

Dre didn't find out about Black's murder charge for killing officer Hall until he came back to town to turn himself in. It didn't surprise him at all, it sounded like something Black would do.

Sitting in the NW-3 dayroom of the DC Jail playing chess, Dre and Black talked about their case and how they felt as though they could beat the murder charge for the old lady that Lil' Mousy had shot at the gas station.

"You ain't gotta worry 'bout that shit. You outta here." Black knew that they would beat the murder of the old lady, but deep down inside he knew that he had fucked up his chances of freedom when he killed Hall.

"All I can look for is some kind of cop," Black said about his murder charge for Hall. "They talking 'bout natural life for killin' dat hot ass nigga Hall."

"So how you plan on going at dat joint?" Dre asked.

"They ain't gon give me a cop dat I can do, so I'm have to wrestle wit da natural life and hope dat Mia can find a legal loop hole in da case somewhere down da line," Black said, sounding as if he had already given deep thought to his options.

"Whatever happen I'ma be able to deal wit it. Fuck it," Black said as he check mated Dre for the third time.

Kelley got out of the cab in front of Pamila's house at 9:30 Friday night. She couldn't wait to see the older woman so that she could be the first to hear the news that Kelley was pregnant with Mann's child. She just found out she was pregnant last week and couldn't wait to see what Mann had to say. Kelley had a feeling that she would end up getting pregnant by Mann because when he came up Ohio to see her on his surprise visits he would make love to her as if there was no tomorrow. All of his energy wasn't in vain, Kelley thought as she knocked on the door.

Tyesha answered the door. Seeing it was Kelley, she opened the door and gave her a big hug. Tyesha had grown to love Kelley like a big sister over the years.

"What's up big girl?" Kelley said to Tyesha as she picked the big child up. Tyesha said that she was just downstairs beating up on Quick in a race car video game.

"Where is mommy?" Kelley asked. Tyesha ran upstairs to get Pamila as Kelley closed the door and took a seat on the sofa. Quick walked upstairs to see who had just came in the house.

"What's up girl?" Quick said as he walked over and hugged Kelley, "Mann know you in town?" Kelley told Quick that she was only going to be home for the weekend and that Mann knew she was coming over.

Looking down at his watch, Quick said, "I gotta move to make so I'ma see you before you leave." Kelley laughed as Quick zoomed out the door. He was still Quick, Kelley thought.

"So what's da big surprise?" Pamila said as she sat down across the room from Kelley, "you pregnant or something?" Kelley's mouth dropped to the floor when she heard Pamila's words, she couldn't believe how the woman hit it right on the nose. Kelley was only about 5 weeks pregnant and she knew she wasn't showing at all.

"How did you know?" Kelley asked, no longer smiling.

"Come on now," Pamila said as she got up and came to sit down right beside Kelley, "I been around a long time. Not too many things would bring you all the way back home."

Pamila was right, Kelley only came home to see what Mann wanted her to do about the baby. She felt that he would want her to stay in school as long as she could, but she wanted to come back to DC and finish her education at Howard University.

"So what you gon do?" Pamila asked. "You gon stay in school until you ready to have your baby, or you gon come home?" Kelley had no plans on dropping out of school until she had her baby. In fact, she was going to stay in school as long as she could before she had to take some time out to have the baby.

"I want to move back down here for a minute and attend Howard until I have the baby," Kelley said.

Eyone Williams

Mann's timing had always been good. Just as Kelley was talking about what she was going to do about school, Mann walked right in the door with Lando. They both walked over and hugged Kelley.

"What's up boo?" Mann said as he sat in a chair beside Pamila. "What y'all in here talking bout?"

Sensing that something was up with Pamila and Kelley, Lando said, "What's up wit y'all? Y'all look like y'all up to something." Pamila stood up and asked Lando to come upstairs with her. Lando caught on quick and went with Pamila.

"What's up?" Mann said as he sat down beside Kelley.

Smiling at Mann, Kelley looked down at her shaking hand and said, "I'm pregnant."

Mann looked down at her stomach and said, "How long you known dis?" Kelley told Mann that she was about 5 weeks pregnant and that she wanted to know what he thought about her coming back home until she had the baby.

"You gon drop outta school?" Mann said with a look of disagreement.

"Naa," Kelley said with a laugh, "I wanna go to Howard until I have da baby." Mann told her that would be a good way to stay in school and still be close to home.

"I'm glad you understand," Kelley said.

Mann looked at her with a crazy look and said, "How else was I supposed to act?"

Kelley leaned over and kissed Mann saying, "I love you."

Kelley wanted to see Lando's son, so she got him to take her to see him after talking to Mann for awhile. Sitting in Lando's bedroom with Nakia and their son Eyone, Kelley could only think of how happy she would be to have Mann's baby.

"How you like being a mother?" Kelley asked the younger girl. She said that she loved having a child of her own, but it was a lot of work. She couldn't go out like she wanted to, but she did get to spend more time with Lando now that she had a baby by him because Eyone somehow kept Lando in the house.

"So it took a baby to slow Lando down," Kelley said as she held Eyone in her arms.

Nakia laughed and said, "I don't know if you would say he done slowed down. You could say that he just be movin' fast around here. You know how Lando and Quick never take a minute to slow down." Both of the girls laughed at the thought of Lando or Quick ever slowing down.

"What da fuck is up wit all dis baby shit?" Lil' Garvin asked Lando as he sat beside Quick and Short Dogg on an old sofa in the alley behind Sam's Liquor store on Georgia Avenue.

Standing under the dim street light at the end of the alley, Lando said, "I can't call it, but I'm glad my son and Mann's baby gon get to grow up together like me and Mann did."

Thinking down the road, Short Dogg said, "Now dat you gotta son you gon have to lay low a lil' bit. You can't be hangin' out here like dis all da time. Anything can happen out here." Quick shook his head in agreement.

"No bullshit," Quick said, "you don't even see niggaz like Mann and Silk out here on da strip joe. They know too much shit happen when a nigga runnin' da streets. You gon have to start thinking like dat too joe." Lando looked at Quick and smiled, Quick could tell everybody else how to slow down, but never thought that he should slow down too.

"I guess dat don't go for you huh?" Lando said with a smile.

Tank and Lil' Moe came down the alley from the other end in Tank's new 300ZX and pulled up right in front of the crowd.

"Shit look like it's going well at Fast Lane," Lil' Garvin said. "Why you ain't got no Z Short Dogg?" Short Dogg told him that he put his signing bonus in the bank in his name so that if the rap shit ain't work he would still have some legal money.

"Dat's smart," Quick said as Tank and Lil' Moe got out the car.

"What's up wit y'all niggaz?" Lando asked as the two younger dudes walked over.

Tank pulled some dice out of his pocket and said, "What they hittin' for?" Everybody started pulling money out of their pockets.

"I guess you think your money long enough to chase mine now you a rapper and shit," Lando said as he grabbed the dice off of the ground and threw a $50 dollar bill under his Nikes.

22

Da Youngins album dropped the first week of June and had already sold 150,000 copies by the middle of July, making Fast Lane Records stronger than it ever was as a record label. Mann took advantage of the strong underground support that Da Youngins were getting and sent them on a small five city tour with PASSION starting in New York City. Mann started out the tour with them, but came back to DC after a week and left Chocolate in charge being as though she proved to have the balls and brains to keep everybody in order and what she couldn't handle, Mann had grown to know that Short Dogg would handle in a way that would not put the record label at any risk. At $6,000 a night, Fast Lane's small tour raked up a quick $80,000 and made hundreds of new fans up and down the east coast.

"I told y'all shit was gon blow up," Mann said as he gave Tank and Lil' Moe their royalty checks from their July album sells. "All things take time. I tried to tell Lando and dem dis shit but they couldn't wait it out." Tank and Lil' Moe understood exactly what Mann was saying. They both had just received a check for $150,000 and their royalty checks for last month were for $50,000. Short Dogg had been paid a little more since he had been around longer and had not only made tracks for Da Youngins album but the PASSION album as well.

Tank folded his check up and slid it into the pocket of his shorts saying, "I'm buyin' moms a house with dis money here." Lil' Moe thought about what Tank had just said, he thought that he would like to do the same thing but his mother was hooked on crack and all he could do was take her out the hood in the flesh, he knew that until she got her life together she would never get to enjoy any of his success.

"I guess I could buy my grandmother a house or something," Lil' Moe said wanting to be able to share his blessing with someone close. Mann laughed, he felt good to have snatched two young souls out of the streets.

"Y'all got da right idea, but keep in mind dat $150,000 don't make you rich. Put some of dat money in da bank at least until next month's royalty check. Da way y'all shit is selling y'all should be seeing checks like dis for da next four or five months," Mann said.

On his way out Landover, Maryland to pick Eyone up from Mann's apartment, Lando and Quick smoked a blunt of weed while Da Youngins CD blasted through the speakers of Lando's Twin Turbo.

Blowing a cloud of smoke out of the window into the cool summer air, Quick said, "I wish Dre and Black was around to see how shit goin out here." Lando felt the same, They both went to see Dre and Black at least once a week with their fake ID's. Lando could see it in their face every time he went over the jail, Dre and Black both knew that they were missing out on all of the shit that Mann had worked for.

"They gon beat dat shit joe," Lando said as he pulled into the parking lot, "I just don't know what's gon happen to Black on dat police joint."

Kelley was sitting in the living room playing with Eyone when Quick and Lando walked in the door.

"You gettin' use to being a mother huh?" Lando asked as he laid on the floor beside Kelley.

Rubbing her stomach, Kelley said, "I can't wait to have my baby." Quick laughed as he walked to the phone to call Wee-Wee.

"Where Mann at?" Quick asked. As always he was at the studio working with Short Dogg and PASSION for their second album which Mann wanted out by the beginning of 1994.

"If you wanna catch Mann dese days you gotta catch him at dat damn studio," Kelley said.

"Mann got da Source Magazine coming to da studio Saturday," Lando said as he picked Eyone up. "They gon have da whole Fast Lane Records family on their cover." Lando was going to make sure that he was around for that, he was starting to like the little spotlight he was getting hanging out at the studio.

"Shit comin' along real swell, partna," Mann said to Dre through the phone behind the glass at the DC Jail.

Looking over at Black who was also in the visiting hall with Mia, Dre said, "I'm glad shit going da way you want it to slim." He truly wanted Mann to succeed. Every time one of PASSION's songs would come on the radio at night, Dre would just think of how he would be a part of the glory if he could beat this murder, but then his loyalty to Black would snatch any feeling of hope away from him when he thought that Black might not be able to be a part of any of the Fast Lane Records era.

"So how y'all case lookin' now?" Mann asked. Dre told him that he felt that he and Black could beat the case, but they had some people saying that they saw them both shooting, which was a lie. Even so, Dre felt confident that he and Black would beat the case.

"I guess it all comes down to what happens with Black's case on the police body then," Mann said. Dre told him that Mia and the law professor that she knew were doing all that they could. As of right now they were going at the case as if Black never knew there were police in the car that pulled up on him being as though they were in an unmarked car which would take away the government's felony murder intent as long as they could prove that Black thought he was being attacked by a car load of street thugs. The plan was one that would take a lot of time, energy, and knowledge of the law to pull off, but Mann knew that Mia would pull all the tricks out of the hat for Black.

"Well I'm 'bout to roll slim," Mann said as he stood up so that he could speak to Black before he left.

"You know where I am whenever you need me," Mann said as he hung up the phone.

Smoke and Serge were sitting on top of an old Cadillac in front of Kisha's house in the baking sun trying to make a few dollars before the young dudes came back outside. Serge was upset that Lando wouldn't front him a half a brick of coke. Serge really burned his bridge with Lando after getting a half a brick about a month ago and giving Lando a sad story about how he fucked the money up. Ever since then, Lando had told them both that they had nothing coming from him or Quick.

"Dese lil' bitch ass youngins get a lil' cash and start thinking they big shit!" Serge said as he vented his anger about Lando. Smoke lit a blunt of weed while his cousin went on about how if it wasn't for Black, he would have been robbed Lando.

"If you so fucked up about da shit why don't you do something 'bout it," Smoke said as he passed Serge the blunt of weed.

"I just might do dat," Serge said, "but if I do I ain't goin at da lil' one, I'm gon for it all."

Smoke got up off the car to look Serge in da face and said, "So what you sayin', you gon rob Mann or somethin'?"

Serge looked Smoke straight in the eyes and said, "Yeah dat's what I'm sayin'. You scared to snatch da nigga wit me."

Smoke burst out laughing as he walked away saying, "You trippin, I ain't tryin to hear dat snake ass shit!"

A couple of reporters and photographers, one from the *Source*, had flooded Fast Lane Studios early Saturday morning trying to get all the information they could about how Fast Lane Records came about. A beautiful tall dark skinned woman in a pair of tight Guess jeans was in charge of the story and the photo shoot. She introduced herself as Grace and told everyone that she wanted them to be as real as they could and to act like she was a part of the family while she got to know everyone.

Smooth as always, Mann had Grace feeling like she had known him for years in only 30 minutes and yet she would never have believed him if he told her the truth on how he built Fast Lane Records. Grace truly thought that Mann had worked hard as a teenager and had saved up to $10,000 to start a little store called Mann's World which gave birth to Fast Lane Records.

"So you were never really a part of the madness that went on around you?" Grace asked. Mann told her that just because he grew up in the streets didn't mean that he had to be a part of them as he grew up.

"I was around, you know," Mann said as he cracked a slick smirk, "I'm not an angel, but I'm not what you would call a real street thug."

Pointing over at Lando and Quick who were standing behind Da Youngins while they took a picture, Mann said, "Dem young niggaz right there, they real street niggaz. Ain't none of 'em over 18 years old and they done seen more and done more than most of dese niggaz out here rappin' 'bout the life they live. Dat's why I put them out on my record label. I put 'em out so they could tell their story and get rich off of it without worrying about going to jail or being shot dead on the streets." Grace was taken off guard by the power of Mann's realness. When she was done talking to him she tried to think of any man she knew that was as strong-willed as Mann and she could think of none as she walked over to talk to PASSION.

"So tell me girls," Grace said with a smile, "which one of you thinks Mann is as fine as I do?" Grace's realness broke the ice well and got all three girls to open right up and tell her about how Mann ran Fast Lane

Records so well. Chocolate was outspoken as always as she took Grace back to the days when they all worked at Bloomingdale's and were all broke.

"Mann pushed us, he inspired us to sing, he made us believe we could make it and not even a year later we are here telling you how it all went down," Chocolate said. After Caramel and Cherry both gave Grace their outlook on how Mann made PASSION the album selling group that they had grown to be, she wished the girls well on their next album and went to see what she could learn about the new rap group called Da Youngins.

"So you not only rap with Da Youngins and make all of the beats for the group, but you also make all the beats for Fast Lane Records as well?" Grace asked Short Dogg as she sat in between him and Lando on the leather sofa in Mann's office. Not wanting to steal the show, Short Dogg told her that he just did whatever he could to help out when he was around and that he was just happy to be making clean money for once in his young life.

Turning to Tank and Lil' Moe, Grace said, "How old are you little guys?"

"I just turned 14 last week," Lil' Moe said.

"You're just a baby," Grace said meaning no harm.

Lil Moe snapped at her, "I'm a grown man! I take care of myself and I been doin dat since I was 9." Grace somehow just realized what Mann meant when he said that Da Youngins were real street niggaz.

"Dis what my man is tryin' to say miss," Tank said, "we young but we been on da streets all our life. It ain't just somethin' we rappin' 'bout."

Pointing his finger at everybody from Lando to Lil' Garvin and Quick, Tank said, "We all done did our dirt in dem streets. While everybody getting rich off da life we live, we got da scars to show."

If Grace never understood the inner workings of real street niggaz before, she did when she was done talking to Da Youngins. Just as she was about to wrap up her story on Fast Lane Records she asked if anyone had anything that they wanted to say.

Lando slowly raised his hand and said, "Yeah, at da end of your story about us I want you to let da world know dat Fast Lane Records got two members behind bars at da DC Jail and dat we love'em and can't wait for 'em to come home." Grace asked what their names were so that she could put them in the story.

"We call 'em Black and Dre   and shit ain't gon be da same til they come home and we got two other members of da family dat ain't here dat we call Silk and Baby-D," Lando said. "Make sure you put dem in there too."

Looking over at Mann, Grace said, "Anything else you wanna say?"

Mann looked around the room and said, "What you see is what you get when you dealin' wit us. Actions speak louder than words. You see how real Fast Lane Records is, let da world know what you seen while you was here wit us. Ain't nobody like us, DC gon bring a whole nother side of da game to da table wit Fast Lane Records."

A month later, people all the way on the west coast were talking about the little DC record label called Fast Lane Records thanks to the five page story in the Source's August issue with Mann, PASSION, and Da Youngins on the cover standing in front of an image of the White House. MTV decided that they wanted a piece of the pie and started playing Da Youngins last video called "Masked Up." Mann was on top of his game and it was no turning back.

Mann had spent all day at the studio today working on a single to PASSION's next album. From 8am until 1am, Mann, PASSION, and Short Dogg had been at work. Dead tired, they all called it a night.

"I'll see you in the morning," Cherry said as she walked out the door into the dark summer night with Caramel and Chocolate. Mann and Short Dogg followed right behind them and went their separate ways.

30 minutes later Mann was pulling up in the parking lot outside of his apartment. Half sleep he looked around and pulled his .40 caliber from under the dash board and got out of his truck walking down to his building. In the dead of the night, he could hear every living thing nearby it seemed. Always on point, Mann heard something run across the parking lot and into the woods. Still walking, Mann went up to his building and let himself in the front door.

As Mann walked up the steps to his apartment, he got a strange feeling in his gut and he stopped dead in his tracks to look over his shoulder to see if he was alone in the hallway, no one was behind him. Mann began to think he was tripping as he turned back around and reached into his pockets for his door key. Out of nowhere two dudes in ski masks popped out of the door to the stairway. Shocked and somewhat off guard, Mann froze as the dudes slowly walked toward him.

"Don't move nigga!" The taller of the two dudes said as he pointed a .357 magnum at Mann, the other dude held a Tec-9 but he somewhat stood behind the taller one. Mann could tell that the two dudes were unsure how they wanted to come at him so he tried to play his cards right.

"What y'all want slim?" Mann said as he slowly raised his hands in the air. The taller dude began to walk closer and closer to Mann as if he was trying to grab him. Fed up with guessing, Mann rushed the taller dude with the .357. BOOM! The .357 went off shaking the walls of the little hallway.

Hit in the chest Mann wrestled the dude for the pistol while the other one tried to get a clear shot. The .357 went off again going through Mann's hand and slamming into his thigh as he and the gunman fell to the ground. Mann managed to snatch the pistol away from the dude as they rolled over on the floor. With the masked man on top of him, Mann fired the pistol twice into his neck killing him. Using the dead body as a shield, Mann fired the last two bullets at the short dude that had started to run down the hallway, but it did no good, he was gone down the stairs.

Coughing blood out of his mouth, Mann struggled to push the dead body off of him. Out of breath, Mann dropped the empty pistol and tried to stand up without success. He was too weak, he didn't have the strength so he did the only thing he had the strength to do; he pulled the mask off of the dead body beside him to see the face of the man that shot him. "Bitch ass nigga!" Mann managed to say when he saw his shooter. It was Serge.

Kelley heard the loud gunshots and ran to the door. She almost passed out when she saw Mann laying on the floor covered in blood.

"Ohmi God!" Kelley screamed as she ran over and tried to pick Mann up.

"Don't," he said, "call an ambulance." Kelley ran inside to do just that as the hallway began to fill with people that wanted to see what was going on.

Mann and Serge were both dead by the time the paramedics and police got on the scene. Kelley broke down when she saw the police cover Mann with plastic.

She rushed the officer screaming, "No! No! Don't put dat on him take him to da hospital, he ain't dead!" As the officer grabbed Kelley with both hands and tried to calm her down.

"Miss we have to do this, that man is dead. Do you know what happened out here?" The officer asked. Kelley couldn't even think straight. She looked down and saw Serge's face for the first time and put everything together, he had to have been the one that shot Mann. Yelling and screaming, she began to kick Serge's dead body. The police grabbed her and took her inside of Mann's apartment to get her away from the dead bodies.

23

Pamila's phone rang at 3:00am, rolling over to see who in their right mind was calling her house at this time of night, she answered the phone and thought she heard Kelley's voice saying, "Pamila." She could tell that someone was crying, but she wasn't sure.

"Kelley?" Pamila asked.

"Yeah, it's me." Kelley said, still crying.

"What's wrong with you girl?" Pamila asked.

"It's Mann."

"What about Mann?" Pamila said in a shaky voice.

"He's......"

"He's what?"

"He's dead," Kelley said. Pamila sat on the phone for almost a minute before saying anything.

"What da fuck you mean he's dead!" Pamila snapped.

Kelley exploded with sobs as she told Pamila how she opened up the door and saw Mann laying on the floor shot. Pamila almost broke down herself, but thought about how this was not the time. She asked Kelley where she was as she let the sting of painful news wear off. Kelley told Pamila that she was at the police station out Maryland and that they needed her to identify Mann's body. Pamila wiped tears out of her eyes and got dressed in a state of shock and disbelief.

Pamila and Kelley both walked in the house an hour later feeling like a piece of their souls was left lying in the morgue.

"I can't believe dis shit!" Kelley said, still crying, "I know they was trying to rob Mann or somethin', dat's da reason they would have shot him," Kelley said as she tried to make some sense of Serge and Mann both lying in the hallway. The police found a pistol on Mann and told Kelley and Pamila that he had to have fought for his life and took the other man's pistol which made Pamila and Kelley both understand what must have went on.

Sitting on the sofa with her face in her hands, Pamila thought of how much trouble was going to come with Mann's death, she knew that Lando and Quick were going to fall into a murderous rage.

"Shit is so fucked up," Pamila said as tears began to roll down her face.

Half sleep, Quick came upstairs to use the bathroom and saw Pamila and Kelley sitting in the living room crying. Walking over in his boxer shorts, he asked what was wrong. Kelley couldn't stand talking about the situation again; she looked over at Pamila who looked as if her whole world had just come to an end.

"Quick," Pamila said with tears running down her face, "Mann is dead." Quick swore he heard her wrong.

"My Mann?" Quick asked in disbelief as he tried to make himself wake up.

"Yeah, your Mann is dead," Pamila said.

Quick could feel his whole body heat up as he sat down beside Pamila and tried to come to an understanding about what she had just told him. Looking over at Kelley, he asked what had happened. Kelley told him everything that she had seen when she opened the door. Quick knew exactly what had to have happened.

"Dem bitch ass niggaz!" Quick said as he got up and started walking towards the basement. He knew that if Serge was dead on the scene of the murder, then Smoke was still somewhere alive and knew all about what had just happened. For the first time ever, Pamila didn't try to stop what she knew was about to happen when she could see where Quick's mind was going.

"Hello!" Lando said as he answered the phone still sleep.

"Get over here joe," Quick said in a deadly voice.

"What da fuck is up?" Lando asked. Quick simply told him the same thing and hung up the phone.

Pissed off and still sleep, Lando walked into Pamila's house ten minutes later and saw her and Kelley still sitting on the sofa in a state of depression. His heart began to beat faster and faster as he shut the door. Something was painfully wrong and he could feel it.

Fearing the answer, Lando looked at Pamila and said, "What's up?" She looked up at him and just shook her head, she knew that Mann's death was going to shake Lando at his foundation and send him plunging back into the streets like he used to be.

Eyone Williams

"What's up?" Lando asked again, sounding more demanding this time.

"Mann is dead," Pamila said with tears running down her face.

No set of words ever said changed Lando's life as drastically as the words 'Mann is dead'. Life as Lando had known it for 16 years was changed in a matter of seconds. The one person that could make all things right as far as he was concerned was gone and would never be back. Lando couldn't believe it. Mann wasn't supposed to die like that Lando thought. He deserved better, he meant too much to too many people. Someone was going to have to pay with their life and anyone in the way would have to pay as well and Lando didn't care who it was.

"What happened?" Lando snapped. Kelley spoke up and told Lando that Serge was lying on the floor shot in the neck when she had opened the door to see where the gunshots came from. Lando immediately saw Serge being wrong and knew that if Serge was a part of Mann's murder then Smoke had to be part of it as well.

"Smoke wasn't there?" Lando asked. Kelley told him that an old lady downstairs on the first floor told the police that a second man had fled the scene after the shooting.

Pamila watched Lando's body language change more and more as Kelley told him what she knew about Mann's murder. It seemed as if Lando could see everything Kelley was saying happening all over again in his mind. Quick came back upstairs dressed in all black as Kelley finished giving Lando the run down on the facts.

"Let's roll," Quick said as he walked towards the door.

Pamila stood up wiping tears from her eyes and said, "I know y'all want to do something about Mann, but I can't deal with worrying about y'all two right now," Pamila said as she tried to talk the two young dudes out of what she knew would be a manhunt. As hard as it was at the time to disregard Pamila's wishes, Lando and Quick told her that they had to go and left to see if they could find out where Smoke may be hiding.

Pamila's heart began to pound as Lando and Quick left the house to somehow try to make a wrong situation right. Kelley knew that Lando and Quick were going to be out of control until they found Smoke, she knew that they were in a state of mind where nothing mattered and this scared her.

"I gotta do something," Pamila said as she tried to think. She knew that she was going to have to stay focused at this painful time in order to save Lando and Quick from their anger.

"Don't you know Mann's friend Silk?" Pamila asked Kelley. Kelley told her she did in fact know him.

"Call 'em, I want to talk to him. He's going to have to help me calm them down," Pamila said.

By noon, Mann's murder was the talk of the city. Every station from WKYS to WPGC had interrupted their broadcast to talk about it, everyone knew that the 20 year old CEO of Fast Lane Records had been shot to death in what police thought was a failed robbery attempt. Chocolate heard the news on the radio on her way to the studio the next morning. She felt as if she had just been shot herself when she heard Mann's name. Not believing what she had just heard she continued on her way to the studio and just knew that Mann would be there when she got there.

Fast Lane Records was full of sorrow when Chocolate walked in the door. She saw Cherry and Caramel sitting on the sofa in the lobby crying, she knew that what she heard was true.

"No!" Chocolate said as the truth hit her hard deep within her soul, "Mann ain't dead!"

Not use to seeing the stronger girl hurt, Caramel quickly got up and hugged her saying, "It's okay, it's okay."

"It's not okay!" Chocolate said as she wept on Caramel's shoulder. Short Dogg came walking down the hall with Tank and saw the three girls all crying. He had just got off the phone with Pamila who had told him all that had went down last night no longer than an hour after he had seen Mann. Short Dogg had grown up a lot after hanging around Mann at the studio and he knew that he had to do what Mann would have wanted done which was hold everything together, so he did that. He calmly told PASSION that he had just talked to Pamila and that she wanted everybody to meet up over her house so that she could talk to them about the situation at hand. Knowing that he had done what Mann would have wanted him to do, Short Dogg still felt nothing but anger in his heart for Smoke and he couldn't wait until he caught up with Lando and Quick.

Dre was just coming out of his cell to get in the shower when he saw the news about Mann's murder on the 12:00 news. Walking into the dayroom in his towel he listened as the news reporter gave bits and pieces of the story. Dre quickly jumped on the phone and called Pamila who told him all that she knew. Dre felt truly helpless for the first time in his life when he got off the phone with Pamila. He went to wake Black up with tears in his eyes.

Black took the news harder than Dre thought. Black began going crazy throwing stuff all around his cell. The fact that Smoke and Serge were Mann's killers was something Black could not accept. He swore that it was his fault for not being on the streets. Dre thought that Black was going to end up taking his anger out on someone in the block by the way he had went off. Dre really didn't know how to calm Black down and if anyone could, it would only be Mann. The only thing Dre could come up with was getting Black to understand that it was nothing that either of them could do, but that they both knew Lando wasn't going to let anyone get away with killing Mann.

Mann's death crushed Pamila. Even so, Pamila knew she was going to have to be the one person strong enough to pull things together before all that Mann had worked so hard for just went down the drain. Pamila had calmed down and was now trying to think of the right words to say to the living room full of people that all some how had dealings with Mann's record label or his store.

Sitting on the sofa between Kisha and Naomi, Pamila said, "I know that everyone here feels the same way about Mann's death as I do, but death is a very big part of life." Everyone listened as Pamila told them that they would miss Mann deeply, but that they had to keep alive all that Mann had started if they wanted Mann's efforts in life to live on. Seeing the look of agreement on the faces of the young people that Mann had helped get out of the streets, Pamila knew she was saying the right things.

"Like any other death," Pamila said as Kisha rubbed her on the back, "we will morn this great loss, but we will not give up on life."

When Pamila was finished talking, she could tell that everyone was in accord with her and she really needed the support that she was feeling before she asked everyone to give her a little time to herself. As everyone began to leave, Short Dogg walked around Pamila with Tank and Lil' Moe.

Pamila asked him if she could speak with him for a minute and pulled him to the side.

"I want to thank you for getting everybody together for me," Pamila said. Short Dogg could tell that the woman respected the way he didn't lose focus and go into a rage of anger like Quick and Lando and she let him know that.

"I only did what I thought would help da situation at hand," Short Dogg said. "It's no doubt dat we all gon feel da loss, but like you said, we gotta keep all dat Mann worked for alive. What goes around comes around so those dat did slim wrong gon get what they got comin'." Short Dogg hugged Pamila and followed everyone else out the door. He was sure he would be able to play a part in whatever was going to come back around for Smoke.

After explaining the whole situation to Tyesha, who really didn't understand how bad the situation was, Pamila went to lay down for a while, she needed some rest. She would have a lot of work to do in preparation for Mann's wake and funeral. Lying in the bed, she wondered what Lando and Quick could have done while they roamed the streets last night. She prayed that they hadn't gotten their selves into something that would bring her more stress at the time. Silk had assured her that he would find them both and talk to them, so Pamila waited to see what he would have to say.

Kelley laid in the bed trying to get some rest, but the thought of having to have her child without Mann wouldn't allow her to sleep. She tried to think like Pamila wanted everybody to think, but it wasn't that easy. The only thing that gave her any sense of peace was knowing that Lando and Quick had been searching the streets all night for the one other person involved in Mann's death. Even so, Kelley knew that the one man she loved was gone and things would never be the same.

Silk caught up with Lando and Quick after beeping them for hours. He told them to meet him at his barber shop so that he could talk to them before they made a bad situation worst. Knowing the love the two younger dudes had for Mann, Silk could only imagine what they could be doing out of anger. As he thought about Mann's death, he became very upset at the fact that the two dudes that Mann knew and had helped out in the past, killed him. The good dudes in the game always got crossed by someone they knew. Silk was hurt, but he knew that Pamila would need his help to pull things together and he was going to give it to her by all means.

Silk was in the back of the barber shop watching the news. Mann's murder was still the top story of the day. Silk shook his head in disgust, the media always found a way to paint a bad picture. Mann was now being portrayed as an ex-drug dealer that found a way to clean his money and open up a local record label called Fast Lane Records. Pissed off, Silk turned the TV off and turned around to see Lando and Quick dressed in all black coming through the front door.

Lando sat down on the sofa in Silk's back office telling him how he and Quick had roamed the streets looking for Smoke all night. Lando and Quick had checked every place they knew that Smoke could possibly be and had come up with nothing at the time. Looking at Lando and Quick, Silk told them that they were not using their heads by grabbing their pistols and looking for Smoke with no plan of where to find him or how they would get away with what they were going to do when they did find him.

"Y'all been around too long to go down out of anger," Silk said. "Y'all both know how Mann would deal wit some shit like dis. He gon think, so y'all gotta think too." Silk told them both that Smoke was going to get what he had coming and they would be the ones to give it to him, but for the time being, they needed to be there for Pamila and Kelley. Lando shook his head, he knew Silk was right and he was going to make sure he didn't cause Pamila any more stress.

For the next few days everyone mourned the death of one of the realest niggaz the DC streets had ever seen. His presence would be missed far and wide without a doubt and it would be awhile before things could get back to normal.

Lando had a lot on his mind, he wanted to say fuck everything and take his anger out on Smoke's family, but he knew Mann wouldn't approve of his actions. Black encouraged Lando to kill Serge's baby mother until he and Quick could catch Smoke. Quick was with the plan, but Lando let them both know that he was against it. Sitting next to Black in the visiting hall, Dre told Lando and Quick to check all through NE where Smoke and Serge had grew up. Lando decided that was the best course of action.

While those that had true love for Mann were preparing for his wake, Lando, Quick, Short Dogg, and Lil' Garvin were outside of an apartment on Maryland Avenue, just a few blocks from Black's mother's house. They had got word that Smoke was laying low over his cousin's apartment, who was Serge's bigger brother. Sliding on ski masks and checking their pistols, the four young killers jumped out of Lil' Garvin's old van and crept around to the back of the apartment with nothing but pay back on their mind.

In the safety of the nightfall they got inside the back door of the apartment building unseen. Standing right outside of the apartment, they could hear people inside laughing and joking. Lando looked back at Quick who had ran across the information of Smoke's whereabouts and asked him if he was sure that Smoke was inside.

With his pistol in hand, Quick said, "I been layin' on dis nigga all day. I know he in here." With no further talking Lando backed away from the door and told Lil' Garvin to kick it open since he was the biggest out of the four.

Lando was the first through the door firing his .45 automatic. Serge's older brother was standing in the middle of the living room with a drink in his hand. Lando hit him five quick times right in the head and stepped over his body as he chased Smoke into the back room with Short Dogg. Quick and Lil' Garvin opened fire on two dudes that were on the sofa smoking weed. With nowhere to run, the two dudes took slug after slug while Lil' Garvin and Quick unloaded.

Smoke ran into the bedroom and tried to get the window open with no success. Realizing that death was in town, Smoke turned around and tried to beg for his life.

"Please!" Smoke begged, "I didn't want anything to do wit dat shit." Balling up in the corner with his hands over his head, Smoke pleaded for his soon to be killers to understand him. Short Dogg slowly walked over to Smoke pointing his Mac-11 at him. Lando walked up behind Short Dogg and pulled out a straight razor.

Placing his .45 to Smoke's head, Lando said, "I should just get dis shit over wit, but it would be too quick." After slicing Smoke's throat, Lando watched for a few seconds before Lil' Garvin and Quick came in the room in a rush to hit the road.

"We ain't got no time for dis shit," Quick said as he walked up and shot Smoke twice in the head. "Let's go!" Quick said as he led everyone swiftly back to the van.

An hour later, Lando walked into the funeral home on Kennedy Street followed by Short Dogg, Quick, and Lil' Garvin. Still dressed in all black jeans and sweat hoods, they leaned against the back wall and looked up front at all of the people that came to pay their respects to Mann. With visions of what had just took place still in his mind, Lando still felt incomplete. Watching people walk by him crying, Lando wondered if anyone felt the loss that he felt. Biting into his bottom lip and shaking his head out of anger, Lando looked down at the floor thinking of what was next. There was no one else to kill, nothing else to do about Mann's murder. All he could do now was deal with his brother's death and go on with life.

Caught up in his mixed feelings of hurt and anger, Lando felt someone tap him on his shoulder. Turning around with a look that could kill on his face, Lando saw Baby-D standing in the door way. Without saying a word, Lando hugged his man patting him on the back, "Yeah slim, niggaz done killed my nigga," Lando said as he held back tears. Baby-D looked around and saw Lil' Garvin, Short Dogg, and Quick all leaning against the wall dressed in black. Being from the streets, Baby-D could tell that they all had been on the hunt for Mann's killer. Baby-D pulled Lando to the side and asked him what had happened.

Standing outside of the funeral home, Lando told Baby-D how Smoke and Serge had tried to rob Mann and ended up killing him. Baby-D couldn't believe that they would try something like that.

"What Black got to say 'bout dis shit?" Baby-D asked as he tried to come to an understanding about the whole situation.

"Black fucked up," Lando said as he looked up and down Kennedy Street. "Black wants me to kill dem niggaz mothers and some more shit, but I can't get down like dat. Both of dem niggaz dead now. Leave it at dat. No matter what I do, I can't bring Mann back." Baby-D felt Lando's pain, he had loved Mann like a brother as well, but he did agree with Lando about life going on.

Back inside, Lando sat down beside Nakia, who was holding his baby in her arms. Lando looked down at his son and began rubbing his little head.

"Dis what da future about," Lando said. He knew that he had to live for his son. Listening to Lando, Nakia was glad to hear him talk in such a way. She thought that Lando was going to go crazy about Mann's death, but he was taking it better than she thought.

Pamila spent less than five minutes at Mann's wake. She couldn't stand seeing him lying in a casket. His 20 years of life went so fast and just when he was starting to make something out of his life it was snatched away. Pamila opened up an old box of pictures as she sat on the bed remembering all the good times and bad times that Mann had brought into her life. Pulling out an old picture of her deceased younger sister and Mann when he was first born, Pamila began to cry again. People took life for granted far too often, they didn't enjoy the times they were blessed with enough, Pamila thought as she looked through more pictures.

Lando walked into Pamila's room and saw her looking at an old picture of him and Mann coming back from the go-cart track.

Lando sat down beside Pamila, putting his arm around her shoulders and said with a smile, "I remember dat day. Dat's when Mann got his car."

Pamila looked over at Lando and cracked a slight smile saying, "Y'all grew up overnight. I can still remember when y'all were babies." Pamila began to think about how hard her sister's death had hit everyone just over ten years ago.

She came across a picture of her sister and handed it to Lando saying, "Do you remember how things were when your mother passed?" Lando looked down at the picture and began to think of the short time he was allowed to enjoy with his mother before death came her way.

Looking back up at Pamila, Lando said, "Yeah, I remember how things were back then. The whole family seemed to pull together." Pamila shook her head in agreement and began to tell Lando how they were going to do the same exact thing this time with Mann's death.

Hugging Lando, Pamila said, "I need you to work with me though. You are going to have to do the right thing. You and Tyesha are all I really have left. I have to hold on to you both as long as the Lord allows me to." Lando felt Pamila's words deep in his heart and without even speaking a word he gave her a look that said he would do all in his power to make things better in the up coming days that would follow Mann's funeral.

Quick knocked on Pamila's open bedroom door and asked if he could come in.

Pamila looked over smiling and said, "You're family, you can always come in." Quick walked over and sat down on the floor in front of Pamila and Lando and began looking at the old pictures. Pamila told Quick how everyone was going to have to work together as a family to recover from Mann's death.

Quick looked up at her and said, "I'ma team player, you know I'm down for whatever."

Pamila had truly grown to love Quick as a son; she leaned over and hugged him saying, "Everything is going to be alright." They all shared one of their first moments of laughter since Mann's murder.

Kelley was lying in the bed with Tyesha explaining to her where people went when they died. Kelley told Tyesha that Mann was in a better place now because he didn't have to worry about anybody doing anything to hurt him again.

Speaking from her young heart, Tyesha said, "If Mann is in a better place, why is everybody so upset?" Kelley looked at the young child in amazement. She had just asked her a question that put everything into perspective. Mann was in a better place. He really didn't have to worry about some broke niggaz trying to rob him, he didn't have to worry about the police, or any other things that he had faced as he journeyed through the fast lane.

On the other side of pain... is love

24

"Daddy! Daddy!" Lando's son said as he came into Lando's bedroom to wake him up so that they could get ready to go to the beach with Kelley and her daughter Marcella who looked just like Mann. Lando sat up on the bed and looked down at his son that was starting to act more like he used to everyday now. At five years old, Eyone thought he was the man of the house and Lando allowed him to feel just that way.

"Where your mother at shorty?" Lando asked Eyone as he stood up to get himself together. Nakia walked into the bedroom just as Lando asked about her.

"Kelley just called," Nakia said as she pulled a Mann's World T-Shirt over Eyone's head. "Pamila told her to tell you that everybody is waiting for us." Lando looked at Nakia and his son and smiled, a lot had changed in the past five years since Mann passed away and Lando could feel it everyday he woke up but instead of it bringing him down it made him feel good to know that he had picked up where his big brother had left off and he was now the one that kept everything together now.

"Is everything packed?" Lando asked as he walked to the bathroom. Nakia told him that everything was ready and waiting on him.

Ready for the trip to the beach, Lando walked down the hallway of the huge house that he had bought to raise his son and future children in. Walking by a huge picture of Mann that hung on the wall over the steps that led to the living room, Lando stopped to reflect on all that he had to be thankful for.

At 21 years old, Lando was where Mann would have wanted him to be and doing what Mann would have wanted him to be doing. He was

Eyone Williams

CEO of Fast Lane Records and had used everything he could get his hands on or hands in to make Fast Lane a name that would be around for years to come. Lando changed no rules, only followed the path that Mann had already laid down and success fell right into his hands as he learned the game as it came to him.

PASSION stayed true to Fast Lane Records and went on to sell millions of records in the five years that passed. Chocolate always paid close attention to every move Mann made when it came to the record label and thanks to her, Lando's job was easy when Pamila turned all of Mann's assets over to him two years after Mann's death. Now working on their 3rd album and still attacking every song like their first, Chocolate, Cherry, and Caramel still gave all their credit to Mann. Chocolate had learned a lot from Mann, she used all she learned to open up hair salons all around the DC metropolitan area. Chocolate named her hair salons 'Styles of Passion' and it was a huge success. Cherry also became very business-minded and opened up a publishing company called Passion's Publishing. Caramel fell deep in love with Baby-D and had his baby, Louis Jr., two years after Mann died. Passion was family.

Da Youngins stuck with the rap game as well even though it took them two albums to attract enough attention to sell a million records. Nevertheless, they had sold a million with their second album and made sure that Fast Lane Records had a heavy hitting rap group on the label as well.

Short Dogg became a sought after producer in the music business once the world found out who was behind the tracks that gave Fast Lane Records it's one and only sound. Growing to love the success that was coming with the music, Short Dogg began to sell tracks for Fast Lane Records as he helped make Fast Lane everything it was growing to be.

Quick came a long way after Mann's death under Pamila's motherly direction and love. He now owned a Mann's World store down the street from Silk's barbershop. He had a little boy by Amber and named the baby after Mann.

Baby-D was now well established in the boxing world and was ranked number 2 on the WBC's top 30 welter-weight boxing list. He literally fought his way out of the streets and the fast lane. Baby-D, Caramel, and their son wanted for nothing. They lived in a huge house right outside of DC in Silver Spring, Maryland.

Silk left the drug game alone right after Mann died and opened several night clubs all over the metropolitan area. He stayed close to Lando and the rest of the youngin's he watched grow up and they all still respected him and saw him as a wise big brother. He paid his respect to Mann by buying Pamila a house and paying for a lawyer to help get all of Mann's financial assets in order. He also paid the rest of Kelley's way through college after she had Marcella. Silk was real as it gets.

Walking down the steps, Lando smiled as he thought about how things were going. Everybody that came along for the ride started out right in the hood, right on the same block. The dope game was over for Lando, Quick, Short Dogg, and Baby-D. Mann would be proud. Even so, Lando knew all too well that with the good came the bad.

Dre came home after being found not guilty of murder on the case that he had with Black. Once back in the streets without Mann by his side, Dre jumped back in the dope game and was moving bricks of coke in no time. As Lando started pulling out of the dope game along with Quick, Dre began to lock down everything that they once had. Lil' Garvin didn't see any sense in going along for the Fast Lane ride if he wasn't rapping so he stayed in the dope game and hooked up with Dre. Two years after Dre hit the streets, the DEA raided five major drug areas and arrested 37 people who they accused of being in a drug ring. Dre was the so-called kingpin on the indictment of 57 counts of racketeering and gun running. Lil' Garvin was the so-called enforcer of the drug ring and was charged with murders as far back as 1989 when he was only 13. As the case grew bigger and bigger, making freedom look unreal for the many co-defendants that hardly knew each other, Dre began to second guess his morals and principles. Sure enough, the government came at him with a deal for him to give up his drug connect and to point the finger at Lil' Garvin and Dre broke. He got off with 2 years, leaving Lil' Garvin no option but to take a plea to 10 years in prison along with many of their other co-defendants.

Lando never forgave Dre for becoming a rat and the only thing that stopped him from killing Dre was the fact that Dre had moved down south somewhere with Tina and his son. Out of all people to turn "hot", Lando would have never guessed it to be Dre, after all this was the same nigga that had stood strong on two murder charges with Black and had never cracked at all, but those were the ones that would get you every time, Lando thought. Grabbing the keys to his car, Lando wondered how Dre could give up all that he had ever been in life to be a witness for the government. Sure things got hard sometimes in life, but that was never a reason to turn on your niggaz Lando thought, Black was a perfect example of standing strong through it all.

Black was doing 25 to life in Lorton's Maximum Security Prison for killing Officer Hall. Mia and her law professor had attacked Black's case from every angle and made the judge and jury understand that he never intended to kill a police officer. Their whole case was that Black was under the impression that Officer Hall and the vice cops were stick up boys and that Black began to shoot at the unmarked car trying to protect himself. By law, the judge had to drop the felony down to a second degree murder because it was no way to prove that Black planned to kill Hall nor did he know he was shooting at a police officer. In the end, Black still had light at the end of the tunnel, he had been locked up for five years and he only had six more years to do before he saw the parole board. Besides that Lando was still paying his trial lawyer to handle his appeal which was now in appeals court and if all went well Black would get his case overturned and he would then fight to get his second degree murder turned into a manslaughter which would get him back into the streets three years sooner. Black began to study Islam and became a Muslim. Islam slowed him down and changed his outlook on life. Mia was so amazed at the change she began to read the Holy Qur'an. Black came a long way as well.

Pamila now had peace. She married Tyesha's father, Jimmy and raised Tyesha well away from the streets. Pamila made sure Kelley, Lando, and Quick also kept their kids away from the streets. She never changed her lifestyle no matter how much money Lando and Quick made, she still worked hard 5 days a week.

Kelley graduated from Howard University with a degree in Psychology but preferred to accept the position of vice president of Fast Lane Records. She lived with Pamila for 3 years after Mann died, but began seeing a dude she met at Howard. After slowly coming out of her shell, she opened up to the dude. Pamila encouraged Kelley to move on with her life and she did just that after a long talk with Pamila. Kelley and Marcella moved in with Kelley's new boyfriend.

Kisha and Naomi were also well off due to Mann. They ran the original Mann's World store. Lando let them run it as they pleased and it was damn near their store. Kisha went back to school and got a degree in business management which helped her run Mann's World better. Naomi got over Lando after awhile and fell for a dude across town named Antoine.

Jazmin also followed her dreams and went away to New York and later graduated from Parson's School of Design with a Bachelor's of Fine Arts. Mann also made a difference in her life.

"Come on, let's get outta here before Pamila call back," Nakia said as she and Eyone came walking out of the kitchen with their bags. Lando looked down at Eyone and smiled, his son was holding Nakia's hand leading her to the door. At only five years old, Lando could see that Eyone wanted to be in control.

"You ready?" Nakia asked Lando as she opened the front door letting the bright summer sun into the living room

"Yeah, let's go," Lando said as he rubbed his son on the head. Just as they were about to walk out of the door, the phone rang. Nakia gave Lando a look like don't answer it. Lando laughed and told her to go ahead to the car.

"I'm right behind you," Lando said as he picked the phone up and watched Nakia and Eyone walk down the front steps to the driveway.

"Hello?" Lando said into the phone.

"Lando is you comin' or what?" Kelley asked.

"Yeah, I'm on my way out da door right now. Where is Quick?" Lando asked.

Kelley told him that Quick was out front with Pamila putting her stuff into his truck.

"Everybody waitin' on y'all so hurry up!" Kelley said as she hung up the phone. Lando laughed as he hung up the phone and began walking out the door. Life in the fast lane wasn't always as smooth as it was now, but like Mann used to always tell Lando, life is what you make it.

The End...

Eyone Williams

Acknowledgements

All praise due to Allah who continues to bless me and open doors for me in this world.

I must express extreme love and respect to my beautiful Queen, my Wife, Aisha. You are more than a Wife, baby girl. You are my best friend, partner, comrade, business partner and so much more. I love you for more reasons than I can express in this space, but I want you to know that we gon' make it, for sure. Without you there would be no Fast Lane or Fast Lane Publications. You believed in the vision and jumped-started the game plan. I got us, baby. Can't nothing or nobody get in our business, we gon' outlive the haters!! Can't wait to see their faces! (smile!)

Much love and respect to my homie, Darren Coleman. Thanks for believing in Fast Lane and my desire to want more out of life. I got your back slim, believe that. I'm still learning the game; I'm just getting started. Once I touch down it's going to be a whole new ball game. Let's get money.

Much love to my comrades that believed in Fast Lane from the jump, when we were way out Arizona holding it down in the struggle. My man Short Dogg, you read Fast Lane page for page as I typed it and you believed in it; that book you're working on—Man's Greatest Weakness—is going to be big, I'm feeling it. Wee-Wee and Poochie a.k.a. Comrade, our talks about the streets took me back to the late 80s/early 90s and kept my memories on point about the murder capital; yall niggaz keep your head up and NEVER LAY DOWN or forget the bond we formed in this struggle. My nigga Black, what's up homes; I had to put you in the joint, much love. Freeway, it trips me out how much you dig my writing; that's love slim. Drive slow homie! Big Vernon a.k.a. Machine, can't forget you champ; I remember when you used to come get the handwritten pages of Fast Lane before it was done. That inspired me.

Much love to all my comrades grindin' in this publishing game. My Fast Lane team: Abdul Malik, Colie "Shaka" Long, Nathan Whelch.

We gon' get right. Rome wasn't built overnight. I'm going to do all I can from my position. My peoples, Lil D and 6400 Entertainment; Seth "Soul Man" and Gorlla Convict Publications; Robert Booker and Sims Sims; my homie Jason Poole and Never Give Up—put that work in slim, we gotta put DC on the map with this writing; my man and brother Abdus Shahid Ali, keep writing homes; my man Scoop, keep it uncut and REAL LIVE; Wahida Clark, I already know you 'bout to do big things; Kwame Teague, keep your head up and keep pushing that fire; C-Murder, that Death Around The Corner was gangsta!

Much love to my peoples that hold me down and keep the buzz alive in the streets: My Pops, Larry Williams; you know how to hustle, let's get money! Tammy Kemp, thanks for being on top of business for the home team. My nigga Karim Mowatt, you hold a nigga down on all levels in them streets; I got your back throughout your struggle. My man Tabi Bonney, I already know that you gon' blow on the rap tip; after all, you the first D.C. artist to have a national video in what? 15 years? Do your thing and hold me a spot; you know my first love is music. Don Diva, Tiff, Kevin and the whole crew; yall real peoples; good looking out on the Panama article. That's going to have people looking for the book—Money Ain't Everything. Thanks for giving me my first shot at writing magazine articles. I got some other pieces in the making.

Much love to my men Panama and Rome. I'm honored to be the one to put the story on paper. Money Ain't Everything gon' take the street lit game to another level.

Much love to my Lattisaw side of the family; the Williams side of the family, in B.C., Va., Ohio and other states, the Jones side, Folkner side; and everybody else that's a part of the family. Thank you all for looking out for me at different times in my life.

My homies in the struggle, I can't name you all but the love is strong, believe that. Zulu, Dominic, Roy, Wayne, Kobi, Bundy, Baby Face, Fly, Hoover and all the men out there with you. Juan, Rah-Rah, Brook, Scrap, Demo, Dogg, Halim, Ali Kitab a.k.a. Lil Rico, Tonio, Monkey-D, Mike Howard, Rome a.k.a. JC, Big Wendell, Mario, Markie, Go-Go, Sop-Sop, Buddy Love, Rick, Fighter Lane, Raff,

Ronald Hughes, Tone, Sean Branch, T.R., Whitey, Garnett, Black Face, Trey, Ben, Mike Boone, Hakim, Redds, B.J., Reel, Face, Bryon, Philly Black, Lil Twan, Dee, T-Man, Sam, Baby-J, E-Dub, Mike P., Bird Man, Smilie, Ned, Black Top, Deon, Rodney Shaw, Chez, Buster, Chico, Mike Owens, Stone, Big Frank, Johann, Talib, Champ a.k.a. Reggie, Squeaky, Big Leon a.k.a D-Bo, both Lil Petes, Fu, Reggie Mack, Marvin, Donald, Shay, Moose, Big Mo, Gees, Kevin Attaway, Butch Woods, Bird, Diamond, Gray Top, Pattrick Patterson, Drew, Fezell, Frank Boston, Twan Hammond, Fish Bone, Sly, Jamaal, Fice, Wimp, Deon Green, Fat Eric, Ty Vire, Montana, Buff, Tip Toe, Mike Woody, Mack Carr, Donnell, Norvell, Fatts, Lil Mack, Harvey, Titus, Lil Roy, Al Jetter, Eazy, Moe-Moe, Whop, Amin, Carl Newton, Toni Lewis, Eddie Mathis, Corey, Crank, Hub, Nate Bailey, Will Johnson, and too many more. If I missed you, I'll get you next time, I'm sure I missed a few, I'm on a deadline.

Much love to my peoples Greg Royster and Rob Jones for always being there for me when I call on you, that's priceless.

Thank you, the reader, for checking me out. Keep your eyes open for more of my work, work that I'm a part of, and work from my Wife, Aisha, she got some fire as well.

ALWAYS REAL,

"E"

Nvision Publishing Order Form

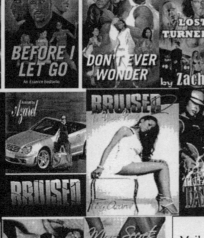

Add $4.25 for shipping via U.S. Priority Mail. Total of 19.25 per book. For orders being shipped directly to prisons Nvision Publishing deducts 20%. Cost are as follows, $12.00 plus shipping for a total of $16.20. For 3 or more books add $2.00 per book for shipping.

Make money order payable to Nvision Publishing. Only certified or government issued checks.

Send to: Nvision Publishing/Order P.O. Box 274 Lanham Severn Road, Lanham, MD 20703:   Purchaser Information

Name _____

Register #_____

Address_____

City_____   State/Zip_____

Which Books_____

# of books_____   Total enclosed $_____

Darren Coleman,

author of the smash hits, *Before I Let Go* & *Do or Die*,

introduces a future legend of the Hip-Hop lit genre...

D.C.'s own,
Eyone Williams

"Eyone Williams is surely one of the best young storytellers of this new era, it takes guts to read this novel, but yet it takes courage to even write a story as vicious as this."

   - *Essence* Best Selling Author of *Larceny*, Jason Poole

"Eyone Williams has laid down a gripping story between on these pages. He takes the readers on a fast-paced journey through the streets that will have the readers ready to dial 9-1-1."

   - *Essence* Bestselling Author of *Thugs & the Women Who Love Them* Wahida Clark